Deathly Deceit

A. W. Lambert

A Wings ePress, Inc.
Mystery

Wings ePress, Inc.

Edited by: Jeanne Smith
Copy Edited by: Christie Kraemer
Executive Editor: Jeanne Smith
Cover Artist: Richard Stroud

All rights reserved

Names, characters and incidents depicted in this book are products of the author's imagination or are used fictitiously. Any resemblance to actual events, locales, organizations, or persons, living or dead, is entirely coincidental and beyond the intent of the author or the publisher.

No part of this book may be reproduced or transmitted in any form or by any means, electronic or mechanical, including photocopying, recording, or by any information storage and retrieval system, without permission in writing from the publisher.

Wings ePress Books
www.wingsepress.com

Copyright © 2019 by A. W. Lambert
ISBN-13: 978-1-61309-632-1
ISBN-10: -1-61309-632-1

Published In the United States Of America

Wings ePress Inc.
3000 N. Rock Road
Newton, KS 67114

What They Are Saying About

Deathly Deceit

Theo Stern, the principal character, is an ex -detective inspector of the London Metropolitan Police. When he returns from Australia after an abortive attempt to rescue his marriage, Stern has no intention of restarting his private detective agency. He closed it when he left; at 63 years of age, it was time to retire.

His former PA, Cherry Hooker, has other ideas. Although Stern has been away for months, Cherry has paid the rent on his office. When he returns, she encourages him to carry on where he left off.

Against his better judgement, Stern restarts his agency and takes on three cases: one via David O'Connor, a senior police officer who engages Stern to help him with a case.

Stern becomes involved with drug and people trafficking, a double murder and arson. During his investigations he's attacked and is seriously injured by a female Polish wrestler, but despite his injuries, manages to crack the cases wide open.

Deathly Deceipt is the sort of book you have to keep on reading. You certainly don't hit the pain barrier at page 3.

Five stars *****
—Andrew R Williams
Author of Arcadia's Children: Samantha's Revenge

Dedication

For the Wings team, whose continued support
means so much.

Prologue

It was a fishing boat, sturdy and fast, its powerful twin 300 horse power engines more than capable of coping with the rain-drenched, wind-battered waters of the heaving North Sea. Other than the dimmed green instrument lighting, the whole journey, long and cold, had been carried out in complete darkness. Now they had slowed, the surging engine sound diminishing to little more than a distant rumble. The two man crew at the helm, their profiles glowing grotesquely green, stared out into the blackness, exchanging sharp conspiratorial whispers.

The two young females sitting huddled to one side had no idea what was being said, their English comprising of little more than a few random and useless words. Both several months short of their sixteenth birthday, they owned only the clothes they were wearing and what meagre possessions they had been able to cram into the small backpacks tucked protectively away at their feet. Alongside each of the backpacks, also protectively guarded, was a package around twelve inches square. It was tightly vacuum-sealed in plastic with a looped strap attached, enabling it to be hung over the shoulder. The two girls had no idea what the package contained, only that it was handed to each of them as they climbed aboard the boat and was an obligatory part of the deal. Despite the money their families had paid up front, refusal to carry the package would have meant they were left stranded. Not that either of them cared. They would have been prepared to carry anything to achieve their aim.

Had their two young faces been visible, it could have been seen they were sickly pale, the result of the constant retching caused by the long hours of unending pitch and roll. It was why they had been clutching the thick plastic supermarket carrier bag in front of them since the start of the journey. The burly crew had travelled this route before; they knew the score. They had a plentiful stock of the carrier bags. At journey's end, like many others before them, the bags would be casually cast over the side, adding to the ever increasing plastic flotsam contaminating the seas.

Every last penny the two girls' loving families had forfeited in order to pay their way to a safe, civilised future had been swallowed up. From the very first day of their tortuous journey, they had been in the hands of others. Sometimes ruthless others. But they had been lucky…they'd come through virtually unscathed. Probably because of their skinny immaturity; there had always been more mature, more desirable pickings for the callus, cold blooded people-smugglers to feed on.

Over time the larger groups among which they'd initially been able to hide themselves during the gruelling cross country marches had dissipated. Smaller groups led off in different directions, they knew not where. Now, all those months later, they were virtually alone. There were just three others on board, all men, huddled together at the rear of the boat. As well as their own meagre possessions, each of the men was also preciously guarding a similar plastic package. The men had never attempted to speak or communicate with the girls in any way. The girls were grateful for this. They had been warned about men, what they could and would do to women given the slightest opportunity. During the long journey, they had seen it happen all too often. Since leaving their loving, protective families, they may not have matured in body, the scarceness of good nutritious food and supreme physical efforts of their long ordeal had meant quite the opposite, but they had very quickly grown wise to the wickedness of the world around them. Now, as far as they knew, they were almost there. This is what their families had sacrificed so much for. This was where they would be safe from the hell of war and butchery, where they would be free to live a life without fear.

This was England, where they had been told they would be welcomed with open arms. Now they need not worry that their families had been unable to pay the whole fee up front. Here work was plentiful. Nannies were essential to look after rich people's children, high class restaurants needed waitresses and hotels were always looking for staff. All these positions, they were told, paid handsomely. The outstanding debt would be paid off in no time at all. Then money could be sent home to support the family. The future, at last, looked bright.

For virtually the whole tortuous trip, when not heaving the foul tasting bile—all that was left in there fragile stomachs—into the plastic bag, their eyes had been fixed on the two men at the controls. Suddenly, they could feel an air of tense expectancy as one of the men whispered harshly and pointed to one side. They looked, following the direction of his pointed finger, and saw the single bright pinprick of light blinking rapidly. The man turned the wheel hard and they heard the rumble of the engine increase just a fraction.

They turned and looked into each other's face, smiling excitedly. They had made it. They were here at last. But still, as they held hands tightly, clinging together, their eyes hanging on to that life-saving speck of light, they felt sick and terrified.

Only moments later, holding their backpacks close, the plastic packages slung around their necks, they were roughly herded to the boat's rail. Each was then manhandled precariously over the side and lowered into an inflatable dingy barely large enough to hold the five of them. The two girls clung together, terrified at being squeezed so tightly together against the men. They need not have worried. The only thing each one of them wanted at that time was to reach dry land safely. And, most importantly, never to release the precious plastic-covered package looped around their necks.

One of the men had been handed a paddle and told to head for the bright, blinking spot of light on the shore. It had been a struggle, the two other men and the two girls using their hands as oars to help propel the tiny craft forward toward the shore.

Finally, feeling the sand rasp beneath them, they climbed out into the freezing, ankle deep water. They stood, uncertain, until a dark shape crunched down the sand toward them. Immediately the shape, recognisable as a large bulky man, produced a knife and thrust it several times into the dingy, which collapsed. Gesturing for them to follow, he grabbed the deflated plastic and commenced dragging it up the beach. Without saying a word the man used hands and feet to crunch the deflated dingy into as small a bundle as he could before tying it tightly with thick string he'd drawn from his pocket. The five, shivering violently, stood silently and watched.

Tucking the bundle under one arm, the man turned to the huddled group. By the light of a small torch and using hand gestures, he made them understand they should remain completely silent and follow him closely. He then turned and headed off along the beach. The group, terrified of losing touch, huddled together and pressed themselves close behind him. The beach ended at the bottom of a cliff that loomed up into the darkness. Here the man stopped. Again by the light of the torch and using sign language, he indicated they had to climb. He weaved his hand from side to side describing a winding track upwards, then demonstrated how the torch would be hooked to the back of his belt, giving them a light to follow. He emphasised again, stay close. Eyes wide with fear in the torchlight, each of them nodded their understanding.

The climb was difficult, the earth underfoot loose leading to slips and slides, but eventually, sporting only cuts and grazes, they all arrived safely at the top of the cliff. The man gave them just a few moments to gather their breath before again urging them forward. They followed a track for some time, then broke away and crossed a field into woodland. Finally the trees parted and they came to a road. Hugging the tree line, they followed the road until they came to a lay-by in which was parked a dark van. The man unlocked the rear doors and threw the destroyed, tightly wrapped dingy inside. Then, waving impatiently, he motioned the five very cold and very frightened individuals to follow suit.

They had no way of estimating time. Just one of them, one of the men, had come through the ordeal with a mobile phone intact. All the others, at some time during their arduous journey, had lost phones, watches and more, all stolen or demanded as additional payment. Sadly, the battery on that solitary instrument had long since died. Therefore, crouched on the unyielding, bare metal floor of the vehicle, they had no concept of time. They were sore and exhausted, their only consolation being the man up front had turned the vehicle's heater to maximum. Now they were at least warm. And, as far as they all knew, they were in the UK. This, the last stage of their long journey, would take as long as it must. And they would endure it because they were safe.

Though they had no way of knowing, it was a little over three hours before they made the first stop. There the rear doors of the van were pulled open and only the three men were ordered out of the vehicle. In just a few minutes the doors were again closed and the van once again moved off. They weren't to know it then, but the two young girls left clinging protectively to each other in the back of the van, would never see any of the men again.

The second stop came no more than ten or fifteen minutes after the first. This time the girls were ushered out of the vehicle. For just a moment they were able to see their surroundings: a narrow house-lined street with pavements and a single street light. Almost instantly they were hustled toward an open door of one of the houses.

One of the young girls looked up at the large bulky man urging her toward the door of the house. She used two of the English words she had known forever. "London? Yes?"

"London yes," the big man said.

She smiled happily. It was all she wanted to hear.

Handing the two girls over to the narrow, dark skinned woman waiting at the door, the man consoled himself that at least he had told the truth; this was London. It was one of the shorter trips. The northern runs were much more exhausting. But as far as the girls, and the men before them, were concerned, it mattered not where they ended up, for them the end result would be just the same.

Before turning back to the van, he watched the two young innocents ushered through the door, the plastic-covered package they had guarded so diligently taken from them as they moved through. Just for that moment, the guilt flooded through him as it always did at this time. Climbing back into the van, he took some consolation from the fact that this was the last time. He'd achieved his aim; he'd got what he wanted. Now it was time to bow out.

One

The landing was good, just the lightest of touches before the huge Boeing triple seven settled its mighty three hundred and fifty tons majestically back on terra firma, the twelve, huge, undercarriage wheels taking the strain, allowing the nose-wheel to sink smoothly on to the Heathrow tarmac. As the pilot brought the massive twin turbines to reverse thrust, bringing the shuddering aircraft to a safe taxiing speed, Theo Stern, together with the majority of the three hundred passengers aboard, breathed a satisfied sigh of relief. Admit it or not, the majority always did at this point in their journey. And on this occasion with good reason. Nine hours from Melbourne to Hong Kong with only a short break before a further twelve from Hong Kong to Heathrow was an endurance test for even the most hardened traveller. But for Stern, the journey had been particularly arduous. He had spent the whole trip agonising whether he should even have made the journey in the first place.

It was just nine months since he had travelled out to Australia in the hope of reconciliation with Annie. It was a last-ditch effort to rekindle the old flame with his ex-wife, and at the time he wanted nothing more. Initially, things did look promising. But as time moved on, it became obvious old gremlins had no regard for location...they came back to haunt wherever you were. They'd tried, of course, both doing their best to accommodate the other's wishes. But, if anything, the gap had widened, Annie becoming more deeply involved in her new life, Stern more frustrated with what he saw as a meaningless existence in a place he didn't particularly like anyway. The end had been inevitable. There was no animosity, no recriminations, just a final sad acceptance that things hadn't changed. They would always be the closest of friends, intimately so, but the old flame that had once burned so brightly had dimmed. The final farewell had been heart-wrenching, but they both knew it was the only way.

Even now, ten thousand miles and twenty-four hours too late, it still taunted him. Could he have done more, tried harder, compromised more? Anything to have made it work? The doubts had plagued him throughout the flight, interrupting his sleep, refusing to let him be.

As the aircraft trundled towards the final gate, he felt exhausted, mentally as well as physically. He had no idea what he was going to do from then on, but of one thing he was sure: he was back home, and one way or another, he had to get a grip on himself and move on.

Half an hour later, his hand luggage, an ancient rucksack, flung over his shoulder, he hauled his single suitcase from the carousel and headed for the green 'nothing to declare' channel.

Among the row of taxi and hire car drivers displaying the names of their pickups was a wide piece of cardboard held up obscuring the holder's face. Scribbled in thick black felt pen, it displayed the single word, 'BOSS.' Seeing it, just for an instant, the despondent tiredness left him and Stern smiled. He couldn't have asked for a more welcome return. He dumped the heavy suitcase in front of the individual and gently pulled down the cardboard.

"Cherry Hooker. Why am I not surprised?"

She was grinning from ear to ear. "Welcome home, boss."

Slowly shaking his head, he studied the impish face, the mischievous, sparkling eyes shining from the pale features framed by the natural fair hair. What was it Annie used to say? Eyes that reflected the heart. He realised he, too, was still smiling. "Thanks, kid. How ya doin'?"

She linked an arm through his and squeezed. "Better now you're back."

Leaving the terminal, they headed across to the car park, Stern shuddering as the sharpness of the cold overcast March morning cut through the thin jacket he was wearing.

Cherry noticed. "It'll be warm in the car."

"Good." He thought for a second. "You still got that shoe box on wheels?" He was referring to the Mini his ex-assistant had owned seemingly forever.

She smiled. "Of course. And why not?"

Stern thought about the last time he had travelled in Cherry's Mini. It was just a half an hour trip, but with his head touching the roof and his knees up to his chin, it was about all he could take.

"How long did it take you to get here this morning?"

"About three hours." She turned away, hiding the grin she couldn't hold back.

Stern sighed but said nothing. He couldn't complain, should be grateful. To be here to collect him at such an hour meant she had set out at around four that morning. That, in itself, had to be worth the cramped return journey home.

They threaded their way between the rows of parked cars, Stern taking little notice of the large, highly polished limousine until Cherry pulled him to a halt in front of it.

Seeing them arrive, a man sitting behind the wheel quickly opened the driver's door and climbed out. "I'll put your stuff in the boot, Mr Stern?" he said, taking Stern's case and rucksack from him.

Stern looked at Cherry. "I thought you said...?"

Cherry smiled up at him with mischievous eyes. "I said I still had the Mini. Didn't say I'd brought it here today, did I?"

"Hooker, you're a diamond."

She held his eyes, genuine affection showing. "Yeah, I know. So, are you getting in the car, or are we spending the rest of the day in the Heathrow car park?"

Two

Stern stood on the tiny second floor balcony looking out over the North Sea. Despite the low, threatening clouds, visibility was good, and the erect turbines of the offshore wind farm stood regimentally clear on the horizon, their blades turning majestically. He lowered his eyes to the beach below where lines of whitecaps pushed along by a stiff onshore breeze cut diagonally across the sand, the froth from one hardly having time to dissipate before another followed suit. It was a familiar scene that over previous years he'd never tired of. Nine months ago, full of hope and anticipation, it was also a scene he'd thought unlikely to see again. How wrong can you be? Strangely enough, despite the still lingering feeling of disappointment and failure, it somehow felt right.

Back then, before he had left, he'd debated whether to rent out the flat, even sell it. But with Cherry prepared to act as caretaker, he'd finally decided to do neither. Just in case, he'd said at the time. Deep down, even then, had he known he was kidding himself, that he and Annie were a lost cause wherever they lived? Whatever, he was pleased with the decision he had made. He turned back into the flat, closing and latching the glass doors, the sound of the wind and surf dying to a background murmur.

Earlier, they had left the M25 behind before the morning rush hour took hold. They'd made the trip in just three hours, door to door. And it had been painless, the seats of the large smooth car deep and comfortable. At the flat, Cherry had ensured the heating was on and a large prepared hotpot was ready, simmering in a slow cooker on the side in the kitchen. Slow cooker? Where the hell did that come from? Cherry had waved away the question, and he'd been too tired to argue. She'd stayed for half an hour, making tea and fussing around him, before saying she had things to do and heading off, promising to make contact later.

Alone, with the flat exactly as he had left it, it felt like he'd never been away. Making himself a fresh mug of tea, he slumped into a chair, his mind trolling back to the time he had left with high hopes of forging a new life with Annie in the sunshine. Now, in a heartbeat, he was back as if nothing had ever happened, the intervening nine months seemingly collapsed into nothingness.

But more worrying than the past was the future. For an instant, his stomach churned, a moment of panic enveloping him. Where the hell did he go from here? What did the future hold for him? He quickly swilled down the tea and pushed himself out of the chair. For a while, he busied himself unpacking and filling the washing machine. Then, the panic easing, unable to think of anything else to do, he made more tea and settled in front of the television. Daytime television was something he had never indulged in. The thought of mindless DIY, gardening and second-rate quiz shows had never appealed, but right now things were much too quiet, some background noise would help. As soon as the TV came alive, and the lunchtime news exploded onto the screen, he wished he hadn't bothered.

A man had driven a car along Westminster Bridge mowing down pedestrians before leaving the car and attacking two police officers guarding the entrance to Westminster with a knife. One of the officers had died. Stern felt his mouth dry, the news engendering an instant flashback.

June 1993, Manchester. A drug bust and Detective Inspector Theodore Stern, on secondment from the London Metropolitan Police force, leading from the front, as he always did.

Later the knife-wielding drug-soaked individual had no recollection of what had occurred, certainly not that he'd come to within an inch of taking Stern's life. He had also ended the career of a dedicated street copper whose whole life had been his work. Physically, Stern had recovered, but out of the force he could only see a bleak future ahead. Stern gave a sad shake of his head. Not a million miles from what he was seeing right now.

Back then, only Cherry Hooker and the launch of Stern Investigations in Norfolk had saved the day. Now, Stern Investigations was dead, wound up nine months ago when he'd headed for a new life on the other side of the world. He was sixty-three years old. A fit sixty-three, it was true, but sixty-three nonetheless. Norfolk was renowned for its older population, but what did it hold for a sixty-three-year-old who was terrified of retirement?

He leaned forward and switched off the television. He had spent nearly the whole of the last twenty-four hours on his backside; he needed exercise. He thought first of the rowing machine in the corner of the bedroom but, deciding against it, he went hunting for his trainers.

It was cold, and rain was falling from low dark clouds. He hadn't worn his running gear since he'd left for Australia, hadn't even taken it with him. He'd forgotten how good it felt. He made his way down from the flat, across the green and down the steps to the promenade. There he stopped and, as he had done so many times before, he spent time stretching cold, complaining muscles that hadn't been treated like this for months. By the time he dropped down onto the beach, he was wet through, but it mattered not, it never had. He reminded himself of his own mantra; if the tide was out, whatever the weather, the time was right. Taking a deep breath of the cold, brine-saturated air, he set off at little more than a jog. Half an hour out, half an hour back, that would be his target.

The first half hour felt good, not too fast, a gentle trot, his brain in neutral, easing himself back into the routine. Before turning for the return run, he took a break, resting against one of the gnarled wooden groins running down the beach into the sea. He scanned his surroundings, realising there wasn't another soul in sight, just the sea, the sand and the crumbling cliffs stretching above him. Despite the cold and wet, the old feeling of wellbeing was creeping back into his bones, reminding him of how much he had come to appreciate this place. Sure, he was a Londoner, born and bred, but there certainly was a special place in his heart for this neck of the woods. He recalled the time when he'd had high hopes of having this and Annie, but it wasn't to be. Australia had beckoned, and Annie hadn't been able to resist. He shoved himself roughly away from the groin and started the return run, pushing harder, angrily telling himself enough was enough. He had tried and failed. Now he had to look forward and build himself a future. Whatever that might be.

Back at the flat, he shed his soddened running gear and climbed into the shower. Running the water as hot as he could bear, he lathered himself from head to foot, his body warming, shedding the outside chill. After drying vigorously, he headed for the bedroom. For a moment, he studied himself in the mirror. Not bad for a sixty-three-year-old, though he wasn't happy with the buzz cut Annie had persuaded him to have. Not quite a crew cut, but not far off. He'd always been proud of his iron grey mop and hadn't really wanted to lose it. It was one sacrifice he *had* made.

He pulled on a pair of jeans and a jumper, happy with the thought that he could let his treasured thatch grow again. He looked at his watch, noting it was after midday...it was over thirty hours since he'd had set out from Melbourne. It hadn't happened yet, probably because of the adrenalin created by the beach run, but the jet lag was sure to hit him soon. Right then, he was hungry. In the kitchen, he lifted the lid from the unfamiliar slow cooker, the aroma of the thick lamb stew deliciously caressing his nostrils. He pulled a deep bowl from the cupboard and slid it onto a tray, adding two slices of buttered bread. Then, spooning a generous portion of the stew into the bowl, he carried the laden tray through to the living room.

The plan was to stay awake as long as he could into the evening, hopefully to get back into a local sleep pattern sooner than later. Whether he would last that long remained to be seen. He hoped a good meal would help.

He had taken only a couple of mouthfuls of Cherry's delicious offering when the telephone on the table alongside his chair rang. Cherry had told him she'd vetted many messages left during his absence, joking about how many were requests for the services of Stern Investigations. He could only think this was one such call. He picked up the phone.

"Stern."

"Theo, it's Dave."

Stern frowned, for the moment unable to recognise the voice, but loath to admit it. He stalled for thinking time. "Hello, Dave, how are you?"

"I'm good, Theo. How are you? Feeling the cold?"

"I am a bit." His mind was in overdrive, still trying to put a name to the voice.

"Theo, Cherry told me you were back, and I thought it only fair to give you a ring."

"Oh?"

"Yeah, I've had an offer for your place upstairs. Chap wants to rent it as office space. Said the way you left it was also perfect for him. Now you're back, I didn't know if you'd want to use it again. Thought it only fair to give you first option."

Ah, now he had it. Dave, the owner of the bakery on Sheringham High Street, above which he had set up and run Stern Investigations. "Thanks for that, Dave. I appreciate it. But to be honest I only arrived back this morning. Don't quite know which end's up right now. Got no intentions starting again, though, so if you have the chance of renting the space again, I guess you should take it."

"Er, d'you want time to give it some thought, Theo?"

Stern frowned, wondering why the question. "No, I don't think so. Why d'you ask?"

"Well, probably I shouldn't say, but Cherry's been up there for the last couple of hours cleaning up, as she put it, making things ready for action."

~ * ~

Cherry arrived back at the flat a little after five that evening. She let herself in with the key given her by Stern when he had left for Australia. Pausing just inside the door, she called out softly.

"It's only me. You decent?"

There was no reply, the flat in complete silence. Moving down the hall, she popped her head around the living room door. Stern was slumped in the armchair, out to the world, his head lolling to one side. On a tray, sitting on the floor alongside the chair, was an empty bowl and half a slice of buttered bread. Cherry tiptoed across the room and removed the tray, at the same time easing the spoon loosely hanging from the fingers of his hand. In the kitchen, she washed the plate and spoon and tidied things away. Glancing in the slow cooker, she smiled, guessing, from what was left, that the boss had a full stomach. Confirmed that everything was safely switched off, she padded softly back into the sitting room. She found a piece of paper and pencil and scribbled a note.

Would like to see you in the office in the morning for coffee and cake. Think you could make nine-thirty?

Looking down at her written words and again at Stern's prone figure, she hesitated for an unsure moment. She was well aware it was a leap of faith that could go badly wrong. But short of Annie herself, Cherry thought she knew the boss better than anyone. Sometimes better than he knew himself. She was banking on this being one of those times. He was what he was and would never be happy any other way. He just needed a gentle little push. She hoped. Taking a deep breath, she headed for the bedroom and perched the note on his pillow. He had to go to bed sometime.

Back in the sitting room, taking a final look round to ensure all was safe and well, Cherry let herself out and quietly locked the front door behind her.

Three

Mo Stevens is a forty-year-old solicitor. She stands a healthy, powerfully built five ten in her stockinged feet with dark hair cut in a severe style framing a serious, but not unattractive face. At the office, Mo power dresses, normally a crisp, gleaming white blouse, a brooch at the throat, sitting snugly under one of her several London made, closely tailored suits. Three-inch-high heels enable her to confidently eyeball the majority of her taller male clients.

At home, as she is now, she's a different woman. With nothing held in, she's dressed in well worn, stained jeans with holes in the knees and a denim shirt, its frayed collar showing its age, hanging loosely outside. Bare feet slipped into open-toed sandals complete the thrown together, beatnik ensemble she so prefers. And relaxed, with no one to impress, the uncombed butch haircut and makeup free, no nonsense face displays the tomboy she truly is.

Mo lives in a hundred-year-old, fisherman's cottage on the outskirts of Blakeney, one of the most enchanting villages on the North Norfolk Coast. Blakeney village is set on a small hill leading down to a natural harbour surrounded by a fascinating landscape of marshes, sand hills and mud banks, with creeks and channels twisting and turning their way throughout. The village is a favourite haunt for tourists, and its captivating terrain and endless skyscape attract artists from all over the country. Indeed, that is exactly the reason Mo is there. She, like so many other wannabe artists drawn to the area, has secret dreams of one day creating the masterpiece that rocks the world.

But it hadn't always been that way.

Until just a few years ago, Mo, a highly qualified solicitor, had lived in London. She worked for a successful city solicitor's practice with every chance of becoming a future partner. She was two years married, her husband a go-getting sales manager in a major car sales franchise. They lived in a large detached house in a leafy suburb, with an equally large mortgage, and presented the image of the perfect couple. Mo was happy and content with her lot. Happy and content, that was until, purely on a whim, seeking a relaxing hobby to ease the pressures of her busy days, she enrolled in evening art classes. As a result, two things happened.

Firstly, Mo almost instantly became captivated with the art of putting paint to canvas. In no time at all, one of the spare bedrooms had been transformed into a studio and when she wasn't away at art classes or browsing exhibitions, she was closeted in her studio totally engrossed in her own little world. Initially, her husband had welcomed her new hobby. He had his golf and regular evenings out with colleagues, so why not. But as the hobby became more of an obsession, he slowly began to feel left out, abandoned even. He made the point, but whatever he said made little difference. Mo was hooked.

The second thing that happened as a result of Mo's new-found passion was Mo's evening class teacher, a charismatic, highly respected local artist, not only took a shine to Mo's art, but also to Mo. A torrid affair followed, the details of which, Mo never did find out how, somehow reached her husband. In a blurred, vitriolic, and seemingly very short time, Mo found herself divorced and living alone in a hastily acquired, not very salubrious flat. The pain increased when her boss, a bit of a puritan, decided her services were no longer required. Her moral behaviour, he told her bluntly, was not conducive to the high, unquestionable standards required of his staff. Particularly, when a good deal of their work revolved around other people's marital problems. In other words, her conduct tarnished the face of the practice. She was out. And just to add insult to injury, her lover, himself a married man, back pedalled so quickly, he disappeared into the sunset quicker than she could say Vincent van Gogh.

Initially, Mo found herself in a tearful, hazy limbo, unable to understand how, in the blink of an eye, she had allowed her happy, comfortable life to be trashed. But with time, questions came to invade her mind. Had she really been happy? If she really was, why did she allow this to happen? Was the torment she was facing destined to have been? Would the path she was truly destined to follow never be found in the wake of other people's grubby waste? Finally, the revelation dawned. No, there was another life waiting out there. It was a spiritually satisfying life she was destined to lead. It was one she had found in her art, and one she was determined to follow.

The divorce settlement had been just sufficient for her to afford the move from the depressing flat to the cottage on the outskirts of Blakeney. Here, she knew, art thrived. And a small solicitor's practice in Norwich, short of qualified staff and not in the least concerned with her past, had been only too pleased to have her. The pay, though not even close to that of her London position, was sufficient for her needs. Anyway, once she had seen the light, she didn't intend to be a solicitor forever. No, Mo felt she had come home, come to a place she was meant to be. And one day, she would abandon the bone aching grind of her current career and become a full-time artist. She would live her life among the thrilling aroma of oil paint, linseed oil and turpentine. Then she would create the masterpiece she dreamed of. Already she had shown at a number of exhibitions across the country and had, indeed, sold some of her work. Nothing big yet but hope sprung eternal.

Now, Sunday mid-morning, Mo was, as always at this time, sitting in front of her easel, her eyes peering out of the large picture window overlooking the coast. Normally, her gaze would be taking in the landscape, her mind assessing the light, imagining tone and form, determining how she would transfer the scene accurately onto the canvas in front of her. But right then, Mo's mind was a million miles from both the scene outside, and the canvas before her.

The cottage, overlooking the coastal dunes, was set apart from the main village. A little remote, she had thought on her first viewing. But so enchanting was the little building and the surrounding area that she just couldn't resist taking the plunge. Initially, at night before retiring, the double check routine had been a must. Twice round all doors and windows to ensure everything was secure, and the alarm system she had installed was live and active. Even then, there were times when she had woken with a start, the old building creaking in the wind, or the outside security light activated by a passing animal. But with time, the sounds became familiar, even comforting. As she came to know the locals and had been assured life in the area was as safe as it could be, she had relaxed and slept soundly.

But it takes just one single frightening incident to destroy confidence, and for Mo, that incident had occurred several days ago. Or more correctly, several nights ago. And not just that once. Last night, it happened again.

Mo took a deep breath, thoughtfully tracing the line of her bottom lip back and forth with the tip of her tongue. She should tell someone, of course, the obvious choice being the police. But that posed a problem. Mo's last encounter with the boys in blue was not a happy one. Not her fault, she'd always told herself. She was a victim of circumstance. Sure, she had made a mistake, been sucked in by the sugary charm of her art teacher. She had accepted that and prepared herself for the repercussions it would bring. But the constant and violent recriminations meted out by her husband had been relentless and beyond reason. Finally, he had pushed her too far, brought on that one moment of madness so alien to her character. In truth, the damage she had caused with the Stanley knife to his top-of-the-range company Audi saloon was no more than a reputable body shop could have put right in no time at all. But both her husband and the company he worked for had played it up big time. As a result, Mo Stevens had a criminal record.

Common sense told her it could have little bearing on the present situation. This was a genuine concern, something the police should know about, but how could she be sure? Once you involve the law, even innocently, and they look back at your record, anything could happen. A single slip of the tongue, a careless word by the local bobby, and the whole of Blakeney, even her employer, would know of her sorry past; the mad woman who'd attacked her husband's car with a Stanley knife. If she were capable of that, then...? No, that wouldn't do at all. She had built a respectable image since moving there, she couldn't afford to jeopardise that. So, the police? She didn't think so.

But there was someone she'd heard talked of locally.

Four

Stern hadn't seen the note when he'd dragged himself out of the armchair and staggered into the bedroom at whatever unearthly time it was in the early hours. Hadn't even noticed it when he had left the bed half an hour ago, nearly falling over the heap of discarded clothes on the floor and headed for the shower. And why would he? His eyes were so full of grit he could hardly see where he was going. But he had slept nearly five solid hours. He couldn't be sure what sort of job he made of the shave, but the shower worked its magic. From very hot to cold, finally, eyes open, peering directly into the flow. Then a brisk rubdown finishing the job. It was when he'd padded back to the bedroom, a towel wrapped around his middle, feeling almost human, he'd spotted the crumpled piece of paper lying on the floor alongside the bed. He bent and picked it up, smoothing it out between his fingers.

Would like to see you in the office in the morning for coffee and cake. Think you could make nine thirty?

So, Cherry had come back last night. He must have been dead to the world, never heard a thing. Now here she was giving out instructions. Some cheek. And the office? What was she on about? As far as he was concerned, there was no office. Stern Investigations wrapped up more than nine months ago, and at his age, he had no intentions of starting again. Then he remembered the call from Dave, his ex-landlord. Slumped on the edge of the bed, he felt the irritation rise. What the blazes was she up to?

He dressed slowly, his mind, as it had done repeatedly since he'd left Melbourne, automatically beginning to trawl through the events of the last months, the sadness returning. He shook his head angrily, stopping himself short. *No, enough. Pull yourself together, Stern. How many times, the past is the past? Only the future matters now.* He wandered into the kitchen and made himself coffee, returning to the sitting room, unlocking the glass doors leading to the balcony outside. The sky was clear, but the chilled onshore breeze of yesterday was as brisk as ever. He stood, cradling the mug between both hands looking out across the North Sea, glancing down at the occasional early riser moving along the promenade below. The air tasted clear and clean, but it was bloody cold, completely the opposite of what he had become used to of late. And that breeze was making his eyes water. But even so, it felt good. After a few minutes, the cold getting the better of him, he returned inside and closed the doors.

Back in the kitchen, he slid the half-finished cold coffee into the microwave, thinking again about Cherry's note. As Dave had indicated, she had obviously been spending time preparing the old Stern Investigations office. But preparing it for what? He had given her no indication he wished to start again. In fact, on the drive from the airport he had made it clear he had no intention of reinstating Stern Investigations. So why would she do that? He pulled the freshly heated coffee from the microwave and slumped down at the kitchen table, at the same time noting the kitchen clock showed eight thirty. It reminded him that back then, on most days, Cherry was at the office before him, seldom later than this time. And there was always a cheeky remark to welcome him. But that was Cherry, the way she was. Even in the early dark days.

He thought back, remembering. The then-Detective Inspector Theodore Stern of the London Metropolitan Police. A dedicated street copper, his life's mission to clear the gutters of the bad guys and protect the vulnerable. And at that time, there was no one more vulnerable than Cherry Hooker. Put on the streets by a ruthless father, and controlled by a vicious pimp who thought of nothing but profit, Cherry had sunk into a misty world of rapacious men and drugs. But even then, the spark that much later Stern had come to know and value still burned. And it was that spark that was her undoing. When callously instructed to accommodate several foreign gentlemen at one sitting, she'd rebelled. But rebellion to her unrelenting ruthless pimp meant just one thing.

The station had received the call from a concerned neighbour. "Violent exchanges, distressed screams." Violent exchanges in the East End of London were nothing new, but distressed screams?

When Stern and his men dragged Cherry from the foul smelling flat, she was beaten half to death. Stern had seen it all before, of course, but there was something about the sight of this particular battered young woman that rankled, got completely under his skin. Whatever it was had driven him to support her morally and financially back to fitness and rehabilitation. When fully recovered, Cherry testified against her attacker, bringing him and his cronies down. It was a brave act, and, for her own protection, she was moved into the anonymity of the witness protection programme.

But it wasn't the last Stern was to see of Cherry Hooker.

Stern, then retired, was living in Norfolk. He was standing on the promenade looking out over the North Sea and contemplating a plan slowly germinating in his head when he felt a tap on the shoulder. Cherry Hooker had sought him out. He remembered his own surprise when he turned and saw her. He also remembered her words as if they were spoken only yesterday: "Don't have a job by any chance, do you, boss?' That memory, a treasured one, always brought a smile.

Now, screwing up his brow, he thought for a moment, remembering. God, that was more than thirteen years ago.

He finished the coffee and pushed himself to his feet. She was always a headstrong young woman; her tragic past had made her so. From the day Cherry Hooker had returned to the real world, she had been determined no one would ever push her around again. And no one had. That was, with the exception of Theo Stern, the boss. He was the true father she had never had; the man who had brought her back from the brink, saved her life, literally. He was her hero and, though not always without argument or cheek, from him she would take anything. For him, she would do anything.

Stern pulled on his top coat and gloves and headed for the door. He would do as she asked and go to the office, but if the little minx thought there was the slightest chance they were about to pick up where they'd left off, she had another think coming.

He left the flat and made his way across the green, past the children's play swings and down the steep flight of stone steps to the promenade. It was deserted and, pulling his collar high, he walked quickly, the sharp breeze chilling his cheeks, making his eyes water. Reaching the fisherman's ramp, the beached crab and lobster boats, as always secured to the heavy eyelets set in the concrete slope, he turned up toward the town. Finally, making his way through the short, narrow alleyway, he emerged onto the high street. He stopped for a moment, looking from left to right, noting that nothing had changed. But then, why would it have? He had been away for a little over nine months, what the hell ever changed in nine months?

Slowing his pace, the high street sheltered from the onshore chill, he headed casually along the street. The bakery was no more than a few hundred yards up ahead and, once he was there, he wasn't sure he wanted to succumb to Cherry's demands after all. But he carried on and a few minutes later found himself outside the bakery. Through the glass frontage, he could see Dave sliding several cakes into a paper bag for just a single customer who, thankfully, he didn't recognise. He pushed his way inside.

Immediately the familiar warm, sweet smelling atmosphere drifting from the baking oven at the rear of the shop enveloped him. He breathed deeply, filling his lungs. How often in the past had he enjoyed the wonderful aroma of freshly baking bread and cakes? Almost every morning since the inauguration of Stern Investigations all those years ago. To him, it signalled the start of a new fresh day. And the pleasure had never waned, not one iota. The only drawback was the amount of willpower required every morning to pass the cake-packed counter without cracking and grabbing the largest cream cake on show. A temptation, much to Cherry's chagrin, he had often been unable to resist.

He gave Dave the thumbs up and smiled, raising his eyes skyward questioningly as he passed. Dave understood immediately and nodded, indicating Cherry was already in the office. Stern continued on toward the back of the shop, passing the humming oven on his way to the single staircase leading upwards. He paused on the first step, glancing up, seeing the half-glassed door above, the words *Stern Investigations* still blazoned across the glass. He shook his head and gave a tight-lipped grin. Life could be a bitch sometimes.

Five

Cherry Hooker took a last look around the office. Everything exactly as it had been before. The heating on—he'd need that after the Australian heat—her desk in place, and the makings ready on the table in the far corner of the room. She had already done the rounds of the inner office, Stern's domain, making sure the ancient desk and chair were dusted down, ready for him. He had been away for only nine months, but it seemed forever. Now, he was back where he should be, doing what he was supposed to be doing, what he was best at. She couldn't be more chuffed. He was her hero, had been ever since that day, the best part of twenty years past. When, regaining consciousness in the hospital bed, the first things she saw were his dark concerned eyes peering down at her. In that instant, an unbreakable link had been made. Even during the interminable five years in witness protection, she had known one day she would seek him out. It had always been a given.

When, determined on reconciliation, Stern had decided to drop everything and chase after his ex in Australia, Cherry had been bereft. The hole he was about to leave in her life seemed huge. It was true she had her own love, and marriage was on the horizon, but that was a different kind of love. It was also a love that could never have happened without the boss. It couldn't have, because without Stern she wouldn't have been here in the first place, probably wouldn't have even been alive.

She'd known the chance of reconciliation between the two was remote, knew them both well enough to be able to see the irreconcilable differences Stern was blind to. Or was he? Did he know in his heart he was wasting his time, that it was a lost cause? Back then, before he left, the things he said, the way he acted, sometimes made her think so. But Cherry had smiled and encouraged him, genuinely hoping things would work out, at the same time wishing like mad he'd change his mind. And though, when she learned he was coming home, she had been sad for his sake, she had shamelessly rejoiced.

She had missed the boss and the excitement Stern Investigations had brought to her life immensely. She wanted him back, wanted the special relationship they'd had for all those years back in her life. Her man, the man who very soon was to become her husband, had told her to let it go. Stern was gone, get used to it, find something else. But she couldn't think of a single thing that could match what she'd had before, not one. Besides, something told her he would be back, that Stern Investigations wasn't finished. It was the sole reason she had asked Dave to keep the office in place. Twelve months, she had told him. After that, he could let it go.

On the way home from the airport, Stern had sounded pretty determined it wouldn't happen, that Stern Investigations was a thing of the past. But Cherry knew Theo Stern. He was a copper through and through. It was part of him, in his bones. Kick him out of the Met, strip him of the official authority, do what you would, and it would make no difference. He had copper engraved on his heart. So, he was no longer a young man, and he was no longer in the force, hadn't been for years, but in her eyes, he was the best, always would be. Anyway, what else could he do?

The question was, would he come? Had she pushed too hard leaving the note? Should she have waited, given him more time? She wrinkled her nose distastefully. No, that had never been her way, and the boss knew it. He would have probably been disappointed if she had. She glanced at her watch. It was just after nine. Not too late yet, but still? She wandered back into Stern's office, did another pass, just to be sure everything was as it should be. For a moment, she stood looking out of the window, peering down at the comings and goings on the Sheringham High Street. He used to do this all the time, thinking, gaining inspiration from the constant flow of human traffic. His words, not hers.

She started at the sound of the footsteps on the stairs, slow and deliberate, to her instantly recognisable. Her heart gave a little flip, and she scuttled back into the outer office, taking her usual place at the desk, the laptop open in front of her. Nine months may have passed, but that was just a minor blip. It was time things got back to normal.

~ * ~

Stern pushed open the door and stood silently, his eyes traversing the room, finally coming to rest on her smiling, defiant face. He had known her since she was in her teens, and in all that time, he had never met another woman like her. Cherry would never grace the cover of a fashion magazine; even without Botox, her lips were too full, and her jaw too aggressive. But there was something about her that caught the eye, drew the attention. Could it be those clear, intelligent eyes? Or was it just the soft, naturally fair hair she wore short, framing her pale flawless features? Then maybe, it was none of these things; maybe it was just the confident, determined, way she held herself. Whatever it was, it was hers and hers alone. This morning, she looked as immaculate as ever; the formal, businesslike white blouse tucked into close fitting skirt accentuating her slim figure, the result, he knew, of her regular visits to the local gym. Yeah, he thought, she was one exceptional young woman. But sometimes, she could also be one exceptional pain in the arse.

He held her gaze sombrely for some moments before speaking. "So, what the hell are you playing at, Hooker?"

Cherry lowered her eyes and ran her finger self-consciously along the edge of the laptop, the immaculately manicured, blood red fingernail glinting. "I just thought...Well, you're back, you'll obviously need something to do."

Stern closed the door and pulled off his gloves, stuffing them into his topcoat pocket. Then, without thinking, shrugged out of his topcoat, automatically crossing the room to the coat rack as he had done a thousand times in the past.

The move didn't go unnoticed. Cherry hid the satisfied smile behind a hand.

Spinning round, Stern again scanned the room. "You were supposed to get rid of all this stuff and wrap up the business."

She slid out of her chair and crossed to the little table holding the makings; tea, coffee, and this morning one of Dave's paper bags, the stain of what was inside a giveaway. "I kept meaning to. Just didn't get around to it. Then I got your email saying you were coming home, and I thought. Well I just thought you might..." She flicked the switch on the kettle. "The usual?"

"Yeah, thanks." Again, the answer came automatically. Realising, he could have bit his tongue. Too late. "So, who's paid the rent for the last nine months?"

She shrugged, keeping her back to him, fussing with the new mugs she had bought for the occasion. "Dave didn't seem too worried, didn't push me." It was a lie, of course; Dave wasn't a charity and never denied the rent for the rooms being an essential addition to his income, particularly out of season. And to find that rent she had taken a job, one she hadn't particularly enjoyed doing, at one of the large stores in Norwich. Not that she was about to admit any of that.

But Stern hadn't been a London detective all those years without learning how to interpret body language. Particularly Cherry Hooker's body language. Hell, they'd worked together for twelve years. If he didn't know a thing or two about her by then, he never would. Never mind, he let it go. For then, anyway.

She turned, holding the two mugs. "D'you want this out here or in your office?"

Tight lipped, he shook his head sadly, then pointed toward the door to his room. "Okay, take 'em in there." He glanced back at the table. "What's in the bag?"

She stopped and smiled. "Breakfast?"

In his office, he settled into the old chair behind his desk, its complaining creaks and groans as loud and welcoming as ever. Just as old and just as comfortable, he thought. But he said nothing, his face a mask. Cherry placed the two mugs of coffee on his desk alongside a brand-new note pad and two freshly sharpened pencils and left the room. She returned immediately with the cream cake, his favourite, on a plate which was also new. She was also carrying a hard-backed file. She slid the plate on the desk in front of him, then settled in the chair opposite, curling her legs beneath her as she always had and balancing the file on her lap. Cradling the coffee between her hands, she held his eyes. "Am I in for a rocket, boss?"

He looked from her anxious face to the cake in front of him and back again, another shake of the head. "You're bloody impossible, d'you know that?"

"I just thought..."

"Yeah, yeah, so you said," he growled. He leaned across and picked up the plate. Settling back in his chair, he took a bite of the cake, conscious of the cream sticking to his lips, wiping it away with the back of his hand. He slid the plate back on the desk, reminded of how bloody good Dave's freshly baked cakes were. Picking up his coffee, he swilled down the mouthful. "So, the plan is to con me into reinstating Stern Investigations by keeping the office open and plying me with cream cakes and coffee, is that it?"

"Yes."

Stern sighed. "Don't mess about, just say what you mean, why don't you?"

"You did ask."

"Look, kid, the business has been down for nine months, and I don't have to remind you I am now just two years away from retirement age. Private detective work involves long hours, and it can sometimes be damned dangerous." He held her gaze. "I don't have to remind you of the Campbell case, do I?" He was referring to the case of Melanie Campbell whose son was drowned, and who carried out vengeance killings using her other powerful, but retarded, son as a weapon. That son had beaten Stern to within an inch of his life.

Cherry studied her fingernails. "No, of course I haven't forgotten. How could I? You had us all frightened to death."

"Well, there you go then. Why d'you think I would want to take that risk again?"

She looked up, tilting her head, a soft smile. "Boss, we worked Stern Investigations for more than twelve years, and that was the only time…"

"As far as I'm concerned, once is enough," he snapped. "And I'll remind you again of the age thing."

She waved away the protest. "Boss, you're as strong and as fit as you ever were." She gave him a sly, knowing grin. "Bet you've already done one of your beach runs."

"That has nothing to do with anything."

"I'm right though, aren't I?"

He replaced the coffee mug on the desk and again retrieved the plate, playing for time, slowly, silently devouring the rest of the cake. Finally, dropping the empty plate back on the desk, he again retrieved the coffee, taking a swig. "Look, even if I did decide to have another go, do you remember how long it took us to initially get going? Advertisements in newspapers, shop windows, the lot. Then the vetting by the police. All an absolute pain. Why would I want to go through…?"

"You don't have to," Cherry interrupted.

His eyes narrowed suspiciously. "What?"

"I've spoken to David O'Connor, and he says as far as he's concerned you are still registered, still on their books." She was talking of Detective Inspector David O'Connor of the Norfolk Constabulary to whom, over the years Stern had become close and assisted on a number of cases.

"Now look, madam, you are really pushing your luck here. I don't think you should assume, just because..."

"And you don't have to worry about getting clients," Cherry blurted out excitedly, cutting him short. "I've got two standing by already."

Six

Stunned, Stern's mouth hung open for some seconds before he was able to speak. Then, rocking forward to the tune of the groaning old chair, he eyeballed Cherry angrily. "Just one minute, young woman. Let me get this straight. You're telling me you've already taken on two clients?"

Cherry dropped her eyes, studying her slender finger as it traced a line around the rim of her mug. "Yes."

He took a breath. "I don't believe...Do you have telephone numbers?"

Cherry looked up apprehensively. "Yes, I do." She made to open the folder on her lap.

Stern held up a hand, stopping her. "Don't bother, just call the two clients, and tell them that whatever you promised was baloney." He gave a heavy sigh. "Just tell me Cherry, what part of the sentence 'Stern Investigations is no longer in business,' do you not understand?"

She stopped, the folder half open, her eyes clouding. "I just thought..."

Stern flopped back in the chair, exasperated. "You keep saying that, kid. You just thought, you just thought. Well, just thinking don't cut it. If I'd wanted to start things over, don't you think I'd have made contact and given you the heads up at some time?"

Cherry laid the folder and the mug on the floor beside her chair then straightened, a determined glint in her eye. "Boss, d'you remember when you first came to Sheringham, when the Met put you out to grass, and you followed Annie here?" It was a question, but she didn't wait for an answer. "In no time at all, you were so bored you were pulling your hair out."

"Yeah, yeah, okay I know where you're going with this," Stern interrupted. "But..."

"No buts, boss," she cut in. "If Stern Investigations, or something like it, hadn't happened, you would have topped yourself."

Stern gave a dismissive shake of the head like he wasn't listening.

But Cherry wasn't deterred. "You're a detective, boss. Always have been and always will be. And you're one of the best. Nobody knows that better than me. It's what you do, what you've always done."

Stern stretched his arms, linking his fingers behind his head. "You're wasting your breath, Hooker."

"Okay, answer me this. What are you going to do instead?"

"That's none of your bloody business."

Cherry looked crestfallen, the snapped out, thoughtless rebuke cutting deep.

Stern saw it, and instantly regretted the harsh retort. "Look Cherry," he came back quickly, his tone softening. "I know you loved what we did before, and I have to admit mostly it was good. But there comes a time when you have to call it quits. I believe that time is now. For crying out loud, you're going to be a married woman soon. With that will come a family and all the other responsibilities that go with it. Don't you think..." He was interrupted by the sudden ringing of the telephone on the desk in front of him. He looked to

Cherry, waiting for her to jump to as she had always had in the past. She didn't move. Frowning, he reached forward and picked up the receiver. "Stern"

"Theo, its David O'Connor. Cherry told me you were back. How are you?"

"I'm good, David. And you?"

"Same old, same old, Theo. One over and two unders, as usual."

Stern couldn't help the smile. O'Connor often used the phrase when they'd worked together before. It was the reason, from time to time, he had requested Stern's assistance. One over, two unders. Overworked, understaffed and underpaid. "Things don't change then?"

"Not in our lifetime, my friend. Don't know why I'm still struggling. I've done my thirty, should cut and run."

Stern thought of his own situation; they had to throw him out. "Not you, David, you're cemented to the job."

"Yeah, you could be right. Blowed if I know why though." There was a short awkward pause before O'Connor went on. "Sorry to hear things didn't work out with Annie."

"We can't all have everything our own way, David."

"No. A pity, though. I'd hoped the sun, sea and sand would do the trick."

Stern didn't answer. There was nothing to say.

"So, when did you get back?" O'Connor came in quickly, filling the silence.

"Yesterday. Still trying to stay awake."

"I'm not surprised. You've seen Cherry, of course."

"Yes, she picked me up from Heathrow. She's sitting with me now." Stern's brain, tired as it was, automatically connected a few dots. "But you knew that, didn't you, David? Otherwise, you wouldn't have called this number."

O'Connor chuckled. "Sharp as ever, Theo. Yes, I knew you'd be there. Cherry told me so." A short pause. "Well, she said she hoped you'd be."

"And I guess she also told you she's trying to get me to reinstate Stern Investigations. In fact, knowing what a devious little madam she is, I wouldn't be at all surprised if she hasn't tried to recruit your help. Is that what this call is about, David?"

"No, not quite, Theo. She did confess her hopes, I have to admit. But she didn't ask for my help. Mind you, if she had, I'd have been only too pleased to put in my two pennyworth."

"At least you're honest."

O'Connor chuckled. "Theo, I'm a policeman, of course I'm honest."

Again, Stern smiled. When the two first met, the relationship had been strained, but they had soon become firm friends; Stern relishing being involved with real policing again, O'Connor grateful to be able to draw on Stern's immense experience and advice. They had since worked on several cases together, the relationship becoming closer and more trusting with each. Truth was, like Cherry, O'Connor had also been sad at Stern's decision to follow Annie to Australia. But his friend was back. He was happy about that.

"Well thanks for the call, David," Stern said. "Let me get over the jet lag, get myself back in the land of the living, and we must have a jar together. I'll give you a call."

"That'll be good, Theo." There was another short uncertain pause before, "Could you make it sooner than later?"

"Oh, why?"

"Well to be honest, this isn't only a social call. See, I've got this problem and now you're back...Well I just thought..."

Stern raised his eyes skyward. "I just thought." Lowering his gaze, he looked across at Cherry who was unable to hide the smile. "Have you been teaching him his bloody lines?" he growled.

Seven

He had taken three days. Sleeping, rising ridiculously early—his body clock all over the place—running the beach, eating, down at the pub, sleeping. Sometimes, if the early morning rain was too heavy, even pounding the rowing machine. All the time, amid the effort and sweat, thoughts of reinstating Stern Investigations tormenting his brain. He cursed Cherry for putting him on the spot as she had, particularly so quickly after his return. Hell, he'd hardly been back twenty-four hours when she was lining up clients. Was she kidding? She hadn't given him time to think, assess what he wanted to do with the rest of his life. Oh, he knew why she had done it, of course. Even with the ups and downs, particularly that very last case when Stern had been severely beaten, the twelve years they'd operated Stern Investigations had been special. It wasn't just the cases and the clients. Their relationship, too, was unique. Cherry, always an open book, made no secret of the fact that he was much more to her than just the boss. Admitting openly, he was the father figure she had always craved and never had. Likewise,

Stern had often thought, if he'd had a daughter of his own, he couldn't have asked for better. So, no, he couldn't blame her for wanting more. But, as he had said to David O'Connor; you can't have everything your own way, and she'd had no right to put him on the spot like she had. He'd been angry and had it not been for David O'Connor's call, would have made her switch off the two so-called clients and wrap things up there and then. Instead, biting his tongue, he had waved a warning finger at Cherry and left the office without another word.

It was the morning of the fourth day, and after the best night's sleep he'd had since his return, he was feeling almost human. Last night, he'd turned in at around midnight and surfaced just after nine thirty this morning. He'd been pleased to see a clear sky and, though the breeze was still sharp off the sea, his run had been relaxed and easy. Back in the flat, he'd shaved, showered and breakfasted on marmalade toast, a banana and fresh coffee. Afterwards, sitting on the tiny balcony cradling his coffee, watching the off-shore wind turbines gently turning on the horizon, his head was clear, and he felt genuinely rested. It was then, breaking into his comfortable reverie, Cherry's words had climbed into his head. '*So, what are you going to do instead then?*' He sighed heavily and reached for the phone, punching in a still well-remembered number.

"Thought you'd kicked me into touch."

"Sorry, David, it's taken me a while to get my head round things. D'you still want to talk?"

"I'd appreciate it." David O'Connor sounded tired.

"I'm all yours today, if it's convenient."

"A beer tonight?" Until the time Stern had left, they'd regularly had a weekly drink together after work. Week about; one week on O'Connor's patch in Norwich, the next in the Sheringham area, Stern's home turf.

"You sound bushed," Stern said. "Shall I come to you?"

"I am, and yes, that'd be good."

"Usual time?"

"Thanks, Theo. Like old times, eh?"

"Yeah, like old times. See you later." Stern ended the call, thinking he wasn't sure he wanted the old times back, but O'Connor's calls usually meant an involvement in real police work. He had to admit to a familiar, not unpleasant, apprehension at the prospect.

Since leaving the office three days before, he hadn't heard from or tried to make contact with Cherry. Now, the guilt was setting in. For years, she had worked hard for him, being as much an influence in the success of Stern Investigations as he was. Cherry's presumption that on his return he would obviously be receptive to reinstating Stern Investigations was misguided, and her actions to that end out of order. But his angry reaction to her no doubt good intentions was uncharacteristic and equally uncalled for. He could only put it down to tiredness, possibly tinged with the still lingering disappointment of his unsuccessful trip. He needed to put that right. He dialled another familiar number. It was answered almost immediately.

"Hello boss." Her voice was soft, hesitant, unlike her.

"Hi, kid. Where are you?"

"At home." Cherry was living with her long-term boyfriend, Rob, who was a boat builder employed by a large holiday boat hire company based on the Norfolk Broads, the extensive series of rivers and lakes spread across Norfolk. They lived in a riverside cottage close to his work, some forty minutes' drive from Sheringham.

Stern looked at his watch. "What you doing for lunch?"

"Nothing special."

"Fancy coming over?"

"Yes, but…"

"See, yesterday I saw a car advertised in the local rag," he interrupted quickly. "Looks like a good buy, and now I'm back, I'm going to need wheels. Thought I'd go and take a look at it this afternoon." Before leaving for Australia, Stern had sold his treasured Hyundai coupe he'd enjoyed driving so much. He was sorry about that now. "You know I can never make up my own mind. How about I buy you lunch, and we go take a look together? We can have a chat about things, too."

"Are you sure, boss?" Again, the unfamiliar, uncertain tone. "I know I was out of order. I should have…"

"Am I sure?" he cut her off quickly. "Now would I be calling if I wasn't sure?"

~ * ~

They'd eaten at a café on the Sheringham high street, initially the mood uncharacteristically awkward, Cherry particularly quiet. Stern was not happy with that. He couldn't remember a time when the relationship had ever been strained. He wasn't about to let it happen now. He pushed his empty plate to one side.

"Okay, so here's how we stand," he said abruptly, his eyes firmly holding hers. "Apart from being exhausted and full of jet lag after a thirty-hour journey, I was also pretty miffed about making a hash of things out there."

"Boss, I know…"

He held up a hand, stopping her short. "No, don't interrupt. You, on the other hand, had taken it for granted that I would welcome starting Stern Investigations again. In fact, you had held onto things here in the hope that would happen." He fixed her with his best scowl. "I'm right, aren't I?"

Cherry held his gaze. "Yes."

"And you continued paying Dave the office rent, didn't you?"

"Uh-huh."

He screwed up his nose. "Bad idea, kid."

She looked up. "I know, but I just…"

He scowled. "Don't you dare say I just thought."

Silently, they held each other's gaze for some moments before broad smiles began to spread across both faces.

"So," Stern went on. "Consider yourself reprimanded for being such a presumptuous madam and taking me for granted, and along with that accept my apologies for being such a miserable old git and a total grump."

Cherry's smile broadened further. "Reprimand and apology accepted with pleasure, boss."

"Good. Now as I see it, we have two very important decisions to make. Firstly, we must get out of here and go find me those wheels."

"And second?"

Stern pushed himself out of the chair. "The second one we make in the morning at the office. Nine o'clock sharp." He waved a finger. "And don't be late."

Eight

Stern was feeling buoyant. He'd never dreamed for one moment he would ever own another Volkswagen Scirroco. It was the latest model, of course, and nothing like the old 1980's model he'd owned before...the one he wouldn't let a garage near and spent every spare hour working on himself. Old with a heavy bunch of miles under its belt, but nonetheless his pride and joy. It had been immaculate, cleaned and polished regularly, not a mark on it. That was until some crazy bozo tried to kill him by driving him off the road into a damn great oak tree. The oak won the contest, his treasured Scirocco, completely totalled, coming a battered second. He thought back to that time, the case of the treacherous ex-Commander Harry Rogers and his dirty deeds. When was that? Back in 2006, if he remembered correctly.

The Hyundai coupe followed the death of his pride and joy, but though a pleasure, it didn't quite measure up to his original love. Now he was back where he'd started. He'd test driven the new model— not quite new, but with only five thousand miles on the clock it was hardly run in. He was happy with that. Of course, it had none of the quirks of the original. Those little idiosyncrasies that put a capital D in driving. For a start, this one had brakes that actually worked. It had power assisted steering, too. With time he could foresee a great relationship developing. There was just one small problem. Today was Monday, and with a full service, and whatever else to be carried out by the garage, the car wouldn't be ready for collection until Wednesday. So, this evening it was a taxi to Norwich for his meet with David O'Connor. Not too much of a disappointment. It meant he could have an extra pint if he fancied it.

He was dropped off at David's local, a short distance from the central market square, just before eight. It had been little more than a year since his last visit, yet it seemed an age. Nevertheless, with the prospect of being involved in proper police work again came the old eagerness within. He found himself smiling. Sixty-three and the urge was still there. He would never admit it, but Cherry was probably right, what else would he do?

Inside, he found O'Connor waiting, an almost finished pint in front of him. He was sitting at a small table tucked away in one corner, slightly removed from the main area. It was their preferred place, away from prying ears, when O'Connor wanted a little privacy. Stern went straight to the bar and collected two pints of his favourite local real ale and weaved his way across.

He eased himself down and slid the fresh pint in front of his friend. "Evening, David."

"Theo, good to see you. How are you?"

"Better. Last night I made a full night for the first time since I returned. Feel like I'm back in the real world at last."

O'Connor finished the dregs of his first pint and pushed the empty glass to one side. "Glad to hear it." He pulled the fresh pint closer. "When we spoke on the phone, I got the impression you were a little peeved with Cherry."

Stern took a drink and wiped the froth from his lips with the back of his hand. "You're right, I was. Shouldn't have been, I guess. She means well."

O'Connor raised his eyebrows. "So, what then?"

"Well, she took it for granted I'd be back in harness as soon as I returned. Would you believe, she even kept the office on while I was away, paid the rent herself. Admitted she was prepared to foot the bill for twelve months in the hope I returned."

O'Connor laughed. "She's a one off, Theo, and no mistake. And she was right, wasn't she? You're back. Anyway, you can't blame her, she loved working with you. Thinks the sun shines out of you know where. You buggering off like you did must have been a wrench for her."

Stern gave a shake of the head. "Yeah, I accept all that, but what she did was barmy."

O'Connor studied him closely across the table. "So, I take it you don't want to get back in harness then?"

Stern sniffed. "Didn't say that. Just don't like being taken for granted."

"So, do you, or don't you?" O'Connor was grinning now.

Stern returned the grin, a little sheepishly. "Let's just say I'd be interested to know why you asked me here."

"Okay, at least that's a start," O'Connor said. "So, does the name Eddie Butler mean anything to you?"

Pulling at his bottom lip, Stern thought for a beat, finally shaking his head. "Can't say it does. Who is he?"

"He's a London businessman. Got a damned great house on the edge of Wroxham Broad. And that's only his holiday home."

Stern remembered the time, way back, when he and Annie had borrowed a friend's cabin cruiser that was moored on Wroxham Broad. They'd spent a whole week exploring the rivers and broads. Now a bitter sweet memory.

"His family home is somewhere in Kensington," O'Connor went on.

"Mmmm," Stern mused. "One of the most expensive areas in London. He's got a few bob then."

"Looks that way. Seems he made his wadge in property dealing. Word has it he started as a street trader in the East End. The period between then and now is cloudy, but however he did it, he built things up from there and is now one wealthy dude. He's been holidaying on our patch for a while and keeps a pretty low profile. Though I'm told he does support local charities from time to time."

"A wealthy do-gooder then," Stern said.

"On the surface," O'Connor came back. "But then a couple of months back, we received this." He reached into his pocket and pulled out a creased envelope. He handed it to Stern.

Stern studied the envelope for a moment. "By post, local postmark."

"Yup"

Stern slid a single sheet of paper from the envelope and unfolded it. The writing was an untidy scrawl. He read it softly to himself.

To the senior officer.

Every wealthy businessman has at some time been involved in dodgy dealings. He wouldn't be wealthy if he hadn't. But, some wealthy businessmen are always involved in dodgy dealings and some, despite how they look, are outright vicious criminals. You have one such man on your manor.

Beware Eddie Butler.

Yours Sincerely

A law-abiding citizen.

Stern looked back at O'Connor. "A few weeks back, you say?"

"Yes. We took little notice at the time. We get all sorts of crackpot complaints and accusations through the post, texts, emails, the lot. Disgruntled employees, unhappy neighbours, council bashers. You name it, we get it."

"So, what made you react to this?"

O'Connor looked toward the piece of paper in Stern's hand. "Since receiving that we've had several others, each accusing Butler of various crimes, from running drugs to running brothels, and everything in between. And with each one, the sender is getting more frustrated because, as far as they're concerned, we're not reacting. Which is not quite true. Just to satisfy our own curiosity, we did quietly check Butler out. We came up with nothing more than I've already told you. As far as we could see, Butler is just another wealthy businessman who enjoys taking the occasional break in the quiet of the Norfolk countryside. He spends his weekdays in the City, where his office is located, and relaxes here at weekends. Particularly in the summer. When he's here, he keeps a low profile, and nobody sees much of him. But, as I said, he can be generous if approached by a local charity. That's about it."

"Age?" Stern asked.

"Mid-sixties."

"Married?"

"Yes. His wife is younger, though I don't know by how much. Foreign woman. She sometimes spends the week here, especially in the summer. Other times, she travels back and forth with her husband. A local guy keeps his eye on the place when the Butlers are not there."

Stern held up the envelope. "Were all the notes posted locally?"

"Some. Others from further afield. But all from around the East Anglia region."

Stern inclined his head. "Fingerprints? Traces of anything?"

O'Connor smiled. "No nothing."

"Okay, so what's changed your mind? Why, after your initial checks on Butler found nothing, is your mystery letter writer not a crackpot anymore?"

"Good question." O'Connor leaned closer, dropping his voice. "About three weeks ago, a body was dragged from the Wensum. The body was male and subsequently identified as a local man called Charlie Croker. He was a forty-seven-year-old builder's labourer."

Stern understood. The River Wensum ran through the centre of Norwich. It connected to the other rivers and Broads throughout the county.

"A post mortem revealed that Croker was full of booze," O'Connor went on. "There were also traces of amphetamines, subsequently identified as speed, in his system. It was therefore concluded that

Croker had been out on a bender and accidently fallen into the river and drowned. The eventual verdict: death by misadventure."

Stern took a drink, then said, "Something tells me there's a big *but* coming here."

"You're not wrong," O'Connor came back. "Almost immediately after the verdict was announced in the local rag, we get another letter from our mystery writer." He pulled another envelope from his pocket and handed it across.

Stern slid the sheet from the envelope and read.

To the senior officer.

You haven't been listening, have you? Well maybe this will make you sit up. I knew Charlie Croker well, knew him for years. And I'll tell you this for free. Charlie was T-total. In all the time I knew him, Charlie never touched a drop. And I should know; he was on my team. His dad was an alcoholic, died from it. Charlie vowed never to follow in the old man's footsteps and never did. Never knew him to dabble in drugs either. How about that? And here's something else. Charlie may have worked on the building, but that was only his day job. Check out what he did at night and what happened when he wanted out, tried to quit!! When he tried to quit working for BUTLER.

Time you started listening.

A law-abiding citizen.

Tight faced, Stern thought for some moments. "Team? What's that all about?"

O'Connor shook his head. "No idea. We need to do some more digging."

"Looks like it," Stern agreed. "But it seems, if we're to believe the mysterious letter writer, Croker didn't drink or take drugs. Yet when he was pulled from the Wensum, he was full of 'em."

"That's right," O'Connor agreed. "And from what it says in the note there, he worked for Butler on the side. Or should I say at night."

"Was Croker married?" Stern asked.

"No, he was a lifelong bachelor, a loner. Lived in a rented flat, a high rise off Rouen Road in Town. D'you know it?"

"Rouen Road." Stern eased back in the chair and thought for a moment. "Runs down from the castle, parallel with King Street, right?"

"That's it. The high rise is just before the two roads join. Can't miss it."

"Yeah, I think I've got it." Stern leaned forward again, elbows resting on the table.

"Okay, so where do I come in, David?"

"Well, as always, I've got about half the manpower I need to cover my workload." He grimaced. "Not that my bloody boss will ever acknowledge it. To him, compared to most of the other stuff that keeps me awake at night, this is seen as low priority. He thinks it's a crank, told me to bin it." He held Stern's enquiring gaze. "But truth is, Theo, I think there could well be something in it. I think we should do a bit more digging before we kick it into touch."

Stern smiled. "And you want to hand me the shovel, right?"

Nine

It was a cold morning with low bloated clouds that at any moment threatened a downpour. As he trudged quickly along the promenade hunched in a heavy topcoat with the collar pulled up close around his ears, Stern hoped he'd be inside before it hit. Emerging onto Sheringham High Street, he made his way quickly along to the bakery and pushed his way inside. Giving Dave a wave, he weaved his way among several waiting customers, and headed to the back of the shop, and the stairway leading up to the Stern Investigations office. Strange how until only a day or so ago he'd thought it had long since been wrapped up, that Stern Investigations was no more. Now here he was, back where he had started, with absolutely no change at all. Hell, he even had a Scirocco again. Well, he would have tomorrow. He smiled at the prospect. No worries there. He checked his watch as he climbed the stairs and entered the office. Just a minute or so after nine. As he expected, Cherry was already there. The office was comfortably warm, and the coffee was bubbling.

"Morning, boss."

"Morning." Crossing the office, Stern eased himself out of the heavy coat and hung it on the rack, rubbing his hands together vigorously. "It's flippin' freezing out there."

"Your blood's still thin." Cherry grinned. "Never mind, only another three or four months, and it might warm up a bit."

Stern headed for his office. "Cheers, that makes me feel a whole lot better."

They'd taken up their usual positions, Stern behind the ancient desk, comfortable in the equally old creaky chair, Cherry in the chair opposite, legs tucked under, coffee mug cradled between her hands. The hard-backed file she'd had on Stern's first visit was on the floor beside her, resting against the leg of the chair. It was as if the interim nine months had never happened.

"Okay," Stern kicked off. "Last evening, I agreed to help David with a problem he has."

"You mean with one of his cases, like we used to?"

"Yes. He feels there's a need for some investigative surveillance over the next week or so, and he just hasn't the manpower to spare. Stern Investigations is still on their books, so he's got the authorisation to use us. On the official books, we will be operating in an administrative capacity. But that's just for the record, okay?"

"I know, like before."

"Yes, like before," Stern agreed. "So, with that in mind, and because you have a couple of clients also hanging on, I've decided to give Stern Investigations another year." He saw the smile, the shining eyes. "Don't get too excited. It's only twelve months. I'll decide what I want to do after that. But," he waved a warning finger, "If I then say it's over, it's over, and no arguments. Agreed?"

Cherry took a breath. "Agreed."

"Okay. That's not to say you weren't well out of order, doing what you did," Stern went on. "But that's water under the bridge. I'll talk to Dave and see if I can come to some arrangement about the money you wasted on the rent."

Cherry shook her head. "Not wasted, boss. Might have been if you hadn't come home. But you did."

Stern smiled and gave a resigned shake of the head. "You are one bloody crazy female, d'you know that?"

Cherry looked across at him, her eyes suddenly clouding. "Maybe I am, boss," she said softly. "But all those years ago you lifted me from a filthy pit and made me what I am today. And my time here, working with you, with Stern Investigations, has been the best years of my whole life. So why would a girl want to give that up?"

Stern felt his throat tighten. He gave a rough cough and reached for the coffee mug. "Yeah, alright, enough of the mush." He took a drink, playing for time, letting the feeling fade. "So, it's twelve months, right?"

"Right."

"Okay, to business then. I'll brief you on David's problem later. First, tell me about those two clients you've lined up." He paused for a beat, a thought occurring. "I told you to dump 'em. You didn't, did you?"

Cherry shook her head. "I was going to, but I thought I'd wait to see what happened at your meet with David."

Stern reached for the coffee mug. "Smart Arse." He took a drink then hoicked the old chair closer to the desk, pulling the new note pad toward him, retrieving one of the pencils. "Okay, let's have 'em."

Uncoiling her legs, Cherry placed the coffee mug on the floor alongside her chair and picked up the file. Opening it on her lap, she looked back at Stern. "Both enquiries were from women," she began. "The first one was worried about her husband."

Stern wrinkled his nose. "Playing away?"

"Maybe, but maybe not," Cherry responded. "The husband tells her he's got himself a second job in the evenings. At the moment, they rent a council house. He tells her he's trying to build up the bank balance, so he can get them on the property ladder, buy their first house. Told her he was doing deliveries, sort of."

Stern frowned. "Deliveries sort of?"

"Yeah I know. Sounds a bit dodgy, I admit," Cherry agreed.

"And his wife thinks the same, I suppose?"

"Well, she's certainly worried on a couple of fronts. Firstly, the work is at night, and he only goes when he gets a phone call."

"And second?"

"The times are not consistent. Sometimes he's only out for a couple of hours, and another time he could be out all night."

"Did you ask her the obvious question?" Stern smirked.

"I did, and she assured me everything between them was fine in that department. She was adamant their love life was as good as ever."

"Age?"

"Didn't ask, but I guess probably in her forties."

"Anything else?"

"Nothing important. I didn't pursue it further. Said we'd call and make an appointment."

"Okay, set that one up for later in the week, Friday if you can."

"Right." Cherry scribbled a note in the file. Turned the page. "The second one is different. This is a young woman who lives in Blakeney. She's a solicitor by profession, works for a small outfit in Norwich. But she's one of the arty type, has aspirations of becoming a full-time painter. Pictures, that is, not houses."

"And her problem is?"

"She lives alone, and her place is on the edge of the village, sits a little apart. Recently, she thinks she's being watched."

"Watched?"

"Yes, at night. Someone at the rear of the house watching her through the window."

"Peeping Tom."

"Looks that way. It's put the frighteners on her. Got her thinking she might be being stalked during the day, too."

"Why does she think that?"

"No good reason as far as I can see. Just paranoia, I think."

Stern gave it some thought. "She should inform the police."

"I told her that, but it seems there's a little something in her past. She wants to stay away from the law."

"Did she tell you what the little something is?"

"No. She said she would explain if we take the case."

"Mmmm, interesting," Stern muttered. "I wonder what this lady has to hide." He brightened, a smile forming. "Yeah, I think we should go and see her. Get the lay of the land."

Cherry frowned. "That's unlike you. First contact, you usually get them to come to the office."

"Well, yes, that's true, but like I said, it might be a good idea to have a look round the woman's place, get the layout. Could you be free tomorrow evening?"

"Wednesday." Cherry gave it some thought. "Well as it happens, it's Rob's darts night. He eats at the pub, so that would fit."

"Good. Give the woman a ring, and set it up. We'll have a bite to eat then we'll head over there." He picked up the mug and drained the last of the cold coffee. "I'll drive."

Cherry frowned for a moment, then her face brightened. "Ah, I get it," she laughed. "It's the new car, isn't it? Tomorrow, you collect the Scirocco. You crafty old devil."

Stern grinned sheepishly. "Well, you don't think I'd have gone in that old tin can of yours, do you?"

Ten

Oliver, Ollie, Preston's pen is poised, his brain searching for the right words. It's important. It'll be no good him scribbling randomly, letting it all out, expelling the mass of hate he feels inside. He has so much bottled up that if he did that, he'd never stop. No, it has to be brief and to the point. And most of all, it has to make them sit up and take notice. Better still, take action. One thing was certain, he wasn't about to stop until they did.

At forty-eight years old, Ollie is no taller than five eight and could generously be described as being portly. Those not so generous, and plenty are, would not be averse to using a less sympathetic adjective. Those same individuals would also not be backward in commenting unfavourably on Ollie's appearance, which does leave a little to be desired. But as far as Ollie is concerned, he has no good reason to be too particular. To be fair, that could be understood because Ollie is one of those individuals who has not been dealt the best of life's hands.

Ollie lives in a small semi-detached bungalow in Sprowston, a suburb on the northern outskirts of Norwich. It's the house in which he was born and raised. The only home he has ever known. The only child of a slovenly lethargic mother who didn't particularly want him in the first place, and a father who, a year after Ollie's birth, seeing the slow deterioration of his wife, decided he could do better elsewhere.

A sickly child, mainly because of the uncaring mother who paid little heed to the health and welfare of her child, Ollie managed to struggle through the first few years of life, thanks in the main to the help of a series of social workers. He did okay at school, but despite this, hated every moment he was there. Ignoring any prospect of formal qualifications, he left as early as he could, thereafter taking whatever menial task paid enough to supplement the social benefits his mother was able to scrounge from the system. As time passed and his mother drifted into a dementia ridden state, Ollie became a full-time carer, caring more for her than she ever had for him.

Dealt a better hand, things could have been different, because the truth was, Ollie wasn't always overweight, and like his father before him, could have been quite a good looking individual. But as a result of a general lack of care during his upbringing, Ollie was plagued with excessive acne which meant, as he got older, shaving became a torment. When eventually things did settle down, the resulting permanent facial pock marks destroyed any potential good looks Ollie may have had. A full beard was the only answer, and an overweight, badly dressed heavily bearded individual would seldom be the top of anyone's popularity list. So, two years ago, when his mother finally passed away, and Ollie became a free man with no purpose, no one to care for, life could have become a very empty space.

Fortunately, however, there were some who did value Ollie's company and could, broadly speaking, be classed as friends. This was thanks to the one particular expertise at which Ollie excelled. Ollie was arguably the best pub dart player in the whole of the county. Indeed, the several trophies displayed in his local's bar were in the main there because of his proficiency at the oche. As a result, within the ranks of his dart playing peers, Ollie was a bit of a celebrity. Neither his general appearance, nor anything else about him, mattered a jot as long as he continued to turn up and maintain the accuracy for which he was so notorious. Winning does that to some. But, as has already been said, one or two of those dart playing peers could be described as friends. Ollie clung to these with all his might because otherwise, in his every day existence, away from the pub environment, Ollie was a no one, an anonymous, not very savoury looking character.

If nothing else, since the death of his mother two years earlier, Ollie had learned two hard lessons. Firstly, if you didn't look the part, people thought the worst. You might be the kindest person, have a heart of gold, but if you looked a bit down at heel, didn't meet the norm, you had to be a bad'n. Stood to reason, right?

Secondly, for the same reason, if they got the chance, most people would happily dump on you. Ollie had quickly learned to counter this one. He learned that if you instinctively felt someone were about to dump on you, it was almost certain they were. So, you dumped on them first, and hard.

Of course, neither of these lessons was always the case. Regarding the first one, for instance. If you had a particular talent, some people thought nothing of how you looked anyway. Ollie was standing proof of that. And there were others, though few and far between, who did see beyond the outer cover. If you had friends like this, you cherished them.

Then there was that second lesson. That, too, wasn't always the case because you couldn't always rely on your own instincts, just occasionally they didn't kick in. Take Eddie Butler, for instance. Ollie never saw that coming, did he? Neither did his closest friend, and that was fatal.

Ollie started to write. The words were coming together. Short, sharp and to the point. He gave a satisfied smirk. This should make them sit up. He paused, the pen hovering, his lips a thin determined line. If it didn't, then it would have to be Plan B. And they wouldn't want that. No, they definitely wouldn't want that.

Eleven

"So, what do you think?" Stern asked as he slid smoothly through the gears, a silly satisfied grin on his face.

Cherry wrinkled her nose and cast her eyes around the interior of the car. "Yeah, it's okay. But, I mean, red."

"Red," Stern snorted. "Is that the best you can come up with? The colour?"

Cherry turned her head away, looking out of the window, hiding the smile. When it came to cars, she knew how to wind him up. "It's a car, boss. It's got four wheels, and it gets you there. They all do that. The only difference is the colour. I'm just saying I'm not keen on red, that's all. Wouldn't have chosen it myself."

"You never said that when we checked it out on Monday."

"No, well, I could see you'd fallen for it. Just didn't want to spoil your day."

Stern let out an exasperated sigh. "Typical woman. You get a top-of-the-range model of a cracking car, and all she can comment on is the colour. And this particular woman drives around in an ancient sardine can on wheels that's a crappy silver."

Cherry turned, feigning indignation. "I'll have you know that ancient sardine can gets me there exactly the same as this does. And it's a lovely silver colour. The same colour as another car once cherished by someone I know. Wasn't crappy then, was it?"

Stern eased the Scirocco through the gate into the local pub car park. The smile had never left his face. It was a game they'd played many times, particularly before the demise of the old Scirocco, which had also been silver. "You can always walk home, you know," he said as they climbed out of the car.

Cherry followed him out, pleased the old banter was still there. Pleased even more at the glint in the boss' eye. Stern Investigations was back on the case.

The Wheatsheaf, a classic vintage pub in the village of West Beckham, said to have been standing for over four hundred years, had been in decline for some time. Several successive tenants had been unable to bring it back to its former popularity. Then in 2014 Stephen and Daniella came on the scene, and things changed. Described as a hidden gem, it had been transformed, becoming once again a popular traditional English pub with a highly praised restaurant and B&B accommodation. Excellent food and real ale, and a genuinely warm welcome from day one, it had won Stern over on his first visit. Thereafter, branded a traitor by his previous local, he had switched his allegiance.

Leaving the car, they entered through the back door. The welcome was as always; a hug from Daniella and a friendly smile from the mountain that was Stephen.

An hour later, both stuffed to the brim, they were back on the road heading for Blakeney. Stern chose to follow the coast road, winding through the coastal villages, the North Sea stretching out beyond the salt marshes, seldom out of sight. Earlier the forecast rain had arrived, heavy for several hours. It had eased and though still cold, the sky was clear.

Stern glanced at the clock. "Seven o'clock, you said, right?"

"Yes."

"Looks like we're spot on time then. Five minutes and we'll be there. So, remind me what we know about this woman."

"She's a solicitor, originally from London, but now works with a company in Norwich. The only other thing she mentioned was her ambition to become a full-time artist. That's about it. Oh, and there's this thing about the run-in with the police. Don't know what that's all about."

They arrived in Blakeney, and the Sat Nav directed them through the village then right into a narrow lane running down toward the coast. The cottage sat several hundred yards from the main village and its nearest neighbour. Stern drove slowly past the small rear garden surrounded by a low hedge and on round to the front of the cottage facing seaward. Here there was a gravel covered area. A car was already parked there. Stern pulled alongside it and killed the engine.

They climbed out of the car and were immediately hit by the stiff sharp breeze cutting in off the North Sea. It was twilight, the sun on the verge of setting, and Stern pulled his topcoat closer as, for a moment, they stood silently looking out across the shimmering sand dunes, the wide open spectacular, uninterrupted sea views clear to the horizon.

"Pretty special, don't you think?" The voice came from behind them. They both turned toward the front of the cottage where a woman stood in the doorway. She was dressed in a white T shirt covered by thick denim shirt hanging loosely open outside stained jeans. The jeans had tears in both knees. She was wearing open-toed sandals on bare feet and was wiping her hands on a large, multicoloured piece of cloth. She was, Stern guessed, in her forties and stocky with short dark hair. She had a pleasant, attractive smile.

They approached the woman, Stern extending his hand. "Spectacular," he said. "Must be pretty nice in the summer, too. I'm Theo Stern."

She took his hand, her grip firm. "It's pretty nice all year round, as far as I'm concerned." She released his hand and held her own up as an apology. "I'm Mo Stevens, and I'm sorry, you'll probably smell of turps now. The price you pay for shaking hands with an artist, I'm afraid. You can wash up inside if you like."

Stern was aware that artists used turpentine and linseed oil in their work. He held his hand to his nose and shook his head. "Not a problem." He indicated toward Cherry. "This is Cherry Hooker. She's my number two. You spoke on the phone." He purposefully avoided calling Cherry his assistant or secretary. He knew she appreciated the thought.

Cherry shook Mo Stevens' hand. "Quite like the smell of turps actually."

Mo smiled. "It's addictive, I can tell you. That and linseed oil." She stood to one side and beckoned them through the door.

Inside, the cottage was sparsely furnished, and it could immediately be seen it was little more than a two up two down. The door through which they entered lead directly into a low ceilinged main room which was both sitting room and studio combined. A sideboard squeezed in alongside a narrow stairway leading to the upper floor covered the whole of one wall. A sofa close to an open door leading to what they could see as the kitchen covered most of another. And, directly opposite, a wide inglenook fireplace housed a glowing log burning stove. The remaining wall, to their right as they entered, faced seaward and was all window. Here, in front of the window, was an easel and the complete paraphernalia of an artist at work. A table and four chairs occupied the centre of the room. Though sparsely furnished, the little room still felt crowded.

Mo closed the door behind them, motioning them to the chairs at the table. "Not much room, I'm afraid."

Cherry eased herself down onto one of the chairs. "Cosy though. And warm."

"Yes, it is, and I love it," Mo admitted. She hovered before joining them at the table. "Can I get you a drink or something?"

Shaking his head, Stern also sat. "No thanks, we haven't long eaten."

Mo joined them at the table. She took a breath. "Well, thanks for coming. I hope you can sort this out for me. Before this happened, my life was pretty well perfect. Now, it's like I'm on tenterhooks the whole time."

Stern leaned forward, elbows resting on the table. "I know it must be unsettling. But before we go any further, I must ask you about your reluctance to involve the law. What you are facing here is a criminal offence and should be reported to the police. You must understand my licence would not allow me to represent a felon. Cherry tells me you're a solicitor, so I'm sure you understand this."

"Well I have to admit," Mo said, "I'm not fully *au fait* with the rules governing a private detective, but you need have no fear about representing me. I'm not on the run or anything like that."

"Even so," Stern persisted. "I'd still need to know..."

"Yes, I do understand," Mo intervened. "It's simple really." During the next five minutes or so, she explained how during her increasingly malicious divorce period she had been driven to deface her ex-husband's expensive Audi. "I was given a warning and made to pay damages," she finished. "It's on my record, though, and I just feel it best to stay away from the police as much as possible."

"Does your current employer know about this?" Stern asked.

"Yes, he does. I admitted everything, told them what I'd done, how I'd been the guilty party. I deserved and expected some retribution from my husband, but in my opinion, he had gone too far. He'd pushed me over the edge. I expected them to show me the door, but they didn't. Instead, they said it would be nice to have someone on the team who had faced the real rigors of life and would understand others' problems at grass root."

"Okay," Stern said. "I don't think what you've told us would influence the police in the slightest if you reported this problem to them. But if you still want us to take it on, it's your choice." He gave her a smile. "But don't forget; the police are free. We charge."

"I understand that, but if you could deal with it, quietly I hope, I would prefer it."

Stern slid the new notebook and pencil supplied by Cherry from his pocket. "Okay, so let's start with the intruder. How many times have you seen him?"

"Twice. Once, a week or so back, then again the day before I called you."

Stern scribbled. "Where did you see him?"

"The first time in the back garden. It was dusk, about this time, and I went to draw the curtains at the back window. He was just standing there on the other side of the hedge, staring. I pulled the curtains quickly and locked the door. A few moments later, I peeped out from behind the curtain and he'd gone."

"Did you see his face?"

Mo shook her head. "Not really. He was wearing a windcheater with the collar pulled up around his ears and a cloth cap, the peak pulled down very low. All I could see was his mouth." She took a breath and swallowed hard. "He was smiling. Well it was more of a sneer than a smile."

"How about size? Height, build?"

"I don't know, really. With him standing on the other side of the hedge, it was difficult to judge how tall he was, but he did look quite heavily built." Mo thought for a moment. "But, like I said, he was wearing a windcheater. It could have made him look heftier than he actually was." She gave a small shrug. "Sorry, not much help I'm afraid."

"Not to worry." He quickly scribbled some more. "And the second time you saw him?"

Mo turned to the other side of the room, indicating to her easel in front of the window facing seaward. "It was about the same time of day as the first time. Possibly a little earlier. I was at my easel trying to capture the late afternoon sunlight moving across the sand dunes." Her eyes darkened. "Suddenly, he was there. It was as if he materialised out of nowhere. I remember moving quickly to the door and throwing the bolt. Then when I returned to the window he was gone."

"It was the same guy. You're sure of it?"

"Yes, I'm sure. He was dressed just the same"

"Just the mouth visible?"

"Yes."

Stern closed the notebook and pushed it to one side. He paused for a second, running a finger across his bottom lip thoughtfully. "Mo, are you still in touch with your ex-husband?"

"Hell no."

"Do you think he knows where you are?"

A worried frown crossed Mo's brow. "I don't think so, but..."

"You can't be sure?"

She shook her head.

"So, if he did know where you were right now, I mean considering his vendetta against you before, do you think this could be him?"

Mo's eyes darkened. "God, I hope not." She hesitated, thinking. "It was just the mouth...that smile. I suppose...Back then, he was so bitter I wouldn't have put anything past him. But now? I mean, it's been almost two years. Surely he wouldn't...?"

"Maybe not," Stern said. "But from your reaction there, you couldn't be sure, right? From what you did see, you couldn't positively rule him out?"

Mo said nothing for a long moment, then slowly shook her head. "No, I don't think I could."

Stern looked to Cherry. "Okay, I think there's a good starting point. Just to be sure we'll check him out." He turned back to Mo. "Do you know anything about what he did after the divorce? I mean, where he lived, where he worked? Anything at all that may help us locate him?"

"I can't imagine he would have moved from the place he worked before," Mo replied. "Back then, the top man only had a year or so to retirement, and my husband was his natural successor. I doubt he'd have given that up. As for where he might be living now, I have no idea."

"Okay, so let's have the address of his work place. That'll do for a start. Oh, and by the way, do you have a photo we could use?"

Twelve

On the return journey from Blakeney, Cherry had come up with the idea. She hadn't been to London in an age, she'd admitted. A day trip would be all it would take. An early train out of Norwich would get her into London's Liverpool Street Station in less than a couple of hours. Mo Stevens had given them the location of the Audi dealer where her ex-husband, Frank Cavendish, had worked at the time of their divorce. From the station, it would take less than an hour to get there. That was by London transport. Probably half that time if the budget could run to a taxi. Then, by using the photograph Mo had given them, she would be able to establish if Cavendish still worked at the dealership. After that, she admitted, she would have to wing it, play it by ear. But she was confident she could make progress one way or another. Whichever way it went, she could be home again by close of play the same day.

Stern wasn't over happy with the 'winging it' part of the plan, but though she may not have been to the capital for some time, Cherry was a Londoner by birth. She was also streetwise enough to look after herself. As for asking about Cavendish at the dealership, he didn't think she could come to much harm in the middle of what he imagined to be a large car showroom.

Her plan would also allow him to concentrate on other things, in particular David O'Connor's problem regarding Eddie Butler and the anonymous notes. Stern finally agreed to Cherry's suggestion and, much to her delight, also authorised the taxi across London. As an afterthought, he had suggested she consider Uber.

Earlier this morning, as they'd agreed, Stern dropped Cherry at Norwich station at around eight. Back in Sheringham, he left the car in the lock-up behind his flat and walked his usual route along the promenade and up into the high street. He was back in the office and reaching for the telephone around half nine.

David O'Connor answered on the second ring.

"David, it's Theo, I was thinking of taking a ride out to the Butler place this morning. Any objections?"

"None at all, Theo. What's the plan?"

"Haven't got one, really. Just thought I'd get to know the lay of the land."

"Couldn't agree more. I've already had one of my lads give it a quick once over. Didn't come up with much other than it's an impressive place. It's called Deep Repose, by the way."

"Imaginative," Stern quipped. "Can't wait to see it. By the way, before I go, what more can you tell me about this Croker guy?"

"No more than I've already told you. With my manpower as low as it is, I was hoping you could take it from there."

"Okay, I'm happy to do that. But just to recap, we're talking about a forty-seven-year-old, unmarried, builder's labourer who was a bit of a loner living in a Norwich highrise."

"Yes."

"And when he was pulled from the Wensum he was full of booze and drugs."

"Right again."

"But, despite this, our anonymous letter writer insisted he was T-total and anti-drugs."

"Correct," O'Connor came back. "Also, that same anonymous writer reported that Croker was doing some dodgy night work for our friend Butler."

"And, for what it's worth, we mustn't forget he played for some team or other," Stern added."

"Yup, that's about it," O'Connor said.

"Okay, thanks David. I'll get back to you when I have anything."

"Theo, same terms of reference as before? Written weekly report with interim reports of any significant findings? Must keep my governor sweet."

"Of course. Wouldn't want to upset the old man, would we? Talk again soon." Stern ended the call with a grin.

His early start meant he hadn't eaten yet so, after a quick trip downstairs to raid Dave's cake rack, Stern made himself coffee. Relaxing back in the old chair, he hoiked his feet up onto the desk. As he munched, he thoughtfully ran through the current situation.

He'd returned from Australia totally despondent with no idea of what the future held for him. Now, in the blink of an eye, he was exactly where he was before he'd left. Stern Investigations was back in action and already had three cases on its books. He looked down at how he was leaning back with legs crossed, his heels resting on the edge of the desk, and gave a slow shake of his head. Hell, how easy it had been for him to slip right back in the groove. And, d'you know what? He smiled. Somehow it felt it was as it should be.

An hour later, having collected the car from the lockup, Stern was back on the road. The overnight rain had continued into the morning, but now the sky was clearing, and a watery sun was beginning to make itself felt. He punched in the address O'Connor had given him. It specified a property called Deep Repose on Oak Lane, Wroxham. He'd visited Wroxham and the surrounding area a number of times in the past but never Oak Lane. Heading out of Sheringham, he took the A149 to North Walsham, said by some to be the capital of North Norfolk, then on to the junction with the A1151 where he made a right. Four or five miles later, the Sat Nav instructed him to make a left. A little further on, another left took him into Oak Lane. It really was no more than a lane bordered by hedges, some meticulously trimmed, large expensive houses and bungalows sitting back in extensive, beautifully manicured grounds. As he cruised slowly along the lane searching for Deep Repose, Stern gave an ironic smile; there was still plenty of money about, even in sleepy old Norfolk.

Since breaking away from the A1151, Stern had worked out his bearings, orientated his mind around the area. If he had it right, the grounds to the rear of the houses to his left ran down to the River Bure. The Bure, after connecting to the Wroxham Broad, meandered further on across the county, eventually terminating at the North Sea. So, if Deep Repose came up on his left, he figured it didn't actually boarder the Broad itself, but the river leading to it. A few moments later, the Sat Nav informed him he would arrive at his destination on his left one hundred yards further on. Here the hedges were high, probably close to eight feet, the only gap filled with equally high ornate wrought iron gates hanging on two three-foot square, brick pillars with round concrete balls sitting on top of each. Beyond the gates, a driveway ran to the front of the property. The gates were closed.

Stern drove past the gates and pulled the car as close to the verge as possible before switching off the engine. Even though the sun was doing its best to warm the mid-March air, the chill cut into him as he climbed out. He pushed his hands deep into his pockets and strolled nonchalantly past the gates. He noted the cleverly scrolled 'Deep' woven into one and 'Repose' in the other. Set in the left-hand pillar, there was a metal panel with a speaker grille and a push button. No entry here without announcing yourself first.

Through the gates, he could see the straight drive cutting directly down through the centre of the front garden. He guessed about hundred yards long. It was bordered on either side by wide neatly cut lawns, the centre of the one to his right sporting an ornate water feature, its fountain, glittering in the sunshine, dancing high. To his left, an expansive fish pond was covered by a heavy protective net. A necessary precaution, Stern guessed. He knew nothing of garden ponds, but being so close to the river, herons would be patrolling daily. They had no favourites. An expensive koi carp from a pond was as tasty as a perch from the river any day. Neat flower beds, yet to show their blooms, surrounded the lawns edges. Just before terminating at a patterned brick weave parking area directly in front of the building, the drive branched left to the forecourt of a lockup garage wide enough to accommodate at least three cars. Here a sparkling metallic blue Mercedes saloon sat centre stage. As O'Connor had said, the whole setup was impressive.

Having no experience of thatched roofing, Stern had never been a great fan. He could only imagine it being full of bugs with a very limited lifespan. And damned expensive to have repaired or replaced. But he couldn't help but be impressed by the specimen he was looking at. He couldn't tell how old the building was. It looked old, he thought Tudor style, with its dark wood box framed beams and white facings, the upper level of the house overhanging the lower. Even the beautifully manicured thatched roof with its straw pheasant strutting its stuff on top.

He strolled for several yards along the road before turning and retracing his steps. This time, with no one around, he stopped in front of the gates and surveyed the area more closely. It was a two-story building and certainly in the Tudor style. Looking more closely, it could be seen that the cleanness of the cut, the straight beams, the flatness of the white facings, hardly wattle and daub, said modern. So, pseudo Tudor, then. He noted that, as well as the large garage situated to the left of the main house, there was another building to the right. This was in the same style as the main building but was little more than a small sized cottage.

There was certainly money here, Stern thought. Big money. But that didn't mean bad money. After all, they only had the word of some crazy letter writer to say Eddie Butler was...What was it now? An outright, vicious criminal? A pretty disturbing accusation, to say the least. They should tread very carefully before taking any notice of such...

"You want something?"

Startled, Stern swung round, his thoughts brought to an abrupt halt by the gruff words.

Stern couldn't see where the hell he'd come from, but he was big, very big, with massive shoulders, a thick neck, cropped hair and a dark bomber jacket with the word 'SECURITY' emblazoned across the breast pocket.

"Er, yeah," Stern stuttered. "I was just…"

Thirteen

It was close to ten thirty when Cherry made her way out of Liverpool Street station and checked out the area for taxis. She didn't know a lot about the Uber cab system, but she had heard that you had to phone to get hold of the nearest. She couldn't be bothered with any of that, and anyway, the boss had only asked her to *try* Uber if she could. Tight old devil. Well she couldn't, so she headed straight for the row of black cabs. It was a generic name and not strictly correct these days, because now they were all colours. It just happened that the one at the head of the queue was black. She pulled open the door and climbed in.

The driver swung round. "Where to, luv?" He was probably in his fifties, pasty faced, bald and overweight. The accent, as cockney as she had ever heard, took her back a very long way.

Cherry pulled out the piece of paper given them by Mo Stevens. It showed the address of the Audi dealership to be just off Piccadilly. She handed it to the driver. "D'you know it?"

He grinned. "Know it, I bought me last motor there. Get a new one every year."

She read the grin and laughed. "In your dreams."

"You're right there, luv. I couldn't even afford a steerin' wheel off one of those things." He eased the taxi away from the kerb and out into a line of traffic. "Can't say 'ow long. Traffic, y'know. Best to do Northumberland Avenue, Pall Mall and St James' this time of day, usually about forty minutes."

Cherry relaxed back in the seat. "I'm in no rush."

He eyed her in the rearview mirror. "So, let me guess, definitely London, right?"

"Sorry?"

"Your accent. Born and bred London."

She smiled, understanding now. "Yes, you're right."

"And, unless I'm mistaken, East End."

"Right again. Bethnal Green, to be precise."

"Don't live there now, then?"

Cherry shook her head. "No, not for a very long time."

"Bet you still miss it though, eh?"

Cherry gave him a wan smile, her mind instantly tumbling back to those early, fearfully dark years she had spent in the East End before Detective Inspector Theo Stern had come into her life. The thought, even now all these years later, creating tension in her. "It was a long time ago."

The driver gave a dismissive shrug of his heavy shoulders. "So, what's with the posh garage, then? You won the lottery or somethin'?"

"No, nothing like that. I'm not here to buy."

"Pity," the driver chuckled. "Thought I might be able to charm ya into buyin' me one too."

"No such luck, I'm afraid."

"So, what you up to then?"

Cherry smiled to herself. Typical chatty London cabby. Chatty and nosy. But that was okay; she had forty minutes to waste. "I'm down from Norfolk carrying out an investigation."

The cabby took a quick glance back. "Investigation? You with the law, then?"

"I am, yes." Well, she was working for the police, wasn't she? Sort of.

"Christ. D'you know what? I've 'ad all sorts in my cab over the years, but never a detective. 'Ow about that. You're me first."

"Lucky you."

"So, what we got then, someone floggin' dodgy motors?"

Cherry was warming to the game. "Come on now, you know I can't discuss a case with you."

"Not even a hint?"

"Well, all I'll say is just keep your eyes on the newspapers in a couple of weeks' time."

He eyed her through the rearview mirror. "Bloody 'ell, you wait till I tell the guys. They won't believe me."

Cherry kept a straight face. "I can promise they will when they read the newspapers. Now don't ask me anymore, alright?"

Cherry paid the driver and climbed from the taxi directly outside the car showroom. "D'you want me to 'ang around?" the driver asked hopefully.

"No thanks. I have no idea how long I'll be."

"Well, you be careful, luv." He gave her a wink and a cheesy grin. "I 'ope you get your man."

She gave him a wave and couldn't help a last word. "I'm like a Mountie, I always do."

During the journey, she had studied the auto magazine purchased at the Norwich station book stall, formulating a plan of action. Now, she stood looking into the extensive showroom for some moments, running through it in her mind. Finally, satisfied, she pushed her way through the large glass door. Inside, there were a number of cars, different models, placed in strategic positions, all highly polished, gleaming in the overhead lighting. Cherry wandered over to the nearest. It was no more than thirty seconds before a salesman appeared at her shoulder.

"Good morning, madam. Can I help?" Dressed in a dark suit over a pure white shirt, a dark blue silk tie tied perfectly at the neck, he was tall, she guessed in his late thirties, good looking, and there wasn't a hair out of place. He was not Mo's ex.

Cherry turned and put on her best defenceless woman expression. "Well, I hope you can. I'm here on behalf of my partner, actually. He's about to change his car. He's had the Jaguar for more than a year now and feels it's getting a bit jaded. Time for a change, he thinks." She shrugged her shoulders apologetically. "You must forgive me; I really have no knowledge of these things. All he asked was for me to get the full SP—his words not mine—on the..." She frowned in mock thought. "Is it the Q-seven SUV?"

Pulling back his shoulders, the man gave her a superior smile. "It certainly is, madam. A first-class selection. Your partner has excellent taste."

Cherry wrinkled her nose temptingly. "Oh yes, he does love his cars."

"He's not able to be here today?"

"No, he's away on business until the weekend. My instructions are to have full details available for when he returns. He likes to know what he's into before he takes the plunge." She gave another little shrug. "I don't know why. He's loaded, and once he homes in on what he wants, there's no stopping him anyway."

The man's face brightened, and he pointed to the far side of the showroom. "We have a Q-seven right here. Would you like me to run over it with you?"

She followed him, weaving through the other vehicles to the immaculate blue car.

The man pulled open the car door for her to see inside. "This is the second-generation Audi Q-seven SUV," he started his spiel confidently. "It is considerably lighter than the original version, which makes it cheaper to run and better to drive."

Cherry slid in behind the wheel, the smell, the newness of the interior invading her nostrils. She feigned scanning the intricate dashboard in great detail. It was a million miles from the simplicity of her aging little mini and, in truth, she had no idea what she was looking at.

"I have to tell you this is the most technologically advanced Audi ever made. It is able to brake, accelerate and even steer itself at speeds of up to thirty-seven miles an hour."

She stopped looking around the interior and peered out at him. "Heavens, I never knew."

"Not many people do, madam. But apart from all the high-tech stuff, it still does the basics brilliantly. Despite being slightly narrower and shorter than the old Q-seven, the interior still has room for seven people and their luggage. It has an optional four-wheel steering system which makes it more stable at higher speeds, and a dream to manoeuvre going slower. There is also an optional air suspension..." He stopped, realising he was losing her. "But why don't we go to the office, and I'll give you the full details? You can then be ready for your man when he returns at the weekend."

Cherry smiled sweetly and climbed out of the car. "That would be wonderful. Thank you so much."

It was an open plan office with five desks. Three were occupied. The man sat her in front of his desk and offered her coffee. She accepted and while he was away she studied the men sitting at the other desks. None matched the photograph in her pocket. She was disappointed, but then, just as the man returned with the coffee—in a china cup and saucer no less—another man emerged from a side office tucked away at the far end of the showroom. Cherry recognised him immediately.

Frank Cavendish stood for some moments surveying the room, his eyes finally coming to rest on Cherry. He strolled across and offered his hand. "Good morning, madam." He wasn't very tall, and of average build, ideal to model the perfectly cut charcoal grey suit he was wearing. A deep blue shirt and immaculately tied burgundy tie completed the smart ensemble. The dark, naturally wavy hair, slightly greying around the ears, complemented the tanned features and deep blue eyes. The smile seemed genuine, the handshake cool and firm. He could, Cherry thought, be considered quite handsome.

"I hope Brian here is looking after you, madam."

Cherry smiled and indicated toward the cup and saucer on the desk in front of her. "Very nicely, thank you."

Brian sat down behind his desk. "This is Mr Cavendish, our manager," he said. "This is Mrs... Er..."

Cherry offered Cavendish her hand. "Murphy," she lied. "Cheryl Murphy." Quick thinking, and the Christian name was true anyway. She looked back at Brian. "And it's Miss, by the way." She lowered her eyes demurely "We don't tie the knot until later this year."

Brian flushed. "Oh, I'm sorry. My mistake." He turned to Cavendish. "I was just about to furnish Miss Murphy with the full details of the Q-seven. Her partner is away until the weekend, but it seems he has set his heart on one."

Cherry smiled. "He certainly has. If it weren't for his silly business, he would be here now. But North Norfolk? He never discusses his business dealings with me but, I mean, North Norfolk? He took me there once. Sloped off to his business meeting and left me to fend for myself. Honestly, it's an awful place. Full of old villages and old people." She looked directly at Cavendish. "Have you ever been there?"

His lips tightening, Cavendish held her gaze for a silent moment before replying. "Personally, no, but I do know a little about the area." Before Cherry could push further, he raised a dismissive hand. "You're in good hands. I'm sure Brian will be able to match any deal you will get elsewhere. The Q-seven is an excellent choice. Your partner will not be disappointed." He made to move away then stopped. "Congratulations for later in the year, by the way."

Cherry smiled sweetly. "Thank you."

Without another word, Cavendish turned and made his way back across the showroom to his office.

Cherry took a sip of the coffee. "Seems like a nice man. Good to work for, is he?"

"Yes, he's okay. Used to be the senior salesman here before the old boss retired. Real ball of fire, he was then." He leaned a little closer, lowering his voice a tad. "Never been quite the same since his missus did the dirty on him a while back."

Cherry laid down her cup. "Oh my, gossip as well as a new car. Please tell me more."

~ * ~

Stern had parked the car and wandered into the station. He grabbed a coffee and stood looking up at the arrivals timetable. Cherry had texted to say she was catching the two o'clock out of Liverpool Street. The arrival timetable, showing it to be due in at three forty-eight, confirmed it to be on time. The station clock showed just before a quarter to four. Only a few minutes to wait. He found a seat and sat people-watching while he finished the coffee. Ten minutes later, as he watched her stride down the platform toward him, he dumped the empty cup in the bin.

"So how did it go?" They climbed into the car, and Stern headed for the car park exit.

"Interesting," Cherry said. "Can't be sure it was Cavendish at Mo's house, but he as sure as hell knows something about it." She glanced sideways toward him. "How about you? How did your day go?"

Stern smiled. "Like you...interesting. I visited the Butler residence. Got a surprising reception." He glanced down at his watch. "Let's leave it for tomorrow. If I don't get you home in reasonable time, Rob will be worried. Might not even let you come out to play tomorrow. Can't have that, can we?"

Fourteen

Ollie Preston was on what he liked to think of as a stake out. The last note he'd sent should have generated some sort of action, but so far as he could see there had been none. Though, he had to admit, it was early days, and he knew the wheels of the judiciary turned at snail pace. Some said the British police were the best in the world, but sometimes he wondered. They were always giving out on television how the support of the public was so imperative to successful policing, yet they didn't respond to factual information shoved under their noses free gratis. Well, they hadn't responded yet, anyway. In truth, Ollie wasn't sure how he would know if they had reacted to his note, other than to see a police presence at Eddie Butler's pad. And that's why he was there, why he'd been there every spare moment he had since he'd sent that last note. Nothing would give him more pleasure than to see a bunch of uniforms swarming all over the big gaff on the other side of the river.

There was, of course, the other reason for him being there. If the police did once again ignore his latest note, as it seemed they had the others, he would have to take matters into his own hands and initiate Plan B. Ollie was not an action man, far from it, but he was honest, with an overriding sense of fair play. Though sometimes he wondered if it was worth it. If he'd followed in his mother's footsteps, he'd have been a scrounging wastrel living off the back of everyone stupid enough to fall for his crafty scams. But he hadn't. He was hard working, even though the jobs he had to take were at the bottom of the labour force ladder. And he would do no one harm. Quite the opposite. He saw the world as a wicked place where evil frequently went unchecked, the wicked riding roughshod over the innocent. At times like this, there was no alternative but for action to be taken. Unless he saw some evidence of action by the police soon, Ollie thought this would be one of those times. If it were, then detailed planning would be essential. In this case, that meant being absolutely certain of every move, of all the comings and goings at the Butler residence both day and night.

Ollie was lounging on the far side of the River Bure, his binoculars focussed on the rear of the huge Tudor building with its grounds running down to the river. He'd never been interested in bird watching, couldn't understand what people saw in it. They were birds, weren't they? Feathered things that left their crap everywhere, and all looked the same. Well, to him they did. And he should know, there were dozens of them in and out of his overgrown garden all the time. Didn't need binoculars to see them there, either. Mind you, the binoculars were coming in very handy right now.

As the sun broke through the cloud, and he popped one of the cans of beer he had brought with him, it felt quite pleasant. Nothing like the warm, friendly atmosphere of the pub on darts night, of course. Nothing quite matched that. But pleasant nonetheless. Besides, he wasn't there for pleasure, certainly not bird watching. He was there on business. He was glad he'd borrowed the tripod and the fancy looking telescope attached to it. He had no idea how to use the thing and didn't intend to use it anyway; the binoculars were perfectly adequate for his purpose. But at least it made his presence look authentic.

He sipped at the beer and studied the scene across the river. There was no movement at all at the property, and he could see that all the rear windows and doors were closed. No one at home. That figured. Butler's business, his legitimate business, was based in London. In the main, he came here only at weekends. The wife, a flash bit of stuff, some years younger than Butler, sometimes stayed during the week. But only sometimes. From watching her, Ollie got the impression she was a town girl. She could probably only take so much raw countryside.

He scanned across to the wide, glass double patio doors. When opened, they led directly onto a deep patio, spreading the whole width of the building's rear. Several sets of garden furniture with tightly furled sun shades protruding from the centre of each table were strategically placed, and to one side sat an enormous stainless steel barbecue. Directly in front of the patio, a deep blue canvas was stretched tightly over a swimming pool, he guessed, from the look of it, equally as big as the local council pool he used from time to time.

Between the high hedges bordering either side of the property, a lawn covering the whole width of the rear area stretched from the swimming pool down to the river's edge. Here, cut into the river bank, was a deep mooring surrounded by decking with protective fenders hanging every few feet. Reversed into the mooring was a boat.

It wasn't huge. Not like some he'd seen poncing up and down the river bragging all the gismos, even radar, looking like they should be on the Med instead of a little river in Norfolk. No, this was long and sleek, and looked fast. The size of the low-slung cabin looked to be good for a couple, no more, but there was something very expensive looking about the craft. Knowing Butler, Ollie guessed the cost probably well outweighed the size. But that was okay. For Ollie's purpose, the more expensive the better.

He had already carried out an extensive check on the front of the house. He thought that aspect too dangerous. The hedges and gates would make entry difficult, and the concentration of security lighting looked to be heavier in the front than at the rear. Also, unless he was mistaken, the distance between the house and the river was too great for the rear security sensors to trigger the lights. As long as he didn't approach the rear of the house, which he had no intention of doing, he would be safe.

Ollie focussed the little binoculars on the name 'Blaze' scrolled along the boat's side.

"Mmmm, so it's Blaze, is it, Butler?" he muttered to himself. "Well, let me tell you, if the law don't get off their backsides pretty soon you'll see just what blaze really means."

Fifteen

It was Friday, and a watery sun was doing its best to warm the morning chill. It wasn't having much success, but at least it wasn't raining. Unusually, they'd arrived at the office simultaneously, Cherry having parked the mini down by the sea front, the only place she could park all day for free. Earlier, Stern had run the beach for best part of an hour before showering and taking the usual stroll along the promenade from the flat. While Cherry climbed the stairs at the back of the bakery and opened the office, Stern hovered at the counter before grabbing a freshly baked Chelsea bun.

Ten minutes later, Cherry followed him into his office carrying the two habitual mugs of morning coffee. Placing Stern's mug on the desk, she settled in the chair opposite. Stern eased himself into the old chair and sank his teeth into the bun, chewing happily, granules of sugar coating his lips.

Cherry wrinkled her nose in disgust. "How could you? It's barely nine o'clock."

Stern grinned through the sugar. He knew how she would react and, for that reason, had purposely left the sugar in place. "It's my breakfast," he mumbled through the mouthful.

"Some breakfast," Cherry humphed. "Why didn't you eat at home, something healthy?"

Stern licked the sugar from his lips. "Didn't have time. Knew you'd give me grief if I was late. You always do."

Cherry gave a shake of her head. "Don't know why I bother, really I don't."

The bun finished, Stern wiped his mouth and fingers on a tissue and reached for the coffee. "So, we have this woman today, right? The one whose husband is coming and going at all hours."

"Yes, she's due in first thing after lunch. Two o'clock."

Stern took a mouthful of coffee, washing down the dregs of the bun. "She have a name?"

"Barford, Doris Barford. Don't have an address, but she did say she lived in Cromer."

"Just down the road then," Stern mused, recognising the nearest other coastal town, a favourite of holiday makers and just five miles farther along the coast road. "That's handy." He slid the mug back on the desk and pulled the chair closer. "Okay, so we have this morning to discuss yesterday's business." He folded his arms and rested his elbows on the desk. "You first."

Cherry took a breath. "Well first of all, I didn't take an Uber, couldn't find one. But it was okay because I got on well with the driver."

"How well."

"Thirty quid."

"Mmmm, not bad, I suppose. Did you find Cavendish?"

"Yes, I did. Like Mo suspected, he's now the manager of the dealership. Bit of a handsome character, too."

"So how did you play it?"

Cherry went on to explain she had played the partner of a rich guy who was after buying a top of the range Audi.

"How did you bring Norfolk into it?" Stern asked.

Cherry smiled, evidently pleased with herself. "I told them my partner couldn't be there because he was away on business, in North Norfolk."

"And?"

"You remember how, a long time ago, you taught me how to watch for the signs, facial expressions, eye movement, body language, that sort of thing. Well, I still don't profess to be an expert, but I'm sure when I mentioned North Norfolk he reacted."

"How?"

"Mouth tightening, eyes narrowing, focussing on me more. A sort of surprised hesitation. You know, like when someone tells you something you least expect to hear. Makes you sit up and take notice. That's how it seemed to me, anyway. So, I asked him if he'd ever been there. He said he hadn't but did know a bit about the area."

"And?"

"Well, that was it as far as Cavendish was concerned. He disappeared after that. But I did chat up one of his salesmen, a guy called Brian. He'd worked with Cavendish since he was senior salesman there. He was happy to talk. He told me that before Mo had her little dalliance with the art teacher, Cavendish was a real go getter. Reckons he was full of vim and vigour, and always up for a laugh. But afterwards, it all changed. According to Brian, as far as anyone knew, there hasn't been another woman since. Even now, no one dares mention anything to do with women or relationships in front of Cavendish."

"Mmmm, seems a hell of a long time. You'd have thought..." Stern stuttered to a halt, in that instant realising what he was about to say, Annie instantly coming to mind. Time, however long, would never change his feelings for her.

Cherry saw, knew instantly. "Maybe not, boss," she came in quickly. "According to Brian, Cavendish doted on Mo. Her betrayal completely devastated him. Immediately afterwards, he went bananas. He stalked Mo for a long time, berating her every chance he got, even in the street."

Stern coughed, refocused. "Right, and that's when she had a go at his car?"

Cherry smiled. "That's right. They'd taken the car back to the showroom after the attack. Seems there wasn't a panel on it that hadn't been gouged. Brian thought it was hilarious."

Stern traced his bottom lip with the tip of his finger. "So, it looks like Cavendish could still be bitter."

"Yup. And like I said, I'm sure he reacted when I mentioned Norfolk. I know that's only going by what you taught me, boss, but I'd lay money on it. There is a small problem, though."

"What's that?"

"Well, according to Brian, the dealership's sales have been down recently, and they've been under pressure from head office to pull their socks up. Seems for some time it's been all hands to the pump to try and improve things. Because of this, Brian told me Cavendish hasn't had a day off for weeks."

"And your point is?"

"Well, you remember Mo told us the last time she saw her stalker man was during the daytime, mid-afternoon. If Cavendish hasn't had a day off for some time, it's unlikely to have been him, don't you think?" She gave a shake of her head. "I mean, even without traffic it has to be at least a three-hour run up here. Can't imagine even a cheated husband doing a round trip like that just to put the evil eye on his ex for no more than a few minutes, can you?"

"Good point," Stern mused, drumming his fingers thoughtfully on the desk. "But if your interpretation of his reaction when you mentioned Norfolk was right, we shouldn't discount him completely."

"Okay. So, we just wait to hear from Mo again, right?"

"Yes, that's what we agreed. The next time the mystery man appears, she'll call us, and we'll take it from there."

"Okay, and for what it's worth, I did get this." Cherry slid her mobile out of her pocket, tapped the face a couple of times and handed it across to Stern.

Stern looked at the picture on the screen. "Mmmm, bit older, more mature, than the one Mo gave us."

"It is. In the showroom, they had a notice board on the wall with large glossy photos of all the staff. I managed to get this before I left. Being current, I thought it might be handy. I'll get a copy run off."

Stern handed the phone back. "You're right, it could be useful. Well done."

Cherry slipped the phone into her pocket. "So how did your day go?"

"Like David said, the Butler property is pretty impressive. It's a big mock Tudor style place called Deep Repose. It's tucked away behind high hedges and protected by equally high iron gates. I checked out the front of the joint on Oak Lane and last night, when I got back to the flat, I pulled up Google Earth. As I thought, the rear of the property runs down to the river. I want to have another run over there, get on the other side of the river and check out the rear of the place."

"Was Butler at home?"

"I think he must have been. There was a posh looking Merc parked outside the front door, and I hadn't been there a minute before Neanderthal man appeared."

"What?"

Stern chuckled. "A security guard, knuckles dragging on the ground. Looked like he could have given Mike Tyson a run for his money. Wanted to know what I was up to."

"Sounds dodgy."

"No, not really. I explained I was on the point of having a new house built, wanted it to be in the Tudor style. Said I was advised if I wanted to see an excellent example I should take a look at Deep Repose."

"And he fell for it?"

Stern was grinning broadly. "Well I don't know about falling for it. More like he was confused."

"Not with you."

"He asked me what the hell Tudor style was."

They were still laughing when Cherry headed out to make more coffee. It was then it came to Stern that, since yesterday morning, Annie hadn't entered his head.

Sixteen

To the Senior Officer.

You should be aware that my patience is fast running out. What are you, bent coppers in league with Butler? On the take? Is that it? Is that why I can see no evidence of you taking me seriously? Well, stand by, Mr Policeman, because unless I see some action in the next day or so, I will be taking matters into my own hands. And believe me, if I have to do that, you will have only yourselves to blame.

A very angry law-abiding citizen.

O'Connor read through the note twice before looking up at his young sergeant. "Same as the others, through the post?"

"Yes, Inspector. This time posted in Fakenham."

"Mmmm, somewhere different again. That's Luton, Cambridge, and now, Fakenham. Not quite as far out as the others, but he does get around."

"It seems that way, sir. Possibly a delivery driver, or a travelling salesman. Unless he gets others to do the posting for him."

O'Connor frowned. "Travelling salesman? Haven't heard that one for a while. Are they still around?"

The young sergeant grinned sheepishly. "Don't know, sir. But didn't they used to get blamed for everything?"

"You've been reading too many old novels, Sergeant," O'Connor snorted. He picked up the note and scanned it again. "Still, a driver of some sort is a possibility I guess. Does the handwriting match the others?"

"Yes, sir, I had it checked out before I brought it to you. No fingerprints or signs of DNA, but it's the same person. That's certain."

O'Connor leaned back in the chair. "Okay, Sergeant. Thanks for that."

As the sergeant left the office, O'Connor, still holding the note, reached for the phone.

~ * ~

As Cherry had assessed previously, Doris Barford was most likely in her mid-forties. She had shoulder length blonde hair which, if her eyebrows were anything to go by, was not natural. Her not unattractive face was pale with little makeup. She was dressed in dark corduroy trousers and a windcheater jacket which she chose to keep on. She smiled a lot, but the smile seemed nervous. Stern beckoned her to the chair opposite. Cherry sat to one side, notepad at the ready.

Stern started by introducing himself and Cherry, detailing his own background and experience and the history of Stern Investigations. He gave a reassuring smile. "Always nice to know who you're dealing with, don't you think?"

She fidgeted uneasily, her hands clasped in her lap. "I had heard about you some time ago," she said softly. "A friend you helped."

"I won't ask who this friend was," Stern said, holding the smile. "But I hope our efforts were successful."

"Yes, they were very pleased."

"Good. Now tell me about you. A little background."

"There's not a lot to tell really, nothing exciting, anyway. I'm married with two young boys. Until the end of last year, we lived in Hampshire...my husband, Steve, was in the military, a regular soldier."

"Aldershot?" Stern asked.

"Yes. During his time, he did a number of tours abroad." Her brow wrinkled. "It affected him quite a lot."

"Not injured, I hope?"

"No, not physically, anyway. But after so many years of military life, particularly the active service side of things, he found Civvy Street difficult to adjust to. You see, he was a driver, he had driven fighting vehicles in a number of conflicts, driving was basically all he knew. So, when he came out, job opportunities were limited, and those he did manage to get bored him silly. He didn't last long in any of them."

"I think I understand," Stern said. "There wouldn't be much outside the military that could come anywhere near what he's been through."

She shook her head sadly and was silent, pensive for a beat before continuing. "Anyway, it was a phone call from my father that brought us here. You see, my family originated from this area, I was born here, and my mother and father still live here. I was talking on the phone to my dad one day, and he said there were always opportunities here for self-employed taxi drivers. He said he knew several, and they were happy and made a fair living. He made it sound interesting; one day never the same as another, always meeting different people, you know the sort of thing."

"Yup, I get the picture."

"Well I talked it over with Steve, and we decided to make a clean break and move here."

"Did your husband find work?"

"Yes, he did. He works freelance for a local company."

"You mean he uses his own vehicle, but the firm finds the customers and takes a percentage?"

"Yes, that's right. But about three weeks ago, he came home and told me he'd had a proposition put to him by one of his fares. The guy said the outfit he worked for was looking for a delivery driver. He said it wasn't full time and was mostly evening work, so Steve could easily fit it in around his day job. A van would be provided, which Steve could keep at home, and he would be paid for each delivery in cash. The only problem was Steve had to react when he was called because the stuff they delivered was perishable and when it was ready to go, it had to go."

Stern looked wary. "Was he told what he would be carrying?"

"I don't think so. Not that he told me anyway."

"Okay, go on."

She took a deep breath. "Anyway, the man gave Steve a telephone number and told him to ring if he was interested. He said not to hang about, though, because they needed someone urgently. That evening Steve told me about it. He also told me how much the man had said he could earn."

It was the way she looked when she said it. "Big money?" Stern said.

Her eyes darkened. "Yes, too big. It was five hundred pounds every trip."

Stern whistled. "That is big."

"I told Steve it couldn't be legit. He said we didn't know that, and, anyway, for a start he'd do it for a short while. That way he could find out what it involved and, at the same time, build up the bank balance." Her eyes moistened, and she looked down, studying her hands twisting in her lap. "Steve's a risk taker, Mr Stern, always has been. He jumps in, both feet, without thinking."

"So, as well as his taxi work, he delivers this stuff, whatever it is, in the evening?"

"Almost always, yes. Sometimes he's away for an hour or two, others, he's gone best part of the night. Comes home in the early hours. The phone rings and whatever the time, he's off."

"Have you talked to him about it again, voiced your concerns?" Cherry said, speaking for the first time. "I mean since he's been doing the job, had a chance to see what it was all about?"

"I've tried to, several times." There was an emotional hic in her voice. "He just waves my questions away. Tells me not to worry, just stay schtum, tell no one, and everything will pan out okay. He keeps repeating that it's only for a short time, and I just have to trust him because, in the end, the benefits will be huge." She turned her attention back to Stern, holding up her hands, a desperate gesture. "For heaven's sake, how can you get huge benefits from being a delivery driver if it's legit, Mr Stern? None of it makes any sense. I mean, sometimes he leaves the house in the morning with his eyes hanging out because he's been up all night. I have a terrible feeling he's got himself mixed up in something really bad, but I just can't make him see it. When he was in the military, he was away for months on end. Sometimes in very dangerous places. That was worrying enough, but honestly if he got himself in trouble with the police...If they sent him to prison. I just couldn't bear to lose him again." Her eyes filled, and tears trickled down her cheeks. She made no attempt to wipe them away.

Stern raised a hand. "Whoa now, don't upset yourself. We mustn't jump the gun here," he said softly. "We can't be sure Steve is doing anything wrong yet, can we? Let's find out what he's up to first and take it from there."

She pulled a handkerchief from the sleeve of her jacket, dabbing her cheeks. "I'm sorry, what with the boys and all, I'm just so worried."

Cherry left her chair and put her arm around the woman's shoulder. "Don't be," she soothed. "Mr Stern is an expert at this type of problem. He'll have your Steve sorted in no time at all."

Stern shot Cherry a warning look. "We'll have to see how things pan out, but we will do all we can," he said. He thought for a moment. "How much warning does your husband get when one of these trips comes along?"

"Not much. Sometimes he gets a call and leaves almost immediately. Other times, it could be an hour or so before he leaves."

"If you get the chance next time it happens, I want you to call us immediately. If I can get to your place before he leaves, I might be able to follow him."

"Okay, I'll try to do that."

"The bad news is there will be a charge for our services, I'm afraid. It will comprise an hourly rate plus travel costs and any additional expenses incurred." He pulled a distasteful expression. "And, of course, the dreaded VAT." He smiled, he hoped reassuringly. "But it is our policy to keep costs at an absolute minimum."

"That would be appreciated, Mr Stern. I do have a little money of my own. It was left to me in my grandmother's will. You can have it all if you make this to go away."

"I understand, and we'll do our best. Now, there will be certain information that Cherry needs to know, including the registration number of the van your husband uses. Once we have that, we can get underway." He paused for a beat. "As a matter of interest, what type of van was Steve supplied with?"

"It's a Ford Transit."

"Colour?"

Mrs Barford hesitated for a moment, thinking. "Black, dark blue, something like that. A dark colour anyway."

"Any markings?"

"No, it's just a plain van."

"Okay, go with Cherry, and she'll take the information we need." Stern thought for a second, then held up a restraining hand. "One last thing. Would you be able to check how many miles the van has done? On the tacho, I mean."

She frowned for a moment, confusion showing. "Yes, I suppose, if that's what you want."

"Good. I'd like you to do that for me as soon as you can, and let us know what it is?"

"Okay, I'll do it when I get home."

"Thank you. Oh, and Mrs Barford, do it without your husband's knowledge, please."

As Cherry escorted Doris Barford from the office, Stern's mobile rang. He checked the display noting it was O'Connor.

"David, what's up?"

"We've had another note. Says if we don't do something soon, they will. Sounds like they mean it, too."

"Still no clues on the envelope, the note paper?"

"No chance. Did you see Butler's gaff?"

"I did. Got warned off by security to boot."

"So what d'you think?"

"Well, I've been giving it some thought," Stern came back. "And I think the only chance we have of identifying this character is through Charlie Croker."

"How so?"

"Didn't the last note you got say our mystery writer knew Croker well?"

There was a pause, O'Connor giving the question some thought. "Yes, it did," he replied finally. "Said they'd known each other for years."

"So, if that were the case, you'd have thought whoever is writing these notes would more than likely have visited Croker's flat."

"You would have thought so, yes."

"Okay, so what's the situation with Croker's flat right now?"

"Give me a minute." Stern could hear O'Connor call out to someone. There was then some indistinct conversation before O'Connor returned to the phone. "Seems our people finished with it this morning. I'm expecting a report later today or early tomorrow. It was only a cursory once over, though. I'm not expecting anything startling. Don't forget, officially this was just an accident. If it weren't for these bloody notes, we would be seeing this as a guy getting stoned out of his mind and falling in the river. Sad, but just an accident."

"That's true," Stern agreed. "So, the flat hasn't been handed back to the council authority yet?"

"No, but that'll happen today or tomorrow, I guess."

"Could you get me the okay to have a look around before you release it, David? I'm busy over the weekend, but Monday would suit, if that were possible. A fresh pair of eyes, particularly with the notes in mind...I'd be happy to be escorted by uniform, just to make it official. I could chat to the neighbours at the same time."

"No problem. I'll arrange for our lads to meet you there. Let's say nine on Monday. That okay?"

"I'll be there."

Seventeen

Saturday dawned bright with the forecast promising it to stay that way. And it had. Stern had owned his new car for just three days and, despite it being in pristine condition when he collected it, he'd spent virtually the whole day at the lock-up behind the flat fussing over it. Unlike his old love, on which he had carried out all maintenance and repairs himself, unwilling to trust any repair shop, this was a different animal. He only had to lift the bonnet to realise with dismay that, other than establishing the whereabouts of the windscreen washer reservoir and the oil dipstick, any necessary work here would be best left to the garage. But keeping his new pride and joy clean, even after only three days, was essential. And there were other things too, not the least being the fantastic sound system with its eight speakers and integral hard disk with enough space to store the whole of his treasured jazz collection. But that would be for later. For the moment, he would make do with the usual stock of CDs in the glove compartment.

Sunday was a more casual day. Stern woke late feeling good, realising the dregs of any jet lag were well behind him. The good weather was holding, so after an extended beach run, he spent an hour relaxing on the tiny balcony, watching the world go by. Come lunchtime, it was a drive to West Beckham and The Wheatsheaf for a superb Sunday roast followed by his favourite bread and butter pudding. Back at the flat, the effect of the meal, and more likely the two post lunch pints, had him dozing for the best part of the afternoon and evening.

Today, Monday, Stern was on his way to Norwich, and the high rise flat where Charlie Croker had lived. It mattered not that the rain had arrived. Alone in the car, he was smiling broadly. The responsive two litre engine purred powerfully under him, and the Scirocco's eight speakers were kicking out a favourite Sidney Bechet album, "Spreadin' Joy," as he'd never heard it. How better to start the new week?

He followed the A140 to the city, crossing the outer ring road, and heading south toward the inner-city area. This was all familiar territory to Stern; over the years, he'd travelled here any number of times while covering previous cases. The city centre, surrounded by an inner ring road, was a maze of one-way streets, so Stern took the easy route, following the road round until he was able to break right at the intersection with King Street, which took him directly onto Rouen Road. He was well aware that parking could be a problem and, if he wasn't careful, expensive. It always was in this area. But he remembered a series of cul-de-sacs leading away from the tower block he'd used before. As in the past, he was lucky, tucking the Scirocco alongside a gleaming Jaguar.

Ten minutes later, he was striding along the fifth-floor balcony of the tower block toward a heavily built young police officer waiting outside Coker's flat.

"Mr Stern?"

"Yes."

"PC Paul Wainwright, sir. Inspector O'Connor instructed I should accompany you during your examination of the flat."

"Thanks, Constable, it's appreciated."

The front door opened into a hallway, the floor covered in polished linoleum, a deep pile rug positioned half way along. On the left, there were two doors. One led into a kitchen, the other a bathroom. On the right, directly opposite the bathroom, was a single bedroom. Stern made cursory check of both the kitchen and bathroom before heading directly to a door at the end of the hallway, the constable following on his heels. The door opened into quite an expansive sitting room, and Stern stood on the threshold, his eyes scanning back and forth.

"Anything in particular you're looking for, Mr Stern?"

Stern shook his head. "I'm sure your people would have done a pretty clean sweep of the place already, Constable. I'm just an extra pair of eyes."

"Hope you don't mind me saying, sir, but it's pretty unusual for us to use a civilian in this classification. An active investigation, I mean. A bit of admin work here and there, but..."

Stern moved into the room. "Yeah, I know what you're saying, Constable, but sometimes, when needs must. Even in the police force."

Following him in, Wainwright gave a nervous little cough. "And when they have someone like you around, of course."

Stern turned and eyeballed the young policeman. "Someone like me?"

"Yes, sir. Some of the older hands at the station know of you, know your background; London CID and all that. Bit of a legend in your day, they say."

Stern humphed. "All scuttlebutt, Constable. Don't believe a word of it."

The constable smiled knowingly. It wasn't only the old hands that had given him the heads up on Stern. The inspector, too, had briefed him, telling him who he would be escorting, telling him to look and learn.

It was a pretty conventional combined sitting room cum dining room covering the whole width of the flat. The heavy pile carpet was light beige and looked expensive and new. The walls, a clean plain white, gave the room a spacious feel. At the sitting room end, the end closest to the door where he stood, a light fabric sofa together with a pair of matching armchairs were positioned against two of the walls. A wide-screen television was strategically placed directly opposite the sofa. Between the sofa and the TV, a round wooden framed coffee table with a glass centre occupied the middle of the room. At the opposite end of the room, a light wood dining room table surrounded by four chairs sat centre stage with a matching sideboard positioned against the wall. Directly opposite the door through which they had entered the room, a broad window looked out over the city centre. The walls were bare of any hanging pictures or photographs.

Stern crossed the room and stood for some moments looking out of the window. "Not a bad view," he muttered.

The constable remained standing by the door. "If you like that sort of thing. Prefer the countryside myself."

Stern turned and headed to the far end of the room. "Each to their own, Constable."

The top of the old sideboard was protected by a typical cloth runner that looked to have been hand crocheted. Standing on this, in the centre of the unit, was a glass bowl holding a single wrinkled apple. The front of the unit comprised two main central doors with a narrower door either side. Above this was a row of three drawers. Stern squatted and pulled open the two main doors. Inside, filling a single shelf, were neatly placed cups, saucers and plates of different sizes. The area below was completely filled with piles of books and magazines. Closing the doors, he made a quick inspection of the areas either side, finding each filled with the usual bric-a-brac that accumulates in any home. A quick rake-through revealed nothing of interest. Stern pushed himself up and pulled open the first of the drawers. It was a cutlery drawer containing an assortment of knives, forks and spoons, all of which looked of good quality and new. The next housed nothing more than a pile of table mats and paper serviettes. It was the third drawer that took his interest. Here, piled to the brim, was a whole host of paperwork.

Stern turned to the constable standing at his side. "How long've we got, Constable? I'd like to go through some of this."

Wainwright shrugged. "The inspector didn't put a time limit on me, Mr Stern. So, I guess you're good to go." He looked at his watch. "Don't want to push my luck, sir, but it's after ten, so if you'd like me to nip out and grab some coffee...?"

Stern grinned. "That's not pushing your luck, Constable, that's what I call initiative." He reached into his pocket, pulled out his wallet and extracted a ten-pound note. "If you can, grab a couple of bacon butties while you're at it."

Eighteen

Cherry arrived at the office just after nine. She followed her usual routine; heat on and coffee brewing, before settling at her desk. She knew she would be alone until at least lunchtime, possibly longer. It didn't bother her. They had three cases running, and she had no doubt there would be more to come. She remembered when they had kicked off Stern Investigations back in 2005. It had been some while before the first case, a woman, had ventured through the door. She had been the first of what the boss came to dub their 'husbands playing away' cases, sometimes traumatic for the client, but for Stern Investigations simple, straightforward bread and butter stuff. All that was needed was proof of the infidelity—this normally requiring the guilty party to be followed, if possible to obtain incriminating photographs. A written report, photographs attached, and it was job done. It was never very difficult. However intelligent, men became total morons when their heads were turned. On the odd occasion when the roles were reversed, it was a little more difficult. Women were much sneakier.

But then, in no time at all, they'd been drawn into much more complicated, sometimes downright dangerous investigations. And it had continued that way. In particular, the Melanie Campbell case; the last case before Stern had left, when he'd been beaten half to death by the crazy woman's crazy son. Cherry was sure this had been one factor in the boss's decision to wrap things up and follow his ex-wife to Australia. His absence had been a miserable time for Cherry, but something had told her he would be back. And she'd been right. Now, Stern Investigations was underway again, and this time the boss had given her a major role to play in one of the investigations. He'd let her off the leash to make the London trip. When reluctantly agreeing to reinstate Stern Investigations again, the boss had said he'd give it twelve months. Cherry was optimistic, believing that once he had the bit between his teeth again, he would carry on. After all, as she had said before, what else would he do? One thing was sure, however long he kept going, she would be by his side.

Cherry was a belt and braces kind of girl. Not only did she create a file for each case on the computer, including an incoming and outgoing finances account chart, she also prepared a hard copy of everything, neatly filed away in a folder in the file cabinet. The Mo Steven case was already on file, both on the computer and in the cabinet. Today, she would use the boss' absence as an opportunity to add to it and write a complete report, including her own observations and conclusions, on her visit to the Audi dealership in London. She had hardly typed the first line into her laptop when the phone rang. She knew who it would be, but she gave the official answer anyway.

"Stern Investigations, how can we help?"

"It's me. Just checking in. Everything okay?"

"Yes, no problems. I'm doing a report on my London trip. How's it going with you?"

"Not bad. I'm at the flat and going through some of Croker's stuff. Need to check up on a couple of bank statements I've pulled out here, but we can do that when I get back. There's something else, though. Like you to check it out for me."

"Okay." Cherry picked up a pen and drew her note pad toward her. Then she hesitated, frowning, noticing his words were unclear, a sort of mumble. "You eating?"

A short pause. "Yeah, but not my fault. I have a very proactive young constable with me who conjured up some coffee and a couple of bacon butties, including Tommy K. He insisted I try one. It would have been churlish of me to refuse."

Cherry sighed. "Bacon butties, more fat. You'll never learn, will you?"

Stern laughed. "Maybe not, but I bet it's tastier than the couple of lettuce leaves and that soggy crispy biscuit you've got for lunch."

She couldn't help smiling. He wasn't far wrong. "Okay, so what d'you want me to check out?"

The serious, business-like tone was instantly back in his voice. "When I've finished here, I'm going to see if I can chat to Croker's neighbours, get to know something about the guy. But among the junk in his sideboard, I found a couple of shields."

"Shields?"

"Yeah, plastic shields. Trophy-type-things, know what I mean?"

"Oh right. Yup, got it."

"Seems Croker won these playing darts, and the name of the pub he played for is engraved on the trophy. Might be a good idea if we paid it a visit."

"Sounds good to me. What d'you want me to do?"

"Well, I've got the name here but not the address. Got a feeling it'll be fairly local, though that doesn't have to be the case. Have a buzz round, see if you can place it?"

"Okay, will do. What's the name of the pub?"

"The Beehive."

"Mmmm, don't remember ever hearing it mentioned locally," Cherry mused.

"No, me neither. Still, see what you can rake up, and we'll talk later, okay?"

"Will do."

Cherry ended the call and minimised the Word document she was using for her report. She then called up Google and typed in Norfolk Pubs.

~ * ~

Stern wrote a list of the various bits and pieces he'd taken from the flat. Among other things, it comprised the two trophy shields, bank statements, bills and a cheque book. He made sure Constable Wainwright checked each item and witnessed his signature. Handing it over to the constable, he suggested it be placed in Croker's file at the station. He suspected anything Croker had on him when he was dragged from the Wensum would still be in that police file. He made a mental note to talk to O'Connor about it.

Leaving Croker's place, they moved along to the flat next. Stern rang the bell. After several rings with no response, they moved to the flat on the other side of Croker's. This time, after a long pause, the door was yanked open. He was short and heavily built with a large belly, emphasised by the fact he was only wearing underpants and a vest. His eyes were sleep filled, and he was angry.

"What the fu…" he growled before stopping, his bleary squinting eyes moving from Stern to the tall uniformed policeman standing alongside him. "Oh, what…I mean…"

"Sorry to trouble you, sir," Stern broke in quickly. "We wondered if you could help us with some information about your neighbour." Stern figured Wainwright's presence and being addressed as 'sir' would prevent him from having to identify himself.

"Neighbour?" The man was obviously still in the throes of waking up.

Wainwright was quick to assess the situation. He stepped forward, accentuating his size and the police uniform, the authority. "Mr Croker, sir. Your next door neighbour?"

"Oh yeah, gotcher, Croker." The man ground his eyes with his knuckles before again focussing on Stern. "Didn't know him all that well, but…" He folded his arms tightly across his chest, the chill of the morning creeping into him. "Look, its bloody freezing out here, you'd better come in."

Inside, they settled in chairs around a kitchen table, the man wrapped in a dressing gown. It had taken no more than a knowing glance of understanding between Stern and Wainwright for the young policeman to know the score. He drew his notebook from his pocket and took the lead.

"So, what can you tell us about Mr Croker, Mr...?"

"Spriggs, George Spriggs." He sniffed heavily. "Sorry about, you know, being grumpy at the door. I work night's y'see. And the wife's out at work. Usually kip through to about mid-afternoon. Bit of a bugger being woke up early."

"That's perfectly okay, Mr Spriggs. We do understand. However, this is important." Wainwright let the silence hang for a moment, waiting.

"I did speak to the others, y'know. Y'know, your lot that came before," Spriggs said.

"Yes, of course," Wainwright said. "And we appreciate that. But since then there have been further developments." He inclined his head toward Stern. "This is Special Investigator Stern working with the CID. He has been brought in to revisit the situation."

Special Investigator? That was some initiative. Stern held his official face, hiding the smile trying to force its way to his lips. He made another mental note to recommend Wainwright for better things.

And it did the trick. Spriggs looked at Stern with renewed respect. "Oh right, got it. So, what can I tell you?"

Wainwright glanced at Stern, his expression saying, 'over to you.'

"Mr Spriggs," Stern came in. "You say you didn't know Mr Croker well?"

Spriggs gave a shake of his head. "No, not really. I don't think anyone knew him that well. He was a bit of a loner. Nice bloke, though. We had a drink now and then, Christmas time, that sort of thing, just to be sociable really." He thought for a moment. "Once, when the wife was away at her sister's, I went with him to one of his matches. One of my nights off. Good night it was, too. Old Croker could sure throw a dart."

"He played for a team, I understand?"

"Yeah, don't ask me who, though. I just went along for a couple of pints."

"Do you know if Mr Croker had family?"

Spriggs smiled for the first time. "Well, he had a young woman visit pretty regularly. Said it was his daughter, but I had my doubts. Never saw or heard of anyone else, though."

"And why did you have doubts about the daughter?"

"Well, for a start, she never stayed for more than a few hours. Always came late evening, around nine or ten o'clock."

"Ah, I see what you mean. Was it always the same woman?"

"Yes, always the same one. Young, she was. Not much meat on her." He gave a dismissive shrug. "Looked nice enough."

"Do you know anything about her?"

"Not much, he kept her to himself. Like I said, she came around nine or ten, left in the early hours. That was it. He did tell me her name was Sally, but that was all."

"How about other visitors? Friends, colleagues from work?"

"No. Like I said, Charlie was a bit of a loner. Other than the girl, I can't remember anyone in particular. Over recent months he had the decorators in. Had some deliveries, too. You know furniture and that." He thought for a moment. "Oh yeah, and he showed me a new carpet he'd had put down. But other than the girl there was no one regular."

Stern reflected back on the nice condition of the flat. It fitted. "Okay, thanks for that. I understand he worked for a builder?"

"Yeah. He worked for Charters."

"Charters?"

"Yeah, local crowd. Got a yard on the Norwich Road, this side of Cromer. Family outfit, father to son, been around forever."

"D'you know what Mr Croker did at Charters?"

"He was a labourer. Did a bit of this and that. Y'know fetching and carrying. Hod carrying, that sort of thing."

Stern thought that tied up with what O'Connor had already told him. "And that was it, was it? Just the one job?" He watched Spriggs closely, immediately clocking the initial, obvious hesitation.

"Er, yeah, as far as I know."

Stern silently held onto Spriggs' gaze until the other man lowered his eyes. The clincher. "Mr Spriggs?"

Spriggs gave another heavy sniff and looked up, doubt clouding his eyes. "Look, I don't know anything about the other business."

"What other business would that be?"

It was as if Spriggs never heard the question. "I work hard and keep my nose out of other people's business. What Charlie got up to in his spare time was nothing to do with me."

For the first time since Stern had taken over the questioning, Wainwright leaned forward, accentuating the uniform, the authority for a second time. "Maybe not, Mr Spriggs, but it's certainly something to do with us. And I'm sure you are aware that withholding information from the police is an offence in law."

Nineteen

Stern left Wainwright in Norwich, thanking him for his help, suggesting if he ever decided to quit the police force he should give Stern Investigations a call. The constable looked double pleased at the compliment and said it had been a pleasure working with such an experience veteran, but the police force was his life. He couldn't see a time when he would consider leaving. However, given the opportunity, he'd relish working with Stern again.

Stern knew exactly what he meant about not leaving the force. Nevertheless, he still waved a warning finger. "Never say never, son."

On his return trip, about three miles outside Cromer on the A140, Stern found Charters. He pulled into the builder's yard and parked the car in a customers' parking slot, safely away from the coming and going of vans and lorries. In the office, he found the boss, Raymond Charter. He was a large, florid faced individual with a booming, thick Norfolk accent and a hail fellow, well met demeanour. He was only too pleased to discuss Croker, not even requesting some form of identification. Stern was pleased about that.

"Damned good worker," he assured Stern. "Not the sharpest knife in the drawer, you understand, but in this business, we don't need all university graduates, do we?" He laughed, a growling rasping sound. "Not that they're all they're cracked up to be these days. No, all you had to do is make sure old Charlie understood what was required of him. Once he knew that, he was away. Couldn't ask for more effort. Damned sorry to lose him." He paused, his large forehead corrugating in a sudden thought. "You say you're with the police?"

"Yes. Name's Stern. I'm a special investigator, brought in by the CID to tidy up one or two details." Stern silently thanked Wainwright for the title and hoped Charter didn't decide to ask for the identity he'd forgotten earlier. That would mean a call to O'Connor, and he didn't want that. He need not have worried.

Charter shook his head sadly. "Strange old business, I have to say."

"Strange?"

"Well, Charlie was a bit of a lone ranger, it's true, and as my father always said; there's none as queer as folk. So what Charlie got up to in his spare time was his business. All I can say is I never ever knew him to take a drink. And I'd doubt any of the lads here had either." He gave an exaggerated shrug of his broad shoulders. "Something to do with his father, I was told. And as for drugs..." Another shake of the head. "Just goes to show, you think you know someone, eh?"

"Was he with you long?"

"Couldn't tell you exactly without pulling his file, but it had to be at least five or six years."

"D'you know if he had any family?"

Charter shook his head. "If he did, he never spoke of them."

A few more questions, and a short time later, Stern thanked Charter for his help and headed for the door. Pausing, he turned. "Do you happen to know if he had any other work, apart from you, I mean?"

Charter shrugged. "Not that I know of. But he had that van of his, so he could have done a bit on the side." He gave a knowing smile. "Plenty of 'em do."

~ * ~

Stern arrived back at the office just after two. As he climbed the stairs, he could hear Cherry speaking on the phone. She gave him a wave as he crossed the office and hung up his topcoat.

"Yes, okay. Mr Stern has just arrived in the office. I'll talk to him, and we'll get back to you directly." Cherry listened for a moment then said, "Yes, this afternoon. Don't worry, we'll be as quick as we can." She said a goodbye and dropped the phone back on its receiver. "That was Mo Stevens. She's had another visitor. Got a better look at him this time, says it's definitely not her ex."

Stern moved across and eased himself onto the corner of her desk. "When was this?"

"Early this morning. She sometimes sits at the window with her bowl of muesli and coffee before heading off to work. This morning, she pulled the curtains and there he was. Seems he did this." She put two forked fingers to her eyes then reversed them and pointed them fang-like at Stern. "You know, the sign for I'm watching you?"

Stern raised his eyebrows. He certainly understood.

"Then he ran a finger across his throat," Cherry continued. "Frightened the poor woman half to death."

"Then what?"

"Nothing. He just turned and walked away. There was a heavy sea mist drifting inshore, and she said he just disappeared into it. She waited a while then ran quickly to her car and drove off. She's still at work in Norwich. She asked if we could go to her place later. Be there when she gets home."

Stern gave it some thought. "This really is a police matter, you know."

"Yes, it is," Cherry agreed. "So, if we do as she asks and go there, we can convince her to hand it over to them."

Stern thought for a moment, pulling at an ear lobe, thinking. "If not, how would it go down with Rob if you were to do an overnight with this woman?"

Cherry thought for a beat, then smiled softly. "Don't know. He always says the bed never gets warm if I'm not in it with him."

Stern knew exactly what she meant. His bed had been exceptionally cold since his return.

"How about you? Would you be happy to spend a night there? I'd do it myself but..." He grinned. "Don't think that would be appropriate, do you?"

"No, probably not."

Stern held up a reassuring hand. "Say no, if you feel uncomfortable about it. I'd understand."

Cherry shook her head. "No, I'm not worried about it at all. I'm up for it if you think it would be worthwhile. But it could be a waste of time. Just one night, he might not surface."

"True, but you never know. I think it's worth a crack."

"Okay, I can give Rob a call." She smiled broadly. "I'll tell him where he can find the hot water bottle."

Stern returned the smile. "He's gonna hate me. But it's not only the overnight bit I had in mind. I thought if we made a copy of that photograph you brought back from London you could spend some time hawking it around the village. You know, shops, cafes, pubs. Never know, someone might recognise him."

"But Mo says it isn't him."

"I know, but I'm trusting on your instinct, kiddo. You said you were sure Cavendish reacted when you mentioned Norfolk at the dealership, right?"

"Yes, but..."

"So, if Cavendish isn't doing the frightening himself, maybe he's paying someone else to do it for him."

"Ah, I see what you mean. You think he might have visited the village at some time to recruit a local."

Stern wrinkled his nose sceptically. "Not a local, I wouldn't think. But if he had recruited someone from London, someone he already knew, he'd have to show them where Mo lived, wouldn't he?" He waved a hand. "Okay, a long shot, I know, but worth a punt, don't you think?"

"I do." She reached for the phone. "I'll call Rob."

"Before you do that, how did you get on with The Beehive search?"

Cherry handed him a piece of paper "No problem. That's the address. It's out in the sticks, a mile or two south of Dereham, just off the A47. Closest I could find was a place called Brandon Parva. Know it?"

"Never heard of it."

Cherry turned her laptop to face him and brought up Google maps. A few clicks later, she pointed at a spot on a local map of the area west of Norwich.

"Blimey, that is out in the sticks," Stern muttered. "Never mind, I'll take a ride out and pay 'em a visit." He slid off the corner of Cherry's desk and made his way into his own office, the old chair giving the usual welcoming creak and groan as he settled down behind the desk. He pulled out his mobile and called up his contacts list, selecting O'Connor's number. It wasn't O'Connor who answered.

"Is he there? It's Theo Stern."

"Mr Stern, didn't expect to speak to you again so soon."

Stern recognised the voice. "Constable Wainwright. Taken over the boss's chair, have we?"

"I wish, sir. No, the inspector called me in to report on this morning's visit to Mr Croker's flat. He's just popped out to visit the gent's. If you like to hang on, he'll be back in a mo."

"Okay I'll do that."

A few moments later, Stern heard Wainwright tell O'Connor he was waiting. Then O'Connor came on the line. "Theo, there's a coincidence, I've just got the constable here bringing me up to date on your visit to the flat. Just a sec." Stern heard O'Connor ask Wainwright to 'give them a minute.' He heard O'Connor's office door open and close again. O'Connor came back on the line. "Thought it best he didn't hear what we had to say. So, how did it go?"

"Not bad. Your lad is a bit of a star. Bags of get up and go and plenty of initiative. Keep your eye on him, David, he's the type of material the force needs."

"Glad to hear it from you, Theo. But I'm ahead of you. He doesn't know it yet but when the time is right I'm hoping to bring him in as my next Detective Constable."

"Yup, I'd go with that," Stern agreed. "A DC has to be his next move. Anyway, I've taken some bits and pieces I'd like to check over," Stern went on. "I've given Wainwright a signed receipt for your records. Most interesting might be Croker's bank statements, I'll come back to you on them. I also found a couple of trophies. Seems Croker played darts for a pub team. Place called The Beehive. Know it?"

"Can't say I do, but if he played darts for a pub, maybe he did take a drink or two after all."

"Don't know about that," Stern came back. "On my way home, I called in on the builder Croker worked for. A chap called Charter. He was adamant; neither he nor any of Croker's co-workers had ever known him to take a drink. He said he'd been told it was something to do with Croker's father being a drunkard."

"Shit," O'Connor breathed. "S'what our note writer said."

"Exactly," Stern agreed. "And, by the way, my theory about the note writer visiting Croker's flat seems to be a no-go. The neighbour said other than a regular visit from a young woman Croker said was his daughter, but the neighbour thinks was a prostitute, there weren't any other regular visitors. Over recent months, he has upgraded the flat, though: decorating, furniture, carpets, that sort of thing. It's one of the reasons I want to give his finances the once over."

"Sounds a good move."

"I think so. And there's more. Seems Croker had a van which, again according to the neighbour, he used regularly at night. The neighbour's a shift worker; works all hours. Says sometimes Croker's van could be missing from the car park best part of the night."

"Looks like we're going to have to start taking our mystery note writer seriously."

"Looks that way, David, but leave it with me for a bit, will you? I'll check things out, including this stuff I brought back. And, by the way, Cherry located the pub, The Beehive, for me. It's near a village

I've never heard of." He looked down at the piece of paper Cherry had given him. "Place called Brandon Pava. D'you know it?"

"Yeah, it's out near Dereham, right."

"Yup, that's the place. I'll take a ride out there, see if I can find out anything worthwhile. I'll get back to you."

"Look forward to it. By the way, Constable Wainwright says if I ever need to supply you with an escort again, he'd like to volunteer."

"And I'd be glad to have him."

Twenty

After talking to Rob, who knew there would be little point in arguing anyway, it was agreed, subject to Mo's agreement, Cherry should stay the night at the cottage. It was unlikely they would be lucky enough to have a visit from the stalker while she was there but, just in case, a plan of action had been agreed. And with Cherry in the cottage, Mo would have the comfort and security of company at least for one night. They had arranged for Stern to return and collect Cherry the following afternoon, thereby giving her a full morning to tour Blakeney with the picture of Frank Cavendish. Cherry called Mo, first ensuring her they'd be at the cottage when she returned from work that evening, then throwing in Stern's idea of her stopover. Mo grabbed the idea with enthusiasm.

They'd closed up shop and driven to Cherry's place in Stalham to collect whatever she needed. From there, leaving Cherry's mini behind, they had driven straight to the cottage at Blakeney. Stern had squashed Cherry's request to use her own car, arguing that a second car parked at the cottage overnight would probably deter the stalker if he was thinking of paying another visit.

It had been agreed that while he was there, Stern would try to persuade Mo to involve the police. Her reason for not doing so seemed pretty puny to him. So much so, he wondered if it was the real reason or if there was something she was holding back. For the moment, he would accept what she was telling them and try to convince her that it was most unlikely the police would hold her past minor misdemeanour against her in any way. She had paid her dues and, as far as the police were concerned, that would be that. Besides, he would argue, his close relationship with David O'Connor would ease the situation for her.

They were waiting when Mo Stevens pulled onto the gravel area at the front of the Blakeney cottage. Inside, Mo changed out of her working clothes into a rumpled plaid shirt hanging outside her old frayed jeans. She made tea, and they settled to talk.

"I appreciate you coming," Mo said. "He really gave me a fright this morning. The way he gestured at me."

"I can imagine. And you're sure it wasn't your ex?"

"Positive. I still couldn't see his face, but the build, the height." She shook her head. "I'm sure it wasn't Frank."

Stern glanced at Cherry, who took the hint. "Mo, I think you are probably right. You see I visited your ex's work place and talked to him."

Mo's mouth dropped open. "You didn't..."

Cherry held up a hand, halting her. "Don't worry. I posed as a potential customer. He knows nothing of what we are doing. But I was able to confirm that it's also very unlikely to have been him on the previous occasions you had a visitor. Seems he's been working all hours. From what his associates told me, he hasn't had a day off for a long time. Of course, I can only go by what I was told. But, if true, it would mean he would have had little time to visit here on the days the stalker appeared."

Mo sighed heavily. "That's something, I suppose."

"Maybe, maybe not." Cherry said.

"Oh?"

"You see, I do have reason to believe he does know you are here."

Deep worried furrows ploughed Mo's brow. "What makes you think that?"

"It's difficult to explain," Cherry admitted. "Just an inkling I got from his mannerisms and what was said during my conversation with him. I did manage to get this." She handed over a print of the photograph she had taken at the showroom. "Pictures of the dealership staff were displayed on the wall. This is the one of your ex."

Mo took the photo and stared down at it. "He's aged," she said softly.

"It's been a while. Probably pressure of work," Stern broke in. He wasn't about to let Cherry go into any detail regarding Cavendish's change of personality since his split with Mo. "What I've asked Cherry to do is to spend tomorrow morning visiting various establishments in the village. Just to see if at any time anyone might have seen him in the vicinity. It may not have been recently. Could have been some time back or..." He gave a shrug, "not at all."

"But why would he...?"

"Can't be sure at this point. But if Cherry's intuition is correct, and he has been here at any time we have to find out why." He smiled, hopefully reassuringly. "But don't let's jump the gun. He may never have been here at all. Let's see what Cherry's search comes up with first, okay?"

"Okay."

"So," Stern went on quickly. "Before we go any further, I'll say again that in my opinion, you should really hand this over to the police."

Mo started sharply, as if she had been struck. "No, that's not... Please, I don't want to do that. I really don't."

Stern frowned, surprised by the reaction. "Why, because of the incident with your husband's car?"

Mo lowered her eyes, nervously twisting a ring on her finger. "Yes, because of that and..." She looked up, fixing him with a decisive look. "I just don't want to, and that's final." She took a breath and pulled back her shoulders determinedly. "Mr Stern, I'm sorry, I don't mean to be rude, but surely if I'm willing to pay for your services, that should be enough?"

Stern studied her closely for a long moment then said, "Are you telling us all we need to know here?"

"Yes."

"You're not holding anything back? Because if you are, then…"

"No, I'm not. And I don't think this is anything to do with Frank. I think there is some loony tune local out there who has latched onto me. All I want you to do is find him and make him stop."

"Well, whatever you think, if you insist on not involving the police, and I do carry on with this, my investigation will be with an open mind. That means not discounting your ex-husband. You do understand that?"

Mo's lips tightened into a thin line. "If that's how it has to be," she said resignedly.

Stern pushed himself out of the chair. "In that case, I will leave you and be on my way." He turned to Cherry. "I'll be back around one tomorrow. If our man does show himself, you know what to do."

Cherry stood up. "I'll see you to the car."

Outside, they walked together across the gravel to the Scirocco.

"She's lying, isn't she?" Cherry said.

"Lying? I don't know. Probably what she is telling us is the truth. I'm more concerned about what she's keeping under her hat." Stern gave a tiny shrug of his shoulders. "Not to worry, we'll run with it, for the moment anyway. Have you got the gun?"

"Yes, I have, "she said, patting her shoulder bag, her unease showing at the admission.

Stern laughed. "Don't look so worried, kid, it's only for show. You know that." He was referring to the replica 9mm Walther PPK hand gun he'd taken from a London villain way back in the 70s. He'd always intended to get rid of it at some time, but for some reason, probably because he was an avid James Bond fan, he'd never got round to it. Just as well really, because, it being impossible to tell from the real thing, he'd used it more than once to great effect in previous Stern Investigations cases. And this was another occasion when he felt it might well come in handy. But he knew Cherry didn't even like holding the thing. "Just keep it under wraps unless you really feel threatened. I promise just seeing it will stop anyone coming near you."

Cherry turned and headed back toward the cottage shaking her head and muttering. "Flippin' James Bond."

Grinning, Stern climbed into the car.

Twenty-one

Stern left Blakeney with the evening ahead of him. After grabbing something to eat, his plan was to head out to Brandon Parva and give The Beehive the once over. If he took one of the narrow lanes directly south out of Blakeney, he could pick up the B1110 directly to Dereham. He'd find somewhere to eat en route and let the Sat Nav take him from there.

Fifteen minutes later, he found what he was looking for. It didn't look much from the outside, just your average small country pub, but the chalk board out front promised proper pub grub. It was good enough for him. Inside, there were low beamed ceilings, cramped little alcoves, and the aroma of something good in the pot. It was still early, and only half dozen people were dotted around the room. Stern crossed to the bar, no more than ten to twelve feet long, nestling comfortably between two gnarled oak uprights. There was an array of four pumps, and, instantly, his eyes homed in on the one labelled London Pride, another of his very favourite real ales. But food first.

"Can I take a guess," he said as the landlord, a large portly character with a jovial expression approached. "Is that beef hotpot I can smell?"

"You have a good nose, sir. And it's freshly made by the expert hand of my very own missus."

Stern grinned happily. "In that case, bring it on, Landlord, and while I'm waiting can I sample the London Pride, please."

He carefully carried the brimming pint across the room, sliding into one of the small alcoves before taking the first mouthful, relishing the sharp cool flavour. No more than five minutes later, the landlord crossed the room carrying a deep plate of the steaming stew. He produced a knife, fork and spoon wrapped in a pure white napkin then stood back looking down at the meal with pride.

"Don't think you'll be disappointed. The missus is famous for it."

Stern drew in the delicious aroma drifting up from the plate. "I'm sure I won't."

"Anything else I can get you?"

"No, I'm good, thanks."

As the landlord turned to leave, a thought struck Stern. "On second thought, d'you happen to know The Beehive? It's out near Brandon Parva, I think."

The landlord stopped in his tracks and turned slowly, a deep frown darkening his brow. "Now, sir, you are a new customer, and obviously a stranger here, otherwise I would be demanding you wash your mouth out with carbolic soap and contribute heavily to the swear box."

Stern found his mouth hanging open in complete surprise at the sudden onslaught. "Sorry," he managed after a moment. "I'm not sure I understand..."

In a beat, the big man's expression changed, and he was again grinning broadly. "No, I don't suppose you do. It's just my bit of fun, so don't take offence."

Stern inclined his head questioningly. "None taken, but why..."

"Do you play darts?" the landlord asked.

Stern shook his head. "Occasionally, nothing serious."

"Well, you see, for some of us here the game's a religion. We're in the local league, high up, too. And this year, we were in line for the trophy, the big one. Most thought we had it in the bag. In the final, we had to play…" He stopped, pretending he was finding it difficult to mouth the word. "Well, we had to play that pub you just asked about."

Stern laughed. "And they beat you."

"Beat us? They wiped the floor with us. Never been so disappointed in my life. We vowed that anyone mentioning their name in this place again would be tarred and feathered and put in the stocks for a week." Laughing, he waved a warning finger at Stern. "So, thank your lucky stars you're not a local. Mind you, if you could bribe a couple of their players to come and play for us, you'd be a hero."

"Interesting you should say that," Stern said. "It's one of their players I'm looking for."

The landlord glanced over his shoulder, noting a couple waiting at the bar. "Tell you what, you finish your meal, and we'll chat later, okay?"

"Sure."

Twenty minutes later, Stern returned a plate and a pint glass, both empty, to the bar. "Best I've eaten for yonks," he said. "My congratulations to the wife."

"I'll pass it on. Now, how can I help you with the…" He jokingly put his hand to his mouth. "You know, that place you asked about."

"You may not have heard about the guy they pulled out of the Wensum a while back. It was minor headlines."

The landlord wore a serious expression. "Someone did say something about it. He was a drunk, wasn't he? Or was it drugs?"

Stern ignored the questions. "Truth is, I'm with the police, and I've been tasked with checking out one or two things relating to the incident."

"Really?"

"S'right, and the reason I asked you about The Beehive was because that man, the one they pulled from the river, was one of their dart players."

This time it was the landlord's mouth that dropped open. "You're kidding me."

"Afraid not. I was on my way to talk to the landlord there."

The big man shook his head. "Well, I suppose word would have drifted down eventually. We only meet when we play, but most of us know each other, even if it's just to say hello." He hesitated for a moment. "Are you allowed to tell me the guy's name."

"Sure, it's Charlie Croker. Did you know him?"

"Old Charlie. It was him, was it?"

"You knew him then?"

"Yeah, I did. Not well, I have to admit. We only met at matches. He threw a great dart. They'll miss him." He paused, a deep frown creasing on his wide brow. "But wait on, they said the guy they pulled from the river was a drunk, didn't they?"

For some reason, Stern already knew what was coming. "They did."

"Well that's a joke, for a start. Like I said, I didn't know the guy that well, but he stood out in their team because he was the only one who drank orange juice. He was ribbed about it all the time. Never saw him touch a pint, ever. Didn't do him any harm though. Apart from that other weird fat bugger, he was the best in their team."

"Weird fat bugger?" Stern asked.

Fifteen minutes later, Stern was back in the car and on his way. He drove with extra care, the Sat Nav taking him through the narrowest of Norfolk lanes. The remainder of the journey took him over half an hour, but eventually he pulled alongside several other cars parked nose forward on a cobbled front standing of The Beehive. It seemed to be the only parking area available. Inside, it wasn't a great deal different from the pub he had just left. It was slightly larger, but nonetheless a rustic Norfolk ale house.

On the basis that he'd already had one pint, and he still had the drive home, narrow lanes included, he ordered a tonic with ice.

He asked the barmaid if it would be possible to talk to the landlord or the owner. She smiled widely, answering in an accent that was certainly not Norfolk.

"Your already talkin' to 'er, luv." She held out a hand. "I'm Pam, Queen Bee at The Beehive."

Stern took her hand, a firm, strong grip. "Nice to meet you, Pam. I'm Theo, Theo Stern." He wasn't surprised at the London accent. These days, he sometimes thought there were more retired Londoners in Norfolk than locals. He explained the reason for him being there.

"Ah right, poor old Charlie. Was a bit of a shock, must admit."

"Mind if I ask you a couple of questions?"

She looked around the room, motioning that it was almost empty. "Not exactly like I'm run off me feet, is it, luv? So 'elp yourself."

"I'm told Charlie didn't drink."

"S'right, he was the only one. Never touched a drop. Not in my presence, anyway."

"Did you read what the paper said?"

"You mean about him being tanked up? Booze and drugs?"

"That's right."

She gave a derisive snort. "Media makeup. Unless Charlie filled his boots in private at 'ome, the booze angle is a load of eye wash. As for drugs..." She raised both hands, submissive. "Who knows what some folk get up to behind their own four walls."

"That's true," Stern admitted. "I know Charlie worked for a builder, but d'you know if he did anything else? Anything on the side?"

She thought for a bit then said, "I think he did. Dunno what, mind. But there was the odd match he couldn't make. The others got a bit miffed when that 'appened."

"Any idea why he couldn't make those matches?"

"Not really. They used to say Charlie always 'ad somethin' on the go. Mind you they got nothin' for playin' darts, did they? So, if he was on an earner now and then, I wouldn't blame 'im, would you?"

"No, I guess not."

Stern finished his drink and thanking her for her help he made to leave, then stopped, and turned back. "Just one last thing. D'you know if Charlie had a particular friend? Someone he associated with more than others?"

She pulled down the corners of her mouth, thinking. "I only know the darts team, and I can't think…They all seemed to get on well together." She gave it some more thought then, as if something had come to mind. "Yeah, now I come to think of it, I do remember Charlie sayin' that 'im and Ollie went back a bit."

"Ollie?"

"Yeah, strange sorta bloke. Big fella, sort of scruffy, like he didn't look after 'imself that well. Know what I mean?"

Stern thought back the description given him by the previous landlord. "And this Ollie also played on the team?"

"Oh yeah, not 'alf. He was their kingpin. The best, they said. Don't think they'd do 'alf as well without Ollie."

"Do you know Ollie's surname? Where he lives?"

She shook her head. "'Fraid not, luv. I know their first names, but that's about it. A long time back, they came and asked if they could put together a darts team to represent the pub in some league or other. All I 'ad to do was put up a dart board. Sounded like a good wheeze to me. Anythin' to pull in a few more punters. So, I said they could. That's about all I 'ave to do with 'em. They come in, drink me beer, sometimes make a lot of noise, 'specially if they're winnin', then wander off."

Stern thanked her again and turned to leave. At the door, he again swung round. "By the way, Pam, when's the next darts match here at The Beehive?"

Twenty-two

Stern had spent the previous evening at the flat in front of the television. Not that he took much notice of the programmes. He was too busy thinking. And he'd had plenty to think about. There seemed little doubt that, whatever the post-mortem showed, Charlie Croker was not a regular drinker. Not in public, anyway. So, as the landlady of The Beehive had suggested, was he a secret drinker? It was possible, it happened all the time. But then, the mystery note writer, who was supposed to have known Croker well, also said he was t-total. Truth was, as far as Stern could see, everyone that knew Croker said he didn't drink. So, what happened on the day he ended up in the Wensum to make him drink so much? And, it seemed, to also take drugs. There couldn't be a more lethal cocktail.

Then there was the note writer's claim that Croker worked for Eddie Butler on the side. One thing was for sure; Croker was up to something outside normal working hours. That was confirmed by statements from both The Beehive's landlady when she said Croker missed dart matches, and again by George Spriggs, the neighbour who talked about Croker sometimes being out all night. Not that either of those testimonies corroborated the note writer's claim that Eddie Butler was involved. And there was nothing to say whoever Croker was working for had anything to do with his death. All very mysterious, and the truth was they'd never know until they found out what Croker had been doing at night. Before he turned in, a plan of action had begun to form. Tomorrow morning at the office, he would go through the stuff he'd collected from Croker's flat then discuss it with O'Connor.

The morning was unseasonably warm for March. Probably because, as well as a completely clear, cloud free sky, there was absolutely no wind. Not even a breeze. It wouldn't last, of course; on the North Norfolk coast it seldom did. The trick was to enjoy it while you could. Stern had done just that, extending his morning run to over the usual hour and loving every minute of it. It was after ten when he climbed the stairs to the office. He smiled as he unlocked the door. Being this late, he wouldn't have been flavour of the month if Cherry had been there. But late or not, he felt refreshed and ready for whatever the day threw at him.

He checked the phone for messages, thankful there were none, then fired up the coffee machine, and took the cream bun he'd purloined as he passed through the bakery into his office. Again, no Cherry to give him grief about the fat or sugar in his diet. Fifteen minutes later, he was sitting at his desk, coffee and bun at the ready, and Charley Croker's belongings spread out in front of him.

Easing back in the chair, he took a bite out of the bun and chewed thoughtfully, his eyes coming to rest on the calendar Cherry had hung on the wall opposite. Calculating, he realised he had been back from Australia just twenty-seven days. He recalled his mood immediately on his return. The feeling of utter failure, his mind in complete turmoil, not knowing what to do or where to go next. He didn't feel he had the energy or the will to do anything or go anywhere. But this morning, he had climbed out of bed feeling completely different. He'd enjoyed a run, stood for ages in the shower, then, in full sunshine, munched through breakfast on his balcony. All the while his mind was in overdrive, trolling through the problems at hand. What a difference! And he knew why. He was back doing what he was made to do, what made life worth living. What a difference twenty-seven days, and that little pain in the butt Cherry Hooker could make. He finished the bun, brushed the crumbs from the desk, and started perusing Croker's stuff.

There were bills, receipts, and some bank statements. He started with the bills. Sometimes what an individual buys, and how he pays for things like goods and services, can reveal a good deal about him. In this case, at first glance, there was nothing untoward. A bill from the local supermarket consisted mainly of groceries, soap, toothpaste, and one or two other innocuous items. Interestingly, no alcohol. But there were several purchases of clothing: a couple of shirts, jeans and a pair of shoes which were not your normal high street price. Certainly not Sheringham High Street anyway. Stern scribbled a note.

There were also a number of receipts for petrol. These were a little more interesting. Stern studied the dates, noting how close some of them were. Also, on each occasion the quantity of fuel purchased was extensive. Stern didn't know what type of van Croker drove, or how much fuel a typical van held, but he was sure sixty to seventy litres had to be close to a full tank. And at such frequent intervals. Croker certainly moved around a lot. Equally as interesting was that every one of the fuel purchases had been made in cash. There were no credit card references on any of them. Stern scribbled some more, making a mental note to ask O'Connor, first, what type of van Croker drove and, also, if the police had retrieved a credit card when they dragged the body from the river. He also retraced his steps, looking back at the previous receipts. All were paid for with cash.

Finally, he pulled the bank statements out from the pile. There were just four sheets, each listing a full month's transactions. They covered the last two months of the previous year, 2016, and January and February of this year. Entries were pretty sparse, comprising in the main of a single monthly input and a few withdrawals. The single monthly input was paid regularly on the first of the month and was for the same amount each month. It was shown as Croker's monthly salary from Charters. The withdrawals were random, and for various amounts, but for the whole of the four months never more than fifty pounds. Stern spent some time scanning each sheet in detail, a concerned frown slowly growing. After some time, he collected his empty mug and crossed to the outer office.

Back at his desk, a refill in front of him, he dialled David O'Connor's number.

"Theo, how're we doing?"

"I'm about to do an interim report, and email it to you. Thought I'd run through one or two things with you first. You got time?"

"As long as it's no more than fifteen minutes. Got a session with the Super. Got a feeling I'm in for a rollocking." He chuckled. "Don't know what for, but I don't ever get called upstairs unless it's to have my backside booted. Getting quite used to it these days. They take away staff and halve the budget, then pull you over the coals because you don't achieve. Great system, eh."

Stern laughed. "It was ever thus, David. Nothing changes."

"No, but it's a right pain, nonetheless." O'Connor sighed. "Okay, Theo what've you got for me?"

"Like I said, I'll send you details, but there's one thing. I've been running through the stuff I got from Croker's flat, particularly bills and bank statements, and something stands out a mile."

"Hit me."

"First can you tell me what sort of van Croker had?"

"Wait one. Knowing you would call I have the file out ready. I have it here." There was a rustle of pages being turned. "According to the report it's a Renault Trafic one-point-nine DCi, whatever that is," O'Connor finally read. "Two thousand and seven model, with a hundred and twenty-five thousand miles on the clock. Been around a bit."

"To all intents and purposes, a two-litre job," Stern mused. "And a diesel. More economic than petrol, but still he topped it up an awful lot." He was silent for a moment, coordinating his thoughts then, "Okay, did your guys find a credit card on Croker's body?"

More pages being turned. "No, I've got the list of belongs here, and there's no mention of a credit card."

"Okay, thanks for that. Now, here's what's bothering me. I found just four monthly statements, two from last year, two from this, and there's not a great deal of difference between them. Croker was paid a regular monthly salary from Charters, the builder he worked for, and he made random withdrawals from the hole in the wall. None of those withdrawals were for more than fifty quid. About right for groceries and other bits and pieces."

"Sounds about right. From what we know, he wasn't a high earner, and he was living alone."

"That's true, but his bills for those four months tell a different story. The flat, for instance, was completely different to what I expected."

"In what way?"

"Well, as you say, the guy wasn't a high earner by any stretch, so I thought it would be a very basic, bog standard one-bedroom pad."

"You're saying it wasn't?"

"Certainly not. It probably didn't register with your guys when they gave it the once-over but comparing it with Croker's outgoings it made bells ring. Look, firstly the flat had been recently decorated. And we know from the neighbour, he had people in to do that. I would also gamble the flooring in the hall, and the tiles in the kitchen were also new. And, again, the neighbour confirmed the rugs and carpets had also been recently put down by a contractor. Add to that the modern furniture, including a wide screen television and in the kitchen a top of the range, all singing and dancing microwave."

"I think I'm beginning to get your drift," O'Connor came back. "Sounds like expensive stuff."

"You better believe it. And David, he filled that van like he owned a refinery. The shoes and clothes, he didn't hold back on those either. For a start, one pair of shoes a hundred notes."

"Bloody hell."

"Right, and there's more."

O'Connor gave a low whistle. "So how did he do it? Was he getting it on credit, on the knock?"

"Nope. And that's the good bit. He paid cash, up front, for everything."

"So, what the hell…"

"As I see it, Croker was getting hold of a regular wadge of cash money from somewhere which didn't find its way into his bank. And I reckon the most likely source of that cash was whatever extra curricula activities he was getting up to."

"Butler you mean?"

"Could be," Stern said hesitantly. "But, remember, it's only our mystery note writer who even mentions Butler. And we can't be sure whatever Croker was up to had anything to do with his death."

"No, but something tells me you don't believe that, do you, Theo?"

Stern sighed. "For some reason, I don't. I mean, we've got both the neighbour and the landlady of The Beehive confirming Croker dabbled in something after his normal working day, but so far, we don't know what. And until we do, we won't know whether it had anything to do with his death or not. I have got one lead I could follow up, but it's a bit nebulous to say the least."

"Oh?"

"Seems Croker was chummy with another guy in the darts team; a bloke called Ollie. He was well known on the dart circuit. Pretty potent at the oche, it seems. Problem is so far, I haven't been able to establish Ollie's surname or where he lives. And, anyway, there's nothing to say he would know any more than the others."

"So, if you don't know his name or address, how are you going to dig him out?"

"No problem. I'm going to a darts match next time they play at The Beehive."

O'Connor chuckled. "Best of luck with that. I'll look forward to hearing what you come up with."

"One more thing," Stern said thoughtfully. "Have you released Croker's flat yet?"

"Don't know, why?"

"Well, it did occur to me that if Croker was picking up cash he wasn't putting in his bank he must have been stashing it somewhere. That somewhere might be in the flat. If you could hold onto it a little longer, I'd like to have another poke around, dig a little deeper."

"Good point. I'll seal it for another day or two. Probably the best I can do, though. Otherwise, I'll have the council all over me about losing revenue."

"A couple of days is good, David. I'll get back to you."

Twenty-three

Stern arrived at Mo Steven's cottage at twelve thirty. As he eased the car onto the gravel parking area, he could see Cherry and Mo lounging on garden chairs each clutching a large mug. He climbed from the car and strolled across to them.

"Alright for some. Others have to work."

"Tea break," Cherry chirped. "Been hard at it all morning."

Stern spun round and looked out toward the coast, squinting into the midday sun. "Natural sun trap," he mused.

"One of the reasons I bought it," Mo said. She pointed to another garden chair sitting against the cottage wall, making to push herself up out of the chair. "Tea or coffee?"

Stern waved a hand. "Nothing thanks." He pulled the other chair over and squatted. "So, how'd things go?"

"Our man never showed," Cherry said. "Or if he did, we didn't see him. I slept like a log."

"Me too," Mo chimed in. "Felt good having someone else in the house for a change."

Stern looked to Cherry. "And this morning?"

Cherry shook her head. "Nothing. Mo took the day off, worked at home. I did the rounds. Needn't have bothered."

Stern gave a shrug. "Ah well, it was worth a try. At least we can write that one off." He glanced at his watch then looked across at Mo. "'Fraid we have to go. Lots on this afternoon. Not much more we can do except wait for the next time." He got to his feet. "But next time, if there is a next time, whenever it is, I want you to do something for me." He pulled a piece of paper from his pocked, holding onto it as he spoke. "First and foremost, don't panic. I'm certain if this guy intended to do you any real harm, physically I mean, he would have already made the move. Can't say I know why he's doing it, but it could be because he's just a loon who gets a kick out of frightening women. If that's the case, we might have a bit of an edge."

Mo frowned. "I don't think I understand."

"Think about it," Stern came back. "To be sure of scaring you, he has to know you've seen him, right?" He didn't wait for an answer. "Which means if you can see him before he knows it, he's likely to hang around for a while waiting to finish the job."

"I get it," Cherry chimed in. "Which would give us time."

"Right," Stern agreed. "So, before you close up at night and again before you open the curtains in the morning, take a crafty peek out front and back. Just make sure, if he is there, he won't see you. Then, if you see him, stay put, don't show yourself, and call this number straight away." He handed her the piece of paper. There was a name and a number scribbled on it. "Then just stay out of sight until that person arrives. Don't open your door unless you hear that name. Understand?"

"Yes, I understand."

Stern took a deep breath, letting it out in a long sigh. "Look, I feel like I'm tinkering around the edges here. Are you absolutely sure you don't want to involve the police?"

Mo shook her head determinedly. "Cherry and I have been talking this morning. She's told me about your background, and the work Stern Investigations has carried out in the past. She has every faith in you, Mr Stern, and after this morning, so have I. I will do exactly as you have told me, and I'm sure we will get this person in the end."

Stern looked at Cherry and shook his head resignedly.

Cherry raised both hands questioningly. "What? All I did was give her a little history lesson."

"Mouth almighty," Stern humphed.

Ten minutes later, they were heading away from Blakeney on the coast road. "Thought we'd grab a bite on the way," Stern said. "Checked out The Beehive yesterday, and this morning I went through Croker's stuff. Turned up a few surprises. I'll brief you over lunch." He glanced sideways, realising Cherry was fidgeting in her seat, a glint in her eye. "What's up with you?"

"I've got some briefing to do, too"

"Oh?"

"Yeah, I lied back there. I didn't want Mo to know how I really got on this morning."

Stern picked up the excitement in her voice. "You did get something then?"

"I did. And now I know why you're the best, boss."

"Cut the bull, Hooker, and get on with it." It sounded like a reprimand, but he was smiling, appreciating the compliment.

And she knew it. "It was exactly as you said. Frank Cavendish was here, and he had another man with him."

Stern pulled into the tiny car park of what looked from the road to be a small country house set back in the trees. It was built at the turn of the century and was initially a private residence. Now, it was a highly popular café used by the locals as well as people from far and wide, particularly in the holiday season.

'We-R-Lunch' opened for just three hours every day, from twelve 'till three, and served just a single main dish and a sweet, which changed daily. Once the day's quota was gone, it was gone. To reserve one of just a dozen available tables set in two small rooms you had to book well in advance. There were no more than half a dozen people who could just walk in and be sure of getting a seat, even if it was in the owner's personal dining room. Theo Stern was one of those people. That was because the proprietor was an ex-London Metropolitan police detective sergeant who on retirement only a few years ago had migrated to Norfolk. He and Stern went back a very long way.

It was March. The holiday season yet to get underway, but still there was just a single vacant table in the place. They stood waiting for no more than two or three minutes before a large individual wearing a striped apron, a cloth thrown over his shoulder, appeared through a door which they could see led to the kitchen.

On seeing them, a broad smile spread across his rugged features, and he barrelled forward, hand outstretched. "Good to see you, mate." He raised heavy eyebrows. "Everything good?"

Stern clasped the big man's hand affectionately. "Yup, everything's good." He turned to Cherry. "Cherry this is Ex-Detective Sergeant Cyril Makepeace, late of the Metropolitan Police Force. And dare I say one of the finest in the business." Then turning back to Cyril. "Cyril, this is Cherry Hooker, my partner in crime."

Cherry, buoyed by the elevation to partner, beamed happily and offered the big man her hand. "Nice to meet you, Cyril."

"And you, Cherry." He held onto her hand a little longer than was usual, his deep eyes holding hers. Finally, he said, "Brilliant."

"So, what's on, mate," Stern asked.

"Fish pie followed by apple crumble."

Stern turned to Cherry. "You won't get better."

Cherry smiled. "I'm sure I won't."

Cyril turned back to the kitchen. "Right, coming up."

They settled down at the table, Cherry looking around, checking out the other tables, mostly occupied by couples, only one with four people squeezed around it.

"Looks popular," she said quietly, the closeness of the other eaters making her inadvertently lower her voice.

"It is. For as long as I've known him, Cyril wanted to cook. He dabbled at it for years, but never got the chance to really get his teeth into it until he retired a few years ago. He bought this place and, in no time at all, made his mark. People fight to get a table here. And when you get your grub, you'll know why."

"I'm sure I will." She thought for a moment then gave him the eye. "So why haven't you told me about Cyril before?"

Stern winked and touched the side of his nose. "You've lived in my pocket for years, kiddo. And there's not much you don't know about me. But I've still got one or two secrets up my sleeve."

"Yeah, especially if it has anything to do with food. I bet Cyril uses full cream butter in everything he cooks, right?"

Stern laughed. "I admit nothing." He leaned a little closer, becoming serious, instantly business-like again. "Okay, so tell me what you've got."

"Well, for a while I thought I was on a loser. I checked the main hotel and all the shops and cafes I could find. None of them recognised Cavendish's picture. I was about to give up and go back to Mo's place when I remembered the other pub, the one on the road leading away from the harbour. It's sort of set back, not so obvious as the main hotel which is spread along the front."

"Go on."

"Well, this place has a courtyard area where people eat when the weather is good. I just wandered in and grabbed the first individual I could find. He was an elderly guy, local and very chatty. Seems he'd worked at the place forever. Bit of a jack of all trades, too. Told me as well as waiting tables, he did anything else they threw at him. Even did a bit of gardening around the place."

"And he recognised Cavendish?"

"He did. Clocked him straight away. Said he remembered him because, as he put it, he wasn't the best of customers. Sharp and dismissive, was how the old boy described him." She grinned. "And worse, he didn't tip." She stopped as Cyril arrived and slid the two plates of fish pie in front of them.

"Enjoy," he said, looking at Stern. "Chat later?"

"Will do."

"Was anyone else with Cavendish?" Stern asked Cherry after Cyril had left them.

"There was. According to the waiter, the two of them tucked themselves away in the corner of the courtyard. They had lunch and were there for about an hour."

"What about the other guy?" Stern asked through a mouthful of fish pie.

"I asked if he could describe him. He said he wasn't very tall and had a number one."

"A what?"

Smiling, Cherry finished a mouthful before speaking. "Come on boss, try and keep up. A number one is a very short haircut. The shortest."

Stern shook his head. "Whatever happened to the crew cut?" He sighed. "Okay, go on."

"He was dressed in jeans and was wearing a sort of bomber jacket." Another amused grin. "And was definitely not local."

"Oh?"

"That's right. According to my chatty friend, if either of them had been local, he would have seen them around at some time, and, anyway, local people were never as ignorant as these two were."

"Good point, I suppose. If anything, Norfolk people are certainly not ignorant." He thought for a second before carrying on. "Okay, so what have we got here? We don't know why, but we have Cavendish paying to have the frighteners put on his ex-wife. Then on the flip side, despite her denials, we have Mo not coming clean about everything. Right?"

"It looks that way."

"So, here's as I see it," Stern went on. "I don't believe this is happening just because of the stroppy breakup. It's has to be something else. Something she doesn't want the police, or even us, to know about. I mean, the excuse about her having a record is rubbish. In a case like this, the police wouldn't even consider her background."

"So, you don't think this is just Cavendish still being vindictive over the break?"

Stern gave a positive shake of the head. "Absolutely not. There's got to be more to it than that."

"It sure beats me," Cherry admitted. "How d'you want to play it from here?"

"Well, we now know the intruder is not Cavendish himself. But it's very likely to be the guy the waiter saw him with at the pub."

"I would guess so," Cherry agreed. "And, like you suggested before, it looks like Cavendish came here just the once to brief the other guy and show him where Mo lived."

"Right," Stern agreed. "But for now, I think we should hold off telling Mo what we know. Let's just wait and see how things pan out, then we'll decide."

"You have a reason for that?"

"Not really. Just a hunch."

They finished their meal, Cherry unusually also going with the apple crumble, though complaining she would regret it. Stern laughing, saying it would put some meat on her bones.

The little room slowly emptying, business over for the day, Cyril came from the kitchen and pulled up a chair. "Okay was it?"

Cherry patted her stomach. "Amazing. I'm stuffed."

Stern chuckled. "It had to be good...she usually survives on a lettuce leaf and fresh air."

Cyril smiled, patting Cherry's arm. "You have to kick over the traces sometimes, Cherry. It does you good. Especially when the boss is paying." He turned and eyeballed Stern. "So, are we all set?"

"Yes, we're all set."

Twenty-four

It was coming onto four o'clock the previous afternoon when Stern dropped Cherry back at her home in Stalham. It was the first time she'd spent the night away from her man since they'd been living together; Stern didn't want to push his luck. Cherry's early life had been a traumatic, frightening mess. She had been abused and used by men, including her own father, from an early age. As a result, since then, the only man she had ever trusted was Stern, the man who'd rescued her from the hell hole she had been driven into as a child. No other man had even got within touching distance. That was until a couple of years ago when Rob appeared on the scene. He was from solid, down to earth Norfolk stock. Steadfast, hard-working, and totally loyal, he stole Cherry's heart. Stern cherished the fact that after all this time, after all she had been through, she was now so happy. He would do nothing to jeopardise that happiness. He knew Rob finished work around five; the least he could do was have Cherry back home to be there when he returned. All the way from Cyril's place she had thrown questions at him. He had batted them away, insisting they would talk in the morning.

This morning, though it wasn't raining, it was dismally overcast with a heavy North Sea mist drifting on shore. Stern's walk from the flat along the promenade and up into the high street had not been a pleasant one. When he climbed the stairs and pushed open the door into the office, Cherry was already there waiting.

He crossed the office and hung up his damp top coat, rubbing his hands across his face. "Nice mornin'."

"Morning, boss." Cherry headed across the office to the already bubbling coffee pot, pulling a section of kitchen paper from the roll they kept there and handing it to him. Then she stood looking at him, her eyes making an exaggerated sweep of both hands. "Where's your breakfast?"

Drying his hands and face with the paper, he strolled over and stood beside her. "I had it at home this morning."

Cherry poured coffee into two mugs. "Oh dear, that'll mean a sugar deficiency round about half ten, right?"

He smiled. "Could well be."

A few minutes later, they had taken up their usual morning positions in Stern's inner sanctum, Cherry the first out of the blocks. "Boss, can I ask you something?"

"Of course." He eased back in the old chair. He'd expected nothing more than for her to carry on from where he'd made her leave off the previous afternoon.

"About your friend Cyril. When you introduced us, he gave me a very strange look. It was as if he was studying me for some reason. Almost as if he knew me. Then he just said 'brilliant.'"

"'Sright."

She frowned, confused. "D'you know why he said that?"

Stern leaned forward, slid his coffee mug to one side and rested his elbows on the edge of the desk. "'Course I do. To start with, your instinct was right; he does know you. Or at least he did. Though you won't remember, Sergeant Cyril Makepeace was my number two back in nineteen ninety-seven when we pulled a certain badly beaten young girl from a crummy flat in Bethnal Green."

Cherry's mouth fell open. "Oh God. I didn't know."

"'Course you didn't. Why should you? He worked in the background most of the time, a great investigative copper. In fact, it was Cyril who did all the detailed work to get you into the witness protection programme."

Cherry shook her head slowly. "I'll be blowed. And I never even knew he existed."

"There was no reason why you should have," Stern came back. "Fact was, most of the time during that period you had no idea what was going on anyway, did you?"

Cherry's eyes darkened at the memory. "No, sometimes even now…"

"And as for the 'brilliant' statement," Stern cut in quickly, recognising the start of a sad memory returning. "Cyril and I have always kept in touch since then, so he knew you were working with me." He smiled. "You have to remember how you looked last time he saw you."

Cherry's eyes cleared, and she smiled. "Oh, I see. Bit of a transformation, eh?"

"You can say that again. Like the man said…brilliant."

Cherry sipped her coffee thoughtfully. "It'll be twenty years late, but I must thank him next time we meet."

"Yeah, he'd appreciate that." Stern cocked his head questioningly. He knew there was more to come. "Is that it?"

"No, not really. Yesterday, I got the impression the two of you had something on the go. Should I know what that something is, or is it another one of those secrets you have up your sleeve?"

Stern swilled down some coffee. "Nope, it is something you should know. See, when Cyril came to Norfolk and kicked off his little café, he knew from the get go it wouldn't engage him full time. And don't forget, like me, he'd been a copper for a very long time. So, once he'd got everything up and running, he called me. Said most evenings he had time on his hands and if there was anything he could do to assist Stern Investigations, he'd be happy to get involved. Said it would keep the old brain cells active, and he would do it in a voluntary capacity. Cyril was in the army, military police, before he was a copper. So, he's got two pensions coming in, plus the café. Money's not a problem."

"Crikey, an ex-Met sergeant," Cherry breathed. "And your old partner, too. Lucky old us."

"Yeah, must admit, it did seem an ideal situation. Having someone to call on when we were both tied up. And basically, for free. But then things took a turn for the worse. The Campbell case came along and..." He stopped, gave a sad shrug of his shoulders and drank some more coffee. "Don't need to remind you what happened there, do I? Anyway, after I recovered, before I knew it I was on my way to Oz. To be honest, I forgot all about Cyril. But recently, when we started again, and the Blakeney case came up, I gave him a ring and..." The telephone stopped him in full flow. He reached across and picked it up and looked at the screen, recognising the caller.

"David, how ya doin'?"

"Not good, Theo." O'Connor sounded serious.

"Why? What's up?"

"It's Butler. I think our note writer has carried out his promised threat."

Stern's stomach lurched. He quickly hit the speaker button, so Cherry could hear. "What's he done?"

"Butler has a boat, an expensive speed boat thing. He moors it on the river at the bottom of his garden. Got his own mooring. Christ knows how much it was worth."

"Was?" Stern cut in, the single word registering.

"Yeah. Last night the whole lot went up in flames. Boat, mooring, the lot."

"What makes you think foul play? Could have been an accident. Batteries, gas cylinders, it happens."

"I know what you mean, Theo, but in this case, I don't think so. There's more to it than just the fire."

Stern felt a shiver of apprehension run through him. "Casualties, you mean?"

"Not as such, no."

"Don't understand."

O'Connor ignored the statement. "What are you doing right now?"

"Having a briefing with Cherry. Another case we've got running."

"Can you leave it?"

"Sure, if you want."

"Constable Wainwright tells me you are now a special investigator with the local CID."

"Yup, seems he promoted me on my last assignment. I'll be looking for a raise, of course."

O'Connor gave a derisive snort. "Don't hold your breath, sunshine. So, how about meeting me at the Butler residence in half an hour?"

"Will do." Stern ended the call and put the phone down. Eyes lowered, he thought for a beat before looking back at Cherry. "Looks like our poison pen man's gone one step further." He climbed out of the chair. "Don't know when I'll be back, but I'll keep in touch, okay."

"No problem. I've got plenty to do."

In the outer office, Stern shrugged into his topcoat and headed for the door. Reaching for the door handle, he stopped and turned back. "By the way, just to finish what I was telling you. The phone number I gave to Mo Stevens was for Cyril Makepeace. He can be at her cottage much quicker than we can."

"That's what he meant when he asked if you were set?"

"S'right. He might be retired, but I still wouldn't want to face up to Cyril on a dark night. Our mystery caller might just find he has a problem on his hands." He pulled open the door. "See you later."

Twenty-five

It was still miserably overcast, but the rain had stayed at bay when, just over half an hour later, Stern turned into Oak Lane and cruised slowly along to the gates at Deep Repose. There was a police patrol car already parked there. It was empty. Stern pulled in directly behind it. Leaving the car, he went straight to the buttoned grill set in the pillar and pressed the button. There was an almost instant rasping response. "Yes."

"Special Investigator Stern. Detective Inspector O'Connor is expecting me."

"Hang on," the voice growled.

Stern was expecting to hear a click and see the gates slide open automatically. It never happened. Instead, the large individual who had challenged him on his last visit appeared, marching along the drive toward him. Arriving at the gate, the security man stood for a moment, his dark eyes narrowing suspiciously. He made no attempt to open up.

"Don't I know you?"

No point in trying to bluff. "You should," Stern said without hesitation. "I'm the guy who's going for the Tudor style like your boss's."

"Oh yeah, right." He still didn't move. "But you're a copper?"

"You don't miss much, do you?" Stern held the other man's gaze, unflinching. "As far as I know, there's no law against a copper building a Tudor house, is there?"

"No, suppose not." He reached into his pocket and retrieved a small remote. The touch of a button, and the heavy gates slid slowly open.

As Stern was escorted along the driveway, he clocked the Mercedes again parked on the forecourt of the wide lockup. This time, alongside it, a chunky Range Rover. Deciding there was no point in delaying the investigation, he pulled out a notebook and flipped it open. Might just as well start with Mr Security. "You know I'm here to assist the inspector with the investigation into the fire?"

"If you say so." The reply was gruff, noncommital.

"So, what's your name?"

"Ron Pace."

Stern scribbled the name. "And you are Mr Butler's security guard, right?"

"Sright. And driver."

"Just you?"

"He only needs me."

"Do you stay here? At the house, I mean. When Mr Butler is here?"

Pace shook his head. "Not at the house, I don't. Mostly, we drive up late Friday afternoon after business. Then, if it's only a day or two, I kip at a B and B in the village, come here during the day. Sometimes the boss stays longer, could be a week or so. Then I go home. He lets me use the Merc."

"Good of him."

"Top man."

"So, you weren't here when the fire started?"

Pace gave a shake of his heavy head. "Nope. When I got in it was all over."

"How long have you worked for Mr Butler?"

"I've been with him forever. Since we were sprats."

"You know him pretty well then?"

"As well as anyone."

"He moved here about five years ago, didn't he?"

"'Sright. When he got tied up with her in there." He looked toward the house.

"His wife?"

"Yeah. His second."

"Does she have a name?

"Katrina."

"Katrina? Sounds Polish, Czech."

"Polish."

"You said 'his second.' So, Mr Butler was married before, right?"

"Yeah. Vera. She died. Bloody shame."

Stern detected genuine sadness. "You liked her?"

For the first time, Pace glanced sideways at Stern. "Everyone liked Vera. Lovely lady she was. One of the old school. I'll tell ya, if it wasn't for her, the boss wouldn't be where he is today."

"Sounds like you don't like this one so much."

Pace sniffed. "Don't know her, don't want to," was all he said.

They'd reached the front door, and Pace thumbed the bell push, the resultant chimes echoing inside. "Might want to talk again before we finish here," Stern said.

Pace shrugged and turned away. "I'm going nowhere."

Seconds later the door was opened. Stern guessed the woman to be probably fifty, no more. She wasn't tall, five six at the most, and heavy set, the white blouse she was wearing over the long black skirt straining under the pressure of heavy breasts. Her bare arms were thick and powerful looking. She had short black hair and dark staring eyes. She immediately stood back and beckoned Stern inside with a single word. "Please."

Stern followed the woman down a long hallway and through a door at the far end that led into an extensive sitting room. On entering, Stern's eyes quickly panned the room noting how the ceiling and walls, beamed with pure white inlays, reflected the Tudor style. The floor, too, tiled with polished light ochre stone tiles, completed the scene. But it was there the theme ended. Throughout the large room, the beautiful furnishings were completely modern including light beige leather armchairs and sofas and gleaming chrome-plated, glass topped tables. It was a tasteful combination and demonstrated just how well modern and ancient could be successfully combined.

"Mr Stern, thanks for coming. Inspector O'Connor has told us all about you. This is a bad business, isn't it?" The man approaching, his hand outstretched, was probably well into his sixties and slightly bowed. He had a full head of hair, salt and pepper grey with more mature lightening at the temples. He was wearing a charcoal grey suit, conservative and business like, and highly polished leather shoes. His accent was broad inner London with, Stern guessed, a determined attempt to add a little culture to his words. The effort was laudable but, as Stern knew well; you can take the man out of London but can't take London out of the man. The handshake was firm and dry.

"Pleased to meet you, Mr Butler, and, yes, this must be most unpleasant for you and the family."

Butler turned to the woman who had shown Stern in. "Thank you, Stefana."

The woman backed out of the room, quietly closing the door behind her.

Butler indicated toward a chair. "Mr Stern, please have a seat."

As he crossed the room, Stern waved a greeting to O'Connor seated opposite. He also clocked Constable Wainwright who had taken up position, discreetly standing to one side of the floor-to-ceiling glass doors overlooking the back garden. His notebook was out and at the ready. He gave Stern a smile.

Butler crossed to a sofa and sat alongside a slim young woman sitting demurely, her hands folded together in her lap. She was wearing a simple blue, perfectly tailored, high necked dress, cut just below the knee. She wore no jewellery other than on the ring finger of her left hand; a large diamond-encrusted engagement ring alongside a thick band of gold. She had long dark hair curled neatly and expertly into a bun at her neck and flawless complexion with, as far as Stern could see, little or no makeup. And in truth none was needed. She sat ramrod straight, model style, and her perfect lips smiled sweetly. Her eyes were dark and serious. Stern gave her no more than twenty-five at most. His thought flipped back to Pace's disdainful 'her in there' comment. Jealousy?

Butler took one of her hands affectionately in both of his. "Mr Stern, I'd like you to meet my wife, Katrina." His eyes shone with pride and obvious affection.

Stern smiled a greeting. "Very pleased to meet you, Mrs Butler."

The smile still in place, she gave a tiny nod of acknowledgement.

O'Connor took the lead. "Theo, as far as we can see, the fire was started in the early hours." He pointed toward the glass doors where Wainwright stood, beyond which Stern could see the lawns leading down to the river where several white-clad individuals were at work. "Unfortunately, the boat was all but totally demolished, but I have forensics going through what's left of the mooring."

"Anything yet?" Stern asked.

"Yes. They have already been able to establish an accelerant was used."

"Petrol?"

"Looks like it."

Stern turned to Butler. "Were you not woken by the fire, Mr Butler?"

"No. Unfortunately I wasn't here. I was in London at my flat when my wife phoned me early this morning. I came as fast as I could."

"Mr Pace, your driver drove you here?"

"Yes."

Stern turned to Mrs Butler. "And the fire never woke you, Mrs Butler?"

She shook her head slowly as if practiced not to disturb her hair. "No, I sleep at front of house," she said softly. The clipped words and distinct accent confirmed the East European descent.

"Were you here alone?" He knew the answer but was making notes. For his report, he needed to record her actual words.

Again, another slow shake of the head. "No, I have mother and..."

Butler rubbed her hand protectively between his. "Katrina's mother, Stefana, is over on a stay with my wife, Mr Stern. You met her when you came in."

As he scribbled, Stern recalled an old saying; *if you want to see how your young intended will look later in life, check out her mother*. Right then, he couldn't imagine the young woman sitting in front of him progressing into anything like the woman who had answered the door. But there you go...age takes its toll in a million ways.

"And, of course, we have the gardener cum handyman," Butler continued. "He has the lodge. Indeed, it was he who was woken by the fire. My wife and her mother knew nothing of it until our gardener came banging on the door to wake them."

Stern recalled seeing the cottage set back from the main building on the opposite side to the large lockup. "Is he here now?"

This time Butler looked to his wife for the answer.

"No, I send him to village for..." she paused, frowning, looking back at her husband.

Butler gave a tolerant smile. "Supplies?"

"Yes, this is it. I send for supplies."

Butler gave her hand an affectionate squeeze. "My wife's English is good, but she still has a little way to go."

"I understand. And your gardener's name?"

"I just know him as Victor," Butler said. "He's a good man, local. Does a damned good job." He looked again at his wife. "Darling?"

"His name is Victor Adams," she said softly.

"Thank you, we would of course require to talk to him immediately he returns," Connor came in.

"Of course. So, there were just the three people here last night?" Stern went on.

"Yes," Butler confirmed. "My wife, her mother and our man in the lodge."

"Do you have CCTV?"

O'Connor answered. "We've checked. It's in the front and directly out back. Doesn't stretch to the river, though."

"Pity." Stern completed his scribbling and turned to O'Connor. "Can we take a look now?"

They made to leave the room then Stern halted, turned back. "Forgive me for asking, Mr Butler, but having not seen the boat, can I ask you what type of craft it was?"

Butler looked grave. "It was a very high spec, two birth river cruiser." He paused, smiling. "A little luxury for my lovely Katrina. A little added extra when I presented her with the house on our first anniversary." He looked down at his wife with adoring eyes. "More of a speed boat, if I'm honest. A bit of an overkill for the broads, but it was what she asked for, and you know how it is."

Stern smiled thinking, *no I don't know how it is*. A house and a speed boat for an anniversary present. She should be so lucky. He was careful not to voice his thoughts. Instead he said, "An expensive item, then. Can I ask if it was insured?"

Butler waved a nonchalant hand. "I expect so, though I can't be sure. My people take care of that sort of thing. But cost is of little importance. No one was hurt. In itself, that is priceless. Wouldn't you agree?"

"I certainly would."

Leaving Butler and his wife, they left the house and headed down the sloping lawn to the river, and the destroyed boat and mooring. Wainwright tagged along.

"So, what d'you think of the lady of the house?" Stern asked O'Connor.

O'Connor gave a shrug. "Nice young thing. Bit timid, I thought. Looks like she wouldn't say boo to a goose. Bit of an age gap, too. Bet old Butler couldn't believe his luck when she took him on."

"I suppose," Stern agreed. "And she hasn't done badly for herself, either. D'you see the size of that ring?"

Arriving at the edge of the water, it was clear the boat had been completely destroyed, and the wooden staging was little more than a pile of smoking ash.

"I take it the boat was made of wood?" Stern said

"It was," O'Connor confirmed. "And when they build them, they have God knows how many coats of varnish finish. Must have burned like a good'n once it got going."

O'Connor left them for a moment to talk to the senior forensics man then moved back to where Stern and Wainwright were waiting.

"They're wrapping things up now. I'll get a full report sometime tomorrow. As of now, all they can tell me is the fire was started deliberately with petrol." He took Stern by the elbow, guiding him toward what remained of the singed staging. "And this." He pointed down at an area of grass close to the still smouldering wood.

Stern crouched for a closer look, being careful to touch nothing. "Is that blood?"

"It is. And take a look at this."

Stern straightened and followed O'Connor a few feet further along the bank, noting the line of blood splatter as he went.

Finally, O'Connor stopped and pointed down. It was hardly necessary. A cluster of blood spots stained the grass. Stern stared down for some moments. "The trail stops here."

"Yes," O'Connor agreed. "Looks like our burner was damaged somehow when he was doing the deed then moved along the bank to this point."

"But no further."

"No. My guess is there was either a boat waiting here or whoever it was swam back across the river."

"Back?"

O'Connor pointed across the river. "Yeah. Our people checked a point directly opposite on the far bank. There's a well flattened area there. Looks like someone has been squatting there for a while. Couple of beer cans and some other discarded rubbish."

"Fisherman?" Stern suggested.

O'Connor shook his head. "Out of season. No more fishing here till the middle of June."

Stern thought for a beat. "So, you're thinking, after watching the place, getting the lay of the land, someone came across and torched the boat."

"It's just a punt, Theo."

"And you think that someone could have been our mystery note writer."

"That's possible too. Don't forget, they did warn us; if we didn't act, they would. Now, we know whoever it was is injured. Nothing major, I wouldn't think, but could be enough for a doctor's visit or a run to casualty for a quick stitch. We can also confirm the blood type from this splatter. As soon as we leave here, Wainwright will do the rounds of local doctors and hospitals, see what he can find. You never know, we might just get lucky. And if he turns out to be the mystery note writer, we will have got a double whammy."

Twenty-six

Mo Stevens woke early. Truth was she hadn't slept very well and was pleased when daylight began to creep through the curtains. Last evening, from the time the light began to fade until it was completely dark, she had spent most of the time moving from one window to another, surreptitiously peeping through the edge of the curtains. No one had appeared. After double checking the place was bolted up tight, she'd retired just before midnight.

She had come to with a start at three, lying for some time trying to figure what it was that had woken her. But other than the usual creaks of the old structure settling as it did every night, there was nothing. The same thing had happened an hour or so later. This time, she'd left her bed and peered cautiously through all the windows. In the blackness outside, she could see nothing.

This morning Mo was sluggish and weary eyed. Nonetheless, she again did the rounds of the windows. As happened frequently at this time of year, an early mist had drifted in off the North Sea, but visibility was still pretty good, and she was relieved there was no sign of her tormentor. She ate breakfast slowly, the curtains drawn tightly closed, her mind trolling back.

Since she had slipped out of London and ended up in this glorious backwater, only one thing had spoiled her new idyllic life. It was the recurring thoughts of Frank Cavendish, her ex-husband. From day one, she'd had no doubt that at some time or other, however long it took, he would find her. He had no option; he couldn't possibly rest until he did. And he had good reason. It was true she'd trashed his car, but that would be the last thing on Frank's mind. Unlike a proud private owner, to those in the car trade a car was a car, just one of hundreds, thousands that would pass through their hands. No, for Frank there was much more at stake than a trashed car.

Of course, her hope was that as time passed, and he moved on with his life, possibly met someone else...She paused, sighing heavily, feeling uncomfortable with the thought. But there was nothing she could do about it now, only hope he would become less inclined to pursue her. After all, she had promised him, made it quite clear that if he backed off, let her alone, he could trust her. But in her heart, she knew it was a forlorn hope.

As far as Frank was concerned, there was too much at stake. Sure, she had made a silly mistake and ruined a perfectly good marriage. But bizarrely, that one single mistake had unearthed a whole new can of worms. One which she had absolutely no knowledge of at the time, but now, she was sure could have brought the marriage to an end anyway. And this time, it had nothing at all to do with her; she was the innocent party. It was all down to him. For that single reason, Mo saw her ex-husband as guilty as she ever was. She had made that clear from the start. Whatever she promised, he would always know she could ruin him at any time. So how much longer would it be before he found her? And what would either of them do when that time came?

She sighed heavily at the thought.

If that wasn't enough, she now had the worry of the stalker.

She thought about her conversations with Stern and Cherry Hooker, relieved Cherry had confirmed it was hardly possible for the stalker to be Frank. From her observations, she had already come to that conclusion, but verification was comforting. And what Cherry had learned made sense. Frank had always been a grafter, always aiming at the next rung of the ladder. Now, being the top man at the dealership, he would already have his sights firmly fixed on the next move upward. He would be spending ninety percent of every day with that in mind. Not a bad thing, because if Cherry was right in thinking Frank knew where Mo was, it was probably only pressure of work delaying the inevitable. After all, there was no rush. If he did know where she was, he could come at any time. But then again, Cherry could be wrong, and maybe Frank still hadn't found her. If so, Mo's reprieve would last a little longer. She vehemently hoped so.

Mo swilled down the last of the coffee and looked at her watch, surprised at the time. She'd been daydreaming longer than she thought and still had to shower and get ready. She collected the breakfast things, dumped them in the sink and hurried into the bathroom. Twenty minutes later, her hair still damp, she grabbed her coat and document case and headed for the door. She hated being late for work and cursed herself for daydreaming so long. But with luck, she still had time. If the traffic into Norwich wasn't too heavy. It was then, as she reached to open the door, she noticed it; the folded piece of paper hanging through the letterbox. It was just a piece of paper, could have been anything, an advertising flyer, a local event, but just the sight of it sent a chill through her. She tentatively pulled it from the letterbox and opened it. The few words were printed crudely in black marker pen.

TIME'S UP. DO THE RIGHT THING OR YOU'RE DONE.

Suddenly anger flared. How dare he? She flung open the door and instantly froze in her tracks. He was there, a dark threatening shape in the mist, casually leaning on her car. He was cleaning his fingernails with a long thin knife.

Twenty-seven

It was heading toward four o'clock, and meal time was over at We-R-Lunch. The place was empty apart from the three of them sitting around one of the central tables.

Earlier, Stern had been about to leave O'Connor at the Butler house when he'd received the call from Cherry. He had instructed her to contact Cyril, suggesting they meet at We-R-Lunch sometime after three, when Cyril had finished his chores. Cyril was still busy when they arrived, so while waiting, Stern had taken the opportunity to brief Cherry on his visit to the Butler house, detailing their findings around the burnt out boat and mooring. Now, all three were settled to discuss the morning's events at Mo Steven's cottage.

"She was in a bit of a state when she called me," Cyril told them. "Said she'd already checked both front and back windows a couple of times and was sure the note wasn't there then. She admitted being late for work and in a rush but was adamant she would have noticed if it had been."

"So, when then?" Stern asked.

"Mo could only think it was when she was in the bathroom. She has one of these electric showers, makes quite a racket apparently."

"She phoned you immediately?"

"Yes, and I got there as quick as I could. Checked all round. Not a sign of anyone."

Stern looked down at the note Cyril had handed to him earlier. *"Time's up. Do the right thing or you're done,"* he read. "What the hell's that supposed to mean."

Cyril shrugged heavy shoulders. "Search me. When I first read it, I asked Mo what it meant. She said she had no idea, but..."

Stern eyed his old colleague. "But what?"

Cyril rubbed at his chin. "Well if you asked me, she knows more than she's saying."

Cherry looked at Stern. "Confirms what you thought, boss."

Stern thoughtfully picked at a thumb nail. "Mmmm, pretty obvious, I think." He turned to Cyril. "Did she say it was the same man?"

"Yup. It was a bit of a misty morning, but she was pretty sure it was the same fella." A small frown touched Cyril's wide forehead. "Bit more threatening this time."

Stern raised his eyebrows questioningly.

"She said when she opened the door, the guy was leaning on her car. He was casually cleaning his fingernails with a knife. When he saw her, he gave her a wave and slowly drew the knife suggestively across his throat. She was terrified. Ran back inside, and threw every bolt on the door, and called me. I left straight away. It took me fifteen minutes max to get there. There was no sign of anyone anywhere near the place when I arrived."

"If only she had taken a peek before opening the door," Cherry mused.

"From what she told Cyril, she already had a couple of times. Anyway, it's a bit late for 'if only's'" Stern came back, the annoyance evident in his words.

"I suppose," Cherry sighed. She looked from one to the other. "So, any ideas where we go from here?"

"Something did occur to me," Stern said, looking to Cherry. "You remember the old fella you spoke to in the hotel in Blakeney?"

"Uh-huh."

"He gave you a bit of a description of the guy with Cavendish, didn't he?"

"Yeah, not very tall, wearing jeans and a sort of bomber jacket."

"And with a crew cut," Stern added.

"That's right."

"And, crucially, not local?"

"So he said."

"A pretty good description," Stern went on. "Probably the best we'll get. Until now, when he pays Mo a visit, he pretty well covers himself up. Now, if it is the same guy your friendly waiter described, we have a much better idea of what he actually looks like." He looked down at his watch, checking the date shown on its face. "Today is the last day of March, isn't it?"

Cyril frowned questioningly. "Is that significant?"

"It could be." Stern scratched his head thoughtfully. "As I see it, other than for a few hardy walkers and bird watchers, the holiday season is still a way off."

The other two said nothing, waiting to see where this was going.

"Which means the majority of holiday lets are sitting vacant, right?" He didn't wait for an answer. "So now we have a guy who's not very tall, has a very short haircut, and at one time, not so long ago, was wearing jeans and a bomber jacket." He raised a finger. "And again, crucially, if your man at the hotel knows his stuff, this guy is not a local. I suggest, to get back and forth to Mo's cottage as quickly he does, he has to be staying somewhere pretty close."

"But everywhere's closed here," Cherry said. "The cottage is only a short walk from just about anywhere in the village."

"True," Cyril agreed. "But, as Theo says, at this time of year, with holiday makers at a minimum, he might stand out among the locals more, be easier to find? Because of what you gleaned from your London jaunt, we have to assume Cavendish just made a flying visit here just to show the other guy the lay of the land. So, he was probably here and gone in no time. I'm not surprised only one person remembered him. On the other hand, the bozo we're looking for has to be staying somewhere around Blakeney. Stands to reason."

"I guess so," Cherry conceded. "Where do we go from here?"

"Not easy," Stern mused. "See, I believe when he's not putting the frighteners on Mo, our man will make a point of keeping his head down. He wouldn't want to be seen by Mo other than when he did his terror act. Certainly not when others are around. He probably only puts his head above the parapet when it's essential."

"What we need is someone on the ground full time."

"Right," Stern agreed. "It can't be any of us; we're all too tied up with other things. Mo works full time and is too frightened of the guy, anyway." He paused, looking to Cyril. "Know any of the locals? Someone, possibly retired, don't know what to do with themselves all day. Welcome a bit of spice in their life."

A smile broke. "Well as it happens, I do know someone. But, Theo, you may well be sorry you ever asked."

Frowning, Stern turned and looked at Cherry.

Shaking her head, she gave a *'Don't ask me'* shrug of her shoulders.

~ * ~

The last part of the short journey from We-R-Lunch was along a track through an area of woodland a few hundred yards inland of the coast road and Blakeney village itself. The track ended in a clearing in the centre of which stood a building.

As the car drew to a halt, Cherry peered out of the window. "Is that a…"

Laughing, Cyril didn't let her finish. "Yup, it's a genuine log cabin."

"A log cabin in Norfolk?"

"You'd better believe it."

They'd used Cyril's elderly Land Rover for the trip and, as they climbed out, they were met by the angry buzz of a chain saw coming from somewhere on the other side of the cabin. At the same time, barking furiously, a huge shape erupted around the corner of the house.

"Jesus. What on earth?"

Cyril put his hands out in front of the other two. "Just stay put." Taking a step in front of them both, he dropped into a crouch. He spread his arms wide and called out to the monster barrelling aggressively toward them. "Hey, Claude, how're doin', old son."

Cherry looked to Stern. Eyes wide she mouthed, "Claude?"

The monster's huge ears pricked forward, and he slowed, but only for a second. Eyes shining with recognition, he again gathered pace finally piling into Cyril's outstretched arms, knocking him back on his rear end, Cyril's arms encircling his neck, but only just. There followed a long moment of roughing, stroking and licking before Cyril was finally able to extricate himself from under the hound, and once again get to his feet. At the same time, the huge beast turned its attention to Stern and Cherry, standing, tongue lolling from one side of his gaping mouth, eyeing them suspiciously.

"What is it?" Cherry said, her voice little more than a whisper.

Cyril continued to ruffle the giant head. "Irish Wolfhound. A beauty, eh?"

"Just talk to him," Cyril said, wiping himself down. "His name's Claude. He's fine with people he knows. As long as I'm here, he'll be okay."

Cherry held out a tentative hand. "Hello, Claude."

The dog moved slowly toward her and sniffed her hand cautiously. Then, unexpectedly, rearing onto his hind legs, it placed its front paws on her shoulders. Standing head and shoulders above her, it decided it was okay to give Cherry's face a good licking.

Under the animal's weight, Cherry staggered back against the car spluttering. "Oh my God, oh my God."

"CLAUDE. Put that person down. You've already had your dinner."

A woman had appeared around the corner of the house and was standing, legs akimbo, a broad grin on her heavily lined, weather beaten face. A smouldering cigarette hanging from the corner of her mouth bounced up and down as she spoke. She looked to be around fifty, possibly a year or two older, and was no more than a whisker over five feet. She was broad, powerfully built, wearing thick leather boots, and a heavily stained boiler suit. A frayed, scruffy flat cap sat at a jaunty angle on her head, long unruly blonde hair splayed out behind. Clasped casually in her heavily gloved hand, hanging by her side, was a large chain saw.

At her command, the dog obediently dropped down onto all fours but continued to stand looking expectantly up at Cherry, who didn't move, even to wipe the animal's saliva from her face.

"Meet Clarissa Albright," Cyril hissed from the corner of his mouth.

The woman pulled the thick gloves from her hands and dropped them together with the saw to the ground. Pulling the cigarette from between her lips, she flicked it down, ground it under a heavy heel, and stomped toward them.

"Cyril Makepeace, you old bugger. What are you doing bringing strangers to the homestead without warning me? Claude's put the fear of Christ into the poor girl." The voice deep with a rasping smoker's edge. She grabbed the heavy chain around the dog's neck and pulled him away. He looked lovingly up at her and sat obediently. She patted his head and pulled gently on one of his ears. "He's a daft old bugger really." She held out a hard callused hand first to Cherry. "Sorry, luvvy, he can be a bit messy. I'm Clarissa, by the way."

Cherry gave a hesitant smile and took the handshake. "No problem. I'm Cherry."

"Nice to meet you, Cherry. When we go inside you can have a wipe down." She turned to Stern. "And who is this handsome gentleman?"

Stern took her hand. "Stern, Theo Stern."

Her eyes widened, and she held onto his hand. "Theo Stern, the detective, late of the Met, now out of Sheringham?"

"'Fraid so," Stern admitted.

Clarissa turned back to Cyril. "You old bugger. You decide to bring a real life, famous detective to the homestead, and you don't warn me? If I'd known, I'd have worn me best dress."

Cyril shook his head. "Clar' you old fraud, you haven't got a best dress."

She laughed, a deep smoker's rattle. "True, but you could still have warned me."

"Sorry, Clar'. Truth is we only decided to come half an hour ago. Mind you, something tells me you might be pleased we did."

She kept hold of Stern's hand and turned toward the cabin. "Let's go inside then. Give Cherry here a chance to have a wash. Then you can tell me what you're after."

Twenty-eight

Cherry slid a fresh mug of coffee on to the desk in front of Stern. "I wonder what made an Ozzie come to live in a backwater like Blakeney."

"She's not Australian. Not by birth, anyway."

"No?"

"No. Cyril tells me she was born in Blakeney, but back in 1970, her folks took the government's offer and emigrated to Western Australia."

"Government's offer?"

Stern took a sip of the hot sweet liquid and smacked his lips. "You know, you're getting quite good at making this stuff."

Cherry wriggled into her usual position on the chair opposite. "Yeah, yeah, like I said, what government offer?"

Stern gave an exaggerated sigh. "So young, so ignorant."

"Okay, so educate me, oh wise one."

Grinning, Stern took another sip before going on. "After the second world war, it was decided efforts should be made to boost the population of Australia and New Zealand."

"Why?"

"Simple. They just didn't have enough people to progress as a country. Back then, particularly, Australia had a tiny population for such a large country so they introduced what they called the Assisted Passage Migration Scheme. It ran from 1945 to 1972, if I remember. It was intended to substantially increase the population of Australia and to supply workers for the country's booming industries. I remember one of their clever politicians called it the Populate or Perish policy."

"And people from here went?"

"By the thousands. And you couldn't blame them. It was a pretty dark time in the UK. They'd just been through five years of war, including the bombings, the blitz in London and other cities. They saw it as a brand new start in the land of sand, sea and sunshine. It cost each adult just ten pounds and all the kids went for free. And you were guaranteed a job when you got there. Not bad, eh?"

"Blimey. I never knew."

Stern chuckled. "The people who went were christened the 'ten pound poms.' By now, many of the early immigrants have passed away or are elderly. But the later ones, like Clarissa, are in their fifties. Proper Australians."

"So that's why her accent is so broad."

"S'right. She could have only been three or four when the family took the plunge, late sixties early seventies. They paid their twenty quid, packed up, and took Clarissa and her brother to a new life. Don't know the details, but from what Cyril told me, Clarissa eventually qualified as an engineer. She married, but there were no kids and, a few years back, she lost her husband. Her ageing parents and her brother are still out there, but she got the urge to come home to where it all started. As soon as she got back, she bought the piece of woodland. She cleared the area and built the log cabin all by herself."

"Wow, a brilliant job, too. I was so surprised how beautiful it was inside."

"It was," Stern agreed. "Anyway, history lesson over. Clarissa is now fully integrated into the village. Part of the local council, and a power to be reckoned with. Also, the good news is, she has her nose into just about everything that's going on in the area."

Cherry gave a sly little smile. "And she has a thing for super sleuth Theo Stern."

Stern took another drink of coffee. "Yeah, she's been a regular customer at Cyril's place since he opened. Almost got her own table at We-R-Lunch. And she's an avid reader of detective novels. Always had a yen to be a bit of a gumshoe herself. Looks like Cyril's been swinging the lantern about us when we were back in the smoke. He knew she'd jump at the chance to help us find our man."

"Well one thing's for sure; if she's got Claude with her when she finds him, he'll give up without a fight."

They both stopped, looked at each other, as heavy footsteps sounded on the stairs and the outer door was opened. Cherry slid off her chair. Sliding her empty mug on Stern's desk, she moved across and peered into the outer office.

"It's David." She grabbed the spare chair leaning against the wall and placed it next to her own in front of the desk.

O'Connor's expression was serious as he strode into the office and slumped down onto the chair. "Thanks, Cherry." He looked across at Stern. "We've had another one, Theo." He reached into his pocket and pulled out an envelope, slid it across the desk.

Stern reached for the envelope. "Posted?"

"Local this time. Norwich. And clean like the others."

Stern pulled out the single sheet of paper. He read out loud.

To Inspector O'Connor. (See, I know your name now.)

I told you if you didn't do something I would. Well, you didn't, and now I have. I'm not a criminal, Inspector, but sometimes it's necessary to act to see justice done.

And this is just the start. All the time you refuse to do something about Butler, I will. And next time, I will be aiming higher.

Still waiting for action.

A law-abiding citizen.

Stern looked up questioningly. "So, the injury couldn't have been too bad."

"Obviously not."

"Your lads find anything else?"

"No, nothing. The fire destroyed best part of everything, and footprints don't show easily in grass. We checked both sides of the river."

"I recall you saying you found discarded beer cans on the far bank. Nothing there, fingerprints I mean?"

O'Connor shook his head. "Just smudges. Whoever it is wears gloves all the time. Possibly why the cut wasn't too bad. There was some protection."

"Quite possibly," Stern said, sliding the note into the envelope and pushing it back across the desk. "He says he's not a criminal, but he's a clever devil, nonetheless." He rubbed the palms of his hands together thoughtfully. "Well, tomorrow we'll see, shall we?"

O'Connor frowned. "Tomorrow?"

"Yeah. You remember I told you about The Beehive, the darts match? Well, it's tomorrow night, and I'm taking Cherry and Rob there for a pint. See if I can rake up more about Croker." He looked across at Cherry, noting the surprised look on her face. "What, didn't Rob tell you I gave him a call?"

"Oops." O'Connor was grinning. "Communications problem, Theo. Unlike you, mate."

Stern shook his head. "Nothing to do with me, David. If her man chooses not to keep her up to date, what can I do?"

Cherry gave a slow shake of her head but said nothing.

O'Connor raised a finger, remembering. "Oh, by the way, the council have been on my back about the flat already."

"Okay, I'll check it out this afternoon." Stern looked at Cherry again. "Fancy a ride out?"

~ * ~

It was just after two when they arrived at the Croker flat. Knowing from past experience such detailed searches often required tools, Stern had brought the toolbox he always carried in the car.

O'Connor hadn't been able to supply Constable Wainwright as before—he was on patrol duty elsewhere—but he had arranged for the local authority to open the flat and allow them entry.

Inside, standing in the narrow hallway, Stern gave Cherry a quick rundown on the layout; the kitchen and bathroom on the left and the single bedroom, directly opposite the bathroom, on the right. Then he led her to the door at the end of the hallway and into the combined sitting room and dining room.

Cherry cast her eyes around the room. "Nice."

"Yeah, not bad for a builder's labourer, eh?"

"Not bad at all. And we're looking for cash, right?"

"We are but remember both the local blues and yours truly have already given it the once-over. So, forget the normal search routine. We're not going to find anything in the usual cupboards and drawers. If it's here at all, it'll be stashed away somewhere you would never expect to find a space. Somewhere nobody would normally look."

"Not easy," Cherry said.

"Maybe, maybe not. Depends on how innovative Mr Croker was." Stern looked around the room and thought for a moment. "Okay, let's forget this room for now. On my last visit I wasn't looking for anything specific, certainly not hidden cash. My bet would be either the bathroom or the kitchen."

"Together or separate?"

"Together," Stern said without hesitation. "Two sets of eyes always better than one."

Half an hour later, they had scoured the kitchen from end to end, Stern insisting they check in, behind and underneath every drawer, even levering away the kick board running along the bottom of the units and checking beneath. They found nothing. It was the same with the bathroom. They lifted the lid from the toilet cistern and removed the front off the bath, checking every inch of possible space. Again, without success.

Frowning, Stern stood tapping the end of the screwdriver he was holding irritably on the edge of the bath. "What have we missed?"

Cherry shrugged. "Nothing as far as I can see. I suppose there's always the chance there's nothing here. I mean, if he did have money, he could have hidden it somewhere else. What about his old van? Was it searched?"

"As far as I know it's in the police pound. But think about it...if you had a wadge of cash, would you leave it in an old van? I mean, parked outside all the time?"

"Good point."

Stern sighed despondently. "Okay, I think we hit the bedroom. If there's nothing there, I guess we'll have to give it best."

"Is it okay if I have another look in the sitting room? You never know...fresh pair of eyes."

"Help yourself."

Only minutes later, Stern was peering behind the wardrobe he'd eased away from the wall when Cherry appeared at the door. She had a very silly grin on her face.

Twenty-nine

It was just before eight, and The Beehive was buzzing, every table taken. Loyal team followers, a few even sporting Beehive emblazoned T-shirts, similar to those worn by the pub's dart team, stood in groups chatting noisily. It was standing room only. Well not quite. Stern spotted a couple of bar stools, probably vacant because they were at the far end of the bar, farthest away from the playing area. He pushed his way through and claimed them, steering Cherry to one and Rob to the other, insisting he was happy to stand.

"Didn't know darts was so popular out here in the sticks," Cherry said.

"Don't know about in the sticks," Stern said. "But I read somewhere that when they play tournaments at the Alexander Palace in London, they get something like forty thousand through the door. I'd say that was pretty popular, wouldn't you?"

There were two people serving at the bar: a young man and Pam, the landlady Stern had met on his first visit. Immediately, they settled, Pam made her way toward them. "Glad to see you again, Theo. Come to see the action?"

"That and to have a chat with a couple of the lads. Okay with you?"

"Fill y'boots, luv. Makes no difference to me." She grinned. "As long as you buy a round."

"Of course, why wouldn't I?" Stern introduced Cherry and Rob and ordered their drinks.

Pam pulled a couple of pints for Stern and Rob and a tonic with ice and lemon for Cherry. "They kick off at eight," she said. "That's when the shoutin' starts."

"Can't wait"

Rob raised his glass to Stern. "Thanks for the invite, Theo. Makes a nice change to join the dynamic duo."

"My pleasure. We should do it more often. I commandeer your girl too much as it is. I'm grateful for your patience. You must put your foot down if you think I'm pushing my luck."

"Some chance," Rob laughed, his eyes drifting to Cherry, the affection obvious. "Ever tried putting your foot down with this woman?"

Cherry gave him a dig in the ribs. "I didn't even know the pair of you had set this up."

Stern winked at Rob. "It's a man thing, kiddo. Just letting you know we can organize some things without your help. Anyway, I hadn't seen Rob in an age. It was time we had a beer together."

Rob took a swig of the beer. "I hear Miss Marple earned her keep yesterday. Came home buzzing."

Stern smiled. "She did, too. Showed me up good and proper."

Cherry uncharacteristically lowered her eyes. "It was luck. I just happened to notice the mark on the carpet."

Rob inclined his head questioningly. "Mark?"

Stern could see Cherry wasn't about to crow about her success. He had driven into her over the years that cases must never be discussed outside the office. She would never break that trust even to Rob. In this case, though, he felt she deserved the praise. "We were helping out David O'Connor, searching a flat, looking for some cash. I'd previously given the flat the once-over, but Cherry asked if she could give the sitting room another look. I didn't think there was much point, but I thought nothing ventured, so I gave her the okay. Would you believe she noticed marks on the carpet looking like at some time one of the armchairs had been moved? She pulled the chair out and noticed its covering was held in place by a zip."

"The money was in the chair?"

"Sure was."

Rob put his arm around Cherry's shoulder. "Clever you."

"It was luck," Cherry insisted. "Anyway, when the boss looked the first time, he wasn't looking for cash. If he had been, he would have found it I'm sure."

Rob looked at Stern. "Am I allowed to ask how much?"

"You can ask, but to be honest we don't know yet. It looked to be a fair stash but as soon as Cherry found it, we called David. He sent a couple of guys to bag and tag it. I've no doubt he'll fill us in sometime."

"All exciting stuff," Rob said. "Makes me want to become a private eye like you two."

"Some chance," Cherry humphed. "Stick to your boats, Popeye, it's what you know, what you're good at."

Rob sighed. "See what I mean, Theo. I've got no chance. I'm doomed to spend the rest of my life toiling in the bowels of other people's boats."

"And you love every minute of it," Cherry chided."

"One hundred and eighty!"

The action had already begun, a cheer and clapping erupting from the group crowded round the playing area. Someone had already scored a maximum. Stern looked to the other end of the bar, catching Pam's eye. He pointed toward the players and mouthed. "Ollie?"

Pam stretched up to look over the heads of the crowd, searching. Shaking her head, she made her way back along the bar. "Can't see 'im, but the 'efty guy throwin' now; that's Archie, the team captain. Talk to 'im, 'e'll put y'right."

"Thanks, Pam, I'll wait till he's free."

It was some time later things came to a halt. Break time, people drifting to the bar to refill glasses. Stern eyeballed the man Pam had pointed out earlier. He had remained at the playing area talking animatedly to another man. Stern left Cherry and Rob and made his way through the crowd.

"Hi, Pam tells me you're the team captain."

The man looked glum. "I am. Not much of a team to be captain of tonight, though."

"Oh, things not going well then?"

"You could say that. You don't happen to be Phil Taylor in disguise come to help us out, do you?"

Stern laughed, recognising the name of probably the most successful professional dart player in the UK. "I wish," he chuckled. "No, my name is Stern, Theo Stern. I'm with the local CID, special investigations." He was warming to the title given him by Constable Wainwright.

The man's brow furrowed. "CID? Not doing anything wrong here, are we?"

Stern shook his head reassuringly. "No, not at all. No one's in trouble. I came tonight hoping to have a chat with one of your team, chap called Ollie."

"You're not the only one," Archie grumbled. "I'd like to have a word with him myself."

"Oh?"

"Yeah, the toe rag should have been here tonight. Let us down big time, he has. Bad enough losing poor old Charlie, but Ollie as well." His lips tightened irritably. "Without both of 'em, we're dead in the water."

"Any idea why Ollie hasn't shown?"

"Yeah, he called. Says he's got flu. Sounded alright to me, though. You'd have thought he'd made the effort, wouldn't you? He knows how important it is." He gave a resigned shrug. "Too late now, of course. He's our main man. He would have taken us through tonight. Now, we're already down the pan. Real bad news for our position in the league."

Stern felt like saying, my heart bleeds for you, but he didn't. Instead, he gave his best 'I'm so sorry' look. "Bad news, eh?"

"You better believe it. Sometimes I wonder why I bother."

Stern couldn't quite figure how someone could get so wound up about a game of darts. Still, it took all sorts. He held the amusement from his face. "What's Ollie's surname, do you know?"

"Yes, it's Preston."

"Do you happen to have his address?"

Archie shook his head. "No, 'fraid not. You can have his mobile number, though."

Back at the bar, Stern downed the last dregs of his pint. "Ollie has unexpectedly not turned up." He grinned. "For poor old Archie, the world has come to an end."

"Shame," Cherry quipped. "Get anything worthwhile out of him?"

"Not much, he's too worried about the team's position in the league. Did get a phone number, though. Problem is our friend Ollie isn't answering. Not tonight, anyway."

People had started to drift back to the playing area and seeing Pam free, Stern beckoned her over.

A tiny frown creased Cherry's forehead. "You've already had one pint, boss. Don't forget you're driving your new baby. And more important you're driving us."

Turning to Rob, Stern gave an exaggerated sigh. "See, it's not only you who has to put up with the nagging. If she's not on at me about fatty and sugary foods, she makes out I'm an alcoholic. Glad she lives with you and not me, mate."

Rob laughed. "She tells me she only has your welfare at heart."

"What can I do for you?" Pam had arrived.

"Can you do us some grub, Pam?"

"Here at the bar?"

"Sure."

"Pie, chicken, sausage. Whichever one you want. All in a basket. All with chips."

"Fantastic. And while you're at it, can you top us all up?" He looked at Cherry and grimaced. "Better make mine a shandy, or I'll get stick from the iron lady here."

It was getting on for ten. The dart match was over, and the majority of fans and players had left. The three of them had finished the food, and Stern had paid the bill. As they were preparing to leave, Pam strolled along the bar. "'Ow was it?"

"Great, Pam. We'll come again," Stern said. He pulled a pen from his pocket and scribbled his mobile number on a beer mat, handing to her. "If you hear anything about our friend Ollie, d'you mind giving us a call?"

"Doubt that'll 'appen, Theo, but if I 'ear anythin', I'll shout."

"Thanks Pam."

Outside, as they were about to climb into the car, Stern's mobile rang. He stepped back and pulled the instrument from his pocket. "Stern."

"Mr Stern, its Doris Barford."

"Mrs Barford. What's up?"

"Steve's just left on a run."

"You didn't have time to call before he left?"

"No. He got the call ten minutes ago. I didn't have a chance..."

Stern could hear the distress in her voice. "Not to worry, it's not the end of the world. What I want you to do is let me know how long he's away, and what mileage is on the clock when he returns. Have you got that?"

"Yes."

"Good. Maybe next time, you'll have more time to warn us. But don't upset yourself. It may take a little while, but we'll sort it for you. Give me a call when you get the info." He ended the call and looked through the car window at Cherry. "Mrs Barford. Her man has just headed out on one of his jaunts. She did phone through the van's mileage I asked for, didn't she?"

"Yes, it's in the file at the office."

Stern climbed into the car. "Good, that's something anyway."

Thirty

After the evening at The Beehive, Stern had dropped Cherry and Rob at Stalham. He'd considered driving to the Barford house and talking to Mrs Barford, seeing if he could acquire some more relevant information about her husband. But on consideration, he'd dismissed the idea. Her husband had left; nothing could be gained by questioning her further. By the time he got home, it was after midnight.

Sunday passed in a blur. He'd slept late, taken a late run, and later still, one of Stephen's super Sunday roasts at The Weatsheaf. He'd dozed through the afternoon and, in the evening, sat watching what he saw as crummy pointless TV. Afterwards, irritated, wondering why he had wasted his time, he climbed into bed before ten and went out like a light.

Monday, he woke to a fine morning, cold but bright. And the tide was out. Problem was, on mornings like this he got carried away. Sharp brine-filled air, the sand yielding beneath his trainers softening every stride, toughening the calf muscles. He couldn't get enough of it, always running farther than intended. By the time he got back to the flat, showered and grabbed a quick bite, he was late. It was after nine thirty when he arrived at the office.

Cherry smiled knowingly as she filled a mug. "Tide out, was it?"

Stern threw his top coat over the hanger. "Yeah, beautiful morning."

"Just had a call from Doris Barford. Gave me the info you asked for."

He took the coffee and set it down on her desk. "Thanks. So, what've we got?"

Sliding onto her chair, Cherry flipped open the Barford file. "Right. The first mileage she gave us was forty-two thousand, four hundred, and twenty miles."

Stern leaned over and scribbled the number on Cherry's pad. "Okay, and this morning?"

"Well, to start with, she said her husband didn't return until around seven. Then, after he left to start his taxi work sometime around ten, she checked the mileage on the van again. This time it showed forty-two thousand, seven hundred, and fifty."

Stern copied the number above the first, doing the sum as he did so. He gave a low whistle. "Three hundred and thirty miles."

"It was about eleven last night when she phoned and told you he'd just left, wasn't it?" Cherry said. "Back at seven this morning. Christ, boss, that's eight hours on the road."

A worried frown creased Stern's forehead. "And he's out there again this morning at ten." He scribbled some more, looked up at Cherry. "That sort of mileage in eight hours? It has to be averaging a good forty. And that would be without stops, which is not likely."

Cherry hesitated. "Boss, this can't be legal, can it? I mean, the cash he's pulling in, the all-night runs, telling his wife to keep schtum."

"Of course not, but what are you saying?"

"I'm wondering, if and when, we pull David in. I mean if we know it's dodgy shouldn't we...?"

Stern shook his head, cutting her off. "I hear what you say, kid, and you're right, it has to be iffy. But right now, we don't know for sure, do we? Okay the guy is delivering something at night, but that doesn't mean it's illegal. Many companies deliver stuff throughout the night." He waved a dismissive hand. "Oh, I know what you mean, and I agree with you. If it's not bent, my name's not Stern. But we don't actually know it. We have no proof. So, at the moment, we are just trying to help a very worried wife find out what her husband is up to. When we crack that, we'll know which way to jump, okay."

Cherry gave an accepting shrug. "You're the boss."

"Okay, so let's recap. This guy is doing late night runs that could take a couple of hours or virtually all night. We don't know about the short runs, but on the all-nighters, he covers three hundred miles plus. And don't forget, before he can deliver whatever it is, he has to collect it first. Maybe more than once. So that three hundred mile trip can't be straight out and straight back, can it?"

Cherry nodded her understanding. "We could be talking closer to home than we might think?"

Stern took a breath and exhaled through pursed lips. "Who knows? Could be anywhere. I mean, Stanstead, Heathrow, Birmingham, and Luton airports could all be possible. Even Gatwick at a push, depending on traffic."

"Traffic at that time of night?"

"No such thing as no traffic these days," Stern mused. "But you're right...it would be light. There are plenty of towns within that range, too. Nottingham, Northampton, Leicester, and Cambridge, all possible. Problem is, surmising and knowing are two completely different things."

"Well one thing's for sure...if he's doing those sort of miles in the time we've just calculated, he's not going to keep it up for long."

Stern edged his rump onto the edge of the desk. "It's times like this when I miss The Met and all its benefits. A simple phone call would have checks carried out on various motorway cameras and, in no time, we'd have number plate recognition. We'd know exactly when and where our man went. Ah, the good old days."

Cherry raised her eyes to the ceiling. "Except back in your time they didn't have motorway cameras, and I'm pretty certain number plate recognition hadn't been invented. Doubt they even had motorways. Didn't need 'em for horse and carts."

"Y'know sometimes..."

She didn't let him finish. "And you seem to forget it was back in those *good old days*," she put heavy emphasis on the last three words, "when some crazy loon stuck a knife in you. Ruined your career, and very nearly took you out for good. Oh yeah, they were the good old days alright."

"Watch it, Hooker, you're treading on dangerous ground again."

Cherry didn't look up. "Anyway, you could always ask David." She knew what the answer to that would be, but before he could reply the phone on Cherry's desk rang.

Cherry picked up. "Stern Investigations." She listened for a moment, a smile breaking, before saying, "just hang on a moment." She cupped her hand over the mouthpiece. "It's Clarissa. She reckons she's nailed the mangy mongrel we're after."

"Already. Hell, that was quick." He took the phone from her, hitting the speaker button as he did so. "Clarissa. You've found him?"

"If the description you gave me is anything to go by, I have, mate." Her voice was thin and metallic over the tiny speaker.

"Two days. Excellent work, Clarissa. How d'you manage it so quickly?"

"Sometimes, it's who you know, mate. Anyway, Blakeney's no bigger than a dried-up billabong. Your man's keeping well out the way, squatting in a caravan on the edge of the village. Me and old Claude flushed him out, no worries."

"Clarissa, you're a diamond. Soon as we're wrapped up here, we'll head over later today. I'll ring you before we set out, okay?"

"Look forward to it, mate."

Stern dropped the phone back on its stand and thoughtfully picked up the coffee mug, draining the last dregs. He looked at his watch. "Half ten. Cyril will be up to his eyes preparing today's lunch.

He'll probably be okay for later, though." He retrieved the phone again, dialled a number. It was answered immediately.

"Cyril, it's Theo. Would you believe Clarissa's found our man?" He chuckled. "Yeah, two days. Not bad, eh? How are you fixed for later, say around five?" He listened for a moment more. "Good man. Best we meet at Clarissa's, I think. Yup, I'll see you there." He ended the call and turned to Cherry. "We've got a lot going on all of a sudden."

Cherry knew from experience the boss had what she had long since christened the 'Stern leapfrog brain.' He was somehow able to flip from one thing to another and back again without losing track of any of it. But by doing so, he frequently lost her. Right then, she felt the need to bring him back to where they were before Clarissa's call. "Yeah, we have, but would it be best to concentrate on the Barford problem first? You know, where we were a minute ago?"

"What? Oh yeah. I was just trying to figure the best way to fit things in." He held up a cautionary finger. "First, let me make another call." He dialled the number.

"David, it's Theo. Just thought I'd let you know our visit to The Beehive drew a blank. Our man didn't show. Flu apparently. I've got his full name and a phone number, though, so I'll have to do some more digging. I'll keep you up to speed." He listened for a moment. "He has? That's good." He scribbled on his pad as he listened. "Okay, will do. Yes, is tomorrow okay? Good, I'll get onto it, keep you informed." He ended the call.

"Everything okay?"

"Yup. The Butler handyman, a guy called Victor Adams, has turned up. David wants me to interview him about the fire. I said I'd drive over there tomorrow. You might as well come, too. It'll keep you up to speed."

Delighted, Cherry slid off the chair. The boss was involving her more and more these days. It was exactly what she wanted.

Thirty-one

Ollie Preston sat in his favourite armchair feeding himself with the fish and chips he'd collected from the corner shop. Greasy fingers between greasy lips. At the shop, before allowing them to be wrapped, he'd smothered them in salt and vinegar from the shop's counter, and back home, was eating them directly from the polystyrene dish. Why bother dirtying a fork and a plate; he'd only have to wash them afterwards.

Ollie was using his left hand, the right hand being heavily bandaged. It made things awkward, and he was annoyed it had happened. Until that point, everything had gone smoothly, exactly to plan. The truth was the adrenalin had been pumping so hard, he hadn't realised he was hurt. Even now he didn't know how it had happened. There was obviously something sharp he hadn't seen. Could have been an exposed nail in the wooden mooring as he clambered quickly away. After breaking into the boat, he had set the fire deep in the hull, but not too close to the engine compartment. He didn't want it to develop too quickly. He needed to be away and back across the river before the thing went up, and everywhere was illuminated by the flames. His ingenious homemade device had worked well. He was proud of that. The one-man inflatable he'd used to ferry himself back and forth across the river had been tucked well away in the boot of the car before he saw the first flicker appear in the window of the boat. He was satisfied he'd have been well on his way home before anyone knew what was happening.

It was a pity about the deep cut to the palm of his hand. When he'd arrived home, he'd washed and treated it with an antiseptic cream before bandaging it tightly. Fortunately, by the following morning, it had stopped bleeding. He knew the gash, some two inches long, should probably be stitched, but it wasn't going to happen. Ollie was no fool; he'd seen the TV police dramas and knew if he'd left any blood at the scene, they'd be checking doctors' surgeries and hospitals. So, he would deal with the situation himself. Over the next few days he had kept the wound scrupulously clean and tightly bandaged. It had done the trick. He was now sure he wouldn't have to seek treatment. He would be scarred, but Ollie was used to scars...under the beard, his face was full of them. The bad news was he'd had to miss the latest dart match. The captain hadn't been pleased, but Ollie thought the flu excuse had worked okay. He didn't see any of the team other than at matches, so no one would know of the deception. He just hoped his hand would be okay for the next match. Fortunately, that was a fortnight away.

The day after his attack on the Butler boat, two things had happened. Firstly, he'd penned another note to the local police warning that unless Butler was investigated he would up his game. A little difficult with the damaged hand, but he had managed it. And he'd had to post this one locally, unlike previous notes he'd sent from the various places the team had played the away games. Not a problem...it would have been as squeaky clean as all the others. And he wasn't kidding. He was determined to see this through to the end, whatever that meant he had to do. Before this, he had lived a pretty boring existence. Now, he was warming to his exciting new role as a modern day vigilante fighting a just cause. He knew well enough he could have just visited the local police station and reported the situation. But this was the lowly Ollie Preston telling tales on a big wig, a wealthy businessman who, by the way, was a bit of a benefactor to the local community. So what reaction would he have got? They would have taken a few notes, given him some consolatory words, and shown him the door, the notes probably hitting the waste paper basket as soon as he'd left the building. So, no, he had to show them he meant business; they had to take him seriously or face the consequences.

The second happening that day was an extensive report of the fire on local TV. Even showing footage of the smouldering mooring, the boat no more than a black oily slick of debris on the water's surface. Until seeing the report, he couldn't be absolutely certain. Now he knew everything had gone according to plan.

The same report had also shown a statement from the senior detective in charge of the investigation. Ollie was pleased to know he could address his notes to a particular individual. Since then, in anticipation, every evening at 6 pm he had sat in front of the TV hoping to see more. It was why he was once again settled waiting for the East Anglia news.

He thought back to how this whole thing had started. How Charlie Croker, probably Ollie's only true friend, had confided in him about how his humdrum life had been turned around. To people like him, he'd told Ollie, good fortune normally came once, if ever. So, how fantastic that at his time of life, fate had targeted him twice and almost at the same time. First, the extra work being so lucrative. Then the girl, his wonderful Sally.

Ollie had been suspicious from the start. If something looks too good to be true, it inevitably is. He had no doubt Charlie had been targeted, but he would be very surprised if fate had anything to do with it. Charlie was a middle-aged man who even Ollie had to admit was not the sharpest knife in the drawer. And, like Ollie, he was lonely. He was also not very well off. How vulnerable can you get? But what Ollie suspected as being Charlie's most important asset was his old van. Ollie had very tactfully voiced his suspicions, but

Charlie was totally besotted. Poor old devil couldn't see beyond the stars in his eyes. Just a few deliveries here and there. No Problem. All he had to do was keep it under wraps, say nothing to anyone, not a soul. Then, when he'd stashed enough...?

But Charlie's good fortune had been bursting to break free. He had been desperate to tell someone. And he had chosen Ollie because Charlie knew if there was one person he could trust to keep his secret, it was Ollie. They had stayed behind after a match, Charlie whispering excitedly. He had it all worked out. A year was all it would take. At the moment, his wonderful Sally could only visit evenings, once, occasionally twice a week, because she worked some distance away and her hours were long. And she, too, she had told him, was saving hard for their future. Things would change when the time came, when they had enough cash behind them. Then Sally, his wonderful Sally, had agreed, they could move away, be together, start afresh. And though chomping at the bit, Charlie had to be patient. The money, he told Ollie, was rolling in, more than he had ever earned in his life, and though only for short visits, he was seeing his Sally regularly.

Despite being highly suspicious, Ollie had to admit he was envious of his friend's apparent good fortune and extreme happiness. As well as a salary from Charters, Charlie was earning big money on the side. He was also seeing a young woman who, if it were true, was promising a long-term future partnership. What more could anyone ask? But the one thing Charlie would never reveal was what he was actually doing to earn that big money. When Ollie pressed, the answer was always the same. Deliveries. Just deliveries.

Ollie couldn't be sure why he'd decided to do it. Probably the envy he felt had played a part. Or simply the concern for his friend's welfare. It mattered not because the long vigil outside Charlie's flat had revealed what Ollie had always feared.

The girl was dropped off at the flat at around ten and collected again just after one. And not by a taxi. To Ollie that said it all. He knew how things worked. He'd been there plenty of times. As a single, not very attractive, adult male, it was the easiest, most uncomplicated way to satisfy certain physical requirements. But this was supposed to be a young woman, his friend's beloved Sally, promising a long-term relationship. Not a casual call girl regularly delivered and collected by her pimp. So, what was going on here? Was there a link between this woman and the lucrative 'just deliveries' his friend had been drawn into?

Ollie had followed the vehicle, a Land Rover, away from Charlie's flat, but as it made its way out of the city he realised he was faced with a dilemma. Just how far would it go, and should he risk tailing it? At such an early hour, after leaving the city, the country roads would be free of any traffic. So, would it be obvious to the driver he was being followed? But Ollie's blood was up. He was convinced his friend was being taken for a ride, could even be in real trouble. What the hell.

He'd stayed well back, using only his side lights wherever possible, and was amazed how his quarry just kept going, seemingly oblivious of his presence. Almost half an hour later, finally creeping down a narrow lane, the Land Rover came to a halt, its stop lights glowing for the last time. Yards back, Ollie doused the lights and killed the engine. Climbing from the car, he edged his way through the darkness, keeping well into the side shrubbery. He saw tall wide gates automatically slide apart, allowing the Land Rover through before almost immediately coming together again.

Keeping close to the thick hedgerow, Ollie sidled up to the closed gates and peered between the ornate ironwork. With automatic security lights blazing, he was able to see the Land Rover as it travelled slowly down a long drive and come to rest outside a wide garage positioned to the left of the large house. A man and the girl climbed from the car and made their way past the front of the house and across to what looked like a small cottage set back on the opposite side of the spacious front garden. The man ushered the girl inside and closed the door.

Tucked away in the hedgerow, Ollie waited for some moments more, but there was no further activity. Finally, the security lights timed out, and the whole area was thrown into darkness. Ollie returned to his car, his mind whizzing. He had no idea who owned the large property, but one thing was sure, for his close friend's sake, he was going to find out.

Ollie snapped out of his reverie, conscious the footage of the smouldering hulk was again on the screen in front of him. Sucking the grease from his fingers, he grabbed the remote and tapped up the volume as the familiar East Anglia reporter came into view.

"...the local police confirmed today that though investigations were ongoing, they had found evidence at the scene of the fire that could possibly lead them to the culprit. They also told our reporter they still had to interview certain individuals of interest. Investigations continue. This is your reporter reporting from..."

Ollie reduced the volume and dropped the remote. He pushed another piece of fish into his mouth. So, they had found blood. He smiled confidently. Well good luck with that.

Thirty-two

They closed the office early, Cherry heading home, and Stern making for a bite to eat at a café on the high street. He'd called Clarissa, confirming he and Cyril would be at her place sometime before six. Clarissa was bubbling, really '*stoked, mate,*' as she put it. During the nine months he'd spent in Australia, Stern could remember only hearing the word once. It was in a bar and used by an old local who at the time couldn't have looked less excited if he'd tried. Stern was raised on London slang and during his time with the Met, it had been part of everyday life. The Ozzie slang was close, but he'd somehow not cottoned onto it.

At the café and again continuing on his way to Blakeney, Stern mulled over their options. But, however he squared things, it always came back to the obvious. Straight in, hit him head on. They knew who he was, though they didn't actually, and they knew what he was up to. Stalking was illegal, and threatening behaviour was worse. If he tried any of the physical stuff, Stern felt he and Cyril were still more than capable of taking care of it. So, there it was. First, they establish the man was actually at home in the caravan, then it was straight in, mob handed.

Cyril was already at the log cabin when Stern arrived. He was sitting, casually sipping a large mug of tea while Clarissa was agitatedly wearing a groove in the carpet. It took Stern back. Of all the number two's Stern had had during his long career, Cyril had been the most laid back. Whether it be on a stake out or moments before a dangerous raid, Cyril was the original cucumber. Cool and controlled as you like. Until it was action stations, then watch out.

Clarissa met Stern at the door, Claude at her side, cigarette clenched in the corner of her mouth. "'Strewth, mate, I'm glad you're here," she breathed, the cigarette violently bobbing up and down with every word. "I've been up and down to the old dunny umpteen times in the last hour." Stern could hear Cyril chuckling away in the background.

"Don't worry, Clarissa. You just show us where he is, and we'll do the rest."

Clarissa looked aghast. "Aw, come on now, Theo. Fair dinkum, mate. I found him, I should be there when we collar the mongrel. Anyway, you'll need Claude to scare the danglers off him."

"She's right, Theo," Cyril came in. "The more the merrier."

Having already had Claude in mind, Stern relented immediately. "No problem. Just thought you'd be a bit nervous."

Clarissa laughed, a rasping, smoker's rattle. "Nervous? Nothing of the sort, Theo. It's the most exciting thing I've done in years. I just can't wait to get going."

They piled into Cyril's Land Rover, Cyril driving with Clarissa alongside, Claude sitting obediently between her legs, tongue lolling from one side of his mouth. Stern was happy to sit behind, away from the dog's slobbering chops. Cyril followed Clarissa's directions, keeping to the coast road, clearing the village by a few hundred yards before turning through a gate into a small field. Cyril halted the car directly inside the gate close to the tall hedge surrounding the field.

There were just four caravans in the field. Each one had a car parked alongside. Early holiday makers, disregarding the weather, taking the opportunity to enjoy the Norfolk coast before the rush, sure to come in a month or so.

Clarissa pointed to a caravan tucked away in the farthest corner of the field. Like the others, there was a car parked alongside it. "That's him," she hissed, her words soft, but hoarse with excitement.

"How the hell did you find him out here?" Stern asked.

"I was having a jar with the farmer who owns the field. Just happened to ask him if he'd seen any strangers around. He told me he had a few early campers in his field. Said mostly they were couples, but there was a guy on his own. Thought I'd come and have a gander. 'Course it might not be him, but if your description is anything to go by, I'd bet Claude's dinner it is."

They were quiet for a while, watching the caravan, the only sound Claude's heavy panting. Finally, Stern broke the silence. "Notice the car?"

Cyril frowned. "What about it?"

"It's an Audi. An A four. Got a few miles under the bonnet I bet, but not in bad nick."

"Is that supposed to mean something?"

"Maybe, maybe not. Just that Mo's ex-husband is head honcho at a top London Audi Dealership."

"Could be a coincidence." Watching Stern, Cyril smiled, remembering one of Stern's frequent mantras from way back: 'If it looks like a coincidence it probably isn't.'

Picking up on the jibe, he too remembering, Stern glanced across at his friend. "Probably isn't, though, right?"

Cyril laughed. "Probably not."

Clarissa looked from one to the other, confused. "Dunno what you two bonzoes are on about, but it's getting as hot as a roo's bum in here. Poor old Claude needs to get out before he catches fire, and I need a fag. So, how're we going to play this?"

"Okay, let's assume it is our man, and he is in the van," Stern said. "You take Claude for a walk, but stay in the field, a casual dog walker, okay? Cyril and I will go across and give him a knock."

Clarissa left the car with Claude and stood nonchalantly by the hedgerow, lighting up and allowing the dog to lift his leg.

"Just like old times," Cyril said as they headed across the field toward the caravan. "How d'you want to play it?"

"Let me take the lead. Jump in when you feel fit."

"Got it." Cyril's mind flashed back, remembering the number of times Stern had said exactly the same words in the past. Never one to arrogantly assume he had it right. Always giving his backup the opportunity to see what he may have missed and act on it.

Approaching the caravan, they could hear music. Their man was at home. Stern rapped on the door, and, immediately, there was movement inside. The door was pulled open, and Stern could instantly see the likeness to the description Cherry had got from the waiter at the Blakeney hotel. Even down to the crew cut and bomber jacket.

"Yeah?" The voice was gruff, a hint of aggression in the single word.

Stern had already decided to accentuate his London accent. "'Ello, mate. You don't know us, but we're up from the Smoke for a few days. I was talking to Frank before we came and seeing as we were coming up anyway he asked me to give you a message."

A heavy frown creased the man's thick forehead. "What?"

Stern inclined his head, eyes narrowing, showing irritation. "Didn't you hear what I said? Frank asked us to drop off here and give you a message."

Now the cautious eye movement, scanning between the two men in front of him. "Er, I dunno..." The aggression giving way to uncertainty.

Shaking his head irritably, Stern gave a heavy sigh. "Gawd mate, we ain't got all day. We've got things on the go. Took us long enough to bloody find you."

Clearly bewildered, the man leaned out from the doorway, his eyes flicking from left to right, looking for something, he didn't know what, just nervous. For a moment, Stern thought he'd got it wrong then, "Yeah, yeah okay. You'd better come inside."

The atmosphere was warm and thick, a heavy smell of frying fat. A small single ringed gas cooker sat directly opposite the door, a frying pan with a single dried up rasher of bacon slowly congealing. Stern glanced to his right…a table with bench seats either side, a thick crudely cut, half eaten bacon sandwich on a paper plate, a half empty litre bottle of vodka, a small radio playing pop music. To his left, at the far end, a single bunk bed, unmade, various items of clothing casually thrown around.

The man moved toward the table before turning. He didn't sit, didn't ask them to. "So, why'd he send you two? Why didn't he phone like usual?"

Neither Stern nor Cyril spoke. They just stood, expressionless, holding the man's gaze. It was a tactic they'd used before, normally creating an atmosphere of extreme tension. It worked.

"Come on, then," the man demanded, rubbing his hands together. "Don't just stand there…"

"What's your connection with Cavendish?" Stern cut him off.

"What? What d'you mean?"

"The inspector asked you a question." This time Cyril, his words curt, demanding.

Eyes now wide, the man's mouth dropped open. "Inspector? I thought you said…"

"You thought wrong, mister." Cyril growled. "Did you know stalking is illegal? And threatening with a knife?" He glanced sideways at Stern. "You can go down big time for that. Right, Inspector?"

"Absolutely, Sergeant," Stern said, his face a hard mask. Another prolonged silence, the tension building further. "What's your name?"

"Look, you can't just burst in here and…"

Stern turned and looked at Cyril. "Do you remember bursting in here, Sergeant?"

Cyril gave an exaggerated shake of his head. "Far as I remember, we were invited in, sir."

"S'what I thought." Stern looked back at the man. "But obviously the gentleman is unhappy with us being here. In that case, I think it best if we continue this conversation back at the station." He turned toward the door.

The man's mouth dropped open. "The station?" he stuttered. "But I ain't done nothing. Why are you doing...?"

Stern swung back, scowling. "What is your name?"

The man's shoulders sagged. "Wheeler, Larry Wheeler, but..."

"Okay, Mr Wheeler," Stern cut him off sharply. "I'll ask again. What's your connection with Cavendish?"

Wheeler hesitated, but this time only for a second. "I occasionally do some work for him." He looked from Stern to Cyril and back. "Look, he told me she owed him big time. I only had to put the frighteners on her for a bit. I wasn't going to do anything. Honest, I wouldn't hurt her. I'm not that sort of..."

"What sort of work? Salesman? Mechanic?"

"Er, no, I was a sort of agent."

"Doing what?"

"This and that. Anything he wanted doing."

"And what did you get out of this little stunt?"

Wheeler raised submissive hands. "Nothing, honest, I just did it as a..."

"As a favour?" Cyril broke in cynically. "D'you really think we came up the Thames on a bike?" He turned to Stern. "I think we have one very dangerous individual here, Inspector."

"I agree, Sergeant. One more off the streets." He turned again to open the door. "Cuff him, Sergeant, and we'll take him down."

"No, no, no," Wheeler babbled, taking a step back, banging into the table, physically trembling now. "I'm not a dangerous man. I've never been in any trouble before, honest." Again, he held out both hands, imploring. "Just let me tell you, please."

Stern stopped and turned back slowly. "You've got three minutes, and it better be good."

Wheeler pointed to the bottle on the table. "Look, I'm out of work. Got a bit of a drink problem." He lowered his eyes, shaking his head sadly. "I'm trying, I really am, but it's so bloody hard, I just can't seem to..." He waved a hand, indicating the surroundings. "Why d'you think I'm living in this pig sty?" He held Stern's eyes, searching for sympathy, seeing none, eventually breaking eye contact. "One day Frank calls me, asks if I want to make a few bob, said it was a piece of cake, no problems. Said he'd see me alright. Told me how his ex had ripped him off and needed to be taught a lesson."

"Ripped him off? How?"

"He didn't say. I did hear she was having it away on the side, but that was a while back." He shrugged. "I wouldn't know, really. Frank just said all I needed to do was put the frighteners on her for a few days, softener her up like."

"Then what?"

"I don't know. That's all he told me. Said afterwards I could hitch up and head off."

"And what *did* you get out of it. The truth this time or..."

"Look I was on the street, sleeping in a cardboard box. I just needed..."

"Just cut the sob stuff," Cyril cut him off. "Just tell us what you got out of it?"

Wheeler gave a resigned sigh. "The car and this heap of crap. And that's the truth."

"And?"

"And a few bob to keep me going. Fifty..." He looked between the two of them then lowered his eyes. "A hundred quid."

Stern felt he had the truth. "Okay Wheeler, I want you to listen to me, and listen good. I'm going to give you a break you don't deserve. But if at any time I hear of a woman, any woman, being hounded like this again, I'll put out a nationwide search for you. Do you understand me?"

"Yes, yes I do"

"Okay, do you have a mobile?"

"Yes, but it's old, pay as you go. And it is mine, I didn't steal..."

Stern shook his head irritably. "Don't care where you got it, just give me the number."

"But I thought you said..."

"Don't worry, you're off the hook right now, but I might need to talk to you again, later." Stern clocked the worry lines creasing Wheeler's face. "If I do, and you can help, there'll be something in it for you, okay?"

"Well yes, thank you." He spelled out the number to Cyril who had already produced his notebook.

"Okay, so when we've finished here, you'll hitch up this pile of junk and find somewhere else to park. And I mean out of Norfolk. Got it?"

"Yes." The relief was palpable.

"Now, outside there is another member of my team with her specially trained guard dog," Stern went on. "She will ensure you do as I have instructed. And be warned...if you value your health, you will do nothing to upset the dog."

Thirty-three

Closely overseen by a threatening, dead-eyed Clarissa and a slathering Claude, a very nervous Larry Wheeler had hooked the caravan to the Audi and quickly left the field.

"'Strewth, mate, I felt like the bloody Gestapo there," Clarissa said, grinning from ear to ear. "This private eye game is bloody good stuff." She looked up at Stern. "You ever need a hand again, Theo, you just shout Clarissa. I'll be there, no worries."

"By the way," Cyril said as they climbed into the Range Rover. 'This 'cuff him sergeant' business. What would you have done if he'd held out his wrists?"

Stern laughed. "I'd have given my sergeant a rollicking for leaving his handcuffs at home."

Back at Clarissa's log cabin, they enjoyed a celebratory drink before leaving, Clarissa again offering her services to Stern whenever he needed her. In a professional capacity, of course, she had quickly corrected, the colour creeping up her neck.

As they drove away, Stern glanced at his watch. "How're you fixed for another hour?" he asked.

"I'm good. What you got in mind?"

"I'd like to nip back and tie things up with Mo."

"Sure, no problem."

Mo must have heard the car crunch onto the gravel area of the cottage because she was waiting at the door as they climbed from the car.

They sat round the table in the tiny sitting room, Stern outlining what had happened, confirming they had sent the man away.

Mo's relief was palpable. "I'm so glad it's over," she said. "Just a crazy peeping tom. What a relief. I really can't thank you enough for dealing with him. Just send me the bill. Whatever it is, I'll be happy to pay."

Stern watched her closely for some moments before speaking again. "I didn't say he was just a peeping tom, did I?"

"No, but I just thought..."

"Look, I think it's time you came clean, don't you?"

Mo's eyes narrowed. "I'm sorry, I don't think I understand."

"I think you do. We might have sent this particular individual packing, but he was not a stalker, or a peeping tom. And he certainly wasn't the root cause of your problem." Again, he eyed her closely, studying her reaction, particularly the eyes, the true indicators. "But I think you were worried that might be the case all along, weren't you?"

"No, certainly not. I..."

"Oh, come on, Mo," Stern snapped, his manner switching, harsh ingrained interrogation mode automatically kicking in. "This guy was sent by Frank Cavendish to put the frighteners on you. We know that now. But you thought it could be him all along, didn't you? It was why you didn't want the police involved." He let the silence hang for a long moment, his face a harsh, uncompromising mask.

"I don't... I'm so..." Mo stuttered, the colour draining from her face.

"Look, Mo," Cyril came in, his voice soft, more sympathetic. "What Theo is saying is we know this guy was just a pawn. He was hired by your ex to harass and frighten you. He told us so. But he couldn't tell us why, but there has to be a reason." He gave her a reassuring smile. "And none of us believe it was because you scratched the old man's car, do we? That was just a red herring, right? So, the point is, knowing what we do now, it's obvious just sending this guy on his bike doesn't solve your problem."

Stern could see the old, well-rehearsed good cop bad cop routine hadn't been forgotten. He got to his feet, his face still a hard mask. "And we can't help unless we know all the facts. So, unless you are prepared to tell us what's really behind this, and I mean all of it, there's no point in us wasting our time here any longer." He raised a warning finger. "But if things turn bad, don't expect me to get involved with this again. I expect my clients to be honest with me. If they're not..." He didn't finish, just shrugged his shoulders and looked at Cyril. "Time we were out of here."

"No, no. Please wait."

Stern said nothing but remained standing.

Mo looked up at him, took a deep breath, exhaling an enormous sigh. "Sit down, please." She waited for him to slide back onto the chair. "It was after the divorce," she began softly. "When everything was settled. We were clearing our stuff out of the house, going our separate ways. Problem was the relationship was so bad neither of us was prepared to be in the house when the other was there. So, through our solicitors, we agreed certain days and times. When he was there, I would stay away, and I went when he was at work." She shook her head sadly. "Stupid, I know, but that was how bad it had got. It was the last time I was there." She stopped for a beat, collecting her thoughts. "You see, it was a big house. Upstairs, as well as our bedroom, we had spares. I commandeered one as my studio, and Frank had another as his home office. We seldom ventured into each other's domain, there was no need. On that last day, I had a good deal of stuff piled on the bed ready to go and needed something to carry it in. At first, after having a good look round and finding nothing, I remembered my holiday luggage, two suitcases, was still in the loft. I'd never been up there, but Frank had, often. He maintained it was important to keep a constant eye on the water tanks and pipe work up there, make sure there were no leaks or overflows. I knew nothing of plumbing or water systems, and wasn't the slightest bit interested anyway. I just accepted it was what you did."

"How often did he go up there," Cyril asked.

Mo gave a shrug. "I don't really know exactly. Probably every couple of weeks. Could be more often, I suppose. I never took much notice. It was just something he did."

Cyril looked at Stern. "Bit of an overkill, don't you think?"

"It is, but I have a feeling there's more to come here." He raised his eyebrows at Mo. "Go on."

She took another deep breath. "Well, I'd seen him go up there, so I knew there was a loft ladder he released by pushing against the loft hatch. Frank used a stick thing, like a broom handle with a hook on one end. It stood just inside the bedroom door. So, I did the same. I let down the ladder and climbed up. There was a light switch on a beam just inside the hatch, and I switched it on. The loft appeared to be completely empty apart from the luggage. All the cases were stacked just inside the hatch, so I grabbed the first of mine and took it down. Then I went back up for the second one. I don't know why, just pure curiosity I suppose, I'd never been up in any loft before, but I went across to have a look at the water tank that had always been so important to Frank. It was then I saw it."

"Saw what?"

"It was an attaché case, tucked out of sight behind the tank. I was intrigued because I'd never seen it before. I pulled it out and tried to open it, but it was locked. For a moment, I was confused. I didn't know if it was Frank's or had been left there by a previous tenant." She stopped, her eyes filling. "I was so stupid. It was just... He had been so nasty to me."

Cyril put his hand on her arm. "Don't worry, take your time."

She pulled a handkerchief from her sleeve and dabbed at her eyes, breathing deeply, trying to compose herself, finally continuing. "After a moment, I concluded it was too clean, too dust free to have been there long. Anyway, Frank had been up there too often not to have seen it. I knew it had to be his. I took it down, and into his office, and searched his desk. I found a key tucked away at the back of one of the drawers." Lowering her eyes, she drifted into silence.

Stern gave her a few moments before urging her on. "It was the key to the briefcase?"

"Yes."

"Come on, Mo. We haven't got all night." It was harsh, but Stern knew this was what it was all about. He needed to push. "So, you opened the case, right?"

Finally, she looked up, holding his gaze for a long moment. Then without saying more, she pushed herself out of the chair and left the room. A few moments later, she returned carrying the briefcase. She laid it on the table in front of them and flipped open the lid. "This is what I found."

Both Stern and Cyril leaned forward, peering into the case.

Cyril whistled. "Christ."

Thirty-four

"How much?" Fidgeting excitedly in the chair, Cherry looked incredulously across the desk.

"Mo said better than ten grand."

"And she stole it from him?"

"She did," Stern came back. "Though whether it was legitimately his in the first place is questionable."

It was the morning after Stern and Cyril had dismissed Larry Wheeler and confronted Mo Preston. Stern was updating an agitated Cherry on events.

"And I missed it all. Didn't even get the chance to see Clarissa do her 'on guard' bit with Claude."

Stern laughed. "You would have enjoyed it. Poor bloke was wetting himself."

"Don't know about poor bloke, boss. He'd been frightening Mo witless, don't forget."

Stern shook his head. "Cherry, he was just a sad alcoholic. Apparently, he did odd jobs for Cavendish, probably to keep the booze flowing. He called himself an agent, but he was just a bit of a gofer whenever Cavendish needed him. He was living on the street, for goodness sake. And Cavendish took advantage of that. Gave him an old car, not worth a lot, probably taken in as part exchange and would have been flogged off to the trade anyway. And a clapped out little caravan more than ready for the scrap heap. Wouldn't mind betting someone paid Cavendish to take it away."

"But what did Mo think she was going to do with the money?"

"Absolutely nothing. She hasn't touched a penny of it since she took it from the house."

"So, what then?"

"She had some silly idea that by hanging on to it she would have something over Cavendish to keep him off her back."

Cherry shook her head. "Don't understand."

"No, it doesn't make a lot of sense, does it?" Stern agreed. "But Mo had no idea he had stashed it away like he had, and certainly didn't know where he'd got it from. She could only think he was on the take, some scam or other. How else could he have got hold of that amount of hard cash lawfully?"

"Wouldn't disagree with that."

"No, but that's when her logic screwed up. You see, it was because after the bust up, after her little fling with the lecherous artist, things got really bad. Cavendish, in particular, hounded her into the ground, never letting up. You remember he drove her to attacking his car."

"I do."

"It all had a profound effect on her. By taking the money, she thought she would have a sort of buffer."

Cherry thought for a moment. "You mean if he came to trouble her again, she would retaliate by threatening to report the money to the police."

"Exactly. For such a switched-on lady, it was muddled thinking, I admit. What she had was just a random case full of cash. I reminded her now she'd removed it from the house, there was absolutely nothing to link it to Cavendish, anyway. And as it turned out, hanging onto it had exactly the opposite effect. Once he located where she was, Cavendish wasn't going to give up till he got his cash back. If we hadn't found Wheeler, he would have carried on until he wore her down. And if she had held on, who knows what he would have resorted to next."

"What a mess," Cherry said dolefully. "Where do we go from here? Or have we done our bit now?"

"No, now she's come clean, told us everything, I've agreed to help her. As far as what we do next, I think our first task is to see if we can establish where Cavendish got the money. Oh, and by the way, we've taken the cash. Mo had it in a kitchen cupboard, not even locked. If someone broke in while she was out they would have found it in no time."

"So where is it now?"

"Safely stashed away at We-R-Lunch. Cyril's got a safe."

"Well, I don't know about you, boss," Cherry said, her expression pained. "But I wouldn't know where to start."

"Yeah, I know it's a tough one. Thing is, if we can get some evidence Cavendish got the money illegally, we can hand things over to the Met., let them handle it."

"It's getting that evidence though, isn't it?"

"It is, but I was mulling it over last night, and I've got an idea there might just be a way." He stopped and pushed himself out of the chair. "But first, we have a certain Mr Victor Adams to interview. So, grab your coat, and I'll treat you to another ride in my super car."

Cherry followed him out of the office. "Sure you don't want to use a decent car for a change? Don't want to wear that thing of yours out. These new-fangled contraptions don't last long, you know."

"My dear girl," he threw over his shoulder as he shrugged himself into his topcoat. "The next time I want to curl myself into your old heap I'll let you know."

"God, you are a snob, boss."

~ * ~

Stern pulled the car to one side of the Deep Repose gates and killed the engine. As they climbed from the warm car, Cherry shivered, pulled her coat closer. The day was calm, the sky clear, but there was a sharp chill in the air. It was early April, and winter wasn't about to let go for a while yet.

Looking through the gate, Stern could see no sign of life, and just the Land Rover was parked in front of the garage. No Mercedes. Then it registered, it being a Tuesday Butler was probably back in London. He pushed the button on the speaker system at the side. There was no response, so he pressed again, this time holding his finger on the button longer. Eventually a click and a voice, male but lighter, less gruff than Pace who'd answered before. "Yes, hello."

"This is Special Investigator Stern calling to interview Victor Adams."

He glanced sideways at Cherry who, eyebrows raised, mouthed, "Special Investigator?"

"Oh yes," the voice came back. "Come to cottage, please." There was a metallic click, and the gates began to slide open.

As they moved through and started down the drive, Cherry was eyeing him, a half grin on her face.

Stern knew why. "Okay, okay but it sounds good, don't you think."

"S'pose so, but where d'it come from?"

"Constable Wainwright promoted me when we gave Charlie Croker's flat the once-over."

She gave it some thought. "So, what does that make me? How about Senior Assistant Special Investigator?"

Stern chuckled. "Why senior?"

"Well, there's no one above me, is there? I mean between me and you."

"At the moment, no, but carry on as you are..." Stern muttered quietly.

"I heard that, and it really hurt."

Making their way down the drive and across the front of the house, they arrived at the cottage. At the door of the little building, a man stood waiting. Stern guessed him to be in his mid-thirties and around six feet. He was lean and wiry with a confident, regular workout stance. His hair was close cropped, and his eyes were close together, alert, even predatory. He was wearing a heavy checked builder's shirt hanging over stained jeans and thick leather boots. The dark tan was real, the result of hours spent outdoors. The smile not so real, more like cautious.

Stern held out a hand. "Victor Adams?"

The hand was callused, the grip firm. "Yes, I am Victor."

"I'm Special Investigator Stern, and this is Senior Assistant Investigator Hooker." He put a slight emphasis on the 'senior,' but kept a straight face.

Adams looked from one to the other, his eyes holding on Cherry longer than Stern, then motioned them inside.

It was a typical cottage, the layout not unlike that of Mo Stevens, though more modern. The front door led directly into the sitting room. From there, three more doors led to other rooms. Two of those doors were slightly ajar, one indicating a small kitchen, the other a bathroom. The other door was closed. The sitting room was sparsely furnished with just a couple of casual chairs facing a TV in the corner and a small dining table with two chairs slid under. Adams motioned Stern and Cherry to the two casual chairs, then slid out a chair from the table, and placed it in front of them for himself.

"Mrs Butler say you need to speak with me."

Stern immediately noticed the accent, his mind flicking back to the original interview with Butler, who described Adams as a local man. He pulled his notebook from his pocket. "Yes, it's regarding the fire."

"I cannot tell you much, I was asleep."

"But the fire woke you?"

"I woke with er, big bang. I don't know…it could be fuel tank." He raised both hands, a resigned gesture. "I know nothing of boats."

Stern scribbled a note. "But you did get up and go to the fire."

"Yes, of course. I put on clothes straight away and run to water." He drew down his lips and gave a dismissive shrug. "But I could do nothing. The burning, the heat. I ran to the house to wake Mrs Butler."

"Did you see anyone there? In the area. On the bank or on the river?"

"No, I saw no one."

"The river's not too wide there," Stern persisted. "With the flames, lots of light, maybe on the far bank?"

Adams gave a positive shake of his head, just a little too positive, too quick. "No, I see nothing."

"Okay. What did Mrs Butler do when she arrived?"

"Katri...er, Mrs Butler, she not come. Just Stefana. Mrs Butler, she stay to call her husband."

The slip didn't go unnoticed. "And you called the fire brigade?"

Adams averted his eyes, suddenly taking an interest in a particular thumbnail. "No, we call no one." He gave another resigned shrug of his shoulders. "Anyway, the boat, it stands on water; there is no need for fire people."

"Mmmm, I see," Stern murmured, scribbling more. "But you did call the police?"

"Mr Butler, when he come, he call the police."

Stern paused, tucking his notebook back into his pocket, watching Adams carefully. "Mr Adams, when I spoke to Mr Butler, he told me you were local, but by your accent I would think different. Could you explain?"

Adams looked pained. "I am local, I live here. Before I work for Mrs Butler, I live in village, do gardens."

"Yes, but where were you born?"

Adams looked down, anxiously wringing his hands.

Stern moved in quickly. "Mr Adams, you do realise it is a criminal offence to lie to the police, don't you?"

Adams' head snapped up. "I do not lie, I never lie."

Stern remained impassive. "Then tell me where you were born."

"I born in Poland, but I live here now. I am English. I show you papers."

Stern shook his head. "No need. How long have you lived here?"

"I live here almost two years, and now I am English, I am local."

Stern pushed himself out of the chair, indicating for Cherry to do the same. "Thank you, Mr Adams. That will be all for the moment." At the door he stopped and turned. "Just one last thing, Mr Adams. What is your real name? I mean the name on your passport?"

Thirty-five

It was around lunchtime when Stern dropped Cherry at the office and headed off to Norwich. Earlier, he'd phoned O'Connor and asked for a meet. He knew O'Connor was always glad to get out of the office, so he suggested tea and a hotdog at one of the stalls in the marketplace. For O'Connor it was just a short walk from the police station, and Stern was happy, he never visited the city without calling in on the particular stall he had in mind. He parked the car in a small pay and display he'd used many times, and made his way across St Andrews, and down Exchange Street to the multi-coloured tented market area. Squirming through the shoppers crowding the narrow passageways between the stalls, he could see O'Connor already there leaning casually at the counter chatting to Bob, the stallholder.

"Mr Stern, as I live and breathe," Bob called as he approached. "Ain't seen you in an age. Why's that, my bangers not good enough for you anymore?"

"Far from it, Bob. Been away, can't wait to get my mitts on one right now."

Bob grinned. "That's my man. The usual?"

"As always."

Bob turned to O'Connor. "And the same for you, Inspector?"

"Might as well, Bob. Don't want to feel out of place, do I?"

Bob filled two polystyrene cups with strong steaming tea and handed them across. Then he turned to the back of the stall and the sizzling hot plate. Bob was particular with his food; everything cooked only on request. The sign on the front of the stall said it all. *'If you don't have time to wait a minute for the best, it's your loss.'* And for market stall food, it was the best. Until his excursion to Oz, Stern's constant returns were testimony to that.

O'Connor took a tentative sip of the scalding brew, smacked his lips. "So, what've you got for me?"

Stern followed suit with the tea, cradling the hot cup in his hands. "Interviewed Victor Adams this morning. Interesting."

O'Connor knew his friend, knew the signs. He cocked his head questioningly. "How so interesting?"

"Well, for a start, I've never met anyone called Adams with a broad Eastern European accent."

O'Connor's eyes narrowed suspiciously. "Eastern European? But Butler said he was local."

"He did," Stern confirmed. "But if you remember, Butler didn't know much about the guy at all. He only knew his first name. It was the missus who told us his name was Adams." He gave a shake of his head. "Not so. His name is actually Adamczyk." He smiled at O'Connor's confusion. "Not sure, couldn't quite get my tongue round it, but I think its pronounced Adamsick. He's Polish, only been here a couple of years. But he's adamant, says now he lives here, he's obviously local."

O'Connor gave a derisive twitch of his nose. "Yeah, right." He considered things for a moment. "I suppose he is legal?"

Stern watched Bob approach with two cardboard plates holding large buns, a long thick hotdog sticking out from each end, fried onions, fat and tomato ketchup dripping from the sides. "A small snack for two of my favourite customers. Even if one has deserted me for best part of a year."

Stern smiled his thanks. "You're a star, Bob."

They ate quietly for some time, huge mouthfuls preventing meaningful speech, constant use of the paper napkins supplied essential. Finally, it was Stern who laid down the half-finished bun, wiped his greasy mouth, and broke the silence.

"Don't know if he's legal, I'll leave that for you to check. But, David, I do know he wasn't telling me everything."

"In what way?"

"A couple of things. To start with, he was first on the scene, said a big bang woke him, and he dressed and ran down to the boat. When I asked if he saw anyone or anything on the banks or on the water, he said no. But his body language said differently. I don't know what, but something did happen that night, I'm sure of it. But whatever it was, our Victor wasn't prepared to tell us what it was."

O'Conner chewed on the final mouthful, swilling it down with the last of his tea and wiping his fingers. "And the other thing?"

"They didn't call the fire brigade. Said there was no point, the boat was on water, anyway."

"It's a point, I suppose. But the water didn't save much of it. The boat was totalled. Not a stick left."

Stern shook his head. "That's just my point. Think about it. You've got a boat sitting there, worth goodness knows how much, and you sit back and let it burn? I don't buy it. Wouldn't you instinctively call the fire brigade?"

"I suppose, but you have to remember Butler wasn't there at the time. Could be without his guidance they just panicked, didn't know what to do."

"Surely not. You see a fire, the first thing you do is to pick up the phone, call the brigade. You don't need guidance for that, do you? It's automatic."

"Okay, I hear what you say," O'Connor conceded. "But I can't think of any other reason why they would sit back and do nothing."

"No, I can't either. But something tells me it might be worth digging a little deeper."

Smiling, O'Connor shook his head. "That bloody nose of yours, Theo. Okay, so how do you want to play it?"

"Well, it might be a good idea if you check out our Polish friend, just to confirm he's kosher. And if it's okay with you, I'll rake around a bit more."

"Sure, just keep me up to speed."

"Will do. By the way, I haven't had a chance to check on our friend Ollie Preston, yet." He grinned. "Too busy running around looking after the local fuzz."

"Yeah, yeah, just let me know if you get something." He looked at his watch. "Anyway, unlike you, I haven't got time to stand around here eating hot dogs. I've got a proper job." He gave Bob a wave and turned to go. "Talk later."

"Yeah, will do." Stern turned to Bob. "Can you knock me up another one, Bob? I'm trying to make up for lost time." He looked back at a surprised O'Connor. "What? A man has to eat, for goodness sake." Then a thought struck him. "Whatever you do, don't tell Cherry."

~ * ~

Stern arrived back at the office around three. Cherry was there with a visitor, Doris Barford. Frowning questioningly, Stern crossed the office to Cherry's desk where they were sitting. "Problem?"

Cherry gave a shake of the head. "No, Doris has some news." She looked to Doris to carry on.

"I came to tell you my husband has a trip tonight. He told me this morning."

"Isn't it unusual for him to be told in advance?"

"Yes, it is. It's never happened before."

Stern collected a chair and pulled it up to Cherry's desk. "Did he say what time?"

"Yes, he said he would be leaving about one, but it shouldn't take more than a couple of hours. He said it was a special."

Stern gave it some thought. "A couple of hours. Not a long haul like last time then?"

Doris shook her head. "No, and I'm glad. It just kills him when he does that."

"Mmmm, I'm not surprised." Chewing his bottom lip, Stern was quiet for a while before continuing. "I guess your husband is out with the taxi right now?"

"Yes, he'll stay out as long as he has a fare."

"Good, I think this is what we've been waiting for. I was on the verge of confronting your husband, anyway. With luck, this will enable us to get something positive to confront him with." He pushed himself up from the chair and headed into his office. A few moments later, he returned carrying a small black instrument the size of a mobile phone in the palm of his hand. "Mrs Barford, this is a GPS tracker," he said, handing it to her. "It's already switched on and active, and it's magnetic. All you have to do when you get home is to place it somewhere out of sight on the van. Think you can do that?"

She took it from him, looking at it uncertainly. "I suppose so."

Stern held her troubled eyes, giving her a reassuring smile. "You don't have to worry, it won't bite. It's easy, just make sure it can't be seen, and that wherever you put it, the magnet holds fast. Has to be on the metal bodywork. Once it's on the van, you can forget it. We'll take it from there."

She cautiously slid the instrument into her bag. "Okay."

"Boss, Doris has a bit of a problem," Cherry broke in. "She needed to tell us about the trip, but now she needs to get back home before her husband gets back. Afraid the bus's timetable won't…"

"No problem, you take her home," Stern interrupted. "And there's little point in coming back here." He turned toward his office. "I'll see you in the morning." He paused at the door. "Expect me when you see me."

After the two women left, Stern sat with his feet up on the desk thinking quietly. All three of the current cases were beginning to come together. As far as the Barford case was concerned, tonight could well put that to bed. Then there was David's mystery note writer. This obviously linked to the boat fire. There were two avenues he needed to follow there. One was Victor Adamczyk, who he would lay money on had something to hide. One way or another, he had to establish what that something was. Then there was Charlie Croker's friend Ollie. His sudden disappearance after the fire was suspicious, to say the least. Stern felt sure, when he managed to get hold of him, Ollie would have a tale to tell. Hopefully, an enlightening one.

But first there was the Mo Steven's case. Pulling his notebook from his pocket, he located the number he was looking for and dialled. It took a number of rings before it was answered, the voice soft, tentative.

"Larry Wheeler?" Stern kept his voice level, authoritative. "This is Inspector Stern. Where are you...we need to talk."

<h1 style="text-align:center">Thirty-six</h1>

Larry Wheeler was not a happy man. He might be a bit of a loser, but he had never been in trouble with the law. Drink was his problem, and he cursed it every time he took a mouthful. But cursing it and giving it up were two different things. Even though he knew if it weren't for the booze he would never have fallen for the bullshit spiel Frank Cavendish had given him. It had started innocently enough, the occasional bottle for a job well done. Then, here and there, a small bonus. It was never very much…a tenner, twenty, but at supermarket alcohol prices enough to keep him going. That's all it was spent on. Rent for the tiny flat he dossed in never seemed a priority, so the final outcome was obvious. Cavendish came to the rescue with the caravan, even found a place at the back of a scrap metal merchant's breaker's yard. Said he couldn't see his friend living on the street. The site was as big a dump as the caravan, but at the time, to Larry, Cavendish was his saviour. He told him so, too, promised to do anything in return. Big mistake.

It was Cavendish who had first christened him his agent. Or to be precise; his agent for second-hand transactions. It was unofficial, of course, Cavendish had made it vehemently clear. Just between the two of them. And at the time, provided Larry could continue his regular visits to the supermarket, he was more than happy to comply.

Larry never did know what the scam was. Didn't know, didn't care. All he knew was it revolved around cars taken in on a part exchange basis. Those not up to the standard required to resell from the main dealership were sold off to the trade; smaller dealers selling lower quality vehicles. Larry delivered the car to the dealer, whichever one of the selected few Cavendish dealt with, got a signature, and returned with the thick sealed brown envelope. Job done.

Probably would have carried on too, but then Cavendish's missus went ape. Someone said she was being given a seeing-to on the side by a painter. Larry never did know the full story, not the sordid details, anyway. It was some while after when Cavendish approached him, reminding him of the time when he had promised to do anything in return for his earlier kindness. And there was a car in it, too.

When the police had ordered him off Blakeney and away from Cavendish's missus, he was so relieved he hit the road pretty damn quick. Then, reality had hit home, and he realised he had no idea where he could go. He had petrol in the car and a few quid in his pocket, but that wouldn't take him far. If he headed back to London, which had been his initial plan, he would never find anywhere to park the van and anyway, prices would rocket. He would also be heading straight back to Cavendish and whatever backlash that would bring. He, therefore, decided to follow the coast road north, find some cheap site to hide the caravan, and see if he could pick up some casual labour. He could stay out of the way for a while and give himself time to figure his next move. He made a mistake, though. He left his phone switched on. First, it was Cavendish pushing to see how things were going. Larry had simply lied, saying any time now he thought the lady would crack. Then things went from bad to worse and for the first time in his life he was on the cops' radar. This Inspector Stern and his sergeant were on their way to question him again. Larry felt like he was between the proverbial rock and a hard place, and he wasn't happy about it, not one bit.

~ * ~

When Stern managed to raise Larry Wheeler on the phone, he couldn't be sure how far he'd travelled. He wasn't unhappy when Wheeler admitted he had only got as far as the village of Holm-next-the-Sea. After they'd put the frighteners on him, Stern had expected him to be much further away. Holm-next-the-Sea, on the tip of the North Norfolk coast, was no more than thirty miles from Sheringham. An hour at most. Stern closed the office just after five and grabbed a leisurely fish and chip meal at the high street café before setting out.

He was half way there when his mobile rang. By the time he'd found a break in the grass verge and pulled in, it had stopped. He checked the screen and saw it was Cherry. He rang back, and she answered immediately.

"Sorry, I was driving, had to pull in. What's the problem?"

"No problem, I just wanted to ask you about the tracker. You never said..."

"No, sorry about that. I intended to brief you when I got back to the office, but Mrs Barford was there, and you had to run her home. There wasn't time. I did intend to ring you later."

"Okay, that's fine. Rob's out with the boys this evening, so I'll be here. Where are you now?"

"I'm on my way to interview Larry Wheeler about Cavendish." He glanced at the dashboard clock. "It's coming on seven, should be back by nine at the latest, okay?"

"Sure, that's fine. Anything I can think about in the meantime?"

Stern smiled. Typical Cherry, always buzzing, never able to wait. "I don't think so. I bought the tracker on line, and got Des to set it up for me." He was referring to the local computer expert based on the Sheringham High Street. Everybody used Des to sort their computer problems.

"Set it up?"

"Yeah, I took the laptop round to him the night before last."

"My laptop?"

He knew he was in trouble. "I know, I know, I should have told you. But you know how it's been. I just got waylaid."

"Boss, you mean all the info for the tracker is on my laptop?"

"Yeah, look I'm sorry..."

"No, it's okay. So, Steve Barford is out tonight with a tracker on his van, and it's all on the laptop?"

"Yes, but remember his wife said he wasn't due to leave 'till around one. And everything will be recorded, so we can check it out in the morning."

Cherry was quiet for a long moment then, "Boss, can I nip back to the office and pick up the laptop?"

"Now?"

"Yes, I can be there and back home in no time."

"Why? You can't lie awake all night watching the laptop screen. Rob would do his nut. Anyway, what would be the point?"

"Well, for a start I can check it's working," Cherry persisted. "Make sure Mrs Barford attached it to the van okay."

Stern gave a resigned sigh. Short of a positive 'no', he was on a loser here. He knew better than to argue. "You're bonkers, you know that?"

She gave a little laugh. "No, boss, I just love my work."

"You'll need the password."

"Okay, shoot." The excitement in her voice was obvious.

"Bechet. Capital B."

"Your favourite jazz man."

"Yup. And make sure you lock the office after you."

Thirty-five minutes later, after searching for some time to find the tiny field where Wheeler had secreted himself, Stern pulled the car alongside the old Audi. Immediately, he climbed out he could see there was a problem; the caravan was on the tilt, one tyre completely flat.

Wheeler was already waiting at the door. He saw Stern look down at the flat tyre. "Just managed to get in here before the bloody thing let go," he said sadly.

"You got a spare?"

Wheeler scowled. "You kidding?" He backed into the caravan. "You'd better come in."

Things were askew inside, but they managed to sit facing each other either side of the table. There was no sign of anything cooking, and more relevant, no sign of any booze.

Wheeler studied Stern with dark-rimmed worried eyes. "Am I in trouble, Inspector?"

Stern held a deadpan expression. He wasn't about to let him off easily. Not yet, anyway. "You do realise that for what you did you could be in very serious bother, don't you?"

Wheeler lowered his eyes despondently. "Yeah, I guess so. But I didn't intend... I mean I would never have hurt her."

"But you terrified her just the same." He gave a dismissive wave of his hand. "But that's not why I'm here. It's not you we're interested in right now. So lucky for you. If you cooperate fully, it's within my power to make things easy for you. Possibly even make this thing go away." He saw the hope spring to Wheeler's eyes. "Do you understand what I'm saying?"

"I do, honestly. And I will cooperate. Just tell me what you want."

"I need to know about the scam Cavendish was pulling."

Hope died as quickly as it had appeared. "But I don't know." He held up his hands, a resigned gesture. "He never ever told me anything about..."

"*Now look,*" Stern snapped out the words harshly. "If you're going to jerk me around."

"No, no, I'm just saying I don't know how it worked. I can tell you what I did, but that's all. Cavendish never confided in me. He called me his agent, but that was bullshit, just to build me up. He could have called me anything, but I was just his errand boy. Honest, Inspector, it's the truth."

Stern studied the pleading face for some time before finally deciding he was being told the truth. "Okay, tell me what you do know. And I want all of it, no convenient lapses of memory, got it?"

Wheeler thought for a moment before starting. "I only know it was to do with second hand cars, trade-ins. I think before, when Frank was the number two at the dealership, the boss man worked it. Then, when he retired, Frank took over. That's when he involved me."

"You mean cars part-exchanged for new ones?"

"Correct. All the salesmen bought and sold, but Frank dealt with the trade-ins, particularly those not at a standard to be resold from the dealership. They either went for auction or were sold on to lesser dealers. That's where I came in. It was my job to deliver the car and get the paperwork sorted."

Stern thought for a minute or two, mulling the situation over. "So, tell me about these other dealers."

Wheeler shrugged. "Just dealers, small outfits happy to take the leftovers."

"Back street setups."

"Well yes." Wheeler lowered his eyes.

Stern watched him closely, checking the telling eye movement. "A bit dodgy?"

"Your words, Inspector, not mine."

"Okay, I get the picture. Cavendish would have his favourites. Those he used regularly."

"Yes, he used three or four regularly."

"Right, so run me through the delivery routine exactly." As he said the words, he could see the tension build across the table.

"Frank would give me the keys and the registration documentation for the particular car. He would also tell me which dealer would be taking it. I would then drive the car to the dealer, get the paperwork signed up, and get a taxi back. Yes, that's all I did."

Stern knew there was something missing, he could feel it. "So, when you returned, you handed the paperwork to Cavendish personally."

"That's right, only to him."

Stern sniffed, his nose wrinkling as if to a bad smell. "What else did you hand over, Larry?" He held up a hand before Wheeler could answer. "And don't forget, you have just this one chance to come clean. Hold back, and I promise the boys in blue will be here to collect you before close of play today."

Wheeler's shoulders sagged. He was done, and he knew it. "A brown envelope." The words were little more than a whisper.

"A thick, sealed brown envelope," Stern persisted.

Wheeler gave a resigned nod of the head.

"Every time?"

"Every time."

Thirty-seven

The raised heartbeat was pumping blood at high pressure through Ollie Preston's veins, his breath rasping in short eager gasps. What was it they said...better than sex? In this instance, he couldn't agree more. Only once before in his whole life had he felt so exhilarated, so damned excited. That was when he'd torched the boat. God, how good had that felt? And even better was the fact everything had gone so perfectly. Okay, so not perfectly perfect, he had cut his hand, and left a little blood. Could have been a bit tricky. But as it turned out, it was no big deal. He hadn't attended hospital or a doctor. Hadn't left any evidence anywhere that could be traced to him. He'd sorted it himself and now, other than a scab, a little tender, it felt fine. So, yeah, he could say it had been almost perfect. So, he was about to do it again. Not the boat, of course, that was done and dusted. No, this was even better, this was something that would really make them sit up. If he was honest, he didn't care if the police were taking notice of his warnings or not. Now it was different, now, it was the thrill of the chase. He had the bit between his teeth, his blood was up, and he was relishing every dangerous minute. It felt so good he could do it for a living. But despite the pleasure of doing it, the reason behind it was the same. He would bring Butler to the law's attention as often as it took to make them realise what was going on. Butler had to pay for what he had done to Charlie, and Ollie was making sure he did.

He'd planned things down to the smallest detail, initially searching out the small inlet in the copse of trees almost a mile back along the A1151. Here, he could leave the car, undetectable unless someone pushed their way into the trees, not likely to happen in the dead of night. It meant quite a trek to the Butler house, but he'd covered that as well. The leather combat boots, thick trousers and heavy bomber jacket, all black. And best of all, the balaclava, only the eyes visible, woolly hat and gloves. Again, all black. Even the rucksack on his back was black. He was totally confident. In the completely dark small hours of the unlit Norfolk countryside, he was invisible.

He had also spent time reconnoitring the Butler residence. Not as last time from the opposite bank of the river, that would have been far too risky. This time, he'd hired a small day boat from a Wroxham boat yard. It was electric, quiet and unobtrusive, the sort seen gliding up and down the river all the time. From there, he was able to survey the security lighting dotted around the big house and its grounds. He was also able to detect the blind spot. It was a small window in the detached cottage sitting to one side of the main house. Where the man had taken the girl the night he had followed the Land Rover from Charlie's flat. To his disappointment, not the house itself as originally planned, it was too well protected. But this would do. For now.

Being some distance away from the house, the rear face of the cottage, with the little window was out of sight of the security cameras and lighting. More importantly it was accessible through the tall hedge dividing the Butler property from its neighbour. Ollie had studied it, checking it from every angle. Finally, he was certain it was perfect for what he had in mind.

Now, moving cautiously along the lane, he was keeping tight against the hedgerow. It was unlikely there would be anyone about at this time in the early hours, but should someone appear, he felt sure, all in black, he could melt unseen into the undergrowth.

With the briefest of flashes from the tiny pen torch he had brought with him, he confirmed he had reached the point where the two properties joined. He stopped, taking several long silent deep breaths in an attempt to calm himself before the next step. This is where he would break through the bushes and make his way along the neighbour's side of the hedge adjoining Butler's grounds. At the point adjacent the cottage, he would again break through the hedge into the area behind Butler's cottage.

He reminded himself he had to be more careful than ever. Breaking through shrubbery such as this was tricky, particularly because it would be so easy to leave evidence of his passing. A shred of cloth hooked onto a branch, a scratch from a sharp branch leaving the tiniest smear of blood, even a single hair. Modern forensics and DNA analysis could identify the tiniest trace of these things. He knew...he had seen it on TV many times. At the boat, he knew he'd been injured, had taken the necessary precautions. Here, it would be easy to leave a trace without even realising it. He must not let it happen. Not if he were to get away with this. And get away with it he would.

He dipped into one of the deep pockets set in each trouser leg and withdrew the sharp garden secateurs he'd purchased only the day before. Working by feel alone, he carefully clipped his way into the hedge. It took the best part of half an hour before he had cleared enough to first slide the backpack through unhindered, then ease himself carefully after it. One down, one to go.

Slowly and carefully, following the dividing hedge between the two properties, he made his way to a point he estimated to be adjacent to the cottage, and the target window. Again, using a brief flash of the torch to confirm his position, he was pleased to see he was only a foot or two out. Again, he reached for the secateurs and started work. It was easier this time, the hedge not so thick, a softer foliage. Less than fifteen minutes later, he was through and standing only a few feet from the wall of the darkened cottage. He moved silently forward, removing the rucksack, and placing it against the wall below the window. He then squatted down, resting his back to the wall, again taking long deep breaths for several minutes, feeling the tension, and the effort of getting so far slowly dissipate. Finally pushing himself to his feet, he turned and surveyed the window frame. It was dark inside, but he could just make out the folds of a curtain drawn closed. He ran his hands silently around the window frame, the adrenalin again picking up when he realised the small flip window at the top of the frame was slightly ajar. Ollie breathed a sigh of relief. On his surveillance trips from the electric boat on the river, he had studied the window through the little binoculars. On every occasion, the little flip window had been open, just slightly ajar as it was now. But that was in the daytime. He had no way of telling if it was closed at night, and a completely sealed window could have been the only sticking point in the whole plan. His decision to chance it anyway had paid off. Now, it should be plain sailing.

In the dark silence, even the plastic zip on the rucksack sounded loud as he gently, inch by inch, eased it open. He was familiar with the position of items inside; several times having practiced exactly what he was about to do in a blacked-out room at home. Before torching the boat, he had carried out a number of very successful tests of what he proudly called Charlie's Revenge. Now, he lifted it carefully from the holdall. It consisted of a small, sealed, liquid-filled plastic drinks bottle with a small tea light suspended centrally beneath in a wire cradle; the same configuration as a hot air balloon with a basket below. Attached to the neck of the bottle was a length of similar wire. The distance between the bottom of the bottle and the tea light was critical...it dictated the amount of time he had to escape, to be well away before things happened. The tests he had carried out had been essential to establish this. And the success of the boat burning had convinced him he had it just right. Now, for the second time, he was about to prove it.

First taking a moment to compose himself, to ease the tremor in his hands, he reached up and tied the free end of the string to the latch of the open window—he didn't want to have to waste precious time doing this while lowering the activated device into the room. This secured, he reached into his pocket and found the zip lighter. Holding Charlie's Revenge up in his left hand, he brought forward the lighter. As soon as the tea light was lit, he had to be swift, quickly lowering the whole thing through the open window to hang at the end of the string inside. He would then make his way back through the hedges to the road and to the hidden car. It would take some time for those in the main house to be woken by the fire—as it had when he had torched the boat—then panic would set in. He would be best part home before anyone even thought of anything but extinguishing the flames.

Ollie held the contraption up, so he could see its vague outline against the very slightly lighter sky. He had to concentrate, had to light it with the first flick of the lighter, to minimise the amount of time the surroundings were illuminated by the lighter's flame. Yes, concentrate, it had to be the first time.

And Ollie did concentrate. He concentrated so hard he failed to hear the sound of a very gentle tread on the soft grass behind him.

Thirty-eight

Later, the forecast was rain, but so far, though the cloud was becoming thicker and lowering, it remained dry. Stern was grateful as he plodded steadily along the beach, his mind in overdrive.

The previous evening he'd left a relieved Wheeler with a promise. As far as he was concerned, no further action would be taken against him. Stern was happy to do that because there were signs the guy was making a genuine effort to get himself together. The farmer whose field the caravan was parked on had offered him work throughout the summer at least. And with the work, as well as free parking of the caravan, the farmer, a genuine soul, had also promised to repair the flat tyre. There was also a small salary. Nothing spectacular, but enough to keep things afloat. The added bonus was Wheeler hadn't taken a drink since Stern and Cyril's first visit. Stern felt, with luck, Cavendish's ex-lackey might just get himself back on track. His last piece of advice before he left was for Wheeler to change his phone, at least get a new pay-as-you-go sim with a new number. That way he would keep Cavendish at bay.

Now, Stern was mulling over the Cavendish scam. He thought he knew how it worked, but without knowing exactly how second-hand car documentation was controlled he couldn't be sure. Not that it mattered. Cavendish was making cash on the side by skimming off his employer. That was fraud and illegal. But illegal or not, the dealership would be very unhappy about it. Stern treated himself to a little smile as he jogged up the steps from the promenade to his flat. He didn't think Mo Stevens would have much to worry about her ex-husband in the future.

Cherry was already in the office, pouring the usual two cups of coffee, when he arrived. She was wearing a white cardigan over a red, neatly fitting polka dot dress. It had become a favourite since she had been told by Dave downstairs how stunning she looked in it. And she did, too. This morning she was her usual bright self, though a little dark around the eyes. He knew why.

He crossed the office and threw his top coat over the hook. "You been up all night?"

She turned, holding the two mugs. "Thanks boss, you look pretty good, too."

Stern took one of the mugs from her. "Tired eyes was all I meant."

Cherry moved across and settled behind her desk. "Point taken."

He strolled over and stood behind her, looking down at the laptop. "What did Rob have to say about it?"

Cherry humphed. "Rob's night out with the boys involves one or two pints. Which means when he hits the sack, he's gone. I could have danced around the place naked under strobe lighting with Status Quo going full volume, and he wouldn't have been any the wiser."

Stern smiled. "The mind boggles." Taking a mouthful of coffee, he focussed on the screen. "So, what did we get?"

"Well, like Doris Barford said, her husband headed out at one. He drove east for best part of an hour and ended up at Winterton. Then…"

"Remind me where Winterton is," Stern broke in.

"On the coast. North of Caister, Great Yarmouth."

"Okay."

"It was difficult to see exactly where he stopped," Cherry went on. "Looked like he was almost on the beach." She shrugged and carried on. "Anyway, he was stationary for about twenty minutes before moving off again. This time for no more than five minutes before he stopped again in a tiny village called West Somerton."

"Don't know it," Stern said, downing some more coffee.

"Neither did I," Cherry agreed. "It's not on our standard road map, but I found it on Google maps. It's a little way in from the coast, close to the River Thurn."

"Okay, what then?"

"He was there for ten minutes max then drove off again. This time, he took the back lanes south until he joined the A47 to Dereham. Then, on the 1075, he continued on to Thetford, where he took the A11, ended up parking near the new roundabout at Barton Mills."

Stern nodded. "I know it. Only recently finished, if I remember." He downed the last of the coffee and crossed the room, replacing the empty mug on the makings tray.

"That's right," Cherry confirmed. "He stopped there for only ten minutes, then headed back up the 1065, and the 148 all the way home." She looked up at Stern.

Stern held her look, raising his eyebrows questioningly, knowing the answer to his next question would be ready and waiting. No need to even ask it.

"Four and a half hours round trip," Cherry said, giving him a smug smile. "Including stops. He was back home by half five this morning, and the van hasn't moved since."

Stern rubbed his chin thoughtfully. "Not quite the short trip he told his wife about then."

"No, but not another all-nighter."

Frowning, Stern eased himself onto the corner of Cherry's desk. "Okay, so first he stops somewhere close to the beach where he waits for twenty minutes. He then does a short hop to a place close to the river where he waits no more than five minutes." He inclined his head, again asking the question. "Right so far?"

"Yup. Then he drives all the way to Barton Mills where he stops again, this time another short one, before driving home."

Stern ran his fingers through his thick thatch. "Three stops. The coast, the river and Barton Mills." He eased himself off the desk and took a couple of paces across the office before turning back. "There's a concealed lay-by at Barton Mills, isn't there?"

Cherry thought for a moment, then snapped her fingers. "You're right, boss. It's behind a tall row of trees. Sheltered from the road. There's a café and toilets there, too. It's where people pull in to take a break, grab a cup of tea and a bite. Cars and lorries."

"True, but not that time in the morning. My guess is, unless a long-distance driver is doing an overnighter, the lay-by would be deserted." He thought some more before heading toward his office. "I think I'm beginning to understand what's going on here. Not sure about the stop at the river, but the rest makes sense." Reaching his office door, he spun round. "And I'm beginning to think the three cases we thought we had may have just become two. But that aside, I think it's time we had a chat with our Mr Barford, don't you?"

Stern just reached his desk and settled back in the old complaining chair when his phone rang. Cherry answered it in the outer office, calling out, "It's David."

Stern frowned, remembering he had spoken to O'Connor only the day before. He picked up his extension. "David, is there a problem?"

"You could say that, Theo. If you consider another corpse in the river being a problem."

Thirty-nine

The body was spotted early that morning by a passing cabin cruiser. It was floating face down, wedged against a reed bank about a mile down river from Wroxham Broad. Eventually pulled from the water by the Norfolk Broads police patrol, it was now in the hands of Norfolk CID, who had started investigations into its identity and cause of death. At this point, cause of death was not considered to be suspicious. Annually, many holidaymakers with little or no experience hire various types of boat to cruise the broads unaware of the dangers they could face. And every year, there is at least one case of death by drowning on the broads. Frequently alcohol is involved. This could yet be one of those cases. However, for some reason, O'Connor admitted to having a bad feeling about this one. He promised to make contact again and update Stern as soon as he received the results of the post-mortem. Meantime, Stern had made other arrangements; he was about to hire a taxi.

Stern parked the Scirocco in a free roadside space a hundred yards or so from the Cromer town centre. He pulled his collar close against the sharp breeze cutting in from the sea. Before he'd left the office, Cherry had contacted Doris Barford who had given her the make and registration number of her husband's car, and the taxi rank he used. Stern hoped Barford would be there and not already away with a fare. Three cars stood line astern in the roadside marked off space for taxis. The first in line was the one he was looking for. Stern moved alongside the car and looked inside. He had never met Steve Barford and had no idea what he looked like. But he knew instantly the large, bulky individual in the car had to be him. And with good reason. Ashen faced, mouth hanging open and head lolling awkwardly to one side, he was slumped in the seat fast asleep.

Stern rapped sharply on the window with his knuckles, and Barford jolted upright. He looked around, for a second confused about his whereabouts. Then, recognition dawning, smiling sheepishly, he wiped away the dribble from one corner of his mouth with the back of his hand. He thumbed down the window.

"Sorry, must have dropped off for a second."

"You looked out to the world to me."

Another sheepish smile. "Must be working too hard." He knuckled his eyes, blinked them into focus. "So, where to?"

Stern ignored the question. "Can I ride up front?"

"Sure." Barford leaned across and released the door.

Stern climbed in and secured the safety belt around him. "D'you know the cliff-top car park in West Runton?" West Runton was a tiny village further along the coast. It had a small unmade car park that ended literally at the cliff edge. It was an ideal place to while away a relaxed hour admiring the dramatic views out over the North Sea. In summer it was popular; this time of year, it was more than likely to be deserted. It was why Stern had chosen it.

"Yeah, I know it," Barford said. "Meeting someone there?"

"Yeah, wanted somewhere quiet to have a chat."

Barford started the car and pulled away from the curb. He looked sideways at Stern, his eyes dark rimmed, heavy lidded. "How you going to get back?"

"Well, I was hoping you would wait. I'll pay for your time, of course."

Barford gave a shrug. "You're the boss. You pay, and I'll wait."

"Thanks." Stern held the silence for a minute or two. "Do this for a living? Full time, I mean."

"Yup, seven days a week. While there's a fare, I'll take it. No option if you want to make a decent living."

"Mmmm, hard graft. It would explain why you're so tired, I guess. Not much of a home life."

Another little shrug of the shoulders. "I do my best."

They travelled the rest of the journey in silence, Barford finally steering the car onto the rugged unkempt surface of the empty car park. Cruising slowly and carefully up to the cliff edge, he cut the engine and hauled on the hand brake. He turned to Stern. "Looks like your meet hasn't arrived yet."

For some moments Stern kept his eyes front, looking out over the white tops, one after the other rolling in on a stiff onshore breeze. Finally, he swivelled quickly round, facing Barford, his back to the door. His words were short, abrupt. "D'you want to go to prison, Steve?"

Barford's head snapped round, his mouth open, as if he'd been slapped in the face. "What? How do you know my..."

"You heard," Stern growled. He didn't move, his expression impassive, eyes probing. "And I'm not in the habit of repeating a question."

Barford turned his heavy frame aggressively toward Stern. "Prison? What are you talking about?"

Stern didn't avert his searching gaze. "I'm just giving you the heads up, letting you know it's a seven to ten stretch for smuggling drugs." He was flying a kite here but attempts to bring drugs into the country via the Norfolk coast were not unheard of. Sometimes even illegal immigrants. And with the evidence given by the tracker, it was a good bet one or the other was happening here. "Seven to ten," he went on. "Don't sound very long, I suppose. If you say it quick. Depends on what you make of it. Bit of a bugger for the wife and kids, though." He watched whatever colour there was in Barford's cheeks drain completely away. But Barford was an ex-soldier, he didn't quit easily.

"I think you're off your bloody trolley, mate. You'd better get out of my car before I throw you out."

This time Stern did move. Shaking his head, he turned and reached for the door handle. "Yup, and I guess a big guy like you could do just that. But, let me tell you, if I leave this car now, the next visit you get will be from our boys in blue." His hand still on the door handle, he looked back and eyed Barford steadily. "They will inform you that they have detailed records of every one of your nightly jaunts." He held the silence, letting his words sink in before upping the pressure. "Because the satellite tracker they fitted to your van gave them all the information they needed."

Barford's whole body stiffened. "A tracker..." he stuttered. "But..."

Stern didn't let him finish. "They will then inform you of your rights and ask you to accompany them to the station. Then, Steve, my old son, it will be the inevitable slippery slope. And I predict seven if you're lucky, but more likely a ten stretch. So, if you insist on trying to bluff it out, I'm out of here, and you're on your own." As he again swung back to the door, making to pull at the door handle, he felt a firm grip on his elbow.

"Jesus, no..." Quivering lips tried, not very successfully, to form a sentence. "I don't know...I just drove like they said..."

Stern released the handle and swung back to face an ashen face and wide dark eyes. His expression showed no compassion for the obviously terrified Barford. "I know exactly what you did, and more to the point, so did you. So, don't come the innocent with me. You were in it for the money, and you didn't give a toss where you went or what you were carrying." Stern was well aware he was pushing his luck here. He only had details of the last trip, and only the one route. Though he could guess, he didn't know for sure what was being carried. Now, if he kept up the pressure, he felt he could find out.

Barford took a bottle of water from under the dash and gulped down several mouthfuls, trying to compose himself. Finally, a little more under control, he took a deep breath. "So, who are you," he asked, his voice a harsh whisper.

"My name is Stern, and I'm a special investigator attached to the Norfolk CID." He was working the special investigator handle to death. But why not, it had worked well so far.

Barford sighed heavily, lowering his eyes, studying shaking hands clasped in his lap. "Christ, up to my armpits then," he murmured.

"That depends." Stern still held the hard, officious tone. "If you insist on maintaining the innocent line, yes. But you can open up, tell us everything, and help us get to whoever's heading up this lot. Then, with luck, you could end up with a suspended. No promises, but it's the best you can expect."

A ray of hope flickered in Barford's dark, troubled eyes.

~ * ~

It was mid-afternoon, and Cherry was impatiently waiting for Stern's return. She didn't know how Barford would have reacted when confronted, but she had no doubt, one way or another, the boss would get what he was after. She just couldn't wait to hear how it went. In the meantime, she had spent the time checking files that didn't need checking and tidying things that didn't need tidying. It was just after three when the phone eventually rang. Over time it had become routine for Stern to call and inform her when he was on his way back from an appointment or meet. She clocked the phone's screen as she picked up. It wasn't Stern. "Stern Investigations."

"Cherry, it's David. Is he there?"

"No, I'm sorry David. He's not. But I am expecting him any time. Can I take a message, or shall I get him to ring you?"

"Both I think, but first a question for you. The guy Theo is looking for regarding Charlie Croker. You know the one at The Beehive pub."

"You mean Ollie Preston?"

Cherry heard the heavy sigh on the other end of the line. "Yeah, that's what I thought. Better get him to ring me as soon as he gets in."

"Sounds ominous."

"You could say that. The body in the river has been identified. It's Ollie Preston. You can tell Theo the doc has brought our notice to a partly healed pretty nasty cut on one of the corpse's hands."

Forty

It was well after five when Stern arrived back at the office. He'd phoned ahead as usual, and Cherry had been sparking, unable to tell him the news fast enough, making it clear, however late, she was going nowhere until he returned, and they'd talked. As he walked through the door, he could smell the coffee brewing and, to his surprise, a large cream bun on a folded paper napkin was sitting next to the makings. Frowning, he threw his topcoat over the hook.

"What's with the goodies?"

"Lots to talk about. Thought we might be here a while. Didn't want you getting hungry. Anyway, Dave was closing shop, it was spare."

"Which means you didn't have to pay for it."

Cherry grinned. "'Course not."

Stern walked across and picked up the bun. "Okay, let's get to it then."

Minutes later, they were ensconced in his office, usual positions, Stern munching a mouthful of cream bun.

"Did David give you anything else?"

"No, just the name, and the news about the cut on the hand. But he said it was important you ring him soonest."

Stern held up the remains of the bun. "Okay, soon as I finish this."

Cherry fidgeted on the chair. "So how did it go with Barford?"

Stern swallowed a chunk of bun and swilled it down with coffee. "I played the special investigator ticket again, and after a little persuasion he came clean. But he pleaded ignorance to any detail." Stern saw the confusion on her face. "He admitted picking up packages and, sometimes people, but swore he didn't know what was in the packages, or who the people were."

Cherry gave a derisive snort. "Rubbish. He must have."

"Of course, he did. He's no fool. He knew what he was up to alright. I gave him the option, tell me all, and he would get consideration for helping the police with their enquiries, or I'd hand him over to the boys in blue. Told him he'd be facing a ten stretch. I don't think we need to worry about him just now, he's going nowhere. Fact, he's probably at home crying on his wife's shoulder as we speak"

"Did you tell him it was his wife who put us on to him?"

"No, that'll be up to her." He wiped his fingers on the napkin and picked up the phone. "And the more I think about it, the more I'm convinced we have a link here. Before we go any further, though, I'll talk to David." He hesitated before dialling. "Are you okay? Shouldn't you be on your way?"

Cherry gave a very positive shake of her head. "Are you kidding? I've already called Rob. He's happy. He's got a microwave curry, and there's footie on the box. I wouldn't have got much out of him if I was there."

Stern shrugged and dialled the number, at the same time hitting the speaker button.

O'Connor's thin metallic sounding voice answered after the first ring. "Theo, thanks for coming back."

"S'okay. I needed to talk to you, anyway. Something I've picked up. But you first."

"Well, as I'm sure Cherry has told you, we've identified the body found in the river as Ollie Preston."

"Yup, she has. She also told me about the damaged hand."

"Just to fill you in on a couple of things. Firstly, the way the guy was dressed."

"That's important, is it?"

"Yes, I think so. See, he was all in black. From head to toe, even a black balaclava."

Stern gave it some thought. "You think he might have been up to something before he went in the river?"

"It's a possibility. Can't think of any other reason for him to be skulking around at night all in black, can you?"

"Suppose not. You said a couple of things."

"I did. It was also the fact the body was pulled from the river not a million miles from the Butler place."

"Interesting." Stern thought for a beat. "So, we have a guy with a damaged hand who went AWOL after the burning of the boat and has now been found in the river close to where the dirty deed was done."

"You've got it. My thinking exactly."

"We're just on the same wavelength, David. Don't forget the last note threatened more action." He thought for a beat. "Any reports of problems at the Butler place last night?"

"No, nothing."

"Well, being all in black as he was, maybe Preston was about to take the action he threatened us with when something happened to stop him."

"Exactly what I was thinking," O'Connor came back. "And you know what that could mean, don't you?"

"I do. It could mean we've found our mystery note writer. But what happened for him to end up in the river, I wonder?"

"Don't know, but there's something else you should know," O'Connor went on. "We haven't had the full report from the coroner yet, so nothing is confirmed. But I've been given an initial heads up. The doc tells me Preston's neck was broken."

"Mmmm, not drowned then."

"Maybe not, but don't let's jump to any conclusions yet, Theo. Not until we get the full SP from the coroner. I'll let you know as soon as it comes in."

"Thanks, I'll look forward to it."

There was a moment's thoughtful silence before either spoke again. Then O'Connor said, "'Course I suppose it could all just be a coincidence. Whatever Preston was up to may have had nothing at all to do with Butler or the note writing."

"Always possible," Stern agreed. "But I keep thinking about the damaged hand. And you know how I feel about coincidence."

"I do. We shall have to see. Anyway, Theo, the point is, as always, I'm up to my eyeballs in the swamp with only a few to keep me afloat. Don't have to cry in my beer to you, do I? If anybody knows the score, it's you. So, I'd appreciate it if you were able to cover for me on this one."

"How?"

"Well, I have Preston's address, and I need to give it the once over. Could you do that for me? See if you can find anything relevant?"

"Not a problem. Where did he live?"

"Norwich north, the Sprowston area."

"Okay, I know it. Let's have the address, and I'll go first thing in the morning."

"Thanks. And there's something else."

"Oh?"

"Tomorrow just happens to be Constable Wainwright's day off. He's asked if he could accompany you. Mufti, of course. And only if you're happy."

Stern didn't hesitate. "I see no reason why not. He's a good man. It's all good experience, too."

"Thanks, Theo. He's with me right now, grinning like a Cheshire. I've given him the address. He's got a bunch of keys found on the body. Pretty sure the front door key will be among them. Something else...there's a car key there, too. Be interesting to see if the car is at the address. If not, I guess we'll have to put out an APB."

"Okay, we'll see when we get there."

"By the way, d'you want Wainwright to pick you up? He says he knows the area quite well."

Stern paused, glanced at Cherry, saw disappointment. "Sure, as long as he has room for three. See, I would've taken Cherry, she's much more observant than I am." He watched the smile break.

They heard O'Connor ask the question of Wainwright. "He says not a problem, bags of room," O'Connor came back. "He'll be at your flat around half nine, okay?"

"Sure, we'll be waiting."

Forty-one

They headed south on the 149 to Norwich, arriving at the city's outer ring road, and breaking left. Wainwright drove confidently, confiding he had completed the police advanced driving course. Leaving the ring road, they took the A1151 Wroxham road for a mile or so before spotting the right turn they were looking for.

"Blue Boar Lane." Stern chuckled. "Interesting name."

Wainwright smiled. "Yeah, don't know the origin but the Blue Boar pub's just up the road. They say it's good." He looked sideways at Stern. "As good as anywhere for lunch, if you are interested later."

"Okay, we'll see how the time goes."

They made another right turn into an estate of mainly semi-detached bungalows. They were typical, Stern thought, of the seventies and eighties era; mostly straight fronted with a one car length drive leading to a garage at the side. Cruising slowly, they finally found Preston's address.

Externally, compared to most of those around it, it looked tired and shabby. The front door and window frames hadn't seen a paintbrush in an age, and the windows themselves were dirty and dulled. The tiny front garden was a square of yellowing grass surrounded by what should have been flower beds but was just a jumble of weeds. The property stood out among its well-maintained neighbours. Wainwright pulled onto the short driveway, and they climbed from the car, for a moment standing surveying the surroundings.

"He was a bachelor," Wainwright said. "Looks like he wasn't too worried about appearances."

Exactly on cue, as if hearing the constable's words, the front door of the attached property was opened, and a small elderly man emerged. He stood for a moment watching them, then, as if making a decision, he made his way across to the low hedge dividing the properties.

"'Bout time you got here," he said, pulling his shoulders back aggressively, an attempt to make full use of every inch of his height. Somehow the fluffy carpet slippers diminished the effect. "Bloody disgrace, if you ask me," he chirped on. "Must have been onto your lot a hundred times. Going to need a second mortgage to pay me bloody phone bill." He waved a hand indicating his neighbour's property. "So? What you going to do about it?"

Wainwright took a step forward, dwarfing the man, looking down questioningly. "Do about what, sir?"

The man gave an exaggerated, frustrated snort, crossing his arms across his puffed-out chest. "About the state of that place, of course. Makes a mockery of all the hard work everybody else puts in. I haven't worked hard all my life to end up living next door to a place like this, you know."

"No, I don't suppose you have, sir. But just who do you think we are?"

As he craned his neck, looking up at Wainwright's imposing bulk the first shadow of doubt crossed the little man's eyes. "The council, of course. You are the council, aren't you?"

Wainwright reached into his pocket and produced his warrant card, holding it down so the man could see. "No, sir, we are the police. But now you're here, could you tell me your name, please?"

Clearly taken aback, the man floundered for a second. "Ah, well I didn't realise, did I? I thought…"

"Yes, of course you did, sir," Wainwright broke in. "But your name, please."

"Er yes, it's Large, Anthony Large. And like I said I didn't…"

"It's perfectly okay, sir." Wainwright casually slid the warrant back into his pocket and retrieved a notebook, purposefully and very slowly making a note of the name. "We may need to speak to you again a little later, Mr Large, but for now that'll be all." He returned the notebook back into his pocket. "Oh, and I'm sorry you can't get any response from the council, but unfortunately, there's little we can do about that. Never mind, you know what they say; if at first you don't succeed…" Smiling, he turned away.

The man immediately spun on his heel and shuffled a little less aggressively than on the outward trip back to his front door, muttering as he went. "Well, they looked like the bloody council to me."

Wainwright produced the bunch of keys found on Preston's body and headed for the front door of the bungalow, commenting softly as he went. "Name fits his attitude more than his stature."

Stern smiled. "And you can bet your boots in five minutes the whole street'll know we're here."

Inside, the layout was typical of many other standard estate-type, two-bedroom bungalows built by the large UK property developers of the period. In this case, the condition inside was a reflection of the outside. The front door opened onto a hallway running from front to back, a narrow threadbare carpet running the whole length. A single light bulb hanging from the ceiling was shadeless, and sad flower-patterned wallpaper, the blooms hardly discernible, covered the walls. Two doors on the right led to bedrooms. The first housed a double bed with a bare, stained mattress, a dark wood wardrobe, and a matching chest of drawers. In the second room, there was a single bed and a small wardrobe with one drawer beneath. The bed was unmade as if someone had just climbed out. The décor in both rooms was as ancient as that in the hall.

The first of the two doors on the left of the hallway opened to a small sitting room, its window looking to the front. It was sparsely furnished, the floor covered in another well-worn carpet, and two armchairs both angled to face an old-style television in one corner. No wide screen here. A well-used, two element, electric fire stood on the hearth in front of an open fireplace grate. The curtains, drawn closed, had at one time been attractive burgundy velvet. Now, they hung limp and dulled. A cursory glance at the two remaining rooms; a kitchen and, at the far end of the hallway, a bathroom, showed the same signs of neglect as the rest of the premises.

After Wainwright, as efficient as ever, produced three pairs of standard police issue thin latex gloves, they decided to split their efforts, each taking separate rooms. While Cherry was assigned the sitting room, and Wainwright the kitchen and bathroom, Stern chose to investigate the bedrooms.

It took only moments to confirm the double bedroom was as abandoned as it seemed. Both the wardrobe and the chest of drawers were completely empty, and a check beneath the stained mattress revealed nothing. The second bedroom, obviously being used, Stern assumed by Preston, revealed little more. First, on opening the wardrobe, he could see Preston had little in the way of clothes. There was a suit, two pairs of trousers, a pair of jeans and a couple of shirts. The suit was dark and shiny with wear. The trousers and shirts had also seen better days. A search of the pockets revealed nothing. The drawer beneath contained some underwear, a couple of ties, and some frayed handkerchiefs. He spent a few moments scanning the room, below the bed, again under the mattress and on top of the wardrobe, before giving it best.

Leaving the bedroom, Stern made his way across the hall to the sitting room where he found Cherry searching beneath the cushions of the armchairs. "Anything?"

Cherry wrinkled her nose. "Not unless you're interested in some crumbs and old crisps. There're even a couple of dried up chips." She brushed her gloved hands together, bits of dust and other debris falling to the floor. "Otherwise nothing."

Stern casually scanned the room. "The guy certainly lived a pretty frugal existence."

They left the sitting room and moved down the hallway. Paul Wainwright was just emerging from the bathroom. He was shaking his head, his mouth drawn down in distaste. "Nothing of interest in there, but I'd give it a miss if I were you." He took a breath, exhaling heavily. "Don't think the windows have ever been opened."

Stern held out a hand. "Okay, let me have the keys, and while you two give the kitchen the once-over, I'll check the garage, see if the car is there."

Outside, Stern found the appropriate key and lifted the up and over door. The garage was empty, but he was immediately hit by the heavy smell of petrol. He crossed to the rear of the area where a small bench had been erected under a window looking out into the back garden. On the bench was a petrol can. It was open, the screw cap lying alongside. Stern lifted the can, feeling the liquid move inside. Its weight indicated it was still at least half full. The obvious source of the heavy smell. He replaced the cap and scanned the rest of the bench top, noting the pliers, wire cutters and the roll of plastic covered wire, the type normally used for various jobs around the garden. A length of this wire had been hooked to the beam directly above the bench and hung down to within a couple of feet of the bench itself. The free end of the wire had been shaped into a hook, as if to hang something on. Stern wondered what that something might be. Other items scattered around were also puzzling. There were a number of small plastic drinks bottles cast to one side of the bench, the bottom of each black and melted, one or two almost completely destroyed. And pushed to the back of the bench were several tea lights, some used, some not. Stern was pondering the scene when Cherry appeared at the garage door.

"Boss, you'd better come and have a look at this."

Forty-two

As far as Stern was concerned, the various finds at the Preston bungalow meant there was little need to continue further. There was now no doubt Ollie Preston was guilty of writing the notes and through the notes had admitted burning the Butler boat. If O'Connor felt it necessary, when his manpower allowed, he could carry out a more detailed investigation of the property and Preston's affairs before handing it back to the relevant authority. Stern had achieved his aim; he had confirmed the identity of the note writer and arsonist. The downside was at this time that individual was dead, which meant any proof of the motive behind his actions had died with him. Nevertheless, Stern was convinced he at least had a handle on the background to a very sorry saga.

A call to O'Connor confirmed it was pointless for them to travel back to Sheringham when they were so close to the Norwich police headquarters. Less than twenty minutes after securing the bungalow, they were in O'Connor's office seated around his desk.

O'Connor was studying the piece of paper handed to him by Stern. He was shaking his head. "Where d'you find this?"

"Large as life. Top sheet of a writing pad on the worktop in the kitchen," Wainwright said.

"Mmmm, says it all I guess," O'Connor mused. "Obviously planned to send it to me after he'd done whatever he intended to do."

"Well whatever it was, he never got round to it," Stern said.

"No, he didn't," O'Connor agreed. "And for your information, the coroner has confirmed Preston's neck was broken."

Stern gave a slow thoughtful nod of the head. "Not drowned then?"

"Nope, he was dead before he hit the water."

Cherry winced. "Which means murder?"

"Looks like it," O'Connor replied. "And I'm getting a little fed up with finding dead bodies in our rivers."

"Well, nobody would have wanted this to happen," Stern said. "But from the wording on this note, he was getting a taste for his daring do's." He took the note from O'Connor.

"*Told you if you didn't do something I would,*" he read out loud. Then, "*Now it's too late. Whatever you do, next time it's the big one. So, stand by, inspector.*"

He slid the note back on the desk. "If he hadn't been stopped, goodness knows what he would have come up with next. A profiler would have probably nailed him from the outset. You know, a loner with no family and with nothing going for him, but a game of darts every now and then suddenly finds some spice in his life."

"It seems in this case that spice all started with the death of his friend. Which he obviously blamed on Butler," Cherry said.

"Mmmm," Stern pursed his lips thoughtfully. "It could have started that way, I suppose. But like I said, he seems to have got a taste for it. Looks like he was going to carry on hitting Butler, whatever David did." He pointed at the note again. "He said so."

O'Connor drummed his fingers on the desk. "You say there was no car at Preston's place?"

Stern shook his head. "No, but there was a car key on the key ring you gave me. A Ford tab."

"Okay, I'll get a search out for that. But let's take a step back. The official verdict on Croker was death by misadventure. He got himself dosed up with a combination of drink and drugs and fell into the river and drowned." He waved a warning finger. "And we only have Preston's notes alleging anything different. Now, ask yourself this; if Preston did know, and could actually prove Croker was moonlighting for Butler, and, as a result, for some reason got himself killed, why didn't he just come in and tell us everything face to face?"

They sat in silence for a time, each with their own thoughts. It was Stern who spoke first.

"What if he was involved?"

"What?"

"What if Preston was also involved in whatever Croker was up to?"

"I get what you're saying," Wainwright said. "You mean when Croker was killed, it ended for Preston as well?"

"It's a thought," Stern mused. "It would give Preston two reasons for being so bitter. First, whatever cash he was pulling in by helping Croker would stop. And he would have also lost his friend. From what we've been told, Croker was probably the only friend he had."

O'Connor eyed Stern closely. "You're suggesting he wouldn't come in because he was scared we might nail him for his involvement in whatever he and Croker were up to?"

Stern rubbed thoughtfully at his chin. "A bit nebulous, I admit, but nothing else comes to mind."

"What about money?" Cherry came in. "We found the stash in Croker's flat, but there was no sign of any in Preston's bungalow." She gave a smile. "There was no indication Preston had spent any either. Not like Croker."

"Good point," Stern came back.

O'Connor raised his hands. "Okay, where do we go from here?"

"Well as I see it," Stern said. "It depends on whether we believe what Preston was trying to tell us or not. If we do, then all roads lead to Butler. But first, there's something else." Eyeing O'Connor, he paused for a moment, collecting his thoughts. "Last time we spoke,

I said I had something to tell you. But when you requested us to search the Preston place, I put it on hold."

O'Connor inclined his head questioningly. "Something to do with this?"

"Possibly. See, round about the same time you approached me about Croker and the mystery notes, Cherry took on a private case. It was a woman who was worried about her husband. He's a taxi driver who'd suddenly started to take on other delivery jobs…" He looked hard at O'Connor. "At night." He saw the interest flare, an instant connection made, O'Connor's training clicking in. He held up a restraining hand. "Yup, I know what you're thinking, David, and I've thought exactly the same. But right now, there's nothing at all to say there's a link. So, before we go off half-cocked, I'd like time to dig deeper."

"D'you know what kind of deliveries this guy's making?"

Stern shook his head. "I have my suspicions, but no solid proof of anything. So right now, a straight answer is no. But I've hit the guy once just to let him know we're onto him. I'm letting him stew for a bit, but he knows I'm coming back." Stern checked his watch. "Today's Thursday; give me 'till close of play Saturday. I'll have the full SP by then. If there is a connection between what this guy's doing, and what Croker was up to, I'll find out. If not, nothing's lost, right?"

O'Connor looked doubtful. "Why Saturday? Why not tomorrow? We could be talking two murders here, Theo. I don't want to hang around."

"I know, I know, but I have another client to visit as soon as we get back to Sheringham today, and tomorrow's already booked. Besides, if what I have is anything like I suspect, we could be onto even more than the murders." He let the words sink in for a beat before pushing on. "Surely must be worth twenty-four hours."

O'Connor finally gave a nod, but only slowly, suspiciously. "Okay, Saturday it is. Meantime I'll see what else I can rake up about Preston and get a search going for that car."

Forty-three

Unable to drag herself away, Mo Stevens stared out of the window in anxious anticipation. The scene outside was as enticing as ever, but just for once, her canvas stood untouched, and her brushes lay idle. Even though she knew, if he came at all, he shouldn't be here for another hour, she couldn't help taking another look at her watch. Just two minutes had passed since the last glance.

Mo's mind flipped back to the call that only yesterday afternoon Theo Stern insisted she make. The one she'd initially adamantly refused to even consider. But Stern and Cherry had driven to her cottage specifically for the purpose. And he had been patient, eventually convincing her, if she wanted this thing to be over, it was what she needed to do. Stern had rehearsed her well, giving her the confidence she needed. But when the time came, she had floundered, only collecting herself when Cherry had laid a hand reassuringly on her arm, giving her a tight smile of confidence.

She recalled how her hands had been shaking, and Stern had dialled for her, handing her the mobile once it started to ring. The call had been answered almost immediately.

"Cavendish."

"It's Mo," she just managed, her mouth completely dry.

The silence was long, sparking immediate tension. "What do you want," he said finally, his voice low...she felt an attempted menace in his words.

She looked down at the piece of paper, her prompt, held in trembling fingers, then at Cherry giving her that encouraging smile.

"Wheeler's been dealt with," she read, trying with all her might to keep the tremor from her voice. "You won't hear from him again."

"What?"

Mo looked up at Stern, his finger held vertically tight across his lips, indicating for her to say nothing. She held her breath, the silence seeming to last for ever.

"What have you done?"

She ignored the question, again reading from her prompt. "You want this over, want what you're after, you need to come here, face me yourself. If you..."

He didn't let her finish. "No way. You hand over what's mine or I'll..."

Suddenly, the anger flared and, for an instant, Mo ignored the prompt. "Or you'll what?" she snapped back. "If you think your stupid errand boy scared me, you'd better think again. He's been dealt with, and there's only one way you'll get your money." The unrehearsed words spat out, the anger drained as quickly as it had erupted. She frantically looked from Stern to Cherry, who was grinning broadly, giving her the thumbs up with one hand and pointing at the prompt with the other. Mo's eyes scanned the sheet, her finger tracing the words, searching for the right place. Finding it she took a deep breath, exhaling slowly. "You know where I am," she read softly. "Be here at three sharp tomorrow, or the police will have everything by four, and I'll see you in court."

"You bi..."

She remembered quickly tapping the red icon on the phone, gratefully cutting him off.

Now, almost twenty-four hours later, there was just an hour to go before she would again come face to face with the man she once loved and thought she would spend the rest of her life with. The man who for some inexplicable reason she had betrayed. As she stared through the window, the guilt flooded over her. How had she allowed it to happen? How had she let her head be turned so easily? And by a man who as soon as he saw danger looming was suddenly no longer there. It was her fault, and her fault alone. But she wasn't alone in her guilt. Though it could never justify her own treachery, the only small consolation she could hang on to was that he, too, had betrayed her. He had squirreled away a great deal of money, illegal money, without her knowledge. Why would he have done that?

She was abruptly pulled from her reverie by the crunch of tyres on the gravel outside. For a heart stopping moment, she thought he had come early. And she was alone. Then, her head clearing of sad memories, she was fully back in the moment, recognising the car, and the two men climbing from it.

The three of them sat round the table, Stern and Cyril Makepeace casually drinking the coffee she had made, Mo's, untouched, cooling in front of her.

"We'll give him an hour tops," Stern said. "If he's not here by then, you'll have to do the right thing. There's no point in hanging onto the money any longer."

Mo knew he was right. The money had been obtained illegally. By keeping it, she was compounding a criminal act. She could even be charged with aiding and abetting. She sighed. "Okay, I just want this to be over."

"It will be," Stern assured her. "It's in your favour that you haven't touched a penny of it, and I will testify that you only held on to the money for your own protection." He gave her a reassuring smile. "You'll probably get another slap on the wrist, but you're used to slaps on the wrist, aren't you?" He turned to Cyril. "Might be a good idea if you make yourself scarce when he arrives, mate. I don't expect him to try anything physical, but you never know."

Cyril gave a knowing smile, thinking back to the days, when they were both a good deal younger, when sometimes it had taken even more than two to pile in and apprehend certain elements of the London lowlife. Cuts and bruises had been the order of the day, sometimes more, but back then, they wouldn't have had it any other way. For them both, it had been far from just a job. It was a dedicated vocation, a way of life. "Sure. I'll be in the kitchen."

It was no more than a few minutes after three when, again, the crunch of wheels on gravel outside alerted them to the arrival of a car. Stern took a furtive peep through the side of the window. "Yup, it's an Audi; he's here."

Cyril stood and headed for the kitchen. "I'll keep an ear out."

Stern took Mo by the shoulders. "No hesitation, okay? Stay positive and most of all, don't let emotion get in the way."

She was wringing her hands anxiously but gave him a sharp, tight lipped nod of her head.

Stern watched from behind the edge of the curtain as Cavendish left the car and stood for a moment looking around the area, his nose wrinkled disdainfully. He was dressed immaculately in a dark blue suit over a slightly lighter blue shirt and burgundy tie. The shoes were soft tanned leather. Despite the expression of contempt, there was a tension in his body and his eyes flicked uncertainly from side to side. Stern smiled and returned to the table, relaxing back in the chair.

Mo answered the knock on the door and, without a word, immediately stood back, allowing her ex-husband to enter. Cavendish strolled confidently into the room desperately trying to hold onto the superior smirk of distain. Then he saw Stern. He stopped abruptly, the expression faltering, eyes again scanning back and forth across the room. His head snapped round to face Mo. "Who the hell is this? You didn't say anything about..."

Saying nothing, Mo moved past him and made her way to the table, taking the chair alongside Stern.

Stern spoke quietly. "What? Didn't say anything about making sure she had a little protection?"

Cavendish stood uncertainly. "Protection? What are you talking about? Why would she need protection?" His nostrils flared aggressively. "And who are you, anyway?"

"Firstly, any woman living on her own has every reason to ask for protection when someone sends a man with a knife to terrorise her."

"What? A knife?" Cavendish waved an erratic finger in the air. "Oh, now come on, I never said anything about a knife. I just told him to..."

"And secondly," Stern snapped, cutting him short. "My name is Stern, and I'm working with the Norfolk CID." A blatant lie, but he needed the clout, and, under the circumstances, he doubted he would be asked for any identification. "I am here at the express wish of your ex-wife and, as a result of this meeting, will be deciding what action should be taken against you."

Cavendish stood stunned. "Against me?" He pointed at Mo. "But she...It was her..." he spluttered.

Stern indicated toward a chair. "I think it would be a good idea if you took a seat."

Cavendish held Mo's eyes, an expression of disbelief flooding his face. "How could you? Why would you do this?"

Seeing her mouth working, words about to pour out, Stern raised a hand in front of Mo's face, motioning her to silence. "Come and sit down, Mr Cavendish. If you want this business resolved to everyone's advantage, we need to talk."

Cavendish stood for a long moment before reluctantly moving to the table and sullenly slumping into a chair opposite Stern. He said nothing, his eyes never leaving his ex-wife's face.

Stern leaned forward and rested his elbows on the table. "Look, Mo has briefed me on this whole sorry situation and has made it clear from the very start she was totally to blame for the collapse of your marriage."

Cavendish gave a derisory snort. "You bet your sweet life she was. If it hadn't been for..."

Stern waved him to silence, stopping the rant mid-sentence. "But what she did had no bearing whatsoever on your fraudulent activities," he continued sharply. "Because that's where this money came from, wasn't it? Your little dodgy deals on the side."

Cavendish glared silently at Stern for a tense moment before breaking eye contact.

Stern pushed on. "And the truth is, you were stashing away your ill-gottens long before your wife went off the rails, weren't you?"

Again, jaw clenched determinedly, Cavendish said nothing.

Stern shook his head. "Saying nothing at this time will get you nowhere. Mo is willing to do whatever is necessary to make things right here. Unless you do the same, there's only one way for this to go, and that's straight to the courts. So, for the good of you both, I suggest you stop this pathetic hard man attitude."

There was another protracted silence before the determination crumbled and Cavendish lowered his eyes. "It just seemed to happen," he said, his voice little more than a whisper. "He said it was the perks of the job."

"He? Who was he?"

Cavendish raised his head, looking to Stern, his eyes dark with worry. "When they made me number two in the dealership, the top man, the manager, briefed me. He said nobody suffered. The customers weren't ripped off, and the other dealers, the back-street guys, had a good deal, too. They were more than happy to come across."

"And the paperwork was kosher, right?"

"Always. We made sure of it. All I had to do was take my cut." He gave a sad shrug of his shoulders. "When he retired, and I got the top job, it just carried on as always. It seemed natural."

"And you never thought to talk to me about it?" Mo asked, the disappointment obvious in her words.

"How could I? You were a solicitor, for Christ sake. It would have put you in an impossible position." He turned back to Stern. "The problem was the money just built up. I couldn't start spending big because it would have raised questions. We had a large mortgage, and, with all the other commitments, our combined income was pretty well spoken for. So, I couldn't just start throwing money about. And for the same reason, large deposits in the bank were also out of the question."

Stern knew all about it. It was a classic dilemma faced by the old-time bank robbers, before sophisticated money laundering came into practice. Loads of cash stashed away but unable to spend a penny. However long it took, the police would be waiting. The first sign of any suspect spending even a few bob more than normal, and they'd be all over it. "So, you just stashed it away in the loft."

"Most of it, yes. I spent a little. Just not enough for Mo to become suspicious. The rest I just kept up there. I thought one day I'd get the opportunity to use it somehow." He shifted his gaze from Stern to Mo. "It was only when I realised you had taken the money I put a stop to it."

"How long ago?" Stern came back.

"Dunno, whenever it was Mo cleared her stuff out and took the money."

Stern looked at Mo, eyebrows raised questioningly.

"Best part of two years, I guess," she said.

Stern turned back to Cavendish. "And you haven't worked the scam since?"

Cavendish gave a positive shake of the head. "I knocked it on the head straight away. I had a few kickbacks from the others, the back-street lads, but I knew it was wrong, and, to be honest, I was happy it was over. My only problem was the money Mo had taken. We weren't the best of friends, and I didn't know what she would do with it. She could have screwed me at any time. You can't imagine. I was walking on egg shells."

"But I would never have…"

"Whoa." Stern turned sharply on Mo, stopping her dead. Then back to Cavendish. "Go on."

"When I did find out where she was, I called her, said she had to give the money back."

"You threatened me," Mo said. Her words soft, regretful. "You said..."

"*Mo*," Stern snapped. "Just be quiet, will you."

Cavendish shook his head. "No, she's right," he admitted softly. "I was that scared, I just didn't know how to...I mean since the divorce we'd been so..." He gave a sad sigh, the right words refusing to come. "From the start, once I knew she had the money, I just expected her to report me to you guys." He looked at his ex, his eyes dark with resignation. "Looks like that's exactly what she's done."

Forty-four

"Blimey, boss, you must be getting soft in your old age."

Stern was smiling a relaxed, satisfied smile. He eased back and hooked his heels over the edge of the desk, the old chair creaking more than usual at the move. "Not so much of the old, Hooker. And as for soft, let's just say as soon as he walked in, I could see something neither of the daft buggers could see themselves. I just played the middle man.

"Don't get you."

"Well, from the time Cavendish climbed out of the car he was putting on the hard man act, but it didn't take a mind reader to see he was a very worried man. And when I hit him with the CID role, he just folded completely. The truth was he'd been terrified the whole thing would come back and bite him since the day she walked off with the money."

"But that was a couple of years back."

"Right, and the man was still a walking wreck. When he realised the game was up, he was only too pleased to get it off his chest."

"He admitted what he'd been up to, where the money came from?"

"Yes, he told me everything. The scam had been started by his boss before him. He'd told Cavendish it was commonplace bunce, said everybody did it. When the boss retired, Cavendish just carried on where he'd left off." He chuckled. "Would you believe the old boss even came in from time to time for a handout? How bazaar is that?"

"So, what happened when he realised Mo had the money?"

"He panicked. After the split, their relationship had been so bad, he thought unless he got to her she would turn him in. So, he started to look for her. It took him ages, and all the time he was expecting a knock on the door. When he eventually found her, he called her and said she should give the money back. But he didn't engage brain; he didn't play it right. He tried the heavy-handed approach from the off. All that did was kindle Mo's fire. She told him where to go."

"So, he sent his man Wheeler to put the frighteners on her?"

"Yes, and he admitted it. Said after she told him to hit the road, he didn't know what else to do."

Leaning forward, Cherry gave him a knowing smile. "So, when did you start to realise there was still something between them?"

"Almost as soon as the daft sod walked through the door. I don't know why, but just the way they looked at each other said something to me. Then I remembered how the salesman at the garage had told you how, even after all this time, Cavendish was still in a state." He chuckled. "But for me, the clincher was when Cavendish explained how scared he had been that at any time she would turn him in. Honest, I had to stop Mo from babbling on about how she would never have done that to him."

Cherry grinned. "I see what you mean. There's obviously still something there, then."

"Of course, there is," Stern said. "Anyway, next thing I knew, they were talking. He was telling her how sorry he was for what he'd done, and she was desperate to tell him how wretched she had always felt about betraying him in the first place. Honest, there were tears squirting out in every direction. Eventually, I could see it was going nowhere. I had to shut them both up and get on with it."

"How d'you manage that?"

"Well, first I asked Mo if she wanted to bring charges against him. By then, I already knew the answer to that one. Then I asked them both what they wanted to do next. In no time at all, they had decided they wanted to sit down and talk it through, decide for themselves where to go from there."

Cherry giggled. "All of a sudden you were redundant."

"Yeah, can you believe it? But I couldn't let it go there, could I?"

She was still grinning. "Absolutely not. Never let it be said the great Theo Stern didn't get the last word."

"Quite correct. So, I told Cavendish I'd decided not to report him to the fraud squad. But only for two reasons. The first was because he had assured me the scam hadn't directly disadvantaged any member of the public; he'd been adamant the original customer got a fair deal whatever happened to the trade-in car. And the second reason was because he'd abandoned the scam the better part of two years before. I warned him I couldn't be responsible if the fraud squad picked up on the scam from some other source. If that happened, he was on his own. I then told Mo unless she wanted it otherwise my involvement was over." He gave a shake of his head. "She was all over me with her thanks, even called Cyril out of the kitchen." He laughed. "You should have seen Cavendish's face when he appeared. After that, I got the distinct feeling she couldn't get us out the door quick enough. I'll never understand women."

"But what about the cash? Ten grand's a lot of loot."

Stern linked his hands behind his head, a satisfied smirk forming. "That was my final coup-de-grace. I told them neither of them should benefit from the proceeds of what I considered a crime. The money had to go to a charity."

"And they agreed?"

Stern smiled smugly. "They did and readily. I believe the pair of them had been walking on egg shells for so long they'd have agreed to almost anything."

Cherry gave a soft sigh. "A happy ending if ever there was one, boss. D'you think they'll get back together?"

Stern gave a snort. "Don't ask me. And don't start going all soggy on me, Hooker. Just get stuck in and make out the bill." He thought for a beat. "And add on an extra ten percent. Cyril and Clarissa should get something for the way they helped us with this one." He dropped his feet to the floor and looked at his watch. "Right, it's time I paid the Barfords a visit. You gave them a call?"

"Yes, I told Mrs Barford you'd be there sometime this morning. She said she'd keep her husband at home."

Stern climbed out of the chair and headed for the outer office, muttering as he went. "Don't think this one will have such a happy ending as the Stevens case."

Cherry followed him out and watched him pull on his coat. "Even if he didn't know any details, he had to know it was iffy, didn't he?"

Buttoning his coat, Stern moved to the door. "Yup, he did. And I think that's what's going to screw him."

~ * ~

Stern was pleased the Barford children were at school. The interview was going to be a very unpleasant experience for the Barfords, particularly the wife who had seen the dangers from the outset. Unfortunately, her husband was from a different mould. Ex-army, a thrill seeker, risk taker. He had seen an exciting break from the mundane task of ferrying mostly older boring people from pillar to post. And the money. Ah yes, it was always the money.

With both Barford's taxi and the van filling the drive, Stern parked the Scirocco at the curb in front of the house. Doris Barford was already at the front door by the time he reached it. She was holding the tracker.

"I don't know if I did right, but I removed this before Steve could find it," she said, handing it to him.

Stern slid it into his pocket. "Did he look for it?"

"Yes, as soon as he came back from seeing you. He said you'd told him he was being tracked. But by then, I'd removed it."

"So, he doesn't know it was you who put it there?"

"No, he doesn't." She straightened her back defiantly, her lips trembling. "But to be honest, I don't care if you tell him. I'm just so fed up with being afraid, Mr Stern. If it takes what we've done to stop this, I don't care what he does or doesn't know."

Stern laid a hand on her arm. "Don't worry. He doesn't have to know anything about your involvement in this if you don't want him to," he said reassuringly. "That'll be your decision."

"Thank you."

She led him into a very comfortably furnished sitting room. Her husband was slouched in an armchair. He was pale and unshaven, his eyes sunken and dark rimmed. Stern guessed sleep wasn't coming easy right now. He eyed Stern suspiciously but said nothing. Refusing an offer of tea, Stern settled in a chair directly opposite the disconsolate husband. Mrs Barford sat in a chair alongside and close to her husband.

Before Stern could say a word, Barford rounded on him. "You told me you were CID," he snapped.

"I did no such thing." Stern kept his voice level, emotionless. "I told you I was a special investigator working for the CID." He reached into his pocket and retrieved his mobile. "I am a thirty-year, time served, detective inspector with the London Metropolitan Police. Now retired, I run a private detective agency and, at this time, I am on secondment to the Norfolk CID." He held out the phone toward Barford. "If you check the contacts menu, you'll see a Detective Inspector O'Connor of the Norfolk CID listed there. You're welcome to give him a call and check my credentials."

Doris Barford angrily grabbed her husband's arm. "Don't you dare question Mr Stern. He's here to help. You should be pleased he is."

Barford looked into his wife's accusing eyes then shaking his head he waved the phone away.

Stern slid the phone back into his pocket. "I have to assume you are not a stupid man, Mr Barford," Stern began, his words taut. "And therefore, it goes without saying you knew what you were doing was illegal."

Barford sat forward. "No, that's not true. How could I? I didn't know what was in the packages. They were wrapped and..."

"And the people?" Stern snapped, cutting him short. "What about the people?"

Barford swallowed heavily. "They were just..."

"Mr Barford," Stern cut in, shaking his head dismissively. "Please don't insult my intelligence. To do so can only end one way." Before carrying on, he let the words hang, the implications obvious. "You were carrying out clandestine trips in the small hours. You were also being paid exceptionally large sums of money for doing so. Far more than anything that could possibly have been legit. You knew perfectly well what you were doing and to expect me to believe otherwise is ludicrous." Again, he paused, allowing the pressure to build. "What you didn't know was that you were doing this for a ruthless organisation that has no qualms at all in carrying out murder."

Doris Barford gasped. "Oh, my God. Steve, what have you done?"

Barford's eyes widened, and his mouth dropped open. "No, no I didn't know that. How could I have?"

"No, maybe you weren't aware of just who you were dealing with. But your crime was not caring. You saw the money and shut your eyes to everything else. Now, I suggest, before more ridiculous denials make matters worse, we start from the beginning, and you tell me everything."

Forty-five

"Honest, he was just another fare." Barford was sitting forward now, his elbows resting on his knees, fists clenched. "I was just talking as you do with any fare. Sitting in the car all day, you'd go barmy if you didn't talk to the customers." He straightened, scratching his head, thinking back. "I could tell by his accent he wasn't local, so I asked where he was from. He told me he was Polish but had lived here for some time. When I asked him what he did for a living, he said he worked for a haulage company."

"Did he give you a name?"

"No, and I didn't ask. At the time, I wasn't interested. It was just chit chat, you know, just to pass the time."

"Okay, go on."

"Anyway, just to keep things going, I told him I was a driver in the mob. He seemed interested and asked me what type of vehicle I drove. I told him everything from an officer's staff car to fighting vehicles and the heavy stuff." He frowned, his mind trolling back for a moment. "Funny, now I come to think of it, I remember the guy didn't say another word until I was about to drop him off. Then, as he was paying me, he told me his company had just lost one of their drivers and was looking for someone to do a few night runs. He said the pay was good, and they supplied the vehicle. He asked if I would be interested. It sounded good, so I asked what I'd be carrying." He stopped and looked across at Stern, his eyes darkening. "I know it was stupid, but the taxi work was driving me mental, and we were just about making ends meet. I hated Doris having to work."

Stern knew instantly this was the turning point. Nothing to be gained by giving him any slack. He kept a straight face. "Okay, I hear you, but let's just get on with it, shall we?"

Barford gave a heavy, resigned sigh. "The guy just stared at me for a bit. Then he said, 'let me worry about that. You just enjoy the payout.'"

Doris Barford's intake of breath was loud in the silence that followed. "You fool," she whispered hoarsely. "I told you…It was so obvious. Didn't you think about me, the boys?"

Barford turned to his wife. "Don't you see? I could have done just a few more trips, built up the bank balance and got out." He lowered his eyes, the words, sounding pathetic, petering out.

Stern felt the anger rise at the man's stupidity. "No, you couldn't, because we've been onto you from the get go." This wasn't true, but it did no harm for Barford to think it was. "And even if we hadn't, from your very first trip, you would have been in too deep for the gang to let you out in one piece." He leaned closer, emphasising what was to come next. "When this man first offered you the work, he told you they had just lost a driver, didn't he?"

"Yes."

"Well, I can tell you we know that driver also tried to get out. He is now dead." Stern could see the words go home like a hammer. "Yes, Mr Barford, we're talking murder here." His lip curled in distaste. "And all for a few bob."

Barford's hand was at his mouth. It was shaking. But Stern wasn't about to let up just yet.

"And now you're a felon and could be spending a great deal of time away from your wife and boys. Like I said before; seven to ten, if not more."

Doris Barford gave a strangled sob. "Mr Stern, you must help us please. I just couldn't bear it if Steve..."

Stern held the woman's pleading eyes for only a moment before turning back to her husband. "Okay, so no more bullshit. You knew what you were doing, knew what you had to be carrying, right?"

Tight lipped, Barford silently held up his hands, a capitulating gesture.

Stern didn't relent. "So, let's have it. And I mean all of it."

Barford looked beaten. "Okay, okay. That first time, when the guy offered me the job, he said I'd be given a trial run. If I did the business, I'd pull five hundred. And that was only the start." He looked at his wife.

She took the cue. "Steve was out in the taxi when they came. I was at home alone. I answered a knock on the door, and a man was standing there holding out a car key on a fob. At first, I was confused then I saw the van parked on the drive. The man gave me the key and told me to tell my husband to wait for a call."

"That's all he said?" Stern asked.

"Yes, that was all."

"Did this man have an accent? Like your husband said, Eastern European?"

"Yes, definitely."

"Then what?"

She shrugged. "Nothing. He just said Steve should wait for a call and walked down to a car waiting at the curb and drove off."

"Did you notice what make the car was, who was driving?"

"I did. It was a Range Rover. And from what I could see, there was a woman in the driver's seat."

"Could you describe her?"

"No, not really. I can only remember thinking she wasn't very big. She looked small behind the wheel. And she looked older. I don't mean old, more like a mature lady."

"Okay." Stern turned back to Barford. "And you eventually got the call?"

"Yes."

"And more calls followed?"

Just a tight nod of assent this time.

Again, Stern eased himself forward in the chair, leaning imposingly toward Barford. "Okay, for a start, you should know we have complete recorded details of one of your trips, from leaving the house to the coast, and on to the Barton Mills lay-by at the A11. This alone will be enough to kick off an investigation that could put you away for a long time. So, if you want me to help you, I need to know everything that happened after that. Every detail, d'you understand?"

Barford swallowed heavily and turned to his wife. "Think I could have a drink of water?"

~ * ~

Stern slumped back in the old chair with a sigh. It wasn't yet three in the afternoon, but he felt tired, bone weary. It occurred to him he was sixty-three years old, and he considered a very fit sixty-three. But right now, for the first time in a good while, he was definitely feeling every one of those sixty-three years.

He had spent a long time with the Barfords going over every detail of Steve Barford's story. Checking and rechecking each point, making notes of routes, journeys and destinations. Not forgetting the cargos. Barford had been an idiot, a greedy idiot. He knew exactly what he was doing and had put money before his own safety and, more importantly, that of his family. Stern had no sympathy whatsoever for the man himself, but his wife and children were a different matter. He had promised to do what he could to minimise the impact of Barford's crimes but minimise was all he could do. He was now convinced both the Ollie Preston/Charlie Croker case and Barford's escapades were linked. This meant, however he played it, he would have to involve David O'Connor. This in turn would mean, at some level or other, Steve Barford would have to pay. By the time he'd left the Barford house, Stern's brain hurt, and he was emotionally drained.

Cherry came into the office carrying a mug and a plate. The mug contained coffee, and one of Dave's large meat pasties sat steaming on the plate. She slid both in front of him then parked herself in her favourite position, legs curled under her, on the chair opposite. "Tell me I'm wrong when I guess you missed lunch."

Stern reached gratefully for the plate. "Can't argue with that."

"You know, when you get to your age, you should at least eat properly."

Stern would normally have reacted to the age comment, but right then, he didn't have the energy. He just took a large bite, the warm spicy meat and pastry attacking his taste buds with gusto. Swallowing the first mouthful, he closed his eyes and gave a satisfied smile.

Ten minutes later, the snack had disappeared, and he was ready to talk. And Cherry was more than ready to listen.

"Okay, here's the bottom line," he began. "Both drugs and people are being brought in along the coast near Winterton." He held up a cautionary hand. "In truth, Barford couldn't be sure it was actually drugs because they were in sealed packages, but I don't think there's much doubt."

Cherry's eyes widened. "But people, too?"

"Yup. According to Barford, both men and women." He pulled his notebook toward him and flipped it open. "And his journey instructions depended on what came ashore. When it was just people, it was never local, always a long run, London, Manchester, Birmingham. On these trips he usually met another vehicle half way. His cargo was transferred, and he came home. When it was London, he mostly met the second vehicle in the lay-by at Barton Mills."

"Like the one we monitored?"

"That's right. Only occasionally did he have to do a complete London run."

"Jeez," Cherry breathed. "How many people are we talking here?"

"Anything from a couple to no more than half a dozen."

Her brow creasing, Cherry thought for a moment. "When we had the tracker on him, he went to the river before taking off to Barton Mills. Why d'you think that was?"

Stern smiled. As always, she didn't miss much. "Because on that occasion, he'd picked up drugs and people. Seems he delivered the drugs to a boat waiting on the river, then took two young girls to Barton Mills where they were taken off in another car."

She gave it some more thought. "There's a link here, boss, isn't there?"

"There is, kiddo. And out of all this, there is one particular fact that convinces me two cases have just become one. You remember the passenger Barford picked up on the first day, the one who offered him the work?"

Again frowning, Cherry tilted her head questioningly. "I do."

"Well, Barford swears to this day he doesn't know who that man was. In fact, he insists he hasn't seen the man since. And I believe him. But one thing he does remember was dropping his fare off smack bang outside the gates of the Butler house."

Forty-six

David O'Connor pulled at his bottom lip, his eyes holding Stern's intently. "We should bring him in, Theo, you know that as well as I do. The man's a criminal, for Christ sake."

Stern leaned forward in the chair. "Of course, I know, but don't forget he came to me of his own free will. He reported what was going on." Stern mentally crossed his fingers for uttering the lie, but he was thinking only of Doris Barford and her boys. Steve Barford was not a criminal, not a bad man. He was a stupid risk taker and, Stern was convinced, given the chance it was unlikely he would stray again. Anyway, he consoled himself, the prisons were too full as it was. He went on quickly. "Okay, I admit it was after the event. He had already carried out some trips and got paid for it. But nevertheless, he has seen the error of his ways and has come clean. In my opinion, if for no other reason, he should be given some slack. Think about it; once we've pulled him, he's no more use to us. All I'm saying is before you do anything rash just hear me out."

It was late afternoon, the only time O'Connor was available, and the four of them were sitting around O'Connor's desk at police headquarters, Norwich. Because of the earlier separate discussions she'd had with Doris Barford, Stern had brought Cherry with him. O'Connor had also decided to be accompanied. He felt it would be good for PC Wainwright's development for him to be present. Stern had given a full account of his interview with Steve Barford and got exactly the response he'd expected from O'Connor. And quite right, too. He was a policeman, his job was to catch criminals and bring them to justice. But Stern was convinced there was more to this than just Barford's misdemeanours. It was just his own speculation, call it policeman's nose if you like, and he knew it could sound speculative. But if he were right, there were bigger fish to fry here, and he would love to fry them. He just had to convince O'Connor to go with him.

O'Connor eased back in his chair, the corners of his mouth turned down sceptically. For a moment, Stern thought he was going to get a no go. But not quite.

"Okay, let's hear what you've got, Theo. But make it good, mate. And quick. If upstairs hear I'm aware there's a guy out there smuggling drugs and people, and I'm not on my way to feel his collar, they'll have my guts for garters."

Stern didn't hesitate, he got straight to it. "First a question. Did you find out anything more about Ollie Preston?"

O'Connor shook his head. "No revelations. Nothing we didn't already know."

"Okay, let's go with what we have then. As far as we know, the only people who were privy to what Charlie Croker was up to at night were Croker himself and Preston. And they're both dead. But what we do have is Preston's notes to you. And if we are to believe those notes, and I think we should, we at least know Croker was night running for Butler. Also, when Croker tried to get out, he was found face down in the Wensum." He waved a hand. "I know the official verdict was accidental death but bear with me. Let's, for the moment, believe Preston was insinuating something more sinister."

"You're making assumptions, Theo," O'Connor broke in. "You're assuming this Barford guy took over from Croker. I think that's a stretch. I mean, even if we believe the notes and accept Croker was working for Butler, we have nothing positive to say Barford took over from him. What's more, although we know what Barford was carrying, we haven't a clue what Croker was up to."

"You're right, we don't know; we don't have anything on Croker. But, like you say, we do know what Barford was carrying. And we do know he was told he was replacing a driver they had lost. I think that's a big enough link for us to make one or two assumptions. Certainly enough for us to give Butler the once-over." He looked to Cherry. She was part of this and should have her say. "Just hear what Cherry found when she checked the time line for me."

"After the boss did his thing with Barford, I checked some dates," Cherry began. "Most importantly I found out Barford was recruited by his mystery fare less than two weeks after Croker was found in the river." She paused, looking to Stern. He motioned her to carry on. "And something else of interest," she went on. "When we had the tracker on Barford, he made a drop at the river before going on to Barton Mills. He told the boss that, at the river, the packages were transferred to a boat, a low river cruiser he called it. I checked the date. It was three days after Butler's boat was torched."

O'Connor turned to Stern. "So, what are you saying?"

"Okay, this is what I think has happened here. For some time, Croker has been used to pick up stuff being smuggled in along the North Norfolk coast. Then I believe, for whatever reason, Croker decides he's had enough, he wants out." He leaned forward to make a point. "For my next assumption," he grinned at O'Connor, "we have to believe that what Preston said in one of his notes was true; that when Croker tried to bail out, he ended up floating in the Wensum. So now, if the goods keep coming in, they need a new driver and quick."

"I see," O'Connor said. "Enter Steve Barford."

"Correct. He's stupid and greedy enough to take over the role. And now, he's admitted to carrying both drugs and people. So, I think it's safe to assume Croker was doing the same before him. Now, think about what Cherry just said about stuff being carried aboard a low river cruiser only a short time after Butler's boat had been torched. Wouldn't it make sense if, before it was burned, the Butler boat was being used to move the goods? Remember it was low slung, more a speed boat than a cruiser. But it had a cabin and was perfectly capable of carrying stuff. And it was low enough to get under the low bridges on the Broads. That was important."

"I know what you mean," O'Connor said. "I've been on the Broads and some of those bridges are flippin' low."

"Exactly," Stern went on. "So, now, as well as having to recruit a new driver, they had to get another boat. And it had to be low slung."

O'Connor still didn't seem totally convinced. "A bit of supposition again, Theo."

"Yup, I agree. But I'm not finished yet. You remember how we couldn't understand why nobody made an attempt to save the boat when it was burning, how they never called the fire brigade?"

O'Connor nodded but stayed quiet.

"Well, when I interviewed the handyman Adams, or whatever his real name is, he gave me some cock and bull story about the boat already sitting on water so why call the brigade. It was hogwash, of course, and knowing what we do now I believe there could well have been another reason. I believe it could have been because there was contraband on the boat." He saw the doubt, the suspicion cloud O'Connor's eyes and raised a cautionary hand. "I know, I'm only surmising the boat was being used to transport drugs in the first place. And I admit I could be wrong. But I don't think I am, so let's just again assume, for the moment, it was. Then by the time they became aware of the fire, the boat was already burning too fiercely for them to get on board and pull the stuff off. So now they faced a dilemma. If they'd called the brigade, the fire could have been doused before the boat was completely destroyed. Then both the brigade and your forensics people would have been all over the remains, right?" He paused for a beat, letting his theory sink home. "Not good if there was still gear on board. So best decision, take the hit, let it burn out. Now, forensics would be checking the surrounding area, the bank and so on. No point in checking the boat." He shrugged his shoulders. "'Cause there's no boat to check."

O'Connor thought for a long moment before responding. "I agree in theory it's all possible, Theo. But to go with it would mean we suspect Butler who, I remind you, is a very influential business man with lots of heavy contacts, of drugs and people smuggling."

Stern gave a shrug. "He wouldn't be the first high roller to go bad. Want me to name a few?"

"No, that won't be necessary. But to make a move on Butler I would need a good deal more than your pretty tenuous assumptions."

"Of course, you would. So how about this. Facts this time." He paused for a moment, collecting his thoughts. "As well as Preston's notes, which I know wouldn't stand up in court, there are a couple of other markers we can't ignore. First, Cherry's partner, Rob, has contacts at the boat hire company used by the smugglers, and he did some checking for us. They said the guy who hired the boat told them he didn't know how long he wanted it for, but he gave them an initial wadge of cash up front." He raised a finger to make a point. "Cash, so there will be no credit card trail. And he gave them an address in Leicester. Now get this. When Cherry checked, she found there was no such address."

O'Connor twitched. "So, the hire company didn't check the man's credentials?"

"Seems not," Stern came back. "They had the cash, why bother."

O'Connor's face tightened angrily, but he said nothing.

"The girl at the hire company did remember the guy, though," Stern went on. "She gave a sort of description...tall, average age, average build. Nothing of much use, but, in particular, she did remember he had an Eastern European accent." Stern paused for effect before following up with, "As, by the way, did the man, the fare, who recruited Steve Barford." He didn't give O'Connor a chance to respond. "And as, by the way, does our Mr Adams, Butler's handyman. And we must not forget Barford dropped the man who recruited him off directly outside the Butler residence." He raised his eyebrows and waited for a response.

O'Connor puffed out his cheeks and exhaled slowly. "Bloody hell, Theo."

Forty-seven

O'Connor had finally succumbed to the argument, though reluctantly. Butler was a highly respected individual, both in business and in the public domain. When in residence in Norfolk, not only did he support several local charities, he also played golf with the chief constable. And you don't go bowling in and accuse a friend of the chief constable of being a drug and human trafficker without positive proof. Sometimes even with what you might think is positive proof. So, softly softly.

After some discussion, it was Constable Wainwright who came up with the suggestion. They were investigating a suspicious death, a body found in the river not a million miles from the Butler residence. As a result, they were searching the banks both sides of the river for clues as to what might have happened to Preston before he went into the river. The section of river bank at the bottom of the Butler rear garden happened to come within the stretch designated to be searched. Once on the property, they would not only carry out a more detailed, if surreptitious, search and, more importantly, take the opportunity to talk again to Butler's handyman, Victor Adams, or Adamczyk, as was his correct name. They would, of course, first need to seek Butler's permission to enter his grounds.

O'Connor made the call to Butler's business office in London, requesting permission for the search to be carried out the next day, Saturday. A helpful secretary informed him that Butler was unavailable but promised to pass on the message and get back to him as soon as she could. In less than twenty minutes, she was back saying Mr Butler was happy for them to again enter his property and check out the river bank there. She also told O'Connor that Butler would be travelling up to Norfolk later that evening, so he would be there when they arrived the following day.

It was agreed that, as Stern was already known by the Butler family to be working with the police, he and Wainwright would cover the Butler grounds. Also, for the search to be seen as authentic, O'Connor would arrange for a uniformed constable to be seen checking both the bank on the other side of the river, and the bank belonging to Butler's neighbour.

The discussion then turned to Steve Barford, O'Connor again asking Stern why he shouldn't be brought in.

Stern had been waiting and was ready. "He's no good to us locked up," he said. "After our little chat earlier, he's ready to cooperate in any way he can. He knows he's in trouble and will do anything to make good and help reduce whatever the court throws at him. And I think we can use him in a couple of ways."

"So, what do you have in mind?"

"When we go in tomorrow, I would like Cherry to be in the area with Barford in her car," Stern suggested.

O'Connor looked worried. "Not sure I like involving Cherry, Theo."

Stern shook his head. "No, not involved. I was thinking of on the other side of the river."

"O'Connor looked perplexed.

"See, I want Barford to identify the handyman, and the man he picked up in Cromer, the man who recruited him, as one and the same. But, we obviously don't want Barford to be seen by Adams. So, if Paul and I could get Adams to accompany us to the river's edge while we carry out the search, and Barford is, say, on the other side of the river, possibly with binoculars..." Stern inclined his head, asking the question.

O'Connor thought for a moment then, "I see. If I remember, after the fire, when we checked the other side of the river, there was a rough area where cars had been parked. Where we found the beer cans and stuff. We thought it may have even been used by Preston before he torched the boat."

"Yes, I remember," Stern agreed. "So, if Cherry can park over there with Barford, with luck, he'll be able to make the identification."

"Okay," O'Connor agreed. "I'll go with that. You said there were a couple of ways we can use him?"

"Yes. I think once we've identified Adams, we'll know we have this end of things nailed down. He's going nowhere so we don't have to hit him, yet. I know it doesn't give us Butler, but once we start to break things down, I think that will come." He held O'Connor's questioning eyes. "With your permission, I'd like to leave Barford out there until he gets his next consignment. You can have the Coastguard on standby to dump on the vessel that drops the load on the coast, and wherever Barford makes his deliveries, your guys could be waiting. How does that sound?"

For the first time, O'Connor gave Stern a semblance of a smile. It was just a twitch at the corners of his mouth, but for Stern it was enough.

Forty-eight

Steve Barford was physically sweating, the memory of Stern's late visit the night before, still raw in his mind. He twisted the binoculars nervously in his lap. "If what your boss told me is true, these guys are killers." He spoke in a hushed tone, even though enclosed in the car on the other side of the river no one else could possibly hear him.

Cherry hadn't been too enthusiastic about Stern's plan in the first place. Now, in the confines of the little mini, the nervous, sweaty man alongside her too close for comfort, she felt decidedly ill at ease. She hadn't liked Barford from the get go. Without any thought for the consequences, or any regard for his wife and boys, he'd been led by pound signs alone. That was unforgiveable. Saying nothing, keeping her eyes focussed across the river, she inched herself sideways away from him.

"If they killed that other guy, like he said," Barford persisted. "And they see me here..."

Cherry kept her eyes averted, not wanting to look at him. "You should have thought of that before you got involved."

"Yeah, but I didn't know then that..."

Unable to hold back, Cherry swung to face him, her expression a tight mask. "Look, I wasn't keen on babysitting you in the first place," she snapped. "So, the last thing I want is you whinging in my ear. You knew what you were up to was wrong, and you're damned lucky Mr Stern is trying to help. He could have kept his mouth shut and just handed you over. And, by the way, he's doing that for your wife and boys, not for you. So, if you don't mind, I'd rather you just keep your mouth shut and concentrate on what we're here for." She held his open-mouthed, surprised look for a moment before looking back across the river.

A florid hue creeping up his neck, Barford swallowed hard and silently turned his gaze in the same direction.

~ * ~

Stern and Paul Wainwright pulled up outside the Butler property. Leaving the car, they approached the gates where, to Stern's surprise, Ron Pace was already waiting. He opened the gates and, without a word, escorted them along the drive to the front door of the house. He stood silently with them until the door was opened, before moving off. Mrs Butler's mother, her scowl as aggressive as ever, ushered them into the same room as before.

Eddie Butler was waiting. This time he was alone. He beckoned them to the sofa and sat opposite. "This is a sad business, Mr Stern," he said.

"It is, Mr Butler, and I'm grateful to you, again, for allowing us onto your property. You see, if possible, we would like to establish exactly where the unfortunate victim went into the water."

Butler looked concerned. "But you don't think it happened in my..."

Stern gave a quick shake of the head, cutting him short. "No, of course not. We have no reason to think your stretch of the bank was involved at all. But for the formal report, your land comes within a pre-designated stretch of the river to be investigated. One of Inspector O'Connor's men will be carrying out a check of your neighbour's property in the same way."

"Yes, I did see a uniform out back of Rupert's place," Butler admitted.

"It's a formality, but it has to be done I'm afraid."

Butler waved a dismissive hand. "That's quite alright, Mr Stern. Is there anything I can do to help?"

"I appreciate the offer," Stern said, getting to his feet. "But there's nothing for you to do. Constable Wainwright and I will be as quick as we can. Should be out of your hair in no more than an hour."

"Not necessary," Butler said with a smile. "Take all the time you need." He paused for just a moment then said, "Am I allowed to ask if it was an accident or...?"

"I'm afraid I can't discuss the case." Stern smiled apologetically. "But I'm sure the local press will have full details in no time."

"Of course, I understand," Butler said. "But are you able to tell me if the man was local? I was thinking if he was, there might be something I could do for the family."

Stern took just a second to study the other man's face, seeing only what appeared to be genuine concern. "I can confirm he was a Norfolk man, but he did not come from this immediate area."

Butler escorted them to the back door and out onto the rear patio where they stood for a moment scanning beyond the patio and swimming pool across the extensive rear garden lawn. Stern felt a very slight nudge of Wainwright's elbow in his side. He didn't respond, knowing the move had been made because, like him, the constable had seen the low-slung river cruiser moored side on to the bank close to the burned out mooring.

Stern turned to Butler. "I see you've replaced the boat."

Smiling, Butler shook his head. "Not really. It's a hire craft and not at all suitable. But it will do until the new one I've ordered becomes available. Takes them a while to build a vessel to a particular spec." He turned back to the house. "Always worth it in the long run, I believe." He turned away. "I'll leave you to it then. Shout if you need anything."

"Oh, just one thing," Stern said, as if a point had just come to him. "It would help if your handyman chappie could accompany us. I'm sure he knows the area like the back of his hand, and it would alleviate any erroneous assumptions we might make about something we come across and don't understand."

Butler didn't hesitate. "Of course, I'm sure he's around somewhere. I'll get Pace to dig him out and send him down to you."

"Many thanks, Mr Butler. It's greatly appreciated."

They made their way to the river's edge and studied the long boat, typical of many used by the Norfolk Broads hire companies.

"Thirty-five, forty foot?" Wainwright suggested.

"Probably," Stern agreed, staring at the registration number printed on the boat's side. "Pity Barford didn't get the number of the boat he delivered the stuff to. We'd have been home and dry with that. Be nice if we could get on board and have a look around."

"Wouldn't mind betting Butler has his eyes on us right now," Wainwright said.

Acknowledging the point, Stern moved some paces from the boat and gestured along the bank, as if discussing tactics. At the same time, he casually checked that Cherry's Mini was in place on the far side of the river. It was there, standing alone under the wide branches of a low hanging oak. Waves of sunlight glittering on the water's surface reflected brightly on the windscreen. Stern smiled. You would never know if there were occupants in the car or not. Perfect.

"So how d'you want to play it?" Wainwright asked.

Stern turned and looked back at the house, the rear of the garage to one side, the handyman's cottage the other. He pointed to the side where the cottage stood. "You take that side, and I'll cover the other. Work your way along the bank and make it look good. Ensure your notebook is visible, study the ground, you know the drill. Check the neighbour's hedge at least up to the cottage and have a quick shufti around that, too. When the handyman makes an appearance, I'll get him down to the water's edge so he's visible from the other side. That done we can wrap this up."

They were about to split up and move along opposite edges of the bank when they saw Ron Pace crossing the lawn toward them.

"Your man's off site," he growled as he came up to them. "Seems like he's gone to the village to get something or other. Be back in a while. I'll send him down soon as."

"Sure, thanks."

The big man hesitated for a beat, as if he were about to say more, then shrugged his wide shoulders and strode away.

Stern and Wainwright made their way along the river bank in opposite directions. Only minutes later, Stern heard a shout. He looked back and could see Wainwright standing with the uniformed constable who had been checking the neighbour's garden. They were waving him over.

Forty-nine

Stern made his way across the lawn to the two officers.

Wainwright introduced the other young constable. "PC Wayford, Mr Stern. Thought you might like to see this." He pointed along the adjoining hedge separating the two properties.

Stern acknowledged the officer and followed him along the hedge to a point directly behind the handyman's cottage.

"Looks like someone's cut a hole through here," Wayford said, pointing to a gap in the hedge. "It's not a natural break. You can see all the cut off bits dotted around."

Stern studied the break in the hedge. "Mmmm, you're right."

"And that's not all," Wayford went on. "Like you to have a look at this." He motioned them through the break and into the neighbour's garden. Here, they followed the hedge until they came to another, taller hedge running at right angles to the first. "This one borders the road," Wayford said. "And whoever it was, came through here in the same way." He pointed to another break in the foliage. "Same thing, see? All the cuttings dotted around."

Stern studied the break in the hedge. "So, you think someone cut their way through here from the road first, then moved along the adjoining hedge until they came to the point behind Butler's cottage?"

Wayford smiled. "Well I'm not a detective, sir, but if you ask me, I would say that's exactly what happened. Either that or they came the other way. Y'know, trying to break out of next door."

Stern returned the smile. "Unlikely I think, but not impossible, I suppose." He thanked Wayford, and he and Wainwright made their way back to the Butler garden. There, in the space between the break in the hedge and the rear of the little cottage, Stern turned slowly, surveying the surroundings, rubbing his chin thoughtfully.

"What do you notice about this patch, Paul? I mean this particular part of the garden?"

For a long time, Wainwright looked around himself, finally raising his hands in defeat. "What am I missing, Mr Stern?"

Stern didn't answer right away but made his way to the break in the hedge, spinning round and scanning the area again for a time. "Unless I'm mistaken," he said finally. "This is probably the only part of the garden not covered by security lights and cameras."

Wainwright followed Stern's eyes. "You're right," he said. "All the lights are positioned around the house, and the cottage is between the house and this small area. It acts as a block."

"Right, and my guess is someone sussed that. They realised they could come through next door's front hedge, make their way along to this spot and come through the adjoining hedge, where the cottage protected them from being detected by the security lights on the house."

"But why?" Wainwright came back. "They would then be trapped in this one space behind the cottage. And, anyway, since the burning of the boat, nothing's happened here."

Stern held the young constable's questioning gaze. "It's true nothing's happened that we know about. But I'm sure something did happen here. This area is shielded from the house, so our gardening friend is not too fussy about the grass here. It's longer, not mown so carefully as that out front. And it's trodden down from the gap in the hedge." He pointed to the area under the window. "And here, in front of the window, it's particularly flattened. No, we might not know about it, but something definitely happened here."

The sound of a vehicle made them both look up and move to the front corner of the cottage where they could see the drive leading up to the house. The Range Rover Stern had seen here previously was just turning in through the gate.

"Looks like our man is back from the village." Stern eased Wainwright behind the cottage. "I'm going back down to the bank, to make sure we get him in full view from across the river. Meanwhile I want you to do a fingertip over this area, see if you can find anything at all out of place."

~ * ~

As she drew onto the parking area, Cherry immediately spotted the hire boat moored beside Butler's burned out mooring on the far bank. Immediately, she turned to Barford. "Recognise the boat?"

He lifted the binoculars to his eyes. "Same type, y'know, long and low. Couldn't be sure it was the same one, though. It was pitch black when I last saw it"

"Same type will do for now," Cherry muttered.

It was the only conversation that had taken place, because later, after Cherry's sharp rebuke, they had sat in silence until Stern and Wainwright appeared out of the back of the house with Butler. They watched them chat for a short while before leaving Butler and wandering down to the water's edge.

"No sign of the handyman, yet," Cherry mused to herself.

"Could be he's out," Barford said, a touch of hope in his voice. "Maybe they won't be able to get him down there."

"The boss'll get him, you can be sure of that."

After seeing the big driver march down and talk to Stern, they watched the pair split and walk in opposite directions along the river bank. Suddenly, Stern turned and retraced his steps, heading for the cottage. Cherry took the binoculars from Barford and focussed on Stern talking to Wainwright and another policeman at the rear of the cottage. After a moment, the three of them disappeared through the hedge into the neighbour's garden.

"Mmmm, looks like they've found something next door," she said, beginning to lower the glasses. "Hang on." She refocused and scanned toward the house. At one of the upper rear windows, Eddie Butler stood watching.

A short time later, Stern and Wainwright reappeared through the hedge and stood talking in the area behind the cottage. After a while, Stern left Wainwright and started to walk back across the lawn toward the river's edge. Cherry handed the binoculars back to Barford and pulled her mobile from her pocket. She hit a single speed dial number and watched until she saw Stern react and fumble for his phone.

"Just thought I'd let you know you're being watched from one of the upper windows in the house," she said when he answered. A pause then, "Yes, it's Butler himself." She listened again. "Yup we've got a great view, and we're ready and waiting." She signed off and slid the phone back into her pocket. "Looks like we're on," she said softly.

~ * ~

Back at the bank, Stern once again cast an eye over the hire boat. All the curtains were drawn firmly together, and the cabin door was closed, almost certainly locked. He would have given anything to get on board and have a good look round, but that would have to wait. He had to focus on the one single reason they were here. They needed to identify Victor Adams as the man who had recruited Barford. Once that was proven, if it were proven, he would have O'Connor's full backing, and they could move big time.

He turned and looked back across the wide lawn. Adams was striding toward him with quick, anxious steps, his face tightly drawn.

"Pace say you want to see me," he said, coming to a halt in front of Stern.

Stern gave his most relaxed smile. "Nothing to worry about. Because of the body found in the river, we're carrying out a check of the river bank. Not just here, but all along." He held the hopefully reassuring smile. "And in cases like this, it's standard procedure to have the land owner accompany us. I talked to Mr Butler, who suggested you would be far more qualified." He spun round and gestured along the river bank. "Half an hour at most."

As he was speaking, explaining, Stern had seen a noticeable relaxation of tight face muscled and stiff posture. He also hadn't missed the fact that Adams had casually manoeuvred himself between him and the boat, his back to the river.

"I thought it was me..."

The false smile was beginning to make Stern's face ache, but he kept it in place. "No, nothing to do with you personally, Victor." He turned and looked along the river bank. "Just want to check along here and the hedge behind the garage. Won't keep you long." A little way along the bank, free from the cover of the boat, he turned and looked across the river. "How wide would you say the river is at this point?" he asked.

Adams turned and followed his gaze, looking directly across the water.

Fifty

The four of them had returned to the Stern Investigations office and were assembled around Stern's desk.

"You're absolutely sure?" Stern said, his eyes fixed determinedly on Barford sitting nervously on the edge of the chair. "There must be no doubt. No doubt at all."

"Yes, I'm sure. It's him."

"He said it was as soon as Adams looked across the river," Cherry came in. "Said it was him straight away."

Stern leaned back in the old chair. "And the boat was the same type you delivered the goods to before?"

Barford gave an uncertain shrug of his shoulders. "Don't know about the specific type, I know nothing about boats. And don't forget, it was dark. But like I said before, it was the same shape and everything."

"And that night at the boat, the guy who took the stuff from you; was that Adams?"

Barford thought some, then shook his head. "No, couldn't have been. He was shorter, stocky, different build altogether."

"D'you see his face?"

Another shake of the head. "Like I said, it was dark. Could only see an outline. Anyway, he was wearing a hoodie. Could hardly see his face at all."

"And you have no idea what was in the packages?"

Barford gave an irritated shake of the head. "I've already told you; they were just plain plastic-covered packages. If there was anything written on them, it was too dark to see anyway."

Stern thought for a beat. "Did you always take stuff to the boat?"

"No, not always. Sometimes when it was just people, they were carrying individual packages. They were on like straps hanging round their necks. Held onto them like their lives depended on it, they did." He thought for a moment. "I do remember once when I dropped them off at a gaff in London. The stuff was whipped off them as they went through the door."

"So, sometimes the boat, sometimes not," Stern muttered.

"Yes."

"Different customers?" Wainwright suggested. "Assuming it is drugs, of course."

"Oh, it's drugs okay," Stern said positively. "You can bet your badge on it. And we'll prove it, too. But all in good time. Right now, we have Adams and, because I don't believe in coincidence, the boat too, both tied to Butler. So, we need to organise ourselves for the next move." He turned to Paul Wainwright. "Whatever we agree here has to be approved by Inspector O'Connor, and, I suspect, someone even more senior. Don't forget Butler's a highly respected guy who, as far as I know, has never hit the headlines. Even more important," he gave an amused grin, "plays golf with David's boss. It will also mean pulling together manpower and cooperation among different policing areas. And I can tell you that's not as straightforward as it might sound. So, we must tread carefully and be absolutely certain of our facts before we brief the Inspector. He's out of commission for best part of today, some senior police officer's collaboration meeting, I think he said. So, when we're sorted here, I want you to get hold of him as soon as he's available. Give him a short heads up and tell him

I need to see him soonest. I'll give him a full brief. If he's up for it, he'll have a good deal of advance organisation to sort out. So, if you can get hold of him before close of play today, so much the better. I'd like to see him tomorrow morning, if possible."

"Okay, I'll get on it."

"But before you go, we need to get things straight here, okay?"

Barford moved uncertainly forward to the edge of his chair. "Er, is that all then? Now I've done what you ask, you know clocked the guy, can I go now? I'm thinking, the wife and kids, they'll be worried."

Wainwright's head snapped round eyes glaring. "Go? Are you kidding? Don't you realise if it weren't for this exercise you would be sitting in a lock-up right now. And I'd have been happy to put you there. As for your wife and children...any worry they have is totally down to you, mate. So, if I were you, I'd sit tight and hear what Mr Stern has got to say."

Lowering his eyes, Barford slid back in the chair. "I just thought now I'd identified the guy..."

Stern shook his head. "Not as easy as that, I'm afraid. That's only part one of the deal. Now, it's on to part two. And in this part, you're a major player. Right now, you're still on the street because of your cooperation with the police. You've knowingly committed a crime, and, at one level or other, you will have to pay. You will just have to resign yourself to that. However, your fate could well depend on how you continue to cooperate, and what happens over the next days."

Barford looked crestfallen but said nothing.

"So, here's what we do," Stern went on, continuing to hold Barford's attention. "I suspect it won't be long before you get a call giving you details of another collection and delivery." He thought for a beat, something occurring. "Normally, you're not given much notice, are you?"

"No, not often," Barford replied. "Usually not very much. I think they have to wait until the boat is almost at the coast. I suppose anything could happen on a crossing, so they wait until they're sure of its arrival. Mostly half an hour, forty-five minutes is about average. An hour max."

"Okay, we'll need to know as soon as you receive a call." Stern opened the draw of his desk and pulled out the GPS tracker. "This is fully charged and ready to go. As soon as you get that call, you are to tuck this away somewhere on the van. We'll then be able to track your every move. All you have to do is carry on as you've done with other trips. The police will take care of everything else."

Barford twisted his hands together, concern darkening his eyes. "But that means I'm doing it again. If the police pick me up…"

Stern held Barford with an uncompromising stare. "On this trip, you need not worry about the police. They will know the score. Right now, you're up to your neck, anyway. As far as I'm concerned, this is your only chance of any kind of redemption." He gave an unconcerned shrug. "But if you'd prefer not to do it, you can go with Constable Wainwright now and take your chances."

Barford's lips tightened, anger bubbling to the surface. "You've already got my balls in a sling, no need to turn the screw," he grumbled.

Stern remained impassive, not reacting to the outburst. "Good. For your wife and kids' sakes, I'm glad." He turned to Cherry. "Cherry, unless David decides otherwise, I'd like you to do the tracking here in the office. You can keep everyone informed by mobile, okay?"

Cherry hid the smile struggling to blossom, the excitement building inside. Unlike when he had first returned from Australia, this was the boss in full flow, back to his old self. It felt good. "Right boss."

"Okay, there's not much more we can do until Inspector O'Connor gets involved." He handed the GPS tracker across the desk to Barford. "You shout as soon as they get in touch, right? And, take it from me, this can only help your cause."

Barford stood and pulled his shoulders back, a determined move. "Yeah, thanks. Can I go now?"

After he had left, Wainwright looked a little uncertain. "Don't suppose he'll do a runner, do you?"

Stern shook his head. "No chance, too much to lose. He's not a criminal. He just let the money blind him. Trouble is, he got mixed up in one of the worst crimes of our day. He'll have to pay, but let's hope for the family's sake, the judge takes his cooperation into consideration."

"Just one more thing before I head out," Wainwright said. He reached down beside the chair and lifted a plastic evidence bag he'd had with him since their return from the Butler house. "The search I did by the cottage. I found this in the undergrowth by the hedge. Thought you'd be interested." He reached into the bag and pulled out a plastic water bottle with a wire cage holding a small round candle hanging from it. The bottle was split down the side and empty, the wire mangled. "Look familiar?"

<h1 align="center">Fifty-one</h1>

With a warm mid-morning sun glinting on shop windows, it felt like spring had truly arrived, and despite it being a Sunday, the Norwich City town centre was buzzing.

The two of them were sitting at a table outside one of the many popular cafés in the pedestrian area. O'Connor's choice, away from Police Headquarters' ears. Until he knew exactly what Stern had to tell him, he wasn't prepared to be overheard. Regardless of police security measures, there was always at least one slack mouth at every station. Here, with people chatting, passing to and fro, going about their everyday business, they were just another pair of guys enjoying a coffee in the sunshine.

O'Connor leaned a little closer, his voice just audible above the hustle and bustle around them. "So, you're now convinced Eddie Butler is involved in people and drug trafficking?"

"And murder," Stern said quietly. "Not personally, of course. I believe he's too clever for that. But everything points to him being behind the whole setup."

O'Connor took a deep breath and puffed out heavily.

"I think Charlie Croker was involved initially," Stern went on. "He was a single bloke and hard up. They probably recruited him by flashing pound notes in front of his eyes. I don't know how long he was involved, but for some reason, he eventually decided to knock it on the head. We know that from Preston's notes. But they couldn't allow that...he knew too much."

"So, he ended up face down in the Wensum," O'Connor finished for him.

"He did. And again, if we're to believe what everybody said about him being T-total, my guess is he was probably force-fed booze and drugs before he went in."

O'Connor sipped his coffee. "This is nasty stuff, Theo. Very big and very nasty. I took another look at the Butler file yesterday. The man's got an OBE for his work in industry, for goodness sake."

"He might have, but like I said before, he wouldn't be the first highly respected individual to tread the dark side."

O'Connor shook his head. "I know it's true. But my boss is going to have a bloody coronary when I tell him."

"Well hold onto your hat because it doesn't end there. With what we found in Preston's garage and again in the shrubbery at Butler's place, I think Preston's vigilante activities came to an end when he tried to torch the cottage."

O'Connor straightened, surprise in his eyes. "You mean he was actually on the Butler property before he was killed?"

"Better than that. I think he was actually killed there."

O'Connor closed his eyes. "Jesus, Theo, where's this all going?"

"I know it's not good but let me explain. You see, I think Preston sussed, as we did, that the only area not covered by security lights and cameras was behind the cottage, the side away from the house. So, he made it his next target. Remember, in his note he threatened there was more to come. When I checked his garage, I found what I now believe to be the makings of a sort of fuse. It was a crude contraption, using a plastic bottle filled with petrol with a tea light hanging under it."

O'Connor frowned. "Don't get you."

Stern smiled. "I know...it confused me at first, too. Then I remembered seeing a crime programme on TV where an arsonist made a fuse out of a condom filled with petrol hanging over a candle. My guess is Preston devised a similar contraption by hanging a tea light under a plastic bottle filled with petrol. The idea being the lower the tea light hung down from the bottle, the longer it took to melt the plastic and ignite the petrol, giving him time to get out of there before it blew. The paraphernalia I found in his garage convinced me that's exactly what he'd been experimenting with. Give him credit; if it was what he used on the boat, it worked a treat. He might have cut himself in the process, but he was obviously well away before anyone noticed the boat going up."

"But he never got to use it on the cottage, did he?"

Stern shook his head. "My guess is he was caught in the act. The trodden down grass behind the cottage could easily have been caused by a struggle."

O'Connor held the cup close to his lips for some time before he spoke again. "So, you're saying he was probably killed there, then dumped in the river."

"Yup. That's my best guess. Seems these people have a fetish for dumping bodies in our rivers."

Stern chose not to interrupt another long silence, O'Connor pulling thoughtfully at his bottom lip. "Okay, Theo, I've got that," he said finally. "Now, what about this Barford guy?"

Stern leaned in. "Barford is where our strength lies. I think using him, we can nail the lot of them. I already have a plan in mind, but it would need your approval and authorisation. Probably someone even higher, because it would mean pulling together police resources outside your patch."

"My boss, you mean?"

Stern shrugged. "Could be, that'll be for you to decide."

"Okay, tell me what you've got, and we'll take it from there."

Fifty-two

Stern and Cyril Makepeace were huddled at a corner table in the We-R -Lunch dining room where Stern was outlining what was probably going to take place in the coming early hours.

"Sometimes they bring in packages, which I'm sure are drugs, as well as a human cargo. The drugs are dumped on a boat moored close to West Somerton. D'you know West Somerton?"

"Yeah, it's just up from Caister. I've got a customer drives over from there. Just for his lunch, would you believe?"

"I believe it," Stern said with a smile. "I had the fish pie and crumble, remember?" He pushed the pleasant memory away. This was business. "So then, the people are taken on to wherever. Barford told us he'd handed over people to be delivered to Birmingham, Sheffield and once even to Liverpool."

Cyril gave a soft whistle. "Christ, that's some round trip."

"It is, but he didn't always go all the way. Sometimes, he'd meet another vehicle somewhere en-route and transfer the cargo. Anyway, I was hoping they'd use the boat tonight, because we're ninety-nine percent sure it's the same one hired by Butler. I was guessing to get from Somerton to Wroxham by river must take a good four hours, which means it would have been back at Butler's place sometime tomorrow morning. If we could have had people waiting both there and at wherever Barford was due to take his human cargo, we could have nailed the whole kit and caboodle, including Butler." He gave an irritated shake of the head. "Unfortunately, that's not going to happen. Unusually, Barford has been given advance warning of his cargo. Seems this time he's only carrying people. He tells me it's straight from the pickup to two addresses in the smoke."

"When is this?"

"Don't know exactly. Barford hasn't been given a time, yet. He probably won't get that 'till an hour or so before he has to go."

"But no mention of the boat?"

"None. And I'm peeved at that. In fact, when Barford reported to us earlier we had a local blue take a look. The boat's still moored at Butler's place."

They sat silently for a moment, Cyril chewing his bottom lip, thinking. "So, where d'you think the people, the immigrants, are coming from?" he asked finally.

"Can't be sure until they're picked up and questioned, but I wouldn't be surprised if wherever they came from originally they ended up at the Calais camp. The Jungle, remember?"

"But that was broken up, wasn't it?"

"It was, but what about the people? There were plenty who just disappeared into the surrounding countryside. And think about it...from Calais to, let's say, the coast along The Hague area in the Netherlands can only be a four or five-hour drive. Let's face it, you could walk it in three of four days. That would seem nothing to what some of these poor souls have already been through. Once there they would probably do anything to get some unscrupulous people smuggler to ship them across to the UK. To the North Norfolk coast."

"It's been done before," Cyril agreed.

"And while there are people willing to pay, it'll be done again," Stern came back. "'Course, in this particular case, I'm only guessing, but I reckon it's as good a bet as any."

"Okay, so what now?"

"Well, I suggested we wait for another delivery," Stern said. "But it was David O'Connor's call, and he figured a bird in the hand…" He didn't finish, just gave a short shrug of his shoulders.

"He has a point, I suppose," Cyril said.

"I know, but it's bloody annoying."

They sat in silence for a long time before Stern, a deep thoughtful frown creasing his forehead, spoke again. "You know, when I was at Butler's place last Saturday, I talked to his handyman, this guy called Adams. We were down by the river, and it's just occurred to me how, while we were talking, he seemed to constantly manoeuvre himself between me and the boat. It was a sort of casual movement, as if he was just unconsciously moving around as we talked. I did notice it but didn't attach any importance to it at the time. You know, some people find it difficult to stand in one place for long, always hopping around as if…" He stopped suddenly, his eyes narrowing.

"What?"

Stern was quiet for some time before going on. "Well, what if it wasn't like that. What if he was deliberately putting himself between me and the boat? You know, trying to divert my attention away from it." He stopped again, his eyes brightening, holding Cyril's questioning gaze. "Now, why would he do that, d'you think?"

Cyril had been a police detective for a very long time. He might be retired now, but age hadn't slowed the brain. It took no more than a millisecond for him to realise what Stern was inferring. "You mean there could already be stuff on board."

"It's a thought."

"I suppose. But risky to keep the stuff at the house, don't you think?"

Stern drew down his lips contemptuously. "Not if you're a highly respected citizen who plays golf with top brass, and no one would even contemplate questioning."

"Okay, so we have a boat moored on Butler property we suspect is carrying drugs. How do you propose proving it? You can't just roll up and demand you search the boat. Someone of Butler's standing would have the world around your ears in a heartbeat."

Stern gave an engaging grin. "Who said anything about turning up and demanding anything?"

Cyril's mouth dropped open. "You don't mean...?" In the past he'd partnered Stern in some pretty precarious situations. Leading from the front was always a given and, sometimes, the line between official and unofficial was decidedly blurred. It was a long time since he'd seen that look but he recognised it now. "Theo, remember we're a couple of oldies no longer on the job, so whatever you're thinking..." He gave a resigned shake of the head. He had a feeling he knew exactly what his friend was thinking.

~ * ~

Cherry and Rob sat side by side in bed, their faces glowing in the light from the screen of the laptop propped up on Cherry's knees. They were studying a map of the local area in the centre of which a single stationary light was blinking.

"So, what are we waiting for?" Rob asked.

"We're waiting for the light to move," Cherry replied softly. She looked at the bedside clock. "Just before one," she muttered. "He should be on the move any time now."

"Then what?"

"I have to report his progress to the boss."

"How?"

"Mobile. I have him on speed dial."

"So, where is he?"

A little frown touched Cherry's forehead. "He's, er, out in the field."

"Which field?"

She dug him with her elbow. "You know what I mean."

"Yeah, I think so. You mean you've got no idea where he is, right?"

"Right now, no I haven't. But when this is over, I will have because he'll tell me everything. He always does. Anyway, wherever he is, I'll bet he's up to his neck in the action. It wouldn't be the boss if he wasn't."

Rob gave a sniff. "So, when you say report progress, it's not just when it kicks off then? When this bloke gets on the move?"

Cherry gave a small shake of the head, her eyes never leaving the screen. "No, they need to know he's following the route he told us about. Not trying to pull a fast one. If he doesn't move soon, it could mean he's taken the tracker off the van. If he's done that, we'll never know where he's headed."

Rob thought for a moment. "Forgive me for saying but shouldn't the police be doing all this?"

Cherry turned, her face just an inch from his. "In this case, the boss is working for the police. He's sort of attached, a special investigator."

Rob took advantage of the closeness and kissed her on the lips. He reached across and switched off the bedside light, sliding down under the duvet. "Which makes you an assistant special investigator, I suppose." He pulled the duvet over his head. "Mmmm, sexy," she heard him mumble. "Never slept with an assistant special investigator before."

A few minutes later, with Rob breathing steadily beside her, Cherry's eyes began to droop. She eased herself up and reached for the glass of water at the bedside. As she did so, from the corner of her eye, she saw the movement on the screen. Sliding carefully out of the bed, she quietly left the room and headed downstairs carrying the laptop and mobile phone. Settling herself at the kitchen table, she hit the speed dial number.

~ * ~

It was a few minutes to one when Steve Barford left the house. He was sweating profusely. Fact was, since the exercise with Theo Stern and the others, when he'd identified his recruiter, there were few times when he hadn't been sweating. Jesus, if he believed what Stern told him about these people, he was dealing with killers. Especially if he tried to call it a day. Which is exactly what he'd intended to do once he'd built their bank balance up sufficiently. Sure, he knew what he was doing was a bit iffy, but who wasn't into something not kosher at some time or the other. And, of course, there was the thrill of it all. The night rides, the delivery of mysterious boxes and packages. He had no idea what any of them contained, and he didn't want to know. By not knowing, he was able to defend, or at least play down, the gravity of his actions. For all he knew, it could have been something quite innocent. The pickups on the shore were more difficult to justify. He finally mollified his own conscience by convincing himself they were obviously being persecuted in their home country, and it was right to bring them to a safe haven. He gave a heavy sigh as he climbed into the van. Who the hell was he kidding? It was about the cash. They'd waved big money under his nose, and he'd dived in, regardless. And like always, it got easier as time passed. However guilty he felt when delivering the goods, it all washed away when the next thick brown envelope arrived. No, he'd got himself involved in a shitty business and put everything at risk, most of all the family. He'd never forgive himself for that. He only hoped, when the time came, they would take what he was doing now into consideration. If they didn't... He shuddered as he turned the ignition key, unwilling to even think of the consequences.

That morning, as soon as he'd received the information, he had called Stern. Stern was out, but his girl, who Barford knew didn't like him very much and made no bones about showing it, had taken the details. It was straightforward; six people collected from a little further down the coast this time, then a direct run into London. He'd given the pickup location on the map...a remote spot at the far end of what they called The Winterton Dunes National Nature Reserve, and both the address and post codes of the two destinations in North London. Cherry had told him that since their meeting, Stern had been in touch with the police, and everything had been arranged. People were on standby, and he was to carry out the collection and delivery exactly as instructed. He wouldn't be impeded, in fact, he probably wouldn't know anything out of the ordinary had happened. When he'd made the final drops, he was to head home and wait to be contacted.

His heart full of trepidation, he headed out of Cromer, the sweat barely diminishing.

Fifty-three

Steve Barford crouched low in the hollow he'd scraped in the sand dunes. Thin reedy plants brushed his face as they moved to a chilled breeze coming off the sea. After a couple of tours in Afghanistan with the mob, he wasn't a great lover of sand and the irritating plant movement annoyed him. Still, there were a couple of benefits to this pickup. First, when his charges arrived, he only had to lead them along an overgrown and very rutted track back to the road where he'd hidden the van behind a hedge. Difficult to follow and quite a distance, but easier than sometimes before when there was a cliff to scramble up. He'd always been terrified of one of them falling and hurting themselves. Especially the young girls. He'd it made clear from the start he was only to deliver unspoiled goods. They would not have been happy if he'd turned up with any of his charges injured in any way. The other benefit, of course, was this time he was doing nothing illegal. Quite the reverse...he was helping the police. He thought so, anyway. Unless Stern was leading him on. If that was the case, then he could be mopped up in one of the expected raids, either here or at the London drops. He sighed in the darkness. When the muck hit the fan, he'd soon find out.

He wondered again when that would be. He assumed the police would have both ends covered, but how it would affect him he didn't know. He'd been told to carry on as usual whatever happened. How he was supposed to do that if things kicked off around him he didn't know. He eased back on his haunches, relaxing lower into the soft sand, never taking his eyes away from the direction of waves he could hear breaking on the beach no more than a hundred feet or so from where he was hunched down. Too late to worry about all that now, he thought. He'd just have to wait and see.

As he stared out into the blackness, a layer of low heavyweight cloud overhead eliminating any semblance of light, he was grateful the weather forecast predicted the rain staying away until later tomorrow. Sitting as he was in pouring rain would not have been fun.

Only minutes later, when he thought he saw the first tiny blink, his heart kicked up a notch as it always did at this point. It was little more than a pinprick of light slightly to the left of where he crouched. He reached into the pocket of the heavy waterproof he was wearing and pulled out the powerful torch. Not yet though. He had to be sure, wait until he got the correct signal; the steady dash dash dash-dash dot dash, morse for OK. Then he could reply with the same. He felt the sweat return and knew the time had come.

~ * ~

Stern felt the mobile vibrate in his pocket. Under the circumstances, he was glad he'd remembered to deactivate the ring tone. He pulled out the instrument and clamped it tightly to his ear. Always conscious of the rumours about damaging mobile phone waves, he would normally have used the speaker, holding it well away from his head. Not this time.

"Cherry." His voice was a hoarse whisper.

"He's on the move, boss. Set out a few minutes ago. Looks like he's heading for the coast as he told us."

"Well done, luv. Let me know when and where he stops."

"Will do. Where are you?"

"Not now, Cherry. Just keep me informed, okay?"

"Er, yeah, I will. Are you okay?"

"Of course, just a bit busy. Talk later." He slipped the phone back in his pocket and turned to Cyril. "Ready?"

"Yup, I've always looked forward to getting to a ripe old age then committing suicide."

Stern grinned in the darkness. "Don't give me that, you're loving every minute of it."

Cyril didn't answer, just eased open the Land Rover door and climbed out, slowly closing the door without latching it.

Stern followed suit and made his way round to the back of the car, waiting for Cyril to open the rear door. "You sure this thing will float?" he whispered.

Cyril latched back the door. "It's a bit bloody late to ask me that, Theo," he whispered.

"I know, but..."

"Look, Clarissa said she'd paddled most of the Bure in it. Said the Abo's have used them like this for generations." He reached into the back of the vehicle for the crudely made canoe. "Now you'd better give me a hand with this before I lose my bottle and head for home."

Between them, they manoeuvred the lightweight craft from the back of the vehicle and carried it to the river's edge, sliding it into the water. There was very little light, but what there was reflected on the river surface showing a pale shimmering ribbon, a path to where they were headed. While Stern held the little craft steady, Cyril climbed in first, grumbling as he did so. "I've got to be out of my mind."

Minutes later, with Stern crouched in the rear, they were both safely aboard and afloat. They sat for some minutes in the shallows ensuring they would stay that way. Finally satisfied, they began to paddle quietly up river.

"I guess no more than ten minutes," Stern whispered. "It'll come up on our left." He pulled the paddle in as he felt the mobile vibrate again. "Cherry."

"He's there, boss. Exactly where he told us."

"Good girl. What time is it?" he whispered.

"Coming on two."

"Okay, you get some sleep. The police will take it from here."

"Will do." She paused. "You sure you're alright, boss."

"Yeah, I'm good," he whispered. "I'll see you later."

~ * ~

Steve Barford returned the okay signal with the torch to show his position, then moved forward and waited at the water's edge. The boat had come closer in shore than in the past when usually there was some form of rubber dingy to dispose of. This time, his charges were lowered bodily over the side into waist deep water and had to struggle toward the beach. This would be a terrifying experience for any one of them if they couldn't swim and, almost immediately, he caught the sound of faint fearful whimpering. He'd been told there would be six in all; two men and four women. He waited in anticipation, hoping they all came ashore safely.

He glanced around anxiously. There wasn't a sight or sound of anyone. Just the very faint rumble of powerful engines gently ticking over, the skipper skilfully holding the boat on station as its cargo was dumped over the side. If the police were here, or even out there on the water somewhere, there was not the slightest evidence of it.

He was pleased to see the first three individuals; a man linking arms with two young females making their way through the surf toward him. Minutes later, the others followed. Again, a man and two women, the man actually carrying one of the women. As they reached him, the man lowered the woman to her feet. Barford briefly flashed the torch on each of them to check they were okay. His stomach sank to see the shivering female that had been carried was no more than thirteen or fourteen years old. Even this terrified pathetic child, like all the others, had the plastic-covered package hanging round her neck. A huge wave of guilt swept over him. Whatever punishment he received, Barford was pleased this would be over soon.

Quickly herding the six together and, as he had done in the past, gesturing how they had to follow him closely, follow the torch, he made his way swiftly up the beach. He never looked back, never intended to. Whatever happened back there, if it happened at all, he didn't want to see. He'd had instructions to carry on as usual, whatever happened. That's exactly what he intended to do.

Even if Barford had stayed and waited to see what transpired after the six unfortunates had left the boat, he would have been disappointed. That was because, unlike the heavily armed police on the two commandeered fast moving inshore lifeboats approaching either side of the smuggler's boat, he wasn't equipped with night vision binoculars and cameras.

Barford and his bedraggled crew were on board the van and well away before the blaring searchlights erupted and froze the two Dutch ex-fishermen turned people smugglers in their tracks.

~ * ~

It had taken longer than expected, the tide, though not very strong on this stretch of river, being in the opposite direction. For a powered craft not even noticeable, but for two elderly, inexperienced paddlers who were having difficulty keeping the rustic craft in a straight line in the first place, much more of a problem. But age never came into the equation, and quitting was not a word recognised by two hardened ex-frontline police officers. Finally, they came to rest alongside the hire craft moored at the Butler property riverside banking. They both shipped their paddles and, for a moment, clung to the outer rail of the boat, catching their breath.

"I don't think the security system stretches this far," Stern whispered. "But if we stay waterside, away from the house, we should be good."

"Fair enough," Cyril answered, the words soft and hoarse. "Must get more exercise. I'm bloody knackered."

Stern grinned in the darkness. Despite the possible danger, he was enjoying this. "Not the powerhouse who used to protect my back then?"

"I'm here, aren't I?"

"You are, mate, and I appreciate it." Stern reached into his pocket and touched the pouch containing the little group of metal instruments he hadn't used for some time. "I'll be as quick as I can, okay," he whispered. "Just try and hold this contraption still enough for me to get on board. I don't want to end up in the drink."

Fifty-four

In Stern's office they had O'Connor on speaker phone. The delight in his voice was obvious.

"We had a guy dug in a little further up the beach. He recorded the whole thing with a night vision camera. As soon as the drop had been made, and we were sure Barford and the group were well on their way, we closed in with a couple of borrowed inshore lifeboats we'd equipped with armed police and powerful spots."

Stern grinned across at Cherry sitting opposite. "A success then?"

"You'd better believe it, Theo," O'Connor came back. "There were just two smugglers on board the boat, and when our guys hit them with the spots and a megaphone screaming 'armed police', they froze in their tracks." He gave a joyful little chuckle. "Would you believe the pair of them even put their hands up. They didn't resist at all, and since being taken in they've admitted to being Dutch fisherman. Said the money being offered was just too good to refuse."

"Won't do them a lot of good now, will it?" Stern mused. "How did the London end go?"

"Just as good. The Met hit each individual drop as soon as the van had left. Word is they used the Sweeney. Would love to have been there."

Stern smiled. It was the first time he'd heard the old cockney rhyming slang description of the Flying Squad for a very long time. The hard case division of the Met had been facing violent criminals on the London streets since 1919, when their transport was a canvas-covered wagon drawn by horses. They were first nicknamed The Sweeney after the notorious fictitious London murderer Sweeney Todd (Sweeney Todd - Flying Squad). Stern hadn't expected to hear a detective inspector in Norfolk using cockney rhyming slang.

"Did they get much out of it?"

"Don't know exact figures," O'Connor admitted. "But it looks like a good hit. The DI in charge gave me a courtesy call first thing. Said they'd pulled several girls from each address and were holding several others, men and women, pending charges. Both addresses are still being searched, but he said from what they've already found, it looks like an Eastern European outfit, probably Polish. Early days, though. Said he'd get back to me when he's got the full picture. Told me the brass down there was double chuffed with what we'd given them. Asked him to send their congrats."

"Good of 'em," Stern said, trying to hold an old prejudice from his words. He remembered his days when some of the brass, or those fat arses squatting in their high backed padded chairs upstairs, as they were frequently referred to by some, weren't held in the highest regard. And it was true that some, though not all, were first and foremost political animals, relishing the limelight of the TV cameras when things went right, suddenly unavailable for comment when the opposite occurred. A lot could well have changed since his day, but he doubted that particular situation would ever change. He gave a derisive sniff but didn't comment further. "What's the situation with Barford?"

"He's good. Like I said, they waited for him to be gone before moving on the targets. He should be well home by now. We will be picking him up, though, Theo. He still has charges to face."

"Of course, and he knows that." Stern had decided not to tell his friend about his little midnight canoe ride with Cyril. It had been a completely illegal move, and if it upset O'Connor, it could well jeopardise the future cooperation he was about to push for. They were friends but, for a copper, however close, friendship could only stretch so far. "How're you going to play the Butler thing?"

"Good question, Theo. I know you wanted us to wait until they delivered something to the boat, so we could nail Butler as well, but you have to agree last night was a winner."

"Of course, but unless we can find proof positive the outfit was linked to Butler, he walks, right?"

"Yes, but at the moment, we only have Barford's word that Adams is the man who recruited him. And he could only say he thought the hire boat moored at the Butler property looked the same shape as the one he delivered the packages to. Add to that Barford's credibility nose-diving as soon as we pick him up and charge him with being part of the outfit. Can you imagine what a field day a good lawyer would have with that? And Butler has good lawyers coming out of his ears."

"So, we need more?"

"We certainly do."

Stern knew exactly what he was coming up with next, but like the previous night's exercise it would need O'Connor's approval. Giving Cherry a wink, he let the conundrum fester for a while before pushing on. Finally, he said, "Okay, so we need to search the Butler property, including the boat."

"What?"

"Look David, I'm absolutely sure Butler is up to his neck in this. He might be a big wig in the city, but as I said before, it wouldn't be the first time someone in his position's gone ape. I think we missed a trick by not waiting until they had a double delivery; people to the Smoke and drugs for distribution up here in Norfolk. Then we could have nailed the whole shebang. Okay, so far, we've done good, can't deny it. But if we're to take the whole thing down, including Butler, we need a plan B. That means finding a direct link to the big man. Can you think of anything better than finding something on his property?"

"No, of course not. But, Theo, to carry out an official search, we have to have evidence, and right now, we've got squit. Okay, we know from the London sting the people were carrying drugs that were sealed in plastic. That doesn't mean the packages Barford delivered to the boat also contained drugs. Like Barford said, they were just packages."

Stern felt the frustration creeping into the back of his throat, but he understood O'Connor's fears. Get it wrong with such a high flyer as Butler, and his whole career could be put in jeopardy. Nevertheless, he couldn't see an alternative. He had to push on. "Are you kidding me? Can you think of anything else they could be smuggling in during the small hours? Especially considering what we got from the London run."

"No, I admit that. But we're talking Butler here. And you know how much clout he has. My boss would skin me alive if he knew I was even thinking I was after a search warrant for the Butler property. Proof, Theo. Rock solid proof. Then we'll be able to move. Legally, I mean. Otherwise it's a no-go."

Stern was getting to where he wanted to be. Plan B. "Okay, forget the search idea then. Just send me in there to update Butler on our progress with the burning of his boat, and the body found in the river. Don't need a warrant for that, do we?"

"No, but I don't get you. What good would it..."

"It gets me in. Legally. Good public relations, too. A crime has been committed against a prominent member of our community. We think the body in the river might well be linked to that crime. A man of his standing, it's only right he should be kept up to date on the progress of our investigations."

"Okay, so it gets you in. Then what?"

"Then I play it by ear. Somehow get myself into the boat, even the cottage. I wouldn't be at all surprised if our dodgy Mr Adams, or whatever his real name is, has something stashed away there, too." From his late canoe trip with Cyril, Stern knew very well the boat was a given. All he had to do was get aboard legally. The cottage would be a bonus.

"And what if there's nothing to find, and you're caught poking around where you have no right to be? The shit will hit the fan, and we'll all get a splatter. Me, in particular, for employing you in the first place. I've got a while to go yet, Theo, but my pension is important to me."

Stern took the point. "Okay, okay I get it. But for a start, I know there will be something there."

"Oh yeah? How?"

"Call it copper's nose or whatever you like, but it's there, I guarantee it." He pushed on quickly before his friend dug any deeper. "If I get dumped, then I'm just a civilian consultant who went rogue, thought he knew better, and stepped way out of his mandate. You immediately give me the order of the boot, and I'll back off. You might get a short sharp kick up the rump for bad judgement in employing me in the first place, and that'll be the end of it. But it won't happen, David, you have my word."

Fifty-five

They'd closed the office at five and headed home. At the flat, Stern had thrown a ready meal lasagne in the microwave and made tea. He was sprawled in the armchair balancing a tray holding the makeshift meal on his knees. As he forked the hot lasagne, chewing tentatively, his mind was in overdrive. He'd managed to convince O'Connor that to get onto the Butler property once more was a priority. Previously, the excuse had been to check the river bank. This time it would be to update Butler on their progress regarding enquiries into the burning of his boat. Of course, the real task was to discover the evidence that Stern knew was there and incriminate Butler personally. So, from what he and Cyril had found when they checked the hire craft the previous night, it was imperative he moved quickly. He didn't want to give them time to make changes or move anything.

Stern also knew, as soon as he deviated from the authorised task of updating Butler, he would be on his own. It was going to be difficult. Taking into consideration who he was dealing with, possibly dangerous. With that in mind, though he would never have admitted

309

it to Cherry, Stern would have appreciated having Paul Wainwright alongside. He'd grown fond of the young constable and recognised the same enthusiasm he'd had himself as a young street copper. Sure, this was rural Norfolk, not the nineteen seventies streets of the East End of London, but nonetheless, Wainwright was exactly what the police force needed, wherever he was based. He had great potential and deserved to go far.

But this was one gig where Stern needed to separate himself from officialdom. O'Connor had made it quite clear if things did go belly up, he was on his own. Well not quite. When he'd outlined his plan to Cherry, she had insisted, as his assistant special investigator, she should be at his side. And for once, he hadn't taken much persuading. He needed someone and, after the little, late night jaunt on the river, he felt it better to lay off an exhausted Cyril for a while. After all, Cherry was his official assistant. She could also be one very tough cookie when necessary. Over the years, she had shown her mettle more than once.

Finishing the meal, he slid the tray onto the floor alongside the chair and relaxed back. As he did so, his mobile sprung to life. He pulled it from his pocket and looked at the screen. "Cherry?"

"Sorry to bother you, boss, but Rob's working late. Would you believe a London customer, bags of cash? His boat needs a complete engine change, and he wants it ready to kick off first thing tomorrow. I reckon poor old Rob will be at it all night."

"And you called to tell me that?"

"No, of course not. I only told you that to let you know, because I'm here on my own, I've been thinking."

"About what?" Need he ask?

"About the case, of course. See, you said we needed to get onto Butler's property as soon as possible, right."

"That's right. Strangely enough, I was just thinking about that myself. I don't want to give anyone the chance to move or get rid of anything. And it is important Butler is at home when we go in."

"Because when we find what we're after, the devious old git can be cautioned and charged personally on the spot," Cherry finished for him.

"Right again."

"Well how about this, then," Cherry came back. "Today's Friday."

Frowning, Stern waited for her to continue. When she didn't he said, "I know, it has been all day."

Cherry gave an exaggerated sigh. "D'you know boss, sometimes I wonder if you really are up to this detective game."

Stern smiled. She'd obviously thought of something she felt important. He would just have to play the game. "Well, it is late. And like you keep telling me, I am getting on a bit."

"Yeah, well don't worry, I'm always here to help you with the zimmer frame." She paused, but only for a beat. "No, seriously, boss, it came to me that Butler's driver told you he drove Butler up to Norfolk on a Friday, didn't he?"

Stern felt the adrenalin instantly kick in. "You're right, kiddo, he did."

"So, like I said, today's Friday," Cherry said, the excitement bubbling.

Stern glanced at his watch. Just before seven. Butler could well be there right now. "Cherry, I've just designated you as genius of the month. Stay by the phone; I'll call you back."

Ending the call, Stern found his notebook and flicked through the pages. Finally, finding what he was looking for, he dialled a number and hit the speaker button. After several rings the phone was answered. "Yes?" It was a woman's voice, and Stern remembered the abrupt tones of Stefana, Katrina Butler's mother.

"Mr Butler, please."

There was a hesitant pause before, "Mr Butler only just here. He very tired."

Holding his hand over the phone, Stern smiled. "Sometimes things do come together," he muttered to himself. He removed his hand. "This is Special Investigator Stern from the police." He spoke sharply, his words clipped, an authoritative edge to his voice. "I wish to speak with Mr Butler. Please ask him to come to the phone."

He heard the aggravated snort at the other end. "You wait."

It was some long moments before Butler came on the line. He did indeed sound tired. "Mr Stern, so sorry to keep you waiting. Not long got here. Bloody traffic. Just managed to shower and change. Stefana said it was important."

A complete change of tone now. Softer, more persuasive. "I do apologise for this intrusion, Mr Butler, but what I need to talk to you about directly relates to the burning of your boat, and the body found in the river."

"You mean the two incidents are linked?"

"There are indications that could be the case, yes. It's why I need to talk to you. It would take no more than half an hour and it would be a great help in our enquiries."

"Well, of course, I'll help if I can. Would tomorrow...?"

"Ah, I'm sorry to say that could be too late," Stern interrupted. "You see, depending on the result of our discussion, immediate action could be necessary."

"You mean you want to talk tonight?"

"Yes, I'm afraid so. Again, I can only apologise, but time could be critical. And again, I promise no more than half an hour."

The heavy sigh was audible over the speaker. "Well I suppose if it has to be." A moment's silence, then, "But I'll need time to grab a bite, put my feet up for an hour. How about sometime after nine? Would that be convenient?"

"That would be perfect. Shall we say nine thirty? And, Mr Butler, I really do appreciate your cooperation." Beaming, he ended the call, immediately calling Cherry back. "We're in," he said as soon as she answered. "Now, I know why I keep you on the books."

"When?" Even the single word resonated Cherry's excitement.

"Tonight. Half nine."

"Right. I'm on my way."

"Whoa, hang on. Are you sure..."

"Boss, I'm sitting here on my own. Probably for the rest of the night. Why would I want to do that when I could be with you on the case?" She didn't wait for an answer. "I'll be at the flat in half an hour."

Over coffee in a local high street café, they spent time going over Stern's plan, which was simply to find some incriminating evidence on Butler's premises. Anything that would give them the authority for a further, more intensive search.

Stern knew the boat was the key, but his knowledge there had been gained illegitimately and, at this point, was unusable. He certainly couldn't go barrelling in demanding to search it. If he did, Butler could have the world down around his ears. Neither could he see a way of persuading Butler to allow them on the boat without a legitimate reason. To try would only create suspicion and probably resistance to any further cooperation. No, initially everything had to be with Butler's permission.

The cottage was a better option. Unlike the boat, he had no concrete evidence to say there would be anything incriminating hidden there. But he had no doubt, with what they already knew, there had to be. Find something in the cottage, and it would be open season at the Butler estate. Boat and all. Time was of the greatest importance because twenty-four hours had already elapsed since he had searched the boat. Twenty-four hours during which things could have changed a good deal.

Fifty-six

The lane to the Butler property was completely unlit and, with heavy clouds above obscuring any moonlight there may have been, only the car's headlights showed the way. Stern pulled the car to a halt outside the gates, leaving the engine idling, the lights on. He climbed out and moved across to the gate and the intercom on the side pillar. This time, after buzzing through and announcing himself, the gates opened remotely, he guessed from within the house. There was no sign of Ron Pace. He must have already signed off and gone to his digs in the village, or even back home to London for the weekend. Stern remembered Pace telling him how Butler generously allowed him to use the car for that purpose. Not for the first time, Stern wondered if Pace knew of, or was even involved in, his boss's nefarious activities. Having worked for Butler for so many years, it seemed almost impossible he wouldn't be. Yet somehow, as gruff and bullish as the big man was, Stern felt there was an air of honesty about him.

At the same time as the gates began to slide apart, the driveway was illuminated by a row of lights stretching from the gate to the house. A quick scan revealed the Range Rover he'd seen on his previous visit parked in front of the garage. The absence of the Mercedes confirmed his previous conclusion about Pace. He returned to the car and drove through the opened gate, following the drive and parking directly outside the front door.

"Remember, just follow my lead," he reminded Cherry as they climbed out.

The front door was opened before they reached it, and they were greeted by the sour, disapproving face of Stefana. She said nothing, just stood to one side allowing them in, then after closing the door, leading them again into the same sitting room as before. Butler was lounging in one of the huge, beige leather armchairs cupping what looked to Stern to be a large whiskey in both hands. He was alone in the room. He smiled, a small tired movement of his lips, and waved them to the sofa.

"Forgive me for not getting up. It's been a very heavy week." He chuckled softly. "I think age is trying to tell me something."

"I do apologise for intruding on your leisure time," Stern said. He indicated toward Cherry. "This is Cherry Hooker, my personal assistant. She's helping with the enquiry."

Butler smiled pleasantly. "An interesting job you have, Miss Hooker."

Cherry gave him her sweetest smile. "It has its moments, Mr Butler. And it's a pleasure to meet you."

They sat side by side on the sofa, Cherry's eyes roaming admiringly around the room. "You have a wonderful home."

"It is nice, isn't it," Butler said. "Sadly, however, I'm hardly ever able to enjoy it. Sometimes, I wish I could spend more time here, but if I'm honest I'm a compulsive workaholic, always have been. Couldn't live without the cut and thrust of the market. It's what lifted me from my lowly beginnings to where I am today." He gave a slow shake of his head. "No, I couldn't do without it. So, unfortunately, I can only manage the occasional weekend and, even more infrequently, a few extra days here. More than that, and I'm itching to get back at it." He looked from one to the other of them. "Sad, eh?"

"Oh, I don't know," Stern came back. "We are who we are in this world, Mr Butler. There's not an awful lot we can do about it."

"Probably not," Butler admitted. "And I'm fortunate enough to have a young wife who is tolerant of my obsession. That is a bonus." He leaned forward and waved a dismissive hand. "So enough about me. You obviously have more important things to discuss."

"Yes, I believe we have," Stern said. "Firstly, I'd like to know if either of two names I have are familiar to you. The first one is Oliver Preston?" He watched closely for the instant initial reaction to the name. However brief, always the indicator.

Butler thought for a moment, his brow creased into deep furrows. He shook his head. "No, can't say I know the name. Is there any reason why you think I should?"

"Possibly. You see we have pretty conclusive evidence to suggest it was Preston who torched your boat."

Butler's jaw sagged. "Good grief. But why...?"

Stern wasn't about to reveal details of the notes received from Preston. It could be perceived as a direct accusation, and it certainly wouldn't help with the main objective of the visit. "Well, you see, when a criminal act of this type is committed, the perpetrator is often a disgruntled employee. Maybe dismissed for some reason, or made redundant, in their eyes, unfairly. Therefore, if you had known him as one of your employees..."

"Ah yes, I see your point." He took a sip of whiskey, his brow furrowing in thought. "I freely admit, in my business competition is tough. You win some, you lose some. As a result, resentment can be caused. But physical retaliation?" He shook his head. "I've never come across it before. I can't say I know the names of everyone in the organisation, particularly at the lower levels, but I can honestly say, I have never heard the name Preston mentioned."

Stern couldn't believe while battling his way up from a London high street barrow boy, to the highly successful business man he was today, Butler hadn't come across physical intimidation in some form or other. Not possible. If nothing else, the presence of Ron Pace constantly at his side belied that statement. He pushed the thought to one side. "Okay, the other name is..." Before he could go further, the door opened, and Katrina Butler came into the room. She was wearing a simple, straight red dress set just above the knee, and unlike before, when her hair was expertly set in a tight bun, this time it was flowing shoulder length, dark and glossy. Again, she wore no makeup.

Butler's face lit up at the sight of her. "Ah, here she is," he chirped happily. "Come in, sweetheart. Mr Stern is just giving me some interesting news about the boat."

She crossed the room and settled in the other armchair, her hands folded demurely in her lap. "You have found who did this?"

"Yes, I believe we have," Stern said. Then looking back at Butler. "And that's where our difficulty lies. Because, you see, Oliver Preston is also the man we found floating in the river only yards from here." Again, he watched Butler closely, noting his every mannerism.

The whiskey tumbler paused on its way to Butler's lips. "Really? How strange. Are you sure?"

"Yes, I'm afraid we are. It's one of the reasons why we're here this evening."

"So, did he fall off a boat or something? An accident of some kind? I mean people don't usually end up drowning for no reason, do they? There has to be a..." He stopped suddenly, his eyes widening. "It wasn't suicide, was it?"

"No, it wasn't suicide, Mr Butler. Sad to say, Preston was dead before he went into the water. His neck had been broken. You see, he was murdered."

Now, Butler looked genuinely shaken, colour draining from his cheeks. He laid the whiskey glass on the table alongside the chair and took a breath. "Well, I have no idea what's going on here, but I have to admit it's damned unsettling." He took a moment, his hand clasped together, as if to compose himself.

Stern watched. Was this an act or was the concern in Butler's eyes genuine? "I'm sorry if this has been upsetting for you, but it was important we establish if Preston was known to you."

Butler shook his head. "To me, no, but just to be sure I will check with our HR department when I return." He paused for a moment then, "You said two names?"

"Yes, I did. The other name is Charles Croker?"

More thought, then another shake of the head. "Don't mean a thing, I'm afraid. Is he something to do with all this?"

Stern shook his head dismissively. "An associate of Preston's, and not as important at this time." He pushed himself up out of the chair, motioning for Cherry to follow. "It's a sad situation we have here, Mr Butler, and, again, I apologies for intruding on you like this. But it's a mystery we still have to solve, and I hope you understand it was important for us to establish if either of these men was linked in any way with you or your company. We now have to continue our investigations into, firstly, Preston's motive for attacking your boat, and his murder. But for now, I think you have helped us all you can. I thank you for that." He paused for just a beat before continuing. "There is just one last thing I'd like to ask."

"Like I said, anything I can do."

"Last time we were here, when we were checking the river bank, one of our constables found something along the fence line behind the gardener's cottage. You wouldn't have noticed because, if you remember, at the time you stayed in the house." He may have stayed in the house, Stern thought, but he sure as hell knew what had gone on. Cherry had seen him studying them from an upstairs window. "It didn't seem much at the time," he went on, "but in the light of recent discoveries, it could be significant. Do you think we could take another quick look while we are here?"

Butler looked completely taken aback. "You mean right now?"

Stern put on his most professional face. "When carrying out a murder investigation time is of no essence, Mr Butler. And it would mean we would have covered everything on this one visit. It need not inconvenience you at all. Just a quick check, and we'll be on our way."

"But it's completely dark out there."

"We have torches, and we know our way. It will take no time at all. With your permission, of course."

Butler shook his head resignedly. "Well of course, if you think it will help."

Katrina Butler got quickly to her feet. "I call Victor. He should be with you."

Fifty-seven

As it transpired, security lights triggered by their movement as soon as they left the house lit the whole area, including the side of the cottage facing the house. It became obvious their torches would only be required behind the little building, in the area away from the house, and adjacent to the boundary fence. As they crossed the wide lawn, they could see Victor Adams already standing directly outside the cottage front door waiting. He hadn't taken long to react to Mrs Butler's call. Legs firmly placed apart, his arms folded across his chest, his posture radiated aggression.

"He don't look happy," Cherry whispered from the side of her mouth.

"Nothing we can't handle," Stern replied. "Just relax." He touched her arm, slowing the pace. "Let's try and get into the cottage first. We'll think about the boat afterwards. Just remember, when I give you the nod, I want you to attract his attention. Do anything to distract him, get him away from me, and give me some breathing space."

"How the hell am I supposed to do that?"

"I don't know," Stern hissed. "You're an assistant special investigator, aren't you? You're supposed to be able to deal with situations like this. Just give him the old come on or something. Y'know, flutter your eyelashes or whatever. Don't care how you do it, just get him away from me. A few seconds is all I need."

"Oh yeah, and how is he supposed to see me fluttering my eyelashes? It'll be pitch black back there."

Stern couldn't help the grin. "Sometimes you're so negative, Hooker."

"Thanks a bunch, boss. I love you, too."

They came to a halt directly in front of the defiant figure.

"You come two time already," Adams said, the irritation clear on his tight features.

Stern held the other man's gaze, eye to eye, and smiled. It was a smile Cherry knew well. It had nothing to do with humour. "You're absolutely right, Victor old lad. We have. And this will make it three times."

"Why you keep coming here?"

The smile had vanished, the words came snapped out, staccato fast and demanding. "I am a British police officer, and right now, I will ask the questions. You are an employee here, and you will do as you are told. Do I make myself clear?"

Adams, shaken by the hostile retort, immediately took a small step back, the aggressive stance instantly faltering, his arms dropping to his side. "I didn't mean to...I do not understand." His words hesitant, the demanding arrogance absent.

Stern maintained the pressure, his voice losing none of its harshness. "You don't have to unlerstand. You have been instructed by your employer to assist us. You do this, and nothing more."

Adams silently lowered his eyes.

Holding for a second, ensuring the scene was set, Stern went on. "Good. Now we need to search the area around the back of the cottage, including the fence which, when we were here last, we found to be damaged."

Adams looked up. "The fence is now good. I repair."

"Why am I not surprised?" Stern quipped. "However, we still need to check the area." While he was talking, Stern clocked the cottage door still being covered by Adams. He could see, though it had been pulled to, it wasn't completed latched closed. Probably because Adams hadn't expected to be called out and wasn't carrying the key, not wanting to lock himself out.

"Okay, this won't take long." Stern flicked on his torch and motioned for Cherry to follow him. They made their way round to the back of the cottage. Adams followed.

"Cherry, I'd like you to check the area along the fence while I look at the rear of the cottage."

"Right, boss." She crossed the several yards separating the fence from the rear of the cottage, playing the light of her torch on the ground, constantly flicking her eyes toward Stern, watching and waiting.

Adams stood uncertain, holding a position in the darkness between the two, his attention mainly on Stern.

Stern made an exaggerated show of first concentrating on the rear wall of the cottage, moving slowly along, traversing the torchlight up and down until he came to the small rear window. Inside, the light was on, and he noticed the top flip pane was standing ajar as it had been on their last visit. Also, as then, the curtains inside were drawn tightly closed. This, he was sure, was to have been Preston's next target. The mangled makeshift petrol bomb Wainwright had discovered here in the undergrowth was a clone to those Stern had found in Preston's garage. It hadn't taken them long to grasp how it was intended to be used. Once lowered through this window, the crudely made delay fuse would have given Preston enough time to be away before the curtains and subsequently everything else went up in flames.

But that hadn't happened. Preston had been discovered and ended up in the river with a broken neck. Stern studied Adams for a brief moment. Could it have been him? O'Connor had shown Stern a photograph of the body dragged from the river. It showed Preston as a chunky guy. In life, he may have been a bit of a handful. So, did Adams look strong enough to have overpowered him, even broken his neck? Stern hoped, if all went well tonight, they would find out.

Standing close to the window, Stern listened for any sound coming from inside. He could hear none. Time to move. He slowly made his way to the corner of the building, kneeling as if he had found something of interest. From here, he could quickly nip round the end of the building, and round to the front door of the cottage in a beat. He briefly flipped the light of the torch up to his face and gave a brief nod of his head.

Cherry, on constant watch, reacted immediately. "Hey, Victor, what the hell is going on over here?" she yelled.

~ * ~

The instant he saw Adams turn toward Cherry, Stern slipped round the corner of the building. A few seconds had him at the front door and inside the cottage. His heart rate had lifted, and he felt a familiar tremble creeping up his spine, his hands shaking just a tad. But crazily, he found himself smiling. Hell, he was enjoying this. The feelings were familiar, it was true, but how long was it since he had last experienced such thrilling sensations? Before yesterday, he would have said a very long time ago, but then only last night, paddling a flimsy canoe on the river in the pitch black came close. What the hell was he thinking...he was halfway through his sixties, for crying out loud, and here he was breaking and entering. Well, not quite breaking, but bloody close, and anyway, he was sure time would show it to be a legally justified act. Legal or not, right now with the adrenalin pumping as it was he was up for this and couldn't give two shakes a lamb's whatsit how old he was.

He quickly pulled the door closed behind him and felt the positive click of the latch falling into place. He needed every second he could muster, and unless Adams did have a key with him out there, his only way back was for Stern to open the door again. Now, he was in, he wasn't about to do that in a hurry.

Stern remembered the layout from his previous visit to the cottage; the front door opening directly into the sitting room with three other doors leading off. In this room, the light was on, and even though the three other doors were firmly closed, he knew two of them led to a kitchen and bathroom. The other room had to be a bedroom. He quickly scanned the room, noting the TV playing silently in the corner, guessing Adams would have engaged mute when he got the call from the house and went outside to meet them. Quickly skirting the table and chairs in the middle of the room, Stern headed for the door of what he knew to be the kitchen. He pushed open the door, flicked on the torch and quickly scrabbled through the room opening every cupboard door, searching every inch. There was nothing unusual. It was a small fully equipped kitchen, nothing more. Leaving the kitchen, he scuttled across to the bathroom. This room was smaller and open with just a shower cubical and a toilet. A quick scan of the room from the doorway was all that was needed. It too was clear.

As he doused the torch and closed the door, he heard raised voices from outside. Then the front door was tried, rattled first, then came the banging and shouting, the words not understandable, not English. Adams had realised Stern was no longer out there with them. Only then, did it come to Stern that in the excitement of getting in here and securing the door to give himself time, he had left Cherry outside with a man, now a very angry man, who they suspected of being a drugs and people smuggler. Possibly a murderer. Not a good idea. He hesitated for a second, torn, something inside telling him that regardless of anything else, he had to check that last room. It would take just a second.

He turned quickly, run across the room and flung open the door to what he knew had to be a bedroom. He didn't need the torch; he knew the light in here was already on.

He stumbled to a halt, transfixed. "Jesus Christ."

Fifty-eight

The first thing Stern saw when pushing open the door was the window in the wall directly opposite. It was the window outside which he'd been standing only moments before. He glanced quickly around the room, noting that, other than a narrow bed pushed into one corner adjacent to the window, the room was completely unfurnished. Unfurnished but not empty. Stacked against the wall directly to his left was a pile of packages, each about eighteen inches square, every one individually vacuum sealed in plastic. But it wasn't these packages that brought the surprised exclamation from Stern. He'd known it was highly likely they'd be here somewhere. No, what stopped Stern in his tracks was the young girl on the bed. Wide eyed with terror, she was frantically scrabbling to pull a single sheet around her thin naked body.

"Please, please, you no kill me," she pleaded.

Just for a second, the unexpected vision in front of him drove the thought of Cherry's dilemma completely from Stern's mind. He held up both hands to show he was not carrying a weapon and stepped into the room. "Don't worry, I'm not going to hurt..."

The sentence ended abruptly with a guttural grunt as a crashing blow to the back of the neck sent him staggering forward, stumbling onto all fours, brilliant flashing lights jamming his vision. Even as he fell, he cursed his stupidity. Basic training, schoolboy error: never enter a room without checking behind the door. But the self-reprimand almost immediately evaporated as a roaring excruciating pain engulfed him. For a moment, head hanging low like a wounded animal, he floundered aimlessly on his hands and knees. Then, fighting the pain, he screwed his head round, peering up, trying to focus on the blurred vision glowering down at him. Standing, legs spread aggressively apart, the figure was squat and broad with thick arms, fists clenched in front. But lines remained blurred, details unclear. He blinked frantically and for just an instant, his sight cleared, and he could vaguely make out the figure. But even though realisation dawned, and he understood, he was unable to stop the vicious kick to the ribs that sent him sprawling into plastic-covered packages piled against the wall. Now, only semi-conscious, an inherent self-preservation mechanism took over and the body automatically rolled itself into a tight protective ball. But a precise second kick found the side of his head and in that instant total blackness descended.

~ * ~

Cherry stood uncertainly outside the cottage. Now, there wasn't a sound coming from inside, and she was afraid for the boss. He should be out by now. She had called his name a couple of times without response before tentatively trying the door, though she knew it would be of no use.

When Adams had realised Stern had slipped away, he had left her and quickly run round to the front door. She had followed but holding back, deliberately keeping out of his reach. Cherry could run and run fast. If Adams came at her, that's exactly what she would do. But he hadn't. In fact, so frantic was he to get back into the cottage it seemed he'd forgotten she was even there. At first, finding the door locked, he had banged frantically, yelling words most of which she couldn't understand. But only for a second or two. Because then, knowing his efforts were useless, he'd turned and run, sprinting across the lawn back toward the house. That was only moments ago, and now she was thinking frantically, her mind in overdrive. Things had somehow gone very wrong in the cottage, and it was obvious to her Adams had galloped because he was frightened of what the boss would have found in there. Now, everything was silent. The door was still locked, there was no sign of the boss, and she stood no more chance of getting in than Adams. But she had to do something and do it fast. She dragged her mobile from her pocket, concentrated the torch beam on its face and dialled a well-known number.

"O'Connor."

Cherry couldn't remember feeling so relieved to hear someone's voice. "David, its Cherry."

"Oh shit..."

She knew this was the response she would get but pushed on quickly anyway. "The boss is locked in the cottage, and I can't hear a thing. I think something has happened, David. I think he's in trouble but..."

"Cherry, I told him when he came up with this crazy idea he was on his own. You can't expect me to come running every time..."

"No, you must listen," Cherry blurted out. "I'm sure the boss has found what he was looking for. We were checking the back of the cottage again, and Adams was with us. Then the boss slipped away and managed to get inside. As soon as Adams realised he'd got into the cottage, he did a runner. He was out of here quicker than light. Now everything's quiet, and I'm sure the boss is in trouble."

"Where's Butler?"

"When we came down to the cottage, we left him up at the house with his missus and her mum."

"So, you're at the cottage, on your own?"

"Yes, I'm outside, and the boss is still in there. But I can't hear anything, and I can't get in. I've called but there's nothing."

The heavy agitated sigh on the other end of the line was loud in her ear. "Okay, look, Wainwright is doubling up in a panda this evening. I'll put a call out to him and get him to you. But, Cherry, my arse is on the line here. Theo had better have found something worthwhile, or the skids'll be under me." The line went dead.

Cherry killed her phone and slipped it back in her pocket. As she did so she heard a sound from inside the cottage. She froze, realising someone was quietly unlocking the door. Initially thinking it had to be Stern, she took a step toward the door and almost called his name. Almost. But then something, some innate sense, said no, wait and see. She moved back and positioned herself just out of sight around the corner of the building.

Slowly the door of the cottage partially opened, and a head appeared cautiously through the narrow gap. Cherry's eyes narrowed, her forehead creasing into a deep confused frown. It didn't make sense, it couldn't be. But it was, and again she was faced with a decision, one she had to make quickly. Then out of the blue it hit her, she had the answer right there, actually hanging over her shoulder. As the door was being pushed further open, she fumbled clumsily through the shoulder bag she always carried, at the same time remembering the boss's words in Blakeney when she'd stayed with Mo Stevens, when he'd made her take it.

"I promise just seeing it will stop anyone coming near you."

As her fingers found the cold steel, she hoped like mad he was right.

Fifty-nine

The standard Ford Focus patrol car leapt forward as Constable Paul Wainwright floored the accelerator. A handbrake turn spun the complaining vehicle through a complete hundred and eighty before the tyres gripped, and it bucked forward, roaring out of North Walsham where the two young constables had been kicking their heels since the start of the shift.

'No histrionics, no lights, no sirens.' O'Connor had warned angrily. 'Just get there soonest and see what bloody mess Stern's got himself into.'

But the mere mention of Theo Stern was enough for Wainwright. There would be no lights or sirens but get there soonest he definitely would. As far as he was concerned, Stern was a legend, an example every young copper should aspire to. If anyone was giving Stern grief, they'd have PC Paul Wainwright to deal with.

PC Doug Hamilton hung onto the door handle as they barrelled into a skidding right turn onto a narrow lane; a shortcut to the A149 and Wroxham. He'd known Wainwright since training, and had always admired his cool, calm temperament. But, as he watched the rev counter needle almost hit the red zone, there was nothing cool or calm about the way his colleague had reacted to the inspector's call. Hell, the poor old Focus had probably never gone as fast in its life.

The lane was just one car wide with the occasional passing area cut into the verge. At this speed, if they met an oncoming vehicle now, they were toast. Hamilton crossed his fingers, hanging onto the knowledge that at least his friend and partner had topped out head of his police advanced driving course.

"So, who is this Stern character?" he managed through gritted teeth.

Wainwright's gaze never wavered from the narrow lane whipping toward them. "He's a top man. You should dig into police records, check out his bio. As far as I'm concerned, he's a star. At college, we had a management study class, you know, different methods of leadership." He twitched the steering wheel a tad to the right, not appearing the least concerned as the nearside front clipped the grass verge and a spray of mud shot up, splattering the side of the car. "There was this case study. It involved an East End of London drug bust. A doss house in Bethnal Green, if I remember. Anyway, the senior detective inspector leading the raid was a real hands-on guy, proper street copper. Thirty odd years on the job. He'd been after this particular villain for a long time. Talk about lead from the front. He went straight in and cornered the guy who, unfortunately, was out of his head on smack or something and had a knife."

Bouncing off the door, Hamilton breathed a sigh of relief as the car actually did a four wheel slide out onto the A149 and Wainwright again floored the throttle. "What happened?"

"The inspector was stabbed within an inch, but not before bringing down the villain."

"Did he survive?"

"He did but was eventually given the push on medical grounds. That's what the official records say, anyway."

"What's that mean?"

"Fact is, he'd always been a bit of a loose cannon and word on the ground says those upstairs grabbed the opportunity to get him out of their hair. After thirty years of service, and with one of the best clean up rates in the Met. Don't make sense to me."

For the first time since leaving North Walsham, Wainwright eased back on the throttle, braking the car into a series of back lanes not familiar to Hamilton. "The case study posed a question: was the way he acted at the bust good or bad leadership?" Wainwright went on. "Almost all of our class said bad, but I think without guys like that, guys prepared to put themselves on the line, we're nothing."

"And that was Stern?"

"It was. He's older now and based here in Norfolk doing private work. But when we're short, the inspector sometimes uses him as backup. He's put me with him a couple of times recently, and I can tell you he's one switched-on guy." He slowed the car to a crawl as in the high hedge to their left a pair wide iron gates appeared in the headlights. The gates were open. Without hesitation, Wainwright steered the car through the gates.

"You know this place?" Hamilton asked.

"Yeah, I was here with Mr Stern before." He drove slowly down the driveway, for a moment surveying the scene in front of them. All the security lights were illuminated, but everything was quiet, just one or two lights on in the main house. There was a Range Rover parked in front of the wide garage to the left of the house, and another car parked outside the front door. It was a Volkswagen. Had to be Stern's new car he'd heard him enthuse over. But O'Connor had said something about trouble at the cottage which was on the other side of the house. Looking across the wide lawn toward the little building, he could see lights on there, too. He carried on down the drive, quietly pulling up alongside the Volkswagen, killing the engine and dousing the lights. Simultaneously, the two officers released their safety belts

Hamilton turned in his seat. "So, what now?"

Wainwright pointed across the lawn. "The inspector said the trouble was at the cottage, so that's where we go."

They climbed from the car and headed across the lawn toward the cottage, noting as they approached, the front door standing wide open. Stopping outside the door, Wainwright called out.

"Hello, this is the police. Anyone there?"

The voice calling from inside was female, the words unnaturally high pitched, fearful. "Yes, please come in."

The two men moved cautiously through the door into a small sitting room. Glancing to his left, Wainwright saw another door. It too was open and framed in the door with her back to him he recognised Cherry Hooker. He quickly moved across the room, coming up behind her and peering over her shoulder.

"Cherry, it's Paul Wainwright," he breathed softly into her ear. "What the bloody hell's going on here?"

Hearing the familiar authoritative voice, Cherry's resolve immediately crumbled. Her arms began to shake violently and the replica 9mm Walther PPK hand gun clasped tightly in both hands she'd held rigidly out in front of her for what seemed an eternity, almost slipped from her fingers. Feeling her knees begin to buckle, Wainwright slid an arm around her waist, pulling her against him for support. With the other hand, he relieved her of the gun. His eyes flicked round the room, quickly taking in the situation.

There were two women sitting on a small single bed pushed into the far corner of the room. One was young, no more than a girl, and slim with pale skin and straggly fair hair hanging below her shoulders. Her legs were curled tightly beneath her and she was clutching a flimsy sheet pulled up closely around her neck. Eyes wide with terror, she had backed herself tightly into the corner, trying to make herself as small as she possibly could.

The other was short and powerfully built with close cut hair and dark penetrating eyes. She was scruffily dressed, as if she had thrown the clothes on, wearing trousers and dark T-shirt pulled roughly down over her bulbous top half. She sat on the edge of the bed, legs akimbo, man like, elbows resting on her knees, her fists clenched. She was wearing a scowl that would have stripped paint. Wainwright recognised her immediately. Seeing Cherry being relieved of the gun, the woman made to get to her feet.

Wainwright didn't know what was going on here but until he did, no one was going anywhere. He waved the woman back down, himself now using the gun taken from Cherry. "Stay where you are," he snapped. He held her challenging gaze for a long moment before she grudgingly and, very slowly, settled back down onto the edge of the bed.

"Nobody moves, understand? Just stay put until this is sorted." He glanced to the other side of the room where a dejected Stern sat crouched amid a pile of plastic-wrapped packages. His eyes were half closed and there was a mat of slowly congealing blood oozing from a deep laceration to the side of his head. Without averting his gaze, he spoke quietly to Hamilton standing at his shoulder.

"Doug, call for backup and an ambulance."

Wainwright held onto the still shaking Cherry, his head bent forward so as to enable him to speak quietly into her ear. "What's the score here, Cherry?"

Cherry swallowed hard, her throat tinder dry. "The woman, she's dangerous. She attacked the boss," she replied, the words little more than a hoarse whisper. "The handyman. He was here too, but he's done a runner. Don't know where he is."

Hamilton was back. "They're on their way. ETA ten minutes."

"Great. Cuff the woman, will you? Behind her."

While Hamilton made the woman stand and turn round, Wainwright kept the gun levelled. Then, once her hands were secured behind her back, he pointed to a space against the wall opposite where Stern remained crouched. "Sit. On the floor," Hamilton instructed.

"You can't," she snarled gruffly. "Mr Butler, he…"

Hamilton, if anything a tad taller than Wainwright, towered over the woman. "I said *SIT*."

For a second time, a face like thunder, she slowly obeyed, turning her back to the wall then sliding down to a sitting position on the floor.

Handing the gun to his partner, Wainwright helped Cherry into the sitting room and sat her in one of the chairs. "You okay here for a bit? I want to check on Mr Stern."

"Yes, please make sure he's okay. I haven't been able to get to him."

Returning to the bedroom, Wainwright knelt in front of Stern. "How y'doin', sir?"

Stern opened his eyes fully for the first time, blinking, trying to focus. "I'm getting there. Good to see you guys."

"We got here as soon as we could." Wainwright gently studied the damage to Stern's head. He could see the bleeding was slowing, the blood congealing. "It don't look too bad. Did the butch woman do this?"

Stern nodded, but only slowly, his lips still tightening at the effort. "She's pretty good with the boot. I think there's a couple of ribs gone, too."

Wainwright glanced back at the woman sitting glowering across at them. "Isn't that Mrs Butler's mum?"

"Supposed to be," Stern said. "But somehow…"

Stern was stopped mid-sentence by the cottage front door being thrown open and a very angry voice. "What the blazes is going on here. Why have I got police cars outside my door without my knowledge? And what the hell are you people doing here?"

Butler came to a blundering halt at the bedroom door, taking in the situation, his gaze coming to rest on the glowering woman sitting on the floor. His mouth dropped open.

"Stefana? What on earth are you doing down there?"

Sixty

Victor Adamczyk crouched in the hedgerow behind the garage. He was breathing heavily, rivulets of sweat running down his face and neck. The sweat wasn't as a result of physical effort; he'd only run from one side of the garden to the other, but more from the sheer panic surging through him. How could it have suddenly gone so wrong? Everything had been so tightly controlled, the cover absolutely foolproof. She had been so confident. 'The British are fools,' she had said. 'They will do anything for sex and money.' And it seemed she had been right. They had chosen their targets with extreme care, and things could not have gone better. Even the disposal of their first problem had gone without a hitch. Accidental death, they'd said. Exactly what she had predicted.

But then came this man Stern. Now everything had collapsed. There hadn't been time to clear the cottage and, of all times, Anna had chosen this night to play out one of her crazy fantasies. And nobody argued with Anna.

Seeing the headlights of a car turn in through the gates, he crouched lower in the bushes. The car moved slowly along the drive to pull to a halt in front of the house. Victor's blood turned to ice as he recognised the vehicle as a police car. He watched as the two police officers climbed out, shrinking even further back into the deep hedgerow. But they never turned toward him. Instead, they headed directly across the lawn toward the cottage.

Victor had no idea what had happened after he'd run. All he knew was the man Stern had got inside the cottage and locked the door behind him, locked himself in with Anna, probably sealed his own fate. That meant it was all over. Now, his only chance was to get away from there. Somehow make his way to a big city. Norwich, or better still, London. He knew people there, others who had been smuggled into the country and disappeared among the masses. But how? And what about Katrina?

The two policemen had disappeared inside the cottage and, looking across at the Range Rover parked in front of the garage, Victor slid his hand down to his pocket. He felt the reassuring outline of the bunch of keys he always carried there. It would only take him so far before he'd have to abandon it. But at least it would get him away from the house and the immediate area. Now was not the time to be thinking of others. The problem was, if he took the car, how long would it be before the alert went out, and they came looking for it? An hour, possibly two at most. And once he'd dumped the vehicle, what then? What would he do after that? He had no money, and the passport and other documentation he had paid so dearly to obtain was all in the cottage. A huge wave of hopelessness enveloped him. It was useless. He would have to surrender himself to these people. These British people who weren't so stupid after all.

As he made to push himself out of the hedgerow, the front door of the house opened, and Eddie Butler appeared. He stood for some moments looking first at the police car parked there then across at the cottage. Then, cursing loudly, he strode off across the lawn toward the little building.

New hope flared in Victor's breast. He would have to be quick, but now there was a way of at least getting money, and money, if you had enough of it, was the key to most things. He broke from his hiding place and ran past the Range Rover toward the house and the front door left ajar by Butler.

~ * ~

Eddie Butler was fuming. How could this have happened? After barging into the cottage and forcing his way passed Hamilton into the bedroom, he had stood aghast at what he was seeing. He looked from the frail looking young girl curled up on the bed, wrapped in nothing but a thin sheet, to the man he knew as Special Investigator Stern huddled on the floor, his face caked in blood. Then, most horrifying of all, his mother-in-law sitting on the floor her back to the wall, her hands shackled behind her. This was a disaster.

But what infuriated him most was, despite his blustered protests and, without any explanation, he was hustled back into the sitting room by the heavy young policeman and made to sit down. He was Eddie Butler, for God's sake. He hadn't been made to do anything against his wishes for years. Yet, here was this lowly crap constable giving him orders. What's more, he was pushing him around, physically enforcing those orders. If only Pace were here. But for the first time in years, Pace wasn't here, was he? Butler hadn't felt so impotent since he was a lad starting out on the street corners flogging the dodgy stuff. Then he was constantly moved on, pushed around by every Tom, Dick, and Harry. He swore then that one day he'd be doing the pushing. And with the ever-loyal Pace he had. Until now. But he still had a voice.

"This is private property," he yelled. "You have no right. You are trespassing on my land." He pushed himself roughly back up off the chair, his face a mask of fury. "I'll have your badges for this. By the time I've finished with you two irks, you'll be lucky to get a job as traffic wardens."

Wainwright moved in quickly, placing a hand on the raging man's shoulder, gently but firmly pushing him back down onto the chair. He spoke strongly but quietly, "Mr Butler, if I were you, I would calm down. Otherwise, I will be forced to restrain you. We have backup on its way, which, without doubt, will include our colleagues from CID. With what we have found here this evening, I'm sure it will be you who will be doing the explaining, not us."

Butler had no option but to sit but glaring up at Wainwright, he wasn't about to stop his tirade anytime soon.

"You cocky shit," he spat. "You have no idea who you are dealing with here. You're dead, you understand? Dead in the water."

Stern emerged from the bedroom. He was unsteady on his feet and was cradling his ribs with one arm. He moved slowly across to where Cherry was sitting. "You okay, luv?"

Cherry looked up at him, her eyes filled with concern. "I'm sorry, boss, I had to watch her. I couldn't get to you. Then when Paul came, my legs just went, I had to sit down. Are you okay?"

His face swelling rapidly, Stern gave her a lopsided grin. "Don't apologise, luv, you did brilliantly. Yeah, I'm okay. Couple of ribs and a bump on the head. Hell, she might have hit me somewhere that really mattered." He turned painfully and looked long and hard at Butler sitting opposite, Wainwright standing over him.

"Time's up, Butler," he said softly, a touch of triumph in his words. "Drugs and people smuggling, not good. But murder. You really have hit the buffers."

Butler shook his head, his lips now a tight line. "I have no idea what you're taking about, Stern."

Stern repeated the lopsided grin. This time there was no sign of humour. "No, of course you don't."

The wail of police sirens could be heard fast approaching.

Sixty-one

Friday evening and a long weekend stretched in front of him. It wasn't Ron Pace's favourite time. Earlier, he had driven the boss up from London and delivered him to Deep Repose. But Butler had early commitments back at the office on Monday. So, Ron had to stay over and be ready for the return journey Sunday evening. And a whole weekend shacked up in the little B&B away from home, and the missus never suited Ron. It was comfortable enough, and the elderly widow who ran it was the nicest person. She cooked great grub, too. She always made him feel at home and seemed to like having him around. They got on well and chatted a lot, but the time still dragged. Even the village pub, pleasant enough and within a few minutes' walk, only eased the boredom a little. Ron wasn't a big drinker...as a driver he couldn't afford to be. So, a couple of hours on a Saturday evening over a single pint was the best he could do. Still, it wasn't all bad news. As an avid crime reader, he had plenty of time to bury himself in a good James Patterson or Michael Connelly novel. One day, he promised himself, he'd write one himself. Yeah, one day.

The window in Ron's little room overlooked the road outside. As a minor country lane, the traffic was minimal during the day and normally non-existent after around seven in the evening. It was for this reason, at some time well after eight, his attention was dragged away from Patterson's *When the Wind Blows* by the sound of a fast approaching car. He laid the book aside and parted the curtains, peering through. It went by at speed and, though there were no lights or sirens, he could see it was a police car. Unusual for any car at this time of night, let alone one in a hurry, and a police car to boot. And heading toward... He frowned, for some unknown reason experiencing a moment of unease. Then pushing it to one side with a shake of the head, he settled back into the book.

It was no more than twenty minutes later when he heard the sirens. Again, he slid back the curtain. This time there were two of them in quick succession, flashing lights and sirens full blast. Pace hardly had time to collect his thoughts when only moments later there were even more sirens and flashing lights. This time an ambulance in full flight. Now, the butterflies in Ron's stomach really erupted.

It was as though he had been expecting it. Not tonight particularly, not any time particularly. And he didn't know what. But for some time, when here in Norfolk, he'd been constantly on edge, anxious, waiting for he didn't know what to happen. Totally unreasonable, stupid even, he had to admit. But then, maybe not. And now this.

Ron Pace had been with Eddie Butler it seemed forever. They were only youngsters when they first met. Eddie had been doing his usual thing with the dodgy goods in a quiet corner of the East End pub. But Eddie, ever the adventurous entrepreneur, had ventured from his own manor, and the local mafia weren't pleased. There were three of them, and Ron knew them all; every one a nasty piece of work. And they were tooled up. Cornered and frightened, Eddie was doing his best to talk himself out of a pretty deep hole. But for once, talk wasn't going to work. Ron, on the other hand, academically never the sharpest knife in the drawer, had always found talk a waste of time in situations like this. Why waste time talking when you were as big and as strong as Ron Pace? And this was Ron's home turf. Better still, it was the Pace family pub. Besides, he liked the look of the young tearaway. Even though he didn't know him, had never met him before, Ron took an instant liking to the little runt desperately trying to talk his way out of being hurt, hurt real bad.

Coming at the three from behind, he took the first out with a single right-hand hammer blow to the kidney area. Then, while the other two stood uncertainly to one side, he gave Eddie a lopsided smile and asked him if he fancied a pint. That was it. That was the start of a lifetime partnership. Ron had been watching Eddie's back ever since.

Then came Vera. The lovely Vera. Not only gorgeous, but one very smart cookie. Butler was besotted from the moment he saw her. "I'm gonna marry her, Ron,' he'd told Pace. And he had. It was just as well he had, too. Vera was honest, truly honest. Not like some of the females Ron had rubbed shoulders with over the years. Vera made sure that from the day they married, all Butler's dodgy dealing came to an end. Instead, she steered him as straight as an arrow, advising him on all the best moves, the best deals, slowly moving him up the ladder. Talk about the woman behind the man. Almost without exception, Butler owed everything he was today to Vera.

But then Vera was taken, and Butler became a lost soul. Though still holding the reins, maintaining overall control, he came to rely more and more on the senior managers in his organisation to hold individual aspects of the business together. And to their credit they had kept things going. Of course, from time to time, when Pace had recognised a little skulduggery going on, like someone taking a slice off the top, he'd had to have a word. He'd said nothing to Butler, and from Pace that was all it took, just a word, and equilibrium was restored.

Butler had met Katrina in a West End hotel where he had been attending a conference. She was a waitress and had paid him special attention from the start. Very special attention. Butler, having had little to do with women since his beloved's death, was vulnerable.

Pace had disliked Katrina as much as he had liked Vera. From the time she placed the first dish in front of Butler, leaning low to advertise her plentiful credentials, he could see she had an aim in mind. In no time at all, she had achieved that aim. She became Mrs Butler.

Then out of nowhere, her mother appeared. Pace liked her even less than the daughter. She was quickly followed by the gardener cum handyman. Pace was sure there was more to him than met the eye, particularly when Katrina spent time in Norfolk without Butler.

He should have voiced his concerns to Butler before, but he knew it would be of no use. The only person Butler had ever taken advice from was Vera, and she was long gone. Everybody else, even Pace, kept their opinions to themselves. But increasingly over time, Pace became more uncomfortable with the situation, and, for some reason, had come to carry a dread that nothing good would come of it. Now that was why, when seeing speeding police cars and an ambulance heading in the direction of Deep Repose, Pace got butterflies.

It was an unreasonable response. After all, events like this were happening all the time. Police cars and ambulances constantly responded at speed to urgent incidents. Nonetheless, with the passing of the urgent vehicles, *When The Wind Blows* instantly lost its appeal. For a moment, Ron Pace hesitated, still looking out of the window, but his mind elsewhere. Then, dropping the book on the table, he grabbed the keys to the Mercedes and headed for the door.

Sixty-two

Arriving at the cottage, it had taken David O'Connor just a few minutes to assess the situation and take control. Having issued instructions, he stood to one side allowing the two constables to escort Stefana Bosko and the frightened young woman, wrapped tightly in a blanket, out to the waiting police vehicles.

He turned to Eddie Butler, slumped dejectedly in the chair. "Edward Butler, I'm arresting you on suspicion of drug smuggling, people trafficking and possible murder. You do not..."

"What?" Butler screamed, exploding from the chair. *"Are you crazy? I have no idea...*

Wainwright again moved quickly, placing himself between Butler and O'Connor.

O'Connor continued without missing a beat. "...have to say anything, but it may harm your defence if you do not mention when questioned something which you later rely on in court. Anything you do say may be given in evidence." He eased Wainwright to one side and stood eye to eye with the raging Butler. "Do you understand what I'm telling you?"

Teeth bared, Butler shook his head vigorously, spittle flicking from the corner of his lips. "No, I fucking don't, and you can go to hell. I want my brief here, and I want him now. Do you understand what I'm telling *you*, you jumped up little shit?" He folded his arms across his chest and deliberately turned his back on O'Connor.

Stern winced, feeling the broken ribs painfully crackle as he was helped out of the chair by the young paramedic. He paused, turning to Butler, forcing the smile and tut-tutting. "Nice language for a respected businessman. And to a police officer, too. Still, like they say, you can take the man out of the East End, but you can't take the East End out of the man. Right, Eddie?"

Butler turned and scowled at Stern. "You too, scumbag. You'll get yours, too."

Stern held onto the smile as he was led to the door. He halted the paramedic alongside O'Connor. "The boat," he whispered. "Don't leave here before checking the boat."

O'Connor gave a brief nod of the head but said nothing.

Cherry rose and made to follow Stern. "I'll go with the boss, see he's okay."

O'Connor put out a hand, holding her back. "No, you won't. We'll need you at the station, Cherry. You'll have to make a full statement." He gave her an encouraging smile, inclining his head toward the door as Stern disappeared outside. "Don't worry about him...he's as tough as old boots." He looked to Wainwright. "Give Cherry a lift to the station."

Cherry made to protest. "It's okay. I can drive the boss's..."

O'Connor gave a sharp shake of the head. "Forget it. The constable will drive you."

Wainwright gently took Cherry's arm. "I'll get Constable Hamilton to follow in Mr Stern's car."

O'Connor spun round and spoke to Butler's back. "Now, we're going to the station, Mr Butler. You can come willingly, or if you insist on being difficult, I will have my officers restrain you. The choice is yours."

Butler spun round and glared at O'Connor, fists tightly clenched, his whole demeanour bowstring taut. He was truly fighting for control. "Listen to me. I know nothing of any smuggling or murder, so whatever you're trying to stitch me up with is not going to work. You and your bunch of bent coppers are heading for the wreckers yard, and I'm going to make sure you stay there." He turned on his heel and strode toward the door.

~ * ~

Ron Pace slowed the Mercedes as he approached Deep Repose. He fully expected the gates to be closed as they normally would be at this time of night. It was why they always kept a small remote control in the car. Sometimes when driving up from London, they would arrive late. It was much easier, and quicker, to open the gates from within the car. Especially if it was raining.

But now the gates weren't closed...they were fully open and inside, every security light was blazing. Cautiously, Pace eased the car through the gates and immediately braked to a halt, his eyes roaming the area. To the left of the house, in front of the wide garage building, the Range Rover was parked in its usual spot. There were lights on in the main house as he expected there would be. One he knew to be the living room downstairs and another upstairs, the main bedroom. Here, he could see shadows, illuminated against the curtains, moving from one side to the other. Nothing unusual about that but looking back down to the front of the house, he noted the front door standing wide open. That was unusual. But not as unusual as the two cars parked directly in front of the house. One was a police car, the other he thought he recognised as belonging to the special investigator guy, Stern. If that wasn't worrying enough, it was nothing compared to the scene on the far side of the wide lawn. Here the two other police cars and the ambulance he'd seen rush past his B&B were parked outside the cottage, all three with their emergency lights still slowly revolving, a number of figures milling around the front door of the little building.

Pace sat for some moments unsure of what to do next. That inner thing was telling him this is what his gut had been warning him about for some time. Ever since that bloody woman had got her talons into Butler and gradually taken control of his private life. Not the business side of things, of course. Only Vera had ever managed that. But in all else, Butler had come to defer to her. Like when she clicked her fingers and got the house here in Norfolk and the boat. It must have cost a fortune. It infuriated Pace. Now, there were police crawling all over the place. An ambulance, too. What the hell had happened here? Who had been hurt? He had no idea what he was going to do, but sliding the car into gear, he slowly drove down the driveway toward the house.

He hadn't moved more than a yard or two when Pace notice the two figures literally burst from the front door of the house. He jumped on the brake and stopped the car again. They were carrying bags...the woman one, the man struggling, stumbling along with two heavy holdalls. They were running, going at a gallop toward the Range Rover. Now, he could see it was that woman and her bloody handyman. But why were they running and where was the boss?

Pace looked from the two frantically throwing the bags into the Range Rover to the activity at the cottage and two policemen, one either side of a woman, walking back across the grass toward the house and the cars parked there. His mind was working hard, but Pace was a driver, a good one, and when necessary a minder who could handle most awkward situations, particularly if it involved anything physical. He was a one task at a time man, and there was too much going on here for his lumbering brain to assess quickly. But slow as he was, he knew he just couldn't sit there and do nothing. He had to act, had to do something and quickly. As the Range Rover reversed away from the garage and swung violently round to head down the drive toward him, he knew what that one thing was. "One thing at a time, Ron," he muttered. "One thing at a time."

Sixty-three

David O'Connor was a friend, but he was first and foremost a police officer. When he'd joined the force many years earlier, he'd made a solemn pledge. Friend or no friend, he would never renege on that pledge. And as an ex, equally dedicated copper, Stern would never have expected him to. That was why today, Sunday, little more than twenty-four hours after having suffered two broken ribs and a kick to the head that left him with a stitched face and concussion, he was sitting opposite O'Connor in an interview room at the Norwich nick.

Stern sat alone, having refused the offer of representation. He refused the compulsory offer of a brief because, technically, he had been working for O'Connor anyway. Officially to update Butler on the progress of the boat fire and Ollie Preston's death. So, O'Connor, whatever he knew about Stern's ultimate intensions, would have no option but to follow the official line. Stern would expect no less and therefore would only have to answer for his own decision to deviate from that particular task. He didn't need the help of a suit, who would have no idea what he was talking about anyway, to explain this.

The side of Stern's face and head was still badly swollen, the dark stitches tracing his jaw line and multi-coloured bruising resembling a split, over a ripe tomato. But the dirt and congealed blood had been cleaned away, taken care of by the excellent A&E staff at the Norfolk and Norwich Hospital. There he had also been x-rayed and, as a result, he was now sporting a tightly strapped rib cage.

"How are you feeling?" O'Connor asked.

"I'm fine," Stern lied. Despite the strapping, any involuntary sudden movement to either side sent sharp pains scything through the whole of his upper body. And the concussion, the pain throbbing through the side of his head, was still with him. Concentration was difficult to the extreme, and he should be in bed swallowing pain killers. But this needed to be over and done before he could afford himself that pleasure.

O'Connor gave a small shake of his head, indicating he was well aware his friend was anything but fine. But he knew the score and pushed down the switches on the recording machine alongside him. After recording the time, those present and the reason for the meeting, he turned back to Stern.

"So, Mr Stern, just to be clear and for the record, you are not under arrest. You are here of your own volition to help the police with their enquiries."

"Yes, I understand."

"Good. Can I just clarify that on the evening of Friday, the fourteenth of April past, as a civilian seconded to the Norfolk police, you were tasked with visiting the businessman Mr Edward Butler at Deep Repose, his property in the Wroxham area."

"Yes, it was regarding the criminal burning of his boat. I was sent to update him on police progress on the case." Stern deliberately chose not to complicate things by also including Preston's body found in the river.

O'Connor didn't pursue it either. "And you did this?"

"Yes, I did."

"But then, for some reason, you chose to exceed your authority by taking things further. Why was this?"

As far as O'Connor was concerned, this was pure bum covering theatre agreed between the two of them before entering the interview room. It had to be made clear to those upstairs that O'Connor had only authorised the task of updating Butler on the case. Anything other than that was completely down to Stern. That way, as Stern had told his friend before, the worst that could happen was an arse kicking for employing Stern in the first place. Now, knowing the outcome, even that was unlikely to happen. Even if it did, it'd be a very gentle kick. But memories fade quickly, so for future posterity it had to be formally placed on record.

Stern was happy to play the game. "As a result of something previously found in the grounds of the house, and new evidence received since, I decided to take the opportunity to recheck an area behind a cottage situated on the Butler estate."

"This is the cottage occupied by the Butler gardener cum handyman?"

"Yes. I admitted it was late, and it was outside my original mandate. But I felt it important, and we were there, on the spot. There was adequate lighting, and as I explained to Mr Butler, it would take just a few moments to complete the check. I felt it would eliminate the necessity of bothering Mr Butler again at a future date and save precious police time. I explained my reasons to Mr Butler, and he immediately gave his permission."

"What was the fresh evidence that prompted you to reinvestigate the area?"

"During the investigation into the burning of the boat, evidence was found to suggest Mr Butler, or his property, was being targeted. Possible by an arsonist. It was thought the cottage could be the perpetrator's next target."

"For the record, can you explain what had been found previously in that area?"

"Yes. The hedge had been broken through, indicating someone had gained access from the property next door. It was felt this could have been an initial exploratory visit to check out the lay of the land. Also, what was thought to be part of a makeshift petrol bomb had been found in that area."

"Once again, for the record," O'Connor went on, "This additional excursion was outside your original directive which was simply to update Mr Butler on the progress of our investigations."

"Yes, and I fully accept the responsibility for my actions. As an ex-London Met detective of over thirty years, the urge to investigate is hard to deny." Stern wanted to smile at the game they were playing. He refrained from doing so. The stitches lining his cheek hurt like hell if he did anything but keep a poker face.

"So, you and your assistant carried out a search of the area behind the cottage."

"Yes, we did. It was while doing this I was attracted to a noise coming from inside the cottage. It sounded like someone crying. The curtains were drawn but not completely, and I looked inside. What I saw appeared to be a scantily clad young female being physically restrained. I immediately called for police backup and made my way inside the cottage to assist. Once inside, I was attacked from behind and knocked to the floor. I don't remember much more until I saw Constable Wainwright bending over to assist me. Soon afterwards, you arrived with backup and an ambulance. After some initial treatment by a paramedic, I was taken to the Norfolk and Norwich hospital. I suggest you know more about what followed at the scene than I do." It wasn't quite the truth but, they had agreed, it was close enough.

O'Connor smiled. They had done what was necessary. The official version was formally on record. As far as he was concerned, Stern's end definitely justified the need. If those upstairs couldn't see it, they could do the other thing.

"Thank you, Mr Stern. I have no doubt we will need to talk to you again, but that will be all for now." He recorded the time and declared the interview over before switching off the recording equipment.

"Okay?" Stern asked.

"Yeah, thanks. You feeling well enough for me to bring you up to speed or do you want someone to drive you home?"

"D'you know how Cherry's doing?" Stern hadn't seen Cherry since the night before last when he'd been escorted away from the mayhem at the cottage by the paramedics. Earlier, O'Connor had told him how they had interviewed Cherry on the night of the incident, but she was there again to give a formal statement of what happened outside the cottage after Stern had gone inside and before Wainwright and his partner had arrived. And, no doubt, to account for the weapon she had been carrying on the night.

"She's been interviewed by Wainwright. They should be done by now. I'll go and check." He was gone only a few moments before he popped his head back through the door. "They're done, waiting out front. I've got an hour before we start on the others. What d'you want to do?"

Stern looked around the little room with its drab grey walls, hard chairs and grubby table stained with dried coffee rings. He'd seen similar rooms so many times in his career. They never seemed to change. "Can we go somewhere a little more comfortable? A strong cup of coffee and a couple of paracetamol would help." He waved a cautious finger. "Not the station canteen, though, if you don't mind."

O'Connor laughed. "Blimey, Theo, after all those years in the force, I'd have thought that'd be your first preference."

Stern snorted derisively through puffed lips. "Yeah, right."

Sixty-four

The coffee shop in the city centre was just a ten-minute slow walk from the police station. And as far as Stern was concerned, slow it had to be. The individual booths with cushioned bench seats either side of the table allowed the privacy required. Stern sat opposite O'Connor and Wainwright, this time with Cherry alongside him. Now, with three large mugs of steaming coffee in front of the guys, and Cherry sipping a glass of spring water, the atmosphere was relaxed, all formality discarded.

Stern had already swallowed the paracetamol tablets Wainwright had stolen from the station first aid box, though he didn't hold out much hope of relief any time soon. The maximum amount taken during the previous day had done little to ease his discomfort. He couldn't expect much more...these things had to take their own course. However, he felt, it wasn't going to stop him finding out what he wanted to know.

He'd spent the whole of yesterday either in bed or lounging uncomfortably in the chair being driven mad by the fact that he didn't know what happened after they'd carted him off to the hospital on Friday night. He'd made calls, but Cherry wasn't picking up and, when he tried calling O'Connor, he was told he wasn't available. He'd learned only this morning that both Cherry and O'Connor had agreed he needed at least twenty-four hours' rest before again being involved. So, they'd both ignored his calls to their mobiles, and O'Connor had given strict instructions at the nick to block all Theo Stern calls for twenty-four hours. It wasn't until late yesterday evening when he'd at last been contacted by the nick to say he would be collected this morning and brought in to give a statement. Now, he was anxious to hear the latest.

"So, after treating me like a stick of rhubarb for the last God knows how long, are we celebrating, or what?" he said.

O'Connor smiled, seeing the eagerness in his friend's eyes. "Sort of."

"Sort of? What does that mean?"

"Well, as always there's good news, and there's bad news. The good news is we have four in custody. Mrs Butler and her so called mother, together with Adams and the young woman you found in the cottage. We have them separated, and yesterday they were cautioned briefly, individually interviewed. That was just the initial process. The serious questioning starts as soon as we get rid of you two today."

"You have Mrs Butler, too?"

O'Connor gave a satisfied smirk. "Yup. While you were getting yourself beaten up, Mrs Butler and her faithful gardener were about to have it away on their toes with quite a stash." He turned to Wainwright. "D'you want to enlighten Mr Stern, constable?"

Wainwright leaned forward, pleased to be given the opportunity to contribute. "When my partner and I were escorting Cherry back to the car, we saw the family Merc drive in through the gates. It didn't go far, just stopped halfway down the drive. Couldn't think why at first. Then we realised the Range Rover parked in front of the garage was also on the move. It was in a hurry, obviously on its way out. Even though the Merc was blocking the drive, it didn't look like it was going to stop. It just swerved onto the grass as if it was going to go round the Merc. But on the grass, it lost traction just for a second before the tyres gripped. Next thing we knew, the Merc shot forward and buried itself into the front of the Range Rover. We were gobsmacked. I left Cherry with Doug and ran toward the wreck. But before I got there, Butler's chauffer had calmly climbed out of the Merc, walked round to the driver's side of the Rover and dragged Adams out. I saw him throw just the one punch, but by the time I arrived, Adams was out cold on the grass. Mrs Butler was screaming blue murder in the car. But most bizarre of all was what the chauffer did next." Wainwright was grinning broadly. "I run up to the wreck and he grabs me by the arm. I thought he was going to hit me too. But he just pulled me to him and said, 'Listen, you'd better believe Mr Butler knew nothing about what these scumbags were up to.' He then let me go, folded his arms and just leaned back against the Merc. Nonchalant as you like."

"I was still dealing with Butler in the cottage at the time," O'Connor came in. "But we heard the crash. We secured Butler in the back of the other car and went across. First thing we did was get Mrs Butler out of the car. She was hysterical and babbling on. Not much of what she said made sense. Anyway, we ended up impounding both cars and ferrying the whole lot of 'em to the station. The bad news is Butler has walked."

"How come?"

"Back at the station, he kicked off again big time. Went ballistic, still claiming he knew nothing of what was going on, and we were trying to stitch him up. He had his brief at the station before his backside hit the chair. Next thing we knew, we had a call from on high instructing us to release him pending questioning at a later date. He was out of there in less than half an hour."

Stern gave a despondent sigh. "Friends in high places again."

"Yeah, but don't worry, we have his passport...he's going nowhere." O'Connor picked up his coffee, sipping thoughtfully. "You know what? I don't think I've ever seen a guy protest his innocence so vehemently before."

"Oh, come on, David," Stern humphed. "You're not trying to tell me you think…"

Holding up a restraining hand, O'Connor gave a quick shake of his head. "I'm not trying to tell you anything, Theo. Just how outraged he was. We'll know a lot more when we've given the others the once-over."

"You said you had the other four in custody," Stern came back. "What about Pace?"

"He went the same way as Butler. But we'll have him back, too. I think there's more to come from him. Something tells me he's an honest broker."

"Yeah, I think so, too," Stern agreed."

O'Connor took another drink. "Anyway, there's more good news." He looked at Cherry. "Thanks to your assistant special investigator." He turned and looked back at Wainwright.

Wainwright took the cue and came in. "That night, after we arrived, I took the gun from Cherry and gave it to Doug Hamilton, my partner. He kept an eye on the bedroom while I helped Cherry into the sitting room. She was a bit of a wreck, obviously in severe shock and was babbling on a bit." He looked across at Cherry. "Sorry, but you were."

"Don't be sorry," Cherry said. "I don't remember much about it. I was so relieved to see you I can't be responsible for anything I said."

"And I'm not surprised," Wainwright conceded. "But most importantly, you insisted I didn't forget he kept calling for Anna. At the time, I was confused, didn't know who *he* was or what you meant." He turned back to Stern. "But this morning when she made her statement, Cherry made it clear." He looked again at Cherry. "D'you want to explain?"

Sixty-five

Cherry sipped some water, hesitating for a moment to collect her thoughts and bring back the events of the night. "When the boss snuck round to the front of the cottage, I tried to hold Adam's attention for as long as I could. But it didn't take him more than a couple of seconds to realise he'd gone," she began. "Then he took off like a rocket and left me standing there. I followed him round to the front of the building and found him pounding on the front door. He was shouting something, most of which was foreign gobbledegook to me. But amongst all the jabber there was one word I thought I did understand. I was sure he kept calling Anna. Said it umpteen times. At the time, I didn't know who was inside the cottage, but I guessed someone in there had to be called Anna. But when we'd talked about the case before, when the boss had told me who was involved, he'd never mentioned an Anna. I was all over the place by the time Paul arrived at the cottage and, to be honest, I can't remember what I said. But it must have seemed important to me at the time."

O'Connor leaned in. "I know Paul has it on record from your interview this morning, but while we're here, tell us briefly what happened then."

"It all happened so quickly," Cherry came back. "One minute he's pounding on the door screaming his head off. Then it looked as if he suddenly realised he was on a loser. He suddenly spun round, and before I knew it, he was galloping off across the lawn toward the house." She paused, more thought, pulling together a time line in her head. "I stood there gobsmacked for a minute. Then I tried the door and called out for the boss. But there wasn't a sound coming from inside. I didn't know what else to do, so I called you, David. You told me you would send Paul. I didn't know how long you would be, so I moved back from the door and waited."

"But then it must have kicked off again," O'Connor persisted. "Because when Paul and his sidekick arrived, you were inside the cottage."

"I was," Cherry agreed. "You see, after I called you, nothing happened for a while. It was just weirdly quiet, not a sound from inside the cottage. I did call for the boss a couple more times but got no response. I didn't know what was happening in there, but I did know if the boss was okay he would have answered me. Then all of a sudden, I heard the door being unlocked. I kept well back and waited for it to open. But it was real slow as if whoever was behind it was wary about coming out, scared of what they might find. It was obvious to me it wasn't the boss. I mean, why would he sneak out like that?" She turned and smiled at Stern, her words still directed across the table. "I've never seen him sneak in or out of anywhere."

Stern took a nonchalant drink of coffee. "See, never was a sneaky person."

O'Connor gave a derisory sniff. "May not be sneaky, but sometimes you can be a real..." He stopped and turned back to Cherry. "Carry on before his head swells even more and breaks those stitches."

"Well, when the door started to open, I had a real bad feeling. I knew something was very wrong, so I moved back around the corner of the building and waited for whoever it was to come out." She shook her head. "I have no idea why at that specific moment I thought of the gun." She turned and looked again at Stern. "I must have remembered what you said when you gave it to me at Mo's place. You said, 'Just seeing it will stop anyone coming near you.'"

Stern grinned broadly. "And it did, right?"

"Yes, it did."

O'Connor looked from Cherry to Stern and back. "Okay, so you remembered the gun, but where the hell did the bloody thing come from in the first place?"

Before Cherry could say another word, Stern gave a little cough. "Afraid that's down to me."

O'Connor gave a sigh and reached again for the coffee mug. "Why am I not surprised to hear that?"

Stern grinned but ignored the jibe. "It was a very long time ago. If I remember, I was a DS at the time. There was this young thug in Bethnal Green. He had a string of petty stuff behind him. Until then, nothing serious. But somehow, he got hold of the gun. Next thing we know, he's strutting his stuff like a modern day Al Capone. The gun was a replica, of course, but it was so good you wouldn't know it from the real thing. Anyway, for a short while, the guy's turning up all over the place knocking off corner shops and the like. But he was as thick as a plank, and it didn't take us long to nail him. When I took the gun off him, I fully intended to hand it in for disposal." He shrugged. "I guess I somehow just never got round to it."

"So how the hell did Cherry get hold of it?"

Stern explained how he had given the gun to Cherry to use as a deterrent against the possible intruder when she had spent the night with Mo Stevens.

"It just stayed in my shoulder bag," Cherry admitted. "And until that door opened I hadn't given it another thought. Who knows how these things spring to mind? Self-preservation I suppose. Anyway, it shook me when I saw Mrs Butler's mother poke her head round the door. I mean, when the boss and I arrived at the house earlier it had been her that opened the front door to us. I can only think she must have snuck back out and across to the cottage while we were first talking to Butler."

"So, what then?"

"Well, I was confused. I mean as far as I knew, she was just a mum, right? But she was dressed real scruffy like. As if she had just thrown herself together. I was still confused, so I stepped out intending to ask her what was going on inside. Next thing I know, she's crouched down and glowering at me like a rugby player going into a scrum. I thought she was about to come at me. I couldn't believe it. I mean, not for a second time. I thought Adams looked miffed before he did a runner, but this woman really put the wind up me. I had hold of the gun, but it was still in my bag, so I pulled it out and levelled it at her." Suddenly, she was smiling at the memory. "I held it out front, two hands, like Cagney and Lacey on tele. You know, like I knew what I was doing. Truth is, I was shaking from head to foot and didn't have a clue what to do next."

They all laughed with her, O'Connor encouraging her on. "So, what *did* you do?"

"Well, I can't honestly remember my exact words, but I think I told her if she took another step I'd blow her head off. I might have even been a little more flowery than that, actually." She looked from one to the other of the men around her, biting her bottom lip, her face flushing.

Unlike O'Connor and Wainwright, it was only the pain in his face preventing Stern from breaking down with laughter. "And she stopped?" he spluttered.

"She did. Just like you said. At first, I couldn't believe it. Then I realised I had control. It boosted my confidence. So, all I could think of was finding out what had happened in the cottage." She looked to Stern. "What had happened to you. So, I ordered her back inside. In the living room, I could see into the bedroom where the boss was on the floor. I realised he was hardly conscious but there was nothing I could do to help him until Paul arrived. I could see the girl on the bed. She was obviously terrified, so I had nothing to fear from her.

But Mrs Butler's mum was a different kettle of fish. I could only think it was her who had injured the boss, and the way she was looking at me I knew she would have a go if I took the gun off her. I made her sit on the edge of the bed and told her if she made a move it would be her last." Another smile. "Must have got that from Cagney and Lacey, too. Thankfully, Paul and his mate appeared pretty quickly. Don't know how much longer I could have stood with the gun out in front of me."

O'Connor drank the last of his coffee and turned to Wainwright, indicating they were leaving. "Right, let's see what we can get out of our three stooges." He looked back at Stern trying to hide a grin without much success. "Did the legendary Theo Stern really let a woman give him a good hiding?"

Stern saw the joke. "She didn't fight fair. Hit me when I wasn't looking. That's not British."

They all laughed. Then O'Connor waved a finger. "By the way, there's still an embargo on your calls to the nick, so don't bother phoning, just take some time to get well. I'll make contact when I have something for you, okay?" He eased himself out of the booth and made to leave. Then stopping, he turned. "Oh, and by the way." He looked toward Cherry. "Whatever you're paying her, it ain't enough."

Sixty-six

As far as Stern was concerned, staying at home, cooped up in the flat for any length of time, had been a no go from the start. He had taken an hour's careful walk each morning, but refreshing as it was, it was no substitute for either the regular twenty minutes on the bedroom rowing machine or his cherished morning beach run. Still, as far as he could tell, things were gradually improving. Over the last twenty-four hours, the effects of the concussion had reduced, and his head had all but cleared. His face, too, was getting better. The bruising, though slowly fading, had become multi-coloured and had spread, covering the whole of one side of his face from jaw line to forehead, including one black eye. A real shiner. The gash in his cheek was more problematic. The stitches had been removed and though healing, it was still crusty and had a tendency to weep, meaning he had to constantly dab at it with a tissue. He was assured this was normal and would eventually clear. The only saving grace was that shaving was out of the question. Normally, this would have been unthinkable. Now, though, as the growth slowly covered most of his damaged features, Stern was happy to let it go. In fact, after forty-eight hours and a little trimming, he began to think he was beginning to look quite distinguished. He might even keep it, grow a full set. The ribs were a whole different ball game. This was probably due to his age. He'd been told by the doctor injuries took longer to heal as you get older. Maybe so, certainly the discomfort in his chest, particularly if he made any sudden twisting move, seemed to be as bad as ever. Nevertheless, as he climbed into bed at the end of the second, long boring day, he was determined to be at the office the following morning.

~ * ~

The morning sky was clear, and a bright early sun was already warming the gentle North Sea onshore breeze when he left the flat. It was before eight thirty, early for him, but he was determined to be at the office before Cherry. For the last couple of days, she'd held the fort, fending off his frequent, probably irritating calls, insisting things were quiet, and there was nothing for him to worry about. Though, just like O'Connor, he didn't think she would have told him if the roof had caved in. The least he could do, just for once, was to have the coffee on the go when she arrived. Even one of Dave's freshly baked cream buns to go with it.

Carefully taking the steps down to the promenade, he made his way along to the fisherman's ramp then up between the shops and onto the high street. It was already busy here, with news agents and most of the other retailers already open for business. As always there were the early shoppers, too, the high street already lined with parked cars. Stern had lived here for thirteen years, and it had never been any different. Sheringham was just a small coastal town, but the little high street was always bustling with activity. Particularly in the summer months when the holiday makers descended in droves. Now, as May approached and the weather was beginning to improve, the B&B's, caravan sites and holiday lets were already beginning to fill.

He made his way along toward Dave's bakery. Parked a few doors down, he couldn't help noticing the gleaming Jaguar saloon.

It stood out among the other less expensive cars lining the kerb. A quick glance at the number plate confirmed it was this year's model, and Stern smiled. It wasn't unusual to see an expensive car alongside the rest here in Norfolk. Norfolk had its monied folk just like any other county.

He pushed open the bakery door and was, as always, met with the warm sweet smell of baking bread and freshly made cakes. It had been the same ever since he'd first rented the upstairs accommodation from Dave. The delicious aroma. As soon as it hit his nostrils, the desire for one of those cakes was irresistible.

Dave gave him a wave from behind the counter. "Is that you behind the hedge?"

Stern approached his landlord, his hand automatically going to the growth on his face. "It's my new disguise. Didn't know if the rent was due. Thought I'd sneak in without you noticing."

Dave looked closer, seeing the damage. "Blimey, mate, I hope the other bloke looks worse."

Stern smiled weakly, feeling his cheek tighten. "You bet. I'll tell you about it when you're not busy."

"Look forward to it. You wanna grab something?"

Earlier, Stern had sat on his balcony and enjoyed breakfast while looking out over a calm North Sea. But that had nothing to do with what he was looking at now. Studying the array of freshly baked cakes and buns lined up on the counter, he pointed to a cream covered doughnut. Perfect. "I'll have a couple of those, please, Dave. I want to get things up and running before she arrives just for once."

Shaking his head, Dave pulled a brown paper bag from a hook and reached for the doughnuts. "You'll have a job, mate. She's already here. And she's got a customer with her." He handed the doughnuts across the counter, waving away Stern's attempt to pay. "Ball of fire, that girl of yours."

"You don't know the half of it, Dave." He turned and made his way past the hot ovens to the back of the shop and the stairs leading up to his domain.

Pushing through the door at the head of the stairs into the outer office, he could see coffee bubbling on the far table where they kept the makings, but Cherry was not at her desk. Then he heard voices coming from his office. He laid the paper bag containing the doughnuts on Cherry's desk and crossed the office, peering through the door. Cherry was sitting at his desk and a large figure, his back to Stern, was standing in front of her. Cherry looked up as he came through the door.

"Boss, what are you doing here?"

"I work here, remember?" Then as the big man turned toward him, "Question is, what you are doing here, Mr Pace?"

Ron Pace, as pokerfaced as ever, studied Stern for a moment before speaking. "The boss wants to talk."

As Stern went across, Cherry left his chair and came round the desk to face him. Coming closer to him, she studied his face for a moment, her eyes darkening with concern. "You sure you're okay?"

"Sure, I'm good, luv. I could kill a coffee, though." He moved round the desk and eased himself slowly down into the old chair.

Cherry looked up at Pace. "D'you want a coffee?"

Pace just shook his head, his eyes never leaving Stern.

"I can't talk to Mr Butler," Stern said. "He may have got the pair of you released, but he'll be called back at any time to answer for the goings on at his place. He could be charged with people smuggling and drug running. Even murder. You do realise that, don't you?"

"Bollocks. He knew nothing about any of it," Pace grunted.

Stern gave a shake of his head. "That's for him to prove. But in the meantime, while he is under suspicion, it would be unethical for me to have any contact with him."

"But you're not a copper, are you? Not a real copper."

"Not any more, no, but..."

"That's why Mr Butler wants to talk to you. He's checked you out. What you did back then. In the smoke, all those years ago. He said you'd know the score. Said you'd understand. You'd know he was telling the truth."

Cherry came back into the office carrying two mugs. She placed one in front of Stern and stood protectively alongside his chair, cradling the other between her hands.

Thanking her, Stern picked up the mug and sipped the coffee. As he did, realisation dawned. He looked long and hard at Pace. "Is it your Jag parked outside?"

The big man gave another of his almost imperceptible nods.

Stern remembered the blacked out rear windows. "And I guess Mr Butler is parked in the back seat, right?"

"Right."

"Why didn't he come in?"

"Didn't want to get you into trouble. Said it would be better if you talk in the motor, then no one would know."

"Thoughtful of him," Stern mused. He drank some more coffee. "You get on well with your guv'ner, don't you, Ron?"

"Been with him since we were kids." Suddenly, without warning, he stepped close, placed both hands on the desk and leaned in toward Stern. "And I can tell you, Mr Stern, he knew nothing about what that bitch was up to. She took the daft old sod for a ride and no mistake. Then brought all her cronies over to help." As if realising he may have overstepped the mark, he straightened, and took a pace back. "Sorry."

It was the first time Stern had seen a softening of the usual hard aggressive stance. "What about Mr Butler's lawyer? He should..."

Pace's jaw tightened. "Nothing but a blood sucker. He takes Eddie's money and plays the game. Does as little as he has to for as much as he can get his dirty mitts on. He's done it for years. No, we just need someone to listen. Someone who's been there. Someone who knows the score." He took a breath. "Eddie knows he slagged you off, and he's sorry about that. He told me to ask you nicely. That's what I'm trying to do."

Stern sighed heavily and looked up at Cherry still alongside him. He raised his eyebrows questioningly.

Cherry gave a little shrug of her shoulders. "He only wants to talk."

Reluctantly, Stern eased himself carefully up out of the chair.

Sixty-seven

It was Sunday and not yet eight. Stern relaxed on his balcony. In front of him was his usual bowl of flakes, honeyed toast and a banana with coffee on the side. May was two thirds gone and, not for the first time this year, the breeze was light and warmed by an early sun. Stern was feeling good. And he had every reason to. He had climbed out of bed at just after six and, for the first time since that fateful Friday night, he had pulled on his running gear and headed for the beach. It wasn't one of his normal runs; more of a stop-start plod really. But he'd kept at it for best part of an hour, and his rib cage seemed to have at last decided not to complain every time he moved. His face, too, was much better. The scabbing had almost all gone, and the bruising had faded. He was still debating about the beard. Cherry, as honest as ever, had dismissed the distinguished idea, telling him it just made him look old. Nevertheless, he'd decided to hang on to it for a while longer. He'd returned from the run feeling refreshed and better than he had for a while. Now after a shower, he was relaxing with a well-deserved breakfast.

As he spooned the flakes into his mouth, he thought about the recent events. He remembered how determined he had been when he stepped off the plane at Heathrow. He'd been distraught about allowing Annie to slip away from him and could only see a bleak nothingness ahead of him. Life had simply stalled. The only thing he had been sure of was Stern Investigations was a thing of the past.

But then, Cherry Hooker had strolled back into his life. Stern Investigations a thing of the past? What idiot said that?

A little more than seven weeks ago, he'd reluctantly agreed to twelve months. Now it seemed like Stern Investigations had never stopped. And though he would never admit it, particularly to the Hooker woman, he didn't think he wanted it to. He was back in the groove, back where he felt he should be. He had to admit it felt good.

The case had been a difficult one. Possibly because what had started as two separate cases had come together as one. Also, because from the start everything had pointed to Butler being the prime suspect. But the doubts had begun to creep in when O'Connor made the point about how adamant Butler had been of his innocence. At the time, Stern had been dismissive, still certain that Butler was involved. But then, Ron Pace had appeared. He'd been so intense, so determined when pleading his boss's innocence, that Stern had agreed to the meeting with Butler in the back of the Jaguar. There Butler had opened his heart, admitting, probably for the first time, how he had been a fool. Stern remembered how, moist eyed, the old man had explained how after losing his beloved Vera, his life had fallen apart. He said he seemed to wander in a wilderness for an age, not caring too much about anything. Then this bright young thing had come into his life. She was gorgeous, and he fully admitted the physical side of the relationship had been the initial draw. But then as time passed, she had made him feel like he was the only one. She had constantly reminded him that age didn't matter…all she wanted in life was to be with him. He'd held Stern's probing gaze with tired dark rimmed eyes, looking every bit his age and more. 'No fool like an old fool, eh, Mr Stern?'

Afterwards, Stern had thought long and hard. He had sent an email to O'Connor informing him of Butler's visit and explaining in detail his discussion with both Pace and Butler. He'd not ventured an opinion, simply because at the time he didn't have one.

He could certainly identify with the vacuum left when losing the love of your life. Not by death, of course, but a loss just the same. So, was it possible that such a shrewd, hard-nosed business man who'd been around the block more than once could be taken for such a ride? The answer was simple; of course, it was. History was littered with such cases. But was it really the case here? Or were Eddie Butler and his faithful minder putting on the show of their lives? He couldn't be sure, and the uncertainty bugged him. If he knew what the outcome was with those in custody, a decision would be simple. But it was almost a week and so far, he hadn't heard a word from O'Connor. More than once, he had almost picked up the phone, but O'Connor had made it quite clear that until he was ready to talk, Stern would get nothing from him.

As he reached for the toast it was as if his thoughts had been transmitted across the airwaves. He picked up the mobile and checked the screen. It was David. He didn't introduce himself, just said, "Thought you'd be out pounding the sand."

"Done that already."

"Clever old you. So, got time for an update?"

"Need you ask?"

"Good. First, we've found Preston's car."

"Well done. Where was it?"

"Can't claim the credit," O'Connor admitted. "That's down to a bunch of council workers trimming hedges about a mile back from Butler's pad. Looks like Preston found a break in the hedge and backed the car into it. Well out of sight of the road."

"Mmmm, ready for getaway after he had torched the cottage. But a mile, bit of a jog."

"Yeah, but who knows, he could have thought if he left it too close to the house it might be found before he got back to it."

"We'll never know, I guess," Stern mused. "What happens to it now?"

"Don't know. Once we've given it the once-over, we'll hand it over to the council. It's an oldie, bit of a wreck really. They'll probably crush it."

"Oh, well, another part of the mystery solved."

"It is," O'Connor agreed. "By the way, what you got planned for the rest of the day?"

"Nothing, it's Sunday."

"Lucky you. To us hard working keepers of the law, Sunday's no different from any other day."

"My heart bleeds for you."

"Just thought I'd let you know we're meeting with the CPS this afternoon at two. Can't get you in on the meeting, but if you want an update, we can meet this evening, and I'll put you in the picture."

Stern's heart gave a little kick. So, David was meeting with the Crown Prosecution Service. It meant he thought he had sufficient evidence on one or more of the defendants to win a conviction. From his own studies, when he first joined the force, Stern knew the CPS had been around in one form or another since the 1980s, probably even before that. But, if he remembered correctly, it was in the late 1990s when it was reconfigured basically to what it was today. It was for the CPS to decide if the police had a solid enough case with enough evidence for a successful prosecution. Stern had retired in 2003, so it was only in the latter part of his career he'd had dealings with the CPS. He knew from experience sometimes it could be frustrating for the police who, when absolutely certain of an individual's guilt, had the case rejected by the CPS for what they saw as insufficient evidence. He hoped O'Connor had done his homework well.

"Yours or mine?"

"Can you come this way again," O'Connor asked. "Looks like today will be a long one. Could do without the drive after work."

"No problem. Shall we say eight?"

"Looks good. If anything crops up, I'll call you."

Stern killed the phone and leaned back in the chair, a satisfied smile lighting his face. Now, he could put this all to bed, find out what progress O'Connor had made. It might also throw some light on whether Eddie Butler was involved, or as he was maintaining, he'd just been taken for a ride. For some reason, Stern was hoping it would be the latter.

Sixty-eight

At a little after eight, Stern walked into O'Connor's local. It was the second meet since his return, and it felt good to get back to their regular get-togethers. There was a secondary reason for Stern being happy to do this run again. Since the attack at the cottage, Stern's new VW had been tucked away in his lockup. He was only too pleased to get behind the wheel and give it a good run, get the oil flowing again. Sensibly, as a precaution, he'd placed a cushion between his chest and the seat belt. He wasn't expecting to do any sudden heavy braking but better safe than sorry.

The place was filling up. O'Connor was already there, seated at their preferred table tucked away in a corner where they could chat securely. Stern grabbed a pint and joined his friend.

"How's it going, mate?"

"It's been a bit of a pull," O'Connor replied. "Virtually slept at the station all week. The wife and kids think I've done a runner." He took a long pull at the pint and gave a satisfied smile. "I think we're there now."

Stern followed suit, wiping the froth from his lips with the back of his hand. "So, fill me in, partner."

There was a twinkle in O'Connor's eye as he leaned in closer to his friend. "First, I have an apology to make."

Stern frowned. "To me?"

"Yup. Back when we met in the café, after you made your statement in the nick, I ribbed you about being taken out by a woman. Remember?"

Stern smiled. "I do. A bit harsh I thought."

"Well, in the light of fresh evidence, I agree."

Confused, Stern shook his head but stayed silent.

"If you remember when she was outside the cottage, Cherry thought she heard Victor Adams call out the name Anna. Well, she heard right. Adams admitted it." He took another pull at the beer before going on. "When we started our interrogations, Butler's wife and her so called mother stayed shtum, refused to answer our questions. Adams, on the other hand, couldn't wait to talk. He's terrified because he's in some heavy dude's bad books back in Poland. He's crying that if we send him back, he'll be topped. So, when we asked him, he admitted calling out Anna because that was the real name of the woman in the cottage. Anna Janowski."

"But she's Mrs Butler's mum?"

O'Connor shook his head. "No, she's not. Our security people have a pretty good relationship with their counterparts in Poland, and as soon as Adams coughed, we checked Janowski out. Fact is, she's nobody's mother and is well known to the Polish authorities. She's got plenty of previous, too, including drugs and, would you believe, GBH. Seems she gets a great kick out of hurting people. She's had plenty of practice, too. She used to be part of the Polish woman's wrestling circuit."

The glass was halfway to Stern's lips when it stopped, his mouth half open. "She's a wrestler?"

"Was," O'Connor corrected. "She was banned from the sport after nearly killing a couple of opponents. Even maimed a referee who tried to intervene. She's one real crazy horse." He smiled across the table. "Seems you were done over by a little more than just any woman, mate. Hence, my apology."

Stern tentatively touched his cheek. "Well I suppose that makes me feel a little better."

"I thought it would. In fact, we're eyeballing crazy Anna for the deaths of Ollie Preston and Charlie Croker." O'Connor gave a hesitant half smile. "If we're right, it looks like you were lucky to get away with a couple of broken ribs and a kicking, mate. Oh, and by the way, Adam's also confessed that the lovely Anna had a penchant for young girls. Her visits to the cottage were not infrequent, it seems."

Stern screwed up his eyes, trying to think back. "You know, back in the cottage, when I was on the floor, I did manage a quick look at her. I could have sworn she was only partly dressed. Afterwards, I thought it was just the bang on the head, but..."

"No, you were right. Seems nobody ever argued with Anna. When she visited the cottage, Adams either left or shut himself in the living room and watched the TV." He grinned. "Probably why she gave you such a kicking. You interrupted her fun."

Wrinkling his nose in distaste, Stern took a drink. "What a bitch." He gave a disbelieving shake of the head. "So, with a record like that, how the hell did she...?"

"Brilliantly forged documentation," O'Connor cut in, pre-empting the question. "She was actually using Butler's wife's real mother's documentation with some very sophisticated alterations. Fooled our normal border checks completely. It took the real boffins to suss it. She was able to come and go as she pleased. We now know, as well as playing the caring mum, she was the gofer, the link between the suppliers in Poland and here. She organised the stuff across Europe, then over to here. It was one very slick outfit."

"You got all this from Adams?"

"We did. Honest, once he started, we couldn't shut him up. He's desperate. Must be into some real hard cases back home. I almost feel sorry for him."

"So what part did he play in the organisation?"

"He was the recruiter at this end. Like Anna did on the other side of the channel, he found likely candidates at this end to transport the gear."

"Charlie Croker and Barford."

"Right. Possibly others we don't know about. Depends on how long they've been working this. We've yet to establish that. Anyway, Victor told us, like others before them, the girls and guys we intercepted in London were picked up in Calais."

Stern gave a satisfied smile. "Yeah, I had a feeling Calais would come into it somewhere. I remember saying to Cyril there were plenty to choose from still hiding out there." He paused, frowning. "But didn't you say Dutch fishermen brought them in?"

"I did. And that confused me, too, until our gobby Mr Adamczyk opened up."

Stern latched onto O'Connor's use of the man's real name. "Pretty good pronunciation, David. I keep forgetting Adams is not his real name."

"Once we had him in custody, we had to use his real name," O'Connor admitted. He smiled. "He was happy to tell me how to pronounce it. According to him, the operation was pretty extensive. It seems the drugs were supplied in Poland. They were then taken overland through Germany. Sometimes, depending what they were carrying, with a detour through Czechoslovakia. Then, if it was just a drug run, they went straight into Holland, Rotterdam, where they just threw big bucks at more than willing fishermen. If people were part of the requirement, they diverted from Germany into France and Calais, where they picked up a few girls and fellas from the hundreds still hiding out trying to illegally hide away on the ferries and lorries."

"I see. Then it was back up to the greedy fishermen in Rotterdam, I suppose?"

"Correct."

"But Victor and Anna weren't behind the setup, were they?"

"No. According to Victor, the force behind the organisation is the Bosko family."

"Who the hell's the Bosko family?"

O'Connor gave a satisfied grin. "Bosko is Mrs Butler's maiden name. Victor admitted the whole family is quite a force in organised crime back in Poland. Particularly her father, the head of the clan. He's one clever dude, apparently. And ruthless with it. Never been nailed. Seems he saw the potential in his very attractive daughter, and sent her over here to select a target, and set the whole thing up. He also recruited Anna Janowski. Her job, as well as organising the Europe end of things, was to keep an eye on his daughter. And it seems Katrina is a chip off the old man's block. Sharp as a razor. Once here, she got herself a place in a top restaurant used by high rollers and waited her chance. Enter Eddie Butler, the perfect foil."

"Christ, what a setup," Stern breathed. "So, the head honcho on this side was the lovely Mrs Butler?"

"According to Adamczyk, yes, she called the shots."

Stern smiled. "What was it you said the first time we met her at the Butler house? Bit timid. Wouldn't say boo to a goose."

For a second, O'Connor's jaw tightened. "Don't remind me. What a wicked deceitful young bitch."

"Talking of deceit," Stern said. "What about Butler? Was he really taken for a ride?"

O'Connor's face tightened. "Well, according to Victor, Katrina said he was a stupid old Englishman ripe for the picking. So, I guess he was."

"Jesus."

They sat quietly contemplating for a moment before Stern spoke again. "That just leaves the young woman we found in the cottage?"

"Ah, yes. Like the others, she was picked up in Calais. But instead of being shipped out, she was brought here and stashed away in the cottage." He raised his eyebrows.

It took Stern only a second. "Don't tell me. A little bonus for our Victor."

O'Connor gave a shrug. "Could be, but he didn't admit to that. He just told us about the lovely Anna's devious fetish. "He wrinkled his nose in disgust "Oh, and by the way, d'you remember Croker's neighbour telling you about the young woman who visited Charlie?"

"Sally?" Stern's eyes widened in surprise. "That was her?"

"It was. Though Sally isn't her real name, of course. She's from Syria and her name is Amira Nassif. She was also more than happy to talk to us. The poor kid had been through hell and back. She told us at first, when they brought her to Butler's place, she was told because her parents hadn't been able to fully pay for her trip she had to do what was necessary to pay the balance. They said it was only temporary, and soon she would be taken to London to a proper job."

Stern gave a sad shake of his head.

"And get this," O'Connor went on. "They made sure she stayed put by telling her that if the British authorities found her there, they would shoot her on the spot."

Immediately, the memory of when he entered the cottage and opened the door to the bedroom hit Stern. The young woman cowering on the bed begging him not to kill her. "And she believed them," he muttered.

"She did, too. She was terrified. Anyway, it seems when Croker started to get cold feet about what he was doing, they brought in Amira. They knew what a lonely old soul Croker was, so they gave him a little extra to keep him happy. Victor used to take her to and from Croker's flat, never letting her off the lead for more than a couple of hours or so at a time. It worked a treat, for a while. But then, Croker got serious about the girl. He made plans to move away from the area and take her with him. Of course, she was keen to go. She admitted she liked Croker very much. She told us he was kind and gentle, but I guess anything was better than what she was going through."

"I can understand that," Stern agreed.

"Anyway, Croker made the fatal mistake of telling Adamczyk he wouldn't be driving anymore because he had found a new girlfriend, and they were moving away from the area."

Stern sucked air through clenched teeth. "Bad move."

O'Connor's face tightened angrily. "The worst thing he could have done. It sealed his fate. Of course, Adamczyk vehemently denies he had anything to do with Croker's death. He's adamant that all he did was to tell Butler's wife."

"Right," Stern broke in. "And from what you've told me, she would have given the lovely Anna her head."

"We can only assume that, Theo. But my guess is you're not far off."

Stern drained his glass. "Hell, David, when I got back from Oz, I said I was finished with all this."

O'Connor laughed. "Theo Stern finished with detective work? Don't make me laugh."

Sixty-nine

Cherry forked some balsamic vinegar-soaked salad into her mouth and, for a moment, chewed thoughtfully. Then, taking a drink of water, she looked across the table at O'Connor. "So, what happens now?"

O'Connor paused slicing through the pork loin on his plate. "Can't be sure, but I would guess Mrs Butler, **Adamczyk**, and Anna Janowski will be looking at a pretty stiff sentence then probably deportation."

"And the young girl?"

"Don't know about her," O'Connor admitted. "It'll be up to immigration. She's been treated appallingly, so I would hope that will be taken into consideration. But, like I said, it's just my guess. The whole investigation is being taken out of our hands now. The big boys are moving in."

"Big boys?"

O'Connor gave a shake of his head and shrugged. "Don't ask, Cherry. According to my boss, the investigation now falls under

The National Crime Agency led by the Home Office Immigration Enforcement people." He raised his eyebrows. "And the UK's Organised Immigration Crime Taskforce."

Stern swallowed the mouthful of curried chicken he'd been chewing and smiled. "Blimey, where'd they come from?"

"Not sure really," O'Connor admitted. "But I've already been given the once-over by a couple of suits up from the smoke. They'll want to talk to you soon, too, so I'd stand by if I were you."

Stern gave a nonchalant shrug of his shoulders and stabbed his fork into another portion of chicken. Nothing new there. He'd done it all before. More than once.

They were sitting round the table at The Wheatsheaf, Stern's treat for the help everyone had given him since he'd been back from Australia. As well as Stern, Cherry and O'Connor, Cyril Makepeace, Clarissa Albright and Paul Wainwright—truly surprised at being asked—were also there. The atmosphere was cheerful and relaxed.

Clarissa, also enjoying the curried chicken, gave a disappointed sniff. "Pity you didn't use me and Claude on that one, Theo. Y'know, we're part of the team now, and we'd have sorted that bloody Anna woman out like we did the mongrel in the caravan." Her eyes sparkling mischievously, she gave a low course chuckle. "Probably got away with a few less bruises, too."

Cherry laughed. "She's probably right, boss."

Stern's face creased into a mock scowl. "Look, you lot, let's not turn tonight into a knock Theo Stern evening. Don't forget who's paying here."

O'Connor raised a hand. "Theo, something I forgot to ask you the other night when we were having a drink. How did you know about the boat and the cottage?"

Stern gave Cyril Makepeace a conspiratorial wink. "Well, I wasn't sure about the cottage. It was more or less a guess. I just knew Adams was involved, and he lived in the cottage, so it had to be searched. I sure as hell didn't expect to find what we did."

"And the boat?"

"Well, let's just say Cyril and I had already had a shufty at the boat."

"S'right, mate," Clarissa came in enthusiastically. "They used my bark canoe, made it meself, just like the old Abo's." She looked at Cyril.

"Real beaut, right Cyril?"

Cyril nearly choked on a mouthful of food. "Er, well..." he spluttered, looking to Stern for support.

O'Connor followed Cyril's gaze, also focussing on Stern. "Bark canoe? What the hell's she on about?"

Stern gave Clarissa the hard eye. "Thanks a bunch, Clarissa."

Clarissa looked surprised. "Strewth, mate, didn't realise you hadn't briefed the old Blues. I'll keep the trap shut from now on."

Stern finished the last spoonful of rice and pushed his plate to one side. "Okay, the night before Cherry and I went to the Butler house, Cyril and I took a little trip down river and had a look in the boat."

O'Connor's mouth fell open, disbelief. "You two? In the dark? In an old Aboriginal bark canoe?"

Stern glanced around the table, saw the others grinning. "Well, yeah, but it wasn't old." He fumbled for words. "Not old like it was made a long time ago. I mean, like she said, Clarissa made it herself. Anyway, it worked, didn't it? We got what we wanted."

O'Connor was smiling. He couldn't help it. He waved a hand. "Well, yeah, I suppose we did. But just give me a moment to get the mental picture of two crazy old sods paddling up the Bure in the dark, in a canoe made from tree bark out of my mind. Then you can tell me what happened."

There were giggles all round.

"Okay, okay, you can mock," Stern said, himself unable to hold back the smile. He looked across the table at Cyril. "But it was us crazy old sods who cracked the case, wasn't it?"

"Too right, mate," Cyril agreed. "The young'ns today have no idea."

Stern's face became serious. "The night I searched the boat, I found the drugs stashed under the beds either side of the forward cabin. They were vacuum sealed in exactly the way Barford had told us. And they were marked."

O'Connor frowned. "Marked?"

"Yup. At first, I didn't understand, but then, when I recognised the markings, it dawned on me. It was why they couldn't wait for Butler's new super, duper boat to be built after the first one was torched. They needed a boat, any boat, because they had deliveries to make. It was only necessary for the boat to have a low profile, so it could get under the low bridges across the river."

"So, these markings?" Wainwright asked. "What were they?"

Stern began to explain. "Think about various stops you can make if you cruise the Bure and the Thurn." He held up his hand counting off his fingers. "Horning, Ranworth Broad, South Walsham Broad, Ludham Bridge. Just some of them."

"The packages were marked with these names?" Wainwright persisted.

"They were. See, Barford told us that when he picked up the stuff from Somerton, some stayed in the van and went to London or wherever with his human cargo. The rest was loaded onto the boat there and then. The boat was then sailed to Butler's mooring. Then, at different times, on the pretence of cruising the river, deliveries were made to those points."

"And remember," O'Connor came back in. "This was an extensive setup. It kicked off in Poland, travelled through Europe, crossed the English Channel and ended up being distributed to all points over here. Including right here on our own Norfolk Broads." He paused for a moment, tight lipped, thoughtful. Then looking at Stern, "I know you don't believe in coincidence, Theo, but in this case, it really did pay a part. When you returned from Oz, Cherry was desperate to get you back in harness. So much so she had already taken on a client."

Stern wrinkled his nose at Cherry. "We don't talk about that, do we?"

"Probably not," O'Connor came back. "But then, I came and asked you for help, too. We weren't to know then that those two cases would become one and lead us down the road we've just travelled. If that's not coincidence, then I don't know what is."

"No argument there, I guess," Stern conceded. "One thing's for sure though. We wouldn't have had such a good result without all of your help."

A glint in her eye, Cherry leaned forward. "And none of us would be sitting here tonight if it weren't for you, boss."

The immediate proceedings and Stern's embarrassment were interrupted by Daniella, the landlady of the hostelry, approaching the table. "Is everything good here?" she asked.

"Yes Daniella, everything is good," Stern said, looking at the faces around the table. "Everything is very good."

Epilogue

Things at Stern Investigations had been quiet for a week. There had been no fresh client enquiries, and the only telephone call had been from Doris Barford to thank Stern for his support. Mainly due to Stern's testimony, her husband had been informed by his council, though nothing was certain, it seemed likely he would get away with a suspended sentence. This because as soon as Barford realised what he was doing was illegal, he had informed the authorities, thereafter assisting them with their investigations. Far from the truth, of course, but in Stern's opinion, sometimes giving a little slack was the right thing to do. It was true Steve Barford had strayed, but he was a chancer, not a criminal. Not in Stern's eyes, anyway. He doubted very much if the ex-squadie would stray from the straight and narrow again any time soon.

Today, Sunday, had been a miserable day. From the time he had climbed out of bed, it had been chilly and overcast with a dampening drizzle drifting off the North Sea. Regardless, he had wrapped up and headed for the beach. Since the attack, he had persevered, slowly progressing from little more than a walk, his ribs even then complaining, to being almost back to where he wanted to be. This morning, despite the weather, he'd completed an hour and felt good for it.

Back at the flat he had showered before taking advantage of a short break in the clouds to pull the car out of the garage and give it a quick wash over. Lunch had been a Sunday roast at The Wheatsheaf followed by an hour's snooze in front of the TV with the sound lowered. Now, still sprawled out in the armchair, the TV switched off, his mind was trawling through the last couple of hectic months. Was it really only eight weeks since his return?

He smiled, thinking of Mo Stevens, and the aggravation she had caused them. From what he had witnessed on the day he'd brought her and her ex together, he wouldn't be surprised if they weren't at least seeing each other again. What a crazy world. Still, she had paid well, and nobody was hurt.

Not so with the Butler case, where two unfortunate individuals had lost their lives. He supposed there was some consolation in that an extensive international drug and people smuggling ring had been taken down. Well, he hoped it had. Since it had been taken out of local police control, they'd heard nothing. But he couldn't help feeling deep sadness for both Charlie Croker and Ollie Preston. One, a sad lonely soul who had been used then callously disposed of when he'd posed a problem. The other because he'd recklessly tried to avenge his friend. All this during a short couple of months. Eight weeks before which he had sworn not to reinstate Stern Investigations.

But then, he hadn't taken into consideration the determination of Cherry Hooker, who twenty years before, as a DCI in the London Met, he had dragged away from a life of drugs and prostitution. Who ever since had considered him her hero. She wanted nothing more than to continue working alongside him and would do almost anything to achieve that. Over the years, the affection had become mutual, he, too, coming to cherish the relationship. She was always there when he needed her, like the daughter he'd never had. But, boy, sometimes she could be a real pain. He knew after committing himself to twelve months she would do her utmost to hold him to it.

He was smiling at his own thoughts when the telephone, on the table alongside, interrupted his reverie. He picked it up and looked at the screen. There was no name just the words incoming call. "Stern."

There was a moment's silence before he heard anything then, "Theo, its Annie."

He felt his heart lurch. It always did when he heard her voice. This time instantly evoking the memory of the heart-breaking moment when he'd realised, despite all his efforts, he'd lost her. Lost her for good. He pushed the thought roughly from his head. "Hello Annie. How are you?"

"I'm fine. Just thought I'd give you a ring. See how you are."

"Yeah, I'm good."

There was a moment's awkward silence before Annie spoke again. "What are you up to?"

"Oh, this and that, you know. Keeping myself pretty busy."

"I thought you might have called."

The words conjured a sudden unreasonable anger in him. "Why?"

Another silence told him the single snapped word had gone home. "You said you would. You said we could still be friends."

He sighed heavily. For the last two months he had buried himself in his work, as time passed, hardly giving his ex a thought. It had proven there could be a life after Annie. There had to be. He had no other option. But he still loved her, always would. That made being just friends difficult. It was also what made him bloody angry. "I know what I said, Annie," he said, keeping his voice level, under control. "But what we had, what I believe we still feel for each other, makes just being friends bloody difficult. I don't know, in time, maybe, but right now..." He stopped. She would know what he was trying to say.

"I just don't want you to be unhappy." He could hear the emotion in her words.

"I know, luv," he said, softening his tone. "But just for a while I think we should ..." He couldn't finish the sentence."

"If it's what you really want."

"Yeah, I think it best. Give me time. I will call you."

"Promise?"

"Yeah. I promise."

He was still staring into space when only a few minutes after a painful goodbye the phone rang again. This time the screen identified the caller. He hit the green button. "Cherry."

"Boss." He could already hear the excitement in her voice. "Sorry to disturb your Sunday, but I just had a call from a woman. She reckons her husband's trying to kill her."

Stern stiffened. "What, now?"

"No, not this minute. She says she thinks he's putting something in her food. Slowly poisoning her."

"Then she should call the police."

"No, that's just it. She says she can't call them."

"Why not?"

"Don't know. She won't tell me. Says she's been told about you and will only talk to you. Says she has plenty of money and is willing to pay. She says..."

Stern started to laugh. He just couldn't help it. It was happening all over again. What a crazy bloody world.

"Boss, are you alright?"

Meet A. W. Lambert

A.W. Lambert was born and raised in Battersea, south London, England. After completing his National Military Service, during which time he was engaged in active service in the EOKA terrorist conflict on the island of Cyprus, he embarked on an engineering career in the British aircraft industry where he also became a qualified pilot. In 1992 he retired from industry to follow his two main passions: the playing of his favourite music, traditional New Orleans Jazz and Creative Writing. After studying with The Writer's Bureau, he developed extensive experience achieving success in magazine article and short story writing before moving into the field of full length Action/ Adventure. A Treacherous Past, his first published novel, introduced retired London Metropolitan Police Inspector, now private investigator, Theo Stern for the first time. Since then follow up novels have seen Stern and AW's other absorbing characters, involved in increasingly intriguing and dangerous scenarios.

After raising two sons; one now living in Boston, USA, the other in Melbourne, Australia, A.W. lives with his wife, Valerie, in a tiny hamlet on the North Norfolk coast of England.

Other Works from the Pen of

A. W. Lambert

A Treacherous Past - When private investigator Theo Stern sets out to find a British Intelligence officer who has mysteriously disappeared, he becomes embroiled in a sinister web of International treachery and violence.

A Fatal Score - Theo Stern's old friend, jazz musician Steve Arnold hits Sheringham. But jazz is the last thing on Stern's mind when he finds that his friend is involved in a sinister tangle of violence and death.

A Lethal Quest - London cabby Frank Barnes is left £250,000 by his estranged mother. But how did she die? Frank seeks answers, but only unearths more questions; the most disturbing of all: is she really dead?

Payback - Racial attacks in the back streets of Norwich and the kidnap of a London gangster. Theo Stern is dragged in to both cases;

one conjuring a nightmare from the past, the other becoming too close for comfort.

Best Served Cold - Anonymous, threatening telephone calls prompt Theo Stern to ask the question: genuine or just a crank? The answer becomes clear when Annie, Stern's wife, is abducted and the terrifying demands begin.

Sleeping Dogs - A piece of an aircraft that's lain hidden since the Second World War is found in a Norfolk wood. Its find sparks a search; two families, each desperate to discover the fate of relatives believed to have been aboard an aircraft that mysteriously disappeared in 1940. But is this find part of that aircraft? Theo Stern is asked to investigate and finds himself embroiled in a web of deceit and half-truths where someone is prepared to mete out savage violence, even commit murder, to hide the truth.

Forbidden Legacy - The theft of a valuable painting and a violent death in a remote Norfolk village leads Theo Stern to a vicious abduction in London and twenty years of unsolved crimes across the UK.

Edge Of Reason - A tragic death in 2006 and a spate of present day brutal murders. What is the link and what, after all this time, has sparked the killing spree?

The Deal - How could a simple teenage handshake in 1996 London cause such havoc seventeen years later and six thousand miles away in Cape Town, South Africa?

Proof of Merit – *'Neither use nor ornament.'* Four simple words, individually nothing spectacular. But put together, a phrase so humiliating it has the power to transform life.

Letter to Our Readers

Enjoy this book?

You can make a difference

As an independent publisher, Wings ePress, Inc. does not have the financial clout of the large New York Publishers. We can't afford large magazine spreads or subway posters to tell people about our quality books.

But, we do have something much more effective and powerful than ads. We have a large base of loyal readers.

Honest Reviews help bring the attention of new readers to our books.

If you enjoyed this book, we would appreciate it if you would spend a few minutes posting a review on the site where you purchased this book or on the Wings ePress, Inc. webpages at: https://wingsepress. com/

Visit Our Website

For The Full Inventory
Of Quality Books:

Wings ePress.Inc
https://wingsepress.com/

Quality trade paperbacks and downloads
in multiple formats,
in genres ranging from light romantic comedy
to general fiction and horror.
Wings has something for every reader's taste.
Visit the website, then bookmark it.
We add new titles each month!

Wings ePress Inc.

3000 N. Rock Road

Newton, KS 67114